THE OFFICIAL
GODZILLA
MOVIE NOVELIZATION OMNIBUS

GODZILLA, GODZILLA: KING OF THE MONSTERS

ALSO AVAILABLE FROM TITAN BOOKS

Kong: Skull Island:
The Official Movie Novelization

Godzilla vs. Kong:
The Official Movie Novelization

Godzilla x Kong: The New Empire -
The Official Movie Novelization

THE OFFICIAL
GODZILLA
MOVIE NOVELIZATION OMNIBUS

GODZILLA: THE OFFICIAL MOVIE NOVELIZATION BY **GREG COX**

GODZILLA: KING OF THE MONSTERS -
THE OFFICIAL MOVIE NOVELIZATION BY **GREG KEYES**

©2025 Legendary. All Rights Reserved.
GODZILLA TM & © TOHO CO., LTD.
MONSTERVERSE TM & © Legendary

TITAN BOOKS

The Official Godzilla Movie Novelization Omnibus
(Godzilla, Godzilla: King of the Monsters)
Print edition ISBN: 9781835414026
E-book edition ISBN: 9781835414033

Published by Titan Books
A division of Titan Publishing Group Ltd
144 Southwark Street, London SE1 0UP
www.titanbooks.com

First edition: August 2025
10 9 8 7 6 5 4 3 2 1

This is a work of fiction. All of the characters, organizations, and events portrayed in this novel are either products of the author's imagination or are used fictitiously. Any resemblance to actual persons, living or dead (except for satirical purposes), is entirely coincidental.

© 2025 Legendary. All Rights Reserved.

GODZILLA TM & © TOHO CO., LTD.

MONSTERVERSE TM & © Legendary

Greg Cox and Greg Keyes assert the moral right to be identified as the authors of this work.

No part of this publication may be reproduced, stored in a retrieval system, or transmitted, in any form or by any means without the prior written permission of the publisher, nor be otherwise circulated in any form of binding or cover other than that in which it is published and without a similar condition being imposed on the subsequent purchaser.

A CIP catalogue record for this title is available from the British Library.

EU RP (For authorities only)
eucomply OÜ, Pärnu mnt. 139b-14, 11317 Tallinn, Estonia
hello@eucompliancepartner.com, +3375690241

Printed and bound by CPI Group (UK) Ltd, Croydon CR0 4YY.

CONTENTS

Godzilla 1

Godzilla: King of the Monsters 303

BOOK ONE

GODZILLA

THE OFFICIAL MOVIE NOVELIZATION

NOVELIZATION BY **GREG COX**

BASED UPON THE SCREENPLAY BY **MAX BORENSTEIN**
STORY BY **DAVID CALLAHAM**
BASED ON THE CHARACTER "GODZILLA" OWNED AND CREATED BY TOHO CO., LTD.

ONE

1954

Nature was at peace.

The turquoise waters of the South Pacific reflected a cloudless blue sky. A coral reef shielded a tranquil lagoon from the sea beyond. A handful of tiny islands formed a remote atoll that was barely a speck on maps of the region. Palm trees swayed above a white sand beach. Warm trade winds rustled thatch huts and coconut groves, as the islanders went about their daily tasks. Bare-chested men, their skin baked brown by sun, tended to their fishing nets and outrigger canoes. Women in white cotton dresses wove baskets and looked after the cooking fires. Naked children played in the sand and surf, chasing after crabs, seabirds, and each other. They slaked their thirst with coconut juice and feasted on breadfruit, bananas, and papayas. A young boy, only eight years old, swam like a dolphin in the warm, refreshing waters of the lagoon, enjoying what seemed like a perfect day in paradise.

Until...

GREG COX

A strange white wake entered the lagoon from beyond the coral reef. The glassy blue water churned and swelled, stirred by the passage of some vast, unfathomable mass beneath the surface. The boy cried out in alarm, and dived frantically out of the way, as a huge dark form rose up from the depths. On the shore, startled villagers dropped everything to gape in fear and wonder, shielding their eyes from the sun, as the conning tower of a large gray nuclear submarine surfaced with a blast of salty spray.

Moments later, the rest of the sub came into view, claiming the lagoon like an invading sea monster. More than three hundred feet long, the intimidating steel vessel dwarfed the islanders' simple outriggers. Paddling in the water several yards away, the boy watched along with his people as a familiar red-white-and-blue flag unfurled via a mechanical winch. Despite his island's remote location and relative isolation from the world, the boy recognized the Stars and Stripes of the United States of America. It had been less than a decade after all since the Americans and the Japanese had waged war over the scattered islands of the South Pacific, but the boy's people had largely been left alone since then. He wondered what had brought the Americans back to the islands.

A shiver ran through the boy, despite the warmth of the sun and water. He knew somehow that the world as he knew it had just changed forever...

Weeks later, Navy helicopters raced away from the island, which had been radically transformed by its new owners. The boy, his friends, family, and neighbors—all 170 natives of the atoll—had been relocated to another island hundreds of miles away. The simple village had been razed. Thatch huts and fire pits were replaced by temporary utility structures, along with massive concrete bunkers built to protect cameras and other test equipment. Frightened pigs and goats were locked inside cages labeled "Test Animals." Some had been shaved and coated in experimental lotions—in the interests of science. They squealed and grunted anxiously as the 'copters departed, abandoning them on the island. An atomic bomb stayed behind to keep them company.

The bomb rested ominously atop a sturdy metal platform constructed by Navy engineers. It was a large, riveted metal egg over eleven feet in length and weighing more than ten thousand pounds. Hand-painted on its nose cone was a snarling lizard, with angry eyes and fangs, pinned inside the cross-hairs of a gun sight.

Fleeing the island, the 'copters passed over the deck of a massive escort carrier floating several miles away from the test site. The *USS Bairoko* was a *Commencement Bay*-class carrier, nearly seven hundred feet long and displacing over ten thousand long tons. Commissioned too late to take part in the War, it had been named after the decisive Battle of Bairoko and pressed into peace-time service. The carrier housed over a thousand souls, including, on this particular mission, a number of scientific observers, many of whom waited tensely on the deck as crucial minutes ticked by. They stared out across the sea at the tiny atoll, which was only a smudge in the distance, and sweated in the heat and humidity. The sun blazed overhead, powered by the same thermonuclear reactions that were about to be unleashed on the defenseless islands.

In the ship's bridge, a sonar screen tracked a large green dot advancing toward the atoll.

"*Countdown commences at thirty,*" a voice blared from the loudspeakers. "*Twenty-nine... twenty-eight...*"

The entire world seemed to hold its breath.

Beyond the carrier, the sea boiled white as a chain of immense, jagged fins broke through the churning froth. Shipboard observers looked on in awe, instinctively backing away from the jaw-dropping spectacle. Each fin was at least the size of a massive rock formation. The mind boggled at the thought of what they might be attached to.

On the island, the test animals sensed what was bearing down on them. They squealed and bleated in panic, bucking and scrambling in their cages. Goats kicked violently against the bars, bloodying their hooves in their frantic attempts to break free. Pigs pawed at the unyielding metal floors of their cages, trying unsuccessfully to burrow to safety. Seabirds abandoned the islands in a flurry of flapping wings. Brightly colored fish fled the lagoon, preferring the dubious safety of the open sea to what was now approaching. Sharks and other predators fled as well.

On the deck of the *Bairoko*, the assembled scientists and military brass braced themselves for what was to come. Protective blast goggles were lowered over dozens of pairs of eyes, the better to witness the historic event. Documentary cameras whirred on tripods that had been lashed to the deck with multiple redundant cables. Ordinary crewmen, lacking special goggles, ducked and covered their eyes as the countdown neared its climax.

"Ten... nine... eight..."

A colossal form rose from sea like a living waterfall, hundreds of feet tall. The immense shape was shrouded by torrents of cascading water and foam, making it difficult to make out more than its gargantuan proportions. For a brief moment, a thundering, primordial roar bellowed across miles and miles of open sea, all but drowning out the amplified countdown.

"Three... two... one..."

A blinding flash of light erupted from island, followed by an immense fireball that could be seen from miles away. The glare was so bright that even the tinted lenses of the blast goggles were not enough to spare the observers aboard the ship, who were forced to avert their eyes. By the time they could turn their gaze back toward the blast site, a gigantic mushroom cloud was billowing up into the sky above the devastated atoll. The sight of the ominous cloud sent an instinctive shudder through all present. Matter itself had just been split apart at its most fundamental level.

A maelstrom of uprooted sand and debris exploded across the atoll, tearing off the tops of trees. The shockwave rippled out across the waves in all directions, racing faster than the speed of sound. The deafening noise of the blast hit the *Bairoku* mere seconds later: a deep, jarring rumble that shook the soldiers and scientists all the way down to the bone. It was a sound to rattle the very rafters of heaven and make a mockery of peace. The serenity of the islands was a thing of a past, as was, perhaps, the monstrous leviathan that has been briefly glimpsed during the final seconds of the countdown.

Or so the observers prayed.

TWO

1999

Dr. Ishiro Serizawa gazed out the side door of the helicopter as it soared over a lush green landscape. Below him stretched a sunlit tropical rain forest clinging to the rugged slopes of the Philippine highlands. Pines and other evergreens dominated the pristine mountainsides, while mahogany and bamboo groves thrived at the lower altitudes, painting a scenic portrait of pure, unsullied nature. A distinguished-looking man in his early forties, with receding black hair and a neatly trimmed mustache and beard, Serizawa enjoyed the view—until he spied his destination.

The strip mine cut like a gash through the verdant wilderness. Acres of natural beauty had been torn away to expose barren ridges of rock and soil. Ugly metal structures crouched upon shelves of naked bedrock that had been carved, blasted, and bulldozed into the side of the mountain. Shanty towns spilled down the slopes, providing housing for the thousands of laborers toiling in the hot midday sun. Mining, for copper, zinc, nickel, and other minerals, was a growing industry in the Philippines, but it came at the expense of the nation's precious flora and fauna. Instead of abundant greenery, the mining complex was dirty, brown and lifeless. Serizawa winced at the damage done to the environment. The older he got, the more he thought that Nature was sometimes best left to its own devices.

His eyes narrowed as he spied what appeared to be a caved-in section of the mine. This was what had drawn him to this desolate location, all the way from his native Japan. He eyed the collapsed mine with a mixture of excitement and trepidation. The early reports had hinted at something truly remarkable, well worth this exhausting journey. Serizawa couldn't wait to see for himself.

The chopper touched down on a flattened stretch of mountaintop, not far from the cave-in. Outside, sweaty laborers operated mucking loaders, scoop trams, and other heavy machinery as they hurriedly excavated loose gravel and sludge from the collapsed mine. The logo of Universal Western Mining was emblazoned on the machinery. Filipino workers backed away from 'copter, raising their arms to shield themselves from the dust and debris thrown up by rotors' wash.

Finally, Serizawa thought. He unbuckled his seatbelt and climbed stiffly out of the 'copter, followed by his colleague, Dr. Vivienne Graham. An attractive Englishwoman in her thirties, she had a dark brown hair cut sensibly short. She had been at Serizawa's right hand for many years now. Her practical attire was rumpled from the trip.

Three other members of their team also exited the chopper and immediately got to work unloading duffel bags and gear. Serizawa took a moment to get his bearings. It felt good to set foot on solid ground and stretch his legs again. He glanced around, looking for someone to escort them to the discovery.

"Doctor Serizawa!"

A stocky, middle-aged American emerged from the chaos surrounding the mine, shouldering his way past busy workers and machinery alike. Perspiration shone on his ruddy face and had soaked through his clothes. Serizawa recognized the man as Oscar Boyd, one of the men in charge of the mining company. He and Serizawa had been in touch earlier.

"Thank God you're here!" Boyd shouted over the whirr of the rotors. He joined Serizawa and his team. "It's just a mess, I'm warning you. Just a total mess."

A squad of armed guards, toting automatic weapons, accompanied Boyd. The men had the stony expressions and ice-cold eyes of hardened mercenaries or guerillas. Not exactly the most reassuring of welcoming committees. Serizawa and Graham exchanged worried looks. The presence of the guns and guards was unnerving, but they had come too far to succumb to second thoughts now. Serizawa trusted that the soldiers were only on hand to provide security, even if the amount of firepower on view struck him as excessive.

"They picked up a radiation pocket out here last month," Boyd said, getting right down to business. He sounded anxious for whatever advice and assistance the scientists might be able to offer. Serizawa's understanding was that Boyd was from the company's main office and had not personally been on hand when the disaster struck. He sounded flustered and out of his depth. "And got all excited thinking they had a uranium deposit. They started stacking up the heavy machinery and..."

As he spoke, he guided them down a slope toward a nearby ridge. Serizawa stepped carefully over the rough, uneven terrain.

"The floor of the valley collapsed into the cavern below,"

Boyd continued. "Just dropped away. Best guess right now is about forty miners went down with it."

He stepped aside to let Serizawa and the others see for themselves. The team found themselves on a rocky ledge, looking out over the valley below—or what was left of it. A jagged chasm, at least a hundred feet long, had swallowed up the floor of the valley. Mangled machinery, shacks, boulders, and other debris could be dimly glimpsed within the shadowy rift, which appeared to descend deep into the Earth. Serizawa gazed down at the wreckage for several moments, taking it all in, before speaking again.

"I need to speak with the survivors," he said.

A tin-roofed storage facility had been converted into an impromptu triage center. Dozens of injured and dying workers occupied rows of cots. Serizawa saw at once that all of the men were suffering from severe radiation burns. Blisters and ulcers and raw red patches afflicted their flesh. Some were still conscious, while the luckier ones had been rendered oblivious by morphine drips. Agonized moans and whimpers echoed off the walls of the building, whose sweltering atmosphere lacked any sort of air-conditioning. Doctors and nurses, overworked and overwhelmed, moved briskly among the rows of patients, doing what little they could to relieve the men's suffering. Unlike their patients, the relief workers had donned hazmat suits for their own protection. Gas masks covered their faces.

Still in his traveling clothes, Serizawa felt uncomfortably exposed.

Graham inhaled sharply beside him, taken aback by the scale of the tragedy. Serizawa shared her horror. From what he could see of the men's burns, few of the miners would last the week, while any survivors would be doomed to years of complications, cancers, and deformities before they finally succumbed to the radiation's pernicious effects. His heart went out to them, knowing there was little that could be done for them at this point.

Steeling himself against the heart-rending sights and sounds, Serizawa approached one of the patients. The man's face was so badly swollen that he looked barely human. Scorched skin peeled and blistered. His hair was falling out. The burns and swelling made it impossible to determine the patient's age, but a glance at his chart revealed that the dying miner was only twenty years old.

So young, Serizawa thought, even as he forced himself to focus on the task at hand. Now was no time for sentiment. He needed hard data and information if the root cause of this catastrophe was indeed what he suspected. Many more lives might well be at stake.

One of his aides had rescued a portable radiation detector from their supplies. The handheld device included an external wand. Serizawa unslung the detector from his shoulder and switched it on. Drawing nearer to the cot, he pointed the sensor at the patient.

The detector clacked rapidly. The needle on the monitor spiked upward, into the red zone.

Serizawa backed away warily, alarmed by the results. He flagged down one of the busy nurses, whose face was largely concealed by her gas mask. He grasped the shoulder of her hazmat suit.

"Can you ask this man what happened?"

The nurse nodded. Leaning over the patient, she spoke to him in Tagalog. A hoarse, whispery voice escaped his cracked and swollen lips, but was far too faint to make out. She leaned in closer as the man repeated himself, gesturing feebly at Serizawa with a bandaged hand.

"He says," the nurse translated, "that people like you... you came here, you raped the earth. You tore holes in her flesh... and now she's given birth to a demon."

The miner slowly rolled over in his cot, using the last of his strength to turn his back on Serizawa and the others. Serizawa did not attempt to refute the man's accusation. He was more concerned with the "demon" the survivor had mentioned. Just the delirious ramblings of a dying man... or a warning?

"Not sure there's a box for that on the insurance form," Boyd said.

The foreman's attempt at lightening the mood fell flat. Lost in thought, Serizawa drew an antique pocket watch from his jacket and quietly wound the stem. He found himself hoping that this *was* a false alarm, but the evidence against that was mounting. The next step was to see for himself, no matter the risks.

A hazmat suit landed loudly at his feet.

Fully suited up, the team made their way into the chasm, steadying themselves on guide ropes that had been set up for the rescue operations. Their flashlights did little to dispel the darkness as they entered a cavern descending steeply into the earth. The sound of his own breathing echoed hollowly inside Serizawa's protective hood, which felt heavy and unwieldy. The weight of the suit, and his limited visibility, did not make the downward trek any easier.

Keeping one hand on the guide rope, he held the radiation sensor out before him. The clacking was nonstop now, the needle pegging the dial. Serizawa couldn't help wondering about the quality and integrity of his hazmat gear. He suspected that Graham and the others were, too. None of them wanted to end up like those wretched souls in the triage center.

While Serizawa monitored the radiation levels, Graham documented the expedition with her digital camera. Periodic flashes lit up the cavern's murky interior, exposing fractured stone walls and twisted metal debris. She gasped as a flash revealed a lifeless human hand extending from the rubble. Flashlight beams swung toward the hand, which belonged to a bloated corpse sprawled upon the rocks. A contorted face was frozen in an agonized rictus. Cloudy eyes gazed sightlessly into oblivion.

"They sent another fifty men down here to search for survivors," Boyd explained, his voice muffled by his protective breathing apparatus. "Half the rescuers never made it back up, they were too weak."

Serizawa did the calculations. That was over sixty-five fatalities so far, not including the doomed and dying men they had just left behind in the triage center. The death count was mounting by the moment and they hadn't even confirmed the cause yet. He feared, however, that this was indeed far more than just a tragic mining accident.

Graham's camera flashed again and again, finding additional bodies scattered in heaps through the cavern. Still more valiant rescue workers, Serizawa realized, who had perished before making it back to the surface. He admired their courage even as he mourned their sacrifice.

Squinting in the shadows, he looked away from the plentiful dead and studied his surroundings. Each flash from Graham's camera offered a glimpse of roughly textured cavern walls and oddly curved calcite formations all around them. It was like exploring the interior of some alien moon or world fresh from the dawn of its creation. The rich, green splendor of the Philippine rain forest seemed very far away.

A work crew from the mine, drafted into service by Boyd, set up globe lights around the spacious interior of the cavern. Serizawa and Graham both gasped out loud as the first of the lights flared to life, giving them a better look at the scene in whole. Thick bands of a porous, calcite-like material ribbed the grotto.

"The rocks, right?" Boyd said, as though anticipating the scientists' reaction. "I've been digging holes for thirty years, but I've never seen anything like it."

Serizawa's eyes widened as he grasped what he was seeing.

"No," he said, his voice hushed in awe. "Not geological. *Biological*." He raised his flashlight, concentrating its beam on the huge shield-shaped calcite formation that made up the ceiling of the grotto. At least twenty meters in length, its contours were clearly recognizable if you knew what you were looking for. "The ceiling... it's bone. It's the sternum. We're inside a ribcage."

Before Boyd could process that, the rest of the globe lights popped, flooding the vast cavern with cold white light. Serizawa turned about, taking in the entire scene. Now that he knew what to look for, the impossible truth was right before his eyes. Gigantic rib bones, curving upwards like the buttresses of a medieval cathedral, formed the walls of the "cavern." A bony spine, composed of huge, boulder-sized vertebrae, ran across the floor beneath their feet, stretching the length of several football fields. Serizawa realized that he was literally standing on the long-buried backbone of some incredibly gargantuan lifeform.

Graham stepped away from Boyd, before the speechless

foreman could start pelting them with questions. Like Serizawa, she rotated slowly to absorb the full magnitude of what they had discovered. Her eyes were wide behind the visor of her gas mask. She drew closer to Serizawa.

"Is it *Him*?" she asked quietly. "Is it possible?"

Serizawa shook his head. "This is far older."

A hush fell over the cavern as everyone coped with Serizawa's stunning revelation. Boyd shook his head in disbelief, while some of the work crew looked like they were on the verge of bolting. Serizawa recalled the myth of Jonah and the whale, as well another legend native to the small Japanese fishing village where he'd grown up...

"Guys!" a voice called out from deeper within the cavern. It belonged to Kenji, a young graduate student who had recently joined Serizawa's team. "You gotta see this!"

The urgency in Kenji's voice could not be missed. Serizawa and the others hurried toward him, while trying not to stumble over the rubble and vertebrae. They found Kenji standing under a beam of natural daylight shining down from above. The sunshine lit up more of the cavern's interior, allowing an even better view of the colossal skeletal remains, but that was not what immediately caught Serizawa's attention. His eyes were drawn to yet another astounding discovery.

Two gigantic sac-like encrustations hung like barnacles from the colossal breast bone that formed the ceiling of the cavern. Each the size of a large boulder, the sacs had a rough, gnarled texture that might have formed from some kind of hardened resin or other secretion. Even more than the skeletal structure of the cavern, the sacs appeared unmistakably organic. Serizawa, whose background was in biology, thought that they resembled the egg sacs of some unknown organism, albeit of unprecedented proportions.

He aimed the radiation sensor at the closest sac, which elicited a flurry of clacking from the detector, but when he turned the sensor toward the further sac, the clacking died off noticeably. The detector registered only the pre-existing background radiation of the cavern.

Interesting, he thought. Theories and possible explanations began to form within his brain. Although he had devoted much of his career to the covert study of unknown megafauna, he had never encountered specimens like these before. *Was it possible that...?*

"*That* one," Kenji pointed out. "The one that's broken. It's almost as though something came out of it..."

Indeed, one of the enormous sacs appeared to have shattered from the inside. Giant chunks of its husk were strewn about the floor of the cavern, dozens of feet below the ruptured specimen. Serizawa made a mental note to have every fragment collected for analysis. The nature of material might provide valuable clues into what sort of organism had produced it.

"Wait," Kenji said. Fear entered his voice as the full implications of his observation sank in. "Did something actually come out of there?"

Serizawa refrained from replying. There were too many unsanctioned ears present and he had no desire to start a panic. Instead he headed toward the sunlight, joining Kenji in a wide circle of warm golden light. Tilting his head back, he peered upward.

High above his head, a ragged hole in the ceiling opened up onto the outside world—almost as though *something* had burst outward from the depth of the cavern, leaving the ruptured sac behind. He exchanged more apprehensive looks with Graham. This was far more than they had anticipated.

Hours later, as their chopper ferried them away from the site, Serizawa got a birds-eye view of the giant sinkhole that had broken through the floor of the jungle. Nearly sixty meters in diameter, the hole was even bigger than it had looked from below. But that wasn't all that alarmed him. Beyond the gaping pit, a massive drag mark stretched across the hilly rain forest, leaving a trail of crushed and uprooted trees and foliage. Acres across, the trail gouged a disturbingly wide path toward the north end of the island—and the open Pacific beyond.

Serizawa could only wonder what had emerged from the pit.

And where it was heading now.

THREE

1999

The alarm clock jolted Ford Brody from sleep. One minute he'd been dreaming about riding a dragon through outer space, the next he found himself back in his bedroom in suburban Japan. Dawn streamed through the window curtains. Only nine years old, the boy smacked the snooze button on the clock and buried his face back into his pillow. Maybe he could get in a few more moments of sleep before his mom dragged him out of bed.

Then he remembered what day it was.

His eyes lit up and a mischievous smile spread across his face. He slid out of bed and tiptoed across the floor, which was littered with toy soldiers, tanks, and dinosaurs. Just last night, right before going to bed, he'd staged an epic battle between the miniature army-men and a ferocious Tyrannosaurus Rex. As usual, the dinosaur had won...

The glow of a heat lamp caught Ford's eyes. Despite his big plans for the morning, he detoured over to his terrarium to check on the butterfly cocoon dangling from a branch inside the glass case. To his slight disappointment, the cocoon had not hatched overnight. He impatiently tapped on the glass, trying to provoke a response, but the pupa inside the cocoon refused to cooperate.

Oh well, Ford thought, shrugging. *Maybe tomorrow.*

In the meantime, he had other business to attend to. There was a reason he had set the alarm to wake him up an hour early. He had a lot to accomplish before his dad woke up.

But as he snuck out into the hall, still in his pajamas, he was dismayed to hear Joe Brody's voice coming from his office at the end of the corridor. Creeping closer, Ford saw his dad pacing back and forth across the work-filled office, talking urgently into the phone:

"—I'm asking—*Takashi*—*Takashi*—I'm asking for the meeting because I *don't* know what's going on. If I could explain it, I'd write a memo."

Shaking his head, Joe ran a hand through his unruly reddish-brown hair. Early morning stubble dotted his anxious face. Glasses perched on his nose. He threw an exasperated look at Ford's mom, Sandra, who hovered in the doorway to the office, listening intently to her husband's side of the conversation. Her short black hair needed combing, and she had a robe on over her nightgown. Ford didn't understand what the problem was, but he figured it had something to with his parents' work at the nuclear power plant. The family had relocated from San Francisco a few years ago so that they could both get good jobs at the plant.

"Because Hayato said it had to come from you," Joe said impatiently.

His mom heard Ford shuffling behind her. She turned away from the office to spot him in the hallway. He crept up beside her, distraught over this unexpected turn of events.

"He's *awake*?" he whispered.

Her face transformed in an instant, going from concerned professional to sympathetic mom right away. She knelt down to look Ford in the eye. She mussed his light brown hair.

"I know!" she whispered back. "He got up early."

Ford's heart sank. Of all mornings for there to be a problem at the plant. "What're we gonna do?"

"Get dressed," she instructed him, flashing a conspiratorial smile. "I'll figure it out."

Sandra watched her son scamper back to his room before turning her attention back to more grown-up affairs. Joe barely looked up as she re-entered the office, which was neatly organized despite all the graphs and reports piled about. Printouts of an unidentified waveform pattern were spread out atop his desk, alongside a stack of zip disks.

"... my data starts two weeks ago," he explained into the phone. "I've got fourteen days of anomalous signal; pulsing between seventy five and a hundred kilohertz, then suddenly today it's like the same thing but an *echo*. I've ruled out the turbines, internal leakage, we've checked every local RF, TV and microwave transponder. I'm still sitting here with two hundred hours of graph I can't explain." He paused, listening to someone at the other end of the line. "No—*No*—the fact that it's stopped is *not* reassuring. That's not good, that's not the message here."

He belatedly noticed Sandra waiting by the doorway. He placed a hand over the phone's receiver. "What's going on?"

"Your birthday?" she reminded him. "Someone is preparing your 'surprise' party..."

Understanding dawned on his face, but she could tell this was the last thing on his mind right now. Flustered, he nodded at her, acknowledging that he'd gotten the message, but making no effort to get off the phone. He held up his hand, signaling that he needed a few more minutes.

Sandra frowned, giving him a gently chiding look, but let him get back to his call. Lord knew she understood how troubling this new data was. She shared her husband's worries.

"... But that's—hang on—*that's exactly my point*," he insisted. "The moment these pulses stopped is when we started having the tremors." He irritably shuffled a stack of zip disks from his desk. "With all due respect, Takashi, and honor. Respect and honor. With all of that, okay? I'm an engineer and I don't like coincidences and I don't like unexplained frequency patterning near a plant that's my responsibility. I need a meeting. Make it happen."

He was still arguing with Takashi as she left to check on Ford, who had already gotten into his school uniform. They waited until Joe disappeared into the master bedroom to change for work, then hurriedly hung a string of cardboard letters over the archway of the office door. The handmade sign read: "HAPPY BIRTHDAY, DAD!"

Grinning, she and Ford admired their work. They high-fived each other. Ford beamed in anticipation of his dad's reaction.

But when Joe emerged from the bedroom, freshly shaven and wearing a suit and tie, he walked right by the banner without even noticing. His phone was glued to his ear and he spoke rapidly in Japanese on his way out the front door. "Come on," he called out to Sandra and Ford, switching back to English. "We gotta go!"

Crushed, Ford looked up at Sandra. "It rocks," she assured

him. "He'll see it when he gets home, I promise."

Her comforting words appeared to do the trick. The absolute trust on his face tugged at her heart. Nodding, he grabbed his backpack and dashed out the door after his father. Sandra followed them, vowing to herself that, freaky signals or no freaky signals, she would see to it that her son was not disappointed.

Besides, it was Joe's birthday after all. He deserved a celebration—after he got the higher-ups at the plant to listen to him.

"Later, Dad!"

Ford sprinted past the family car on his way to the bus stop. Seated behind the wheel, Joe waved distractedly at the boy, while wrapping up his call.

"Good. Finally," he said in Japanese. "Thank you."

Sandra slid into the passenger seat beside him. She clipped a "Janjira Power" ID badge to the lapel of her jacket and handed a matching badge to Joe.

"He made you a sign, you know."

A sign? A pang of guilt stabbed Joe as he realized what she meant, and that he had been utterly oblivious to whatever she and Ford had cooked up for his birthday. Contrite, he put down his phone and looked over at his wife. He'd had no idea …

"He worked so hard," she said. "I think what I'm gonna do, I'm gonna come home early. I'll take the car and pick him up and we can get a proper cake."

Joe was grateful that she was on top of this—and letting him off so easily. "I'm gonna practice being surprised all day. I promise."

To prove his sincerity, he generated his best "Holy Shit!" expression. His eyes bugged out and his jaw dropped as though he had just won the lottery. The effort teased a laugh from Sandra. He smirked back at her, enjoying the moment. Which couldn't last, unfortunately. Not with the matter preying on his mind.

"Look," he said, "I need to know it's not the sensors. I can't call this meeting and look like the American maniac. We get in, don't even come upstairs, just grab a team and head down to Level 5—do 5 and the coolant cask—just check my sensors. Make sure they're working."

"You're not a maniac," she assured him. "I mean, *you are*, just not about this."

He appreciated her effort to lighten the mood, but he had too much on his mind to joke around right now. "There's got to be something we're not thinking of."

"Happy birthday," she said stubbornly.

He turned toward her. An infectious smile penetrated the cloud hanging over him, and reminded him just how lucky he really was. The corners of his lips lifted.

"I don't know what you're talking about," he lied.

She leaned forward and kissed him warmly on the lips. Despite all his worries and frustration, he responded to the kiss, keeping it going even as he fired up the ignition. They reluctantly disengaged as he pulled away from the curb and headed towards the plant, which loomed prominently on the horizon.

His birthday would have to wait.

The Janjira Nuclear Power Plant perched above the coastline, dominating the skyline overlooking the Sea of Japan.

Thick white plumes of steam vented from the plant's cooling towers, while the reactors themselves were secured within three imposing structures of steel and concrete that had been built to withstand even a crashing 747. Adjoining buildings housed the turbines, generators, pumps, water tanks, storage units, machine shops, administrative offices, and other essentials. A row of transmission towers rose from the switchyard adjacent to the plant. High-voltage power lines transmitted freshly generated electricity to the nearby city and points beyond.

After parking the car in the lot, Joe and Sandra hurried off on their respective tasks. Within minutes, Joe was marching briskly down a corridor, trailed by Stan Walsh, his best friend and partner in crime. Another transplanted American, Stan was a few years older than Joe, who was counting on Stan to back him up when they met with Hayato and the others. Joe gulped down black coffee on the run. "#1 DAD" was emblazoned on his mug, a title Joe doubted he was entitled to this morning.

I'll make it up to Ford later, he promised himself, *after I get to the bottom of this.*

A local engineer, Sachio Maki, hurried up to Joe with an anxious expression on his face. He nervously thrust a file of reports at Joe. Juggling his coffee cup, Joe flipped through the folder, which contained some seismographic readings he had never seen before. His eyes bugged out for real this time.

"Whoa." He froze in his tracks, caught off-guard by the data. "What is *that?*"

"Yes," Maki confirmed. "Seismic anomaly."

The region had been experiencing a number of small underground tremors recently, but nothing this dramatic. "This is from when?" Joe asked urgently.

"Now," Maki said. "This is *now*."

Joe blinked, not quite grasping the truth. When Maki said "now" did he really mean...?

"This graph is minutes, not days," Maki explained, spelling it out. "This is now."

"*What?*"

"Wait," Stan said, trying to keep up. "Seismic' as in what? As in earthquakes?" He peered over Joe's shoulders at the graphs. "Are those earthquakes?"

Joe shook his head. "Earthquakes are random, jagged. This is steady, increasing." He flipped rapidly through the remainder of the report, his eyes tracing the steady upward path of the vibrations' intensity over time. "This is a *pattern*."

Just like the inexplicable signals he had been monitoring.

Following Joe's instructions, Sandra headed straight for the sub-level corridors beneath the primary reactor building, pausing only briefly before a large open doorway. Warning signs, printed in Japanese, marked the boundary before them. This was where the buck stopped: the containment threshold where sturdy barriers could be deployed to seal off the area beyond in the event of a significant radiation leak. While the existence of the barriers should have been reassuring, the necessity of them was something she generally preferred not to think about. There hadn't been a Chernobyl-type disaster since 1986, thirteen years ago, but nobody in the industry wanted to take any chances.

She had rounded up a four-person team to assist her in the inspection. They quickly climbed into full-body radiation suits, as required by the Level 5 safety protocols. Multiple layers of thick protective material, along with a self-contained breathing apparatus, made the uncomfortable suit both hot and heavy to work in. Internal helmet lights illuminated their faces. Sandra took pains to maintain a cool, confident expression on hers.

"Alright," she said, leading the way. "Let's make this quick."

Caught up in the anomalous new seismic data, Joe moved more slowly down the hall toward his meeting. He barely registered Stan fretting beside him.

"Can I be your Rabbi here for a minute?" Stan pleaded, sounding like he was on the verge of another ulcer. He popped an antacid. "Before you go in there and pull some China Syndrome freakout on these guys, keep in mind that we are hired guns here, okay?"

Joe understood that Stan was worried about their contracts and careers, but there were bigger issues at stake here, like the safety of the plant and the surrounding community.

"I have operational authority in my contract, Stan."

This didn't seem to allay Stan's anxieties. If anything, he sounded even more apprehensive. "You pull this off-line, it'll be three months before we get back up."

You think I don't know that, Joe thought, but before he could reply the fluorescent lights flickered overhead. Joe glanced up in confusion. *Now what?*

A second later, a sudden rumble shook the entire building.

The tremor hit even harder down on Level 5. Sandra's team froze in surprise. One of her team members, Toyoaki Yamato, looked at her in alarm. "What was that?"

The overhead lights flickered momentarily, but then the subterranean rumbling stopped. Sandra held her breath for a moment, waiting to see if the tremor had truly subsided, before taking charge again. She tried her best to keep her voice steady.

"Just a little farther," she stated. "Let's check the cask and get out of here."

The other workers nodded and quickened their pace. Nobody wanted to linger in the containment area longer than possible.

Including Sandra.

Joe could feel the tension in the plant's control room the minute he and Stan arrived. Banks of sophisticated control panels, gauges, and monitors, manned by a crew of largely Japanese technicians, lined the walls of the chamber, while the main work desk occupied the center of the room. Windows looked over the plant grounds. Glass partitions isolated various support cubicles. Anxious voices exchanged technical data in Japanese.

Joe spotted the men in charge, Haruo Takashi and Ren Hayato, huddled over a bank of monitors. All eyes turned toward Joe, the hubbub of voices quieting somewhat. He could tell right away that there was more bad news coming.

Some birthday this is turning out to be.

"What the hell's going on?" he demanded.

Takashi turned to face him. The Deputy Plant Administrator was a slim young man, who looked like he was having a bad day as well. "Maybe not such a good time for a meeting," he suggested.

"Agreed," Joe said, pushing the seismic graphs on Takashi. "Have you seen this?"

Takashi nodded toward the bank of monitors he had been glued to before. Hayato, the Senior Reactor Engineer, stepped aside so that Joe could see for himself. Joe immediately recognized the distinctive waveform snaking and pulsing across the monitors. It was the same pattern that he had been staring at for days.

"Do we have a source?" he asked crisply. "Where's the epicenter?"

Takashi threw up his hands. He was more rattled than Joe had ever seen him. "We keep trying... nothing..."

Joe shook his head. "It's got to be centered somewhere."

Hayato spoke up. "No one else is reporting. We've contacted every other plant in the Kanto region, Tokai, Fujiyama... they're unaffected."

Joe wasn't sure if that was good news or bad. "Are we at full function?"

Takashi nodded. "Perhaps we should be drawing down. To be safe."

"Is that my call?" Joe asked.

"Right now, maybe yes," Hayato conceded. He was an older man with graying temples, only a few years from retirement. "We're trying to reach Mr. Mori, but he's not answering."

Joe wasn't inclined to wait on the owner of the company. Those weren't profit-and-loss charts on the monitors. This was a safety issue.

As though to drive that point home, another tremor rattled the building. This one was felt even harder and sharper than before. Joe felt the weight of dozens of eyes upon him. He made up his mind.

"Take us off-line," he said.

Stan balked. A shutdown could cost millions—and possibly their jobs. "Joe..."

"Do it. Wind it down." He issued the order in Japanese. "Seal down the reactors."

There was a brief moment of hesitation before the room erupted into a quiet frenzy of activity. Joe suddenly found himself at the eye of storm, overseeing emergency measures he had expected to go his entire career without implementing. The full import of his decision hit home and he felt weak in the knees. A cold sweat glued his shirt to his back. What if he had over-reacted and pulled the plug too soon? This could be the biggest mistake of his career...

Breathe, he reminded himself. *Think.*

He put down his coffee cup on a nearby table, figuring that his heart was already racing fast enough, thank you very much. Diagrams and blueprints were strewn across the table, along with a selection of walkie-talkies on a tray. He snatched one up and started scanning through the channels, searching for a signal. He needed info and he needed it now, damnit.

And he needed to know that Sandra was okay.

Before he could get hold of her, the mug started vibrating across the table, spilling coffee onto the blueprints, which were also shaking as well. Joe glanced in alarm at the monitors, where the pulse pattern was spiking into a new shape. A stronger, secondary jolt, accompanied by a deep sonic thrum that Joe could feel all the way to his teeth, rattled the glass windows of the control room. The walls shook.

Even worse, all the monitors and other electronics lost power for a second, briefly killing the lights, before they popped back on again. Startled technicians swore and shouted and scrambled to check their systems. Agitated voices competed with each other, everybody talking at once.

"No status!" Takashi blurted. "Everything's rebooting!"

"*Calm*," Joe insisted, trying to maintain order. "No yelling."

Takashi got the message, settling down. He regained his composure as Joe raised his voice to be heard over the clamor.

"All personnel not needed for SLCS procedure should begin to evacuate the plant," Joe announced. "You know the drill." SLCS referred to the Standby Liquid Control System, which could be deployed to shut down the reactors in case the control rods failed to insert. He waited long enough to see his order being carried out before raising the walkie-talkie to his lips. A recorded announcement blared over the intercoms in the background. He placed a hand over his ear to tune it out. "Sandra? Sandy, can you hear me? You need to get back up here!"

At first there was no response, as he urgently spun through the channels, but then he heard his wife's voice over the receiver, broken up by bursts of static:

"*—ear me... anyone co... this is... report... damage to t—*"

FOUR

1999

The sub-level monitoring station was practically useless. Every screen was either flickering or dead, making it practically impossible to get reliable readings on the reactor core and cooling systems. Sandra kept one eye on her team, who were trying unsuccessfully to bring the equipment back on-line, as she worked the walkie-talkie.

"It's shaking hard down here, Joe. Do you copy?"

Yamato stepped away from an uncooperative screen. "We've lost the monitors!" he reported. He was sweating visibly behind the visor of his helmet.

"Sensors are down," another technician confirmed.

The team turned toward Sandra, waiting for her to make the call. She hesitated, knowing how much Joe was counting on her to get him the data he needed, but it looked like that wasn't going to happen. The escalating tremors and blackouts had thrown a monkey wrench in their plans, and forced her to put the safety of her crew ahead of her mission. This was no place you wanted to be during an earthquake... or whatever this was.

"We're turning back," she declared. "Let's go!"

Yet another tremor shook the control room, nearly throwing Joe off-balance. He grabbed onto the table to steady himself. Overhead light fixtures swayed violently even as the fluorescent bulbs went dead. All the electronics crashed again, while dust was shaken loose from the ceiling. The discarded coffee cup vibrated towards the edge of the table. Joe lunged for the mug, hoping to rescue it in time, but he was too late. It crashed to the floor and shattered.

So much for "#1 DAD."

The tremor subsided and the lights blinked back on. Everybody held their breath, waiting for the next shock, before frantically trying to resume the shutdown procedure, if it wasn't too late already. No one, least of all Joe, knew when the next tremor would hit—or how big it might be.

"Joe, are you there?" Sandra's voice broke through the static. *"We're heading back through the containment seal—"*

He clutched the walkie-talkie to his ear.

Hurry, he thought. *Please hurry!*

Sandra and the others raced back the way they'd come, moving as fast as they could in the heavy radiation suits. She prayed that was fast enough.

"You need to get out of there," Joe urged via the walkie-talkie. *"If there's a reactor breach, you won't last five minutes, suits or no suits."* She could hear the fear in his voice even through the static. *"Do you hear me?"*

"I hear you," she responded, breathing hard. "We're coming—"

A sonic pulse cut her off, thrumming louder than before. The floor quaked beneath her feet, causing her to miss a step. She threw out a hand to brace herself against a wall, and could feel the vibration even through her insulated gloves. The lights flickered and—

A massive jolt rocked the building to its foundations, as though it had been struck by a titanic sledge hammer. In the control room, Joe and the others were thrown to the floor. The exterior windows shattered, spraying broken fragments onto the floor, while a glass partition cracked down the middle. A file cabinet toppled over, spilling old paperwork over the floor tile. Empty desk chairs bounced and rolled about.

Sprawled on the floor, not far from the broken coffee mug, Joe rode out the tremor, keeping his face covered. Not until the shaking stopped did he cautiously lift his head and look around. Checking to make sure his glasses were still in one piece, he painfully peeled himself off the floor. His nerves were jangled, and he was bruised from the fall, but he was relieved to see that the control room was more or less intact. His eyes sought out the master control monitors, which, miraculously, were still running. Stan, Takashi, and the others began to clamber to their feet as well. Nobody seemed seriously injured, at least not here in the control room.

But what about Sandra and her team?

He peered up at a video monitor. Closed-circuit TV footage showed a crew in full radiation suits dashing though the reactor unit's sub-levels. He didn't need to make out

Sandra's face to know who was leading the team. He pointed anxiously at the screen.

"Sandra and her crew," he exclaimed. "They're in the containment area!"

Takashi looked aghast. "Why?"

Joe didn't have time to explain. "Oh shit," he muttered. What had that last shock had done to the reactor?. He dashed for the exit, shouting back over his shoulder at Takashi. "Put the safety doors on manual override!"

"I can't do that!" the deputy engineer protested.

Joe didn't want to hear it. He shouted back from the doorway.

"PUT THE DOORS ON MANUAL!"

Sandra and the others raced down a concrete corridor, which felt twice as long as she remembered. A stairway, leading to an upper level, finally appeared before them.

Thank God, she thought. *Maybe we can still get out of here in—*

Another jolt nearly threw her off her feet. Yamato stumbled, but she grabbed onto him and kept him from falling. The cumbersome radiation suits made every movement clumsier than it ought to be, and were unbearably hot as well; she was half-tempted to shuck the suit, but that would be insane. For all she knew, there could be a leak at any minute.

The team squeezed into the cramped, dimly lit stairwell. They were all panting now, weighed down by the heavy suits and breathing gear. Sandra's muscles ached and her legs felt like they were made of lead, but adrenalin and panic kept her and the others climbing for their lives.

If they could just make it past the containment threshold…

An emergency stairwell led from the control room to the primary reactor unit. Joe rushed down, taking the steps two or three at a time. His heart pounded in his chest, going a mile a minute, while he prayed that Sandra was heading toward him from the opposite direction. He wasn't sure how much longer he could count on Takashi to keep the containment doors open.

Don't stop, he silently pleaded with her. *Don't slow down for a second. Please!*

Reaching Level 5 in record time, he burst out of the stairwell and skidded to a stop right before the entrance to the containment area. A large button, surrounded by emergency instructions in both Japanese and English, was installed in the wall to one side of the entrance. Joe peered down the long corridor beyond, hoping desperately to see Sandra and the others running toward him, but the hallway was eerily silent and empty, as though it had already been evacuated. He was tempted to run into the corridor to find Sandra, but there was no time to suit up and somebody had to stand by to trigger the manual controls, just in case the worst-case scenario played out, which was looking more and more likely by the moment.

C'mon, Sandy, he thought. *Where the hell are you?*

A closed-circuit video camera was mounted in a corner where the walls met the ceiling. Joe hoped to God that Takashi was still watching this. He shouted up at the camera.

"Takashi! Tell me this door is on manual!"

The other man's voice emerged from the comm system. *"Manual, yes, but Joe—we're starting to breach, you understand me?"*

He understood all right. This was the nightmare that every nuclear engineer dreaded, the one that kept them up at nights, thinking about Chernobyl and Three Mile Island. He feared there was nothing he could to do to save one or all of the reactors.

But maybe he could still save his wife.

"I'm right here," he told Takashi, as forcefully as he could. "As soon as they're through, I'll seal it!"

He hoped that would be enough to Takashi's finger off the panic button, but he wouldn't blame the other man for playing it safe. Takashi didn't have the love of his life still in the danger zone.

"Sandra?" he said into the walkie-talkie. "Can you hear me? I'm here, honey. I'm at the door!"

She held on tightly to the walkie-talkie as she and the others sprinted breathlessly down yet another seemingly endless corridor. Steel-toed rubber boots pounded against the hard concrete floors. The crew had made it up the stairs, but they still had a ways to go before they were beyond the containment area. Joe's voice, coming over the walkie-talkie, urged her on, even though his words were fragmented by harsh blasts of static:

"—ere—for you—checkpoin—aiting—"

Emergency klaxons started blaring behind them like angry foghorns. Flashing red annunciator lights turned the sterile white corridors incarnadine. Sandra glanced back behind her, as did the rest of her team. Panic gripped her heart. They all knew what the sirens and flashing lights meant and why the klaxons were getting louder and closer by the moment. The danger posed by the tremors was no longer just a terrifying possibility. The fiery genie inside the reactor had escaped its bottle and was chasing after them.

They were going to die, unless they made it to safety in time.

Takashi was alone in the control room. The rest of the staff had already deserted the premises, including Hayato. The older man had volunteered to stay behind, but Takashi had convinced him to take charge of the evacuation instead. Hayato was a family man, with a wife, children, and several grandchildren who needed him, while Takashi had put his career ahead of any serious relationships so far. The young engineer stared in horror at a hallway schematic of the lower levels. Blinking red icons indicated the rapid spread of radiation throughout the corridors. His eyes widened in dread as stayed at his post, torn between his duty to contain the disaster and his purely human concern for his friends and co-workers. He could only imagine how excruciating this must be for Joe Brody, even as Takashi worried whether the American engineer would really be able to do what was necessary, no matter the cost.

Takashi wasn't sure he could, not if it was his true love at stake.

Joe stared anxiously past the threshold, frozen in fear. He listened numbly to Takashi's fractured voice over the intercom. Static interference mangled the transmission, rendering it barely comprehensible:

"*Brody—we—ah—each—*"

"What?" Joe asked, straining to make out what was being said. "Say again?"

"Catastrophic radiation breach!"

Joe had thought he couldn't be any more scared, but this nightmare just kept getting worse and worse. Utter horror transfixed him. This couldn't be happening...

"Seal the corridor," Takashi pleaded, *"or the whole city will be exposed!"*

Keep going, Sandra thought. *Just a little further!*

Terror overcame exhaustion as she and her crew sprinted down a corridor, despite the best efforts of the earthquake to slow them down. An earth-shaking rumble caused the floor to quake beneath their feet, tossing them from one side to another. Yamato tumbled headfirst onto the concrete floor, forcing Sandra to turn back and help him to his feet. His visor had survived the fall intact, thank goodness, and they were about to resume their flight when—

The air rippled behind them as a billowing cloud of radioactive vapor and particulate matter blew in from the far end of the corridor. The oncoming vapors set off the radiation sensors in the ceiling, causing the emergency klaxons to sound directly overhead. Flashing red lights accompanied the sirens. The hot gases and steam rushed toward Sandra and the others with frightening speed. Unable to outrun it, her eyes wide with horror, she braced herself as the cloud blasted past them like a red-hot gust of wind, knocking them all to the floor. Buffeted by the blast, she felt the heat of the vapors through the multiple layers of her protective suit. She held her breath instinctively, despite the gas mask protecting her air supply.

Oh my God, she thought. *Have I been exposed?*

But that wasn't the worst part. The cloud kept on going, triggering sirens further ahead. It flooded down the corridor toward the containment threshold. Sandra and Yamato traded stunned looks. They all knew what would happen if the irradiated cloud reached the checkpoint first, what would *have* to happen for the safety of the entire community. They needed to be on other side of that boundary before it was too late.

Panicked, they all scrambled to their feet and ran madly for the checkpoint.

"Five seconds... four seconds... "

Takashi counted down over the intercom as Joe stood like a statue right outside the containment area, staring bleakly at the empty corridor beyond. He remembered kissing Sandra in the car less than an hour ago, tried to remember the last thing he said to her before they went their separate ways this morning. Had he said he loved her, or even said goodbye?

He knew he couldn't wait much longer.

"*Joe,*" Takashi said, reaching the end of his countdown. No doubt he was tracking the progress of the radiation leak as it spread through the lower levels. "*You have to shut it down... now.*"

Looking away from the entrance, Joe stared at the manual control button on the wall. He tried to step toward it, but his feet didn't want to move. He forced himself to take one step toward the button, two, three... until the button was within reach. He raised his hand, clenched his fist.

God forgive me, he thought.

Static squawked from the walkie-talkie. Fragmented bursts of his wife's voice came over the speaker:

"*—Joe—ear—an—*"

His heart surged in his chest. He clutched the walkie-talkie hard enough to turn his knuckles white. Desperation filled his voice.

"Sandra?... *Sandra?*"

Perversely, the static abated long enough for him to hear her clearly at last, perhaps for the last time.

"Joe. It's too late! We're not going to make it!"

Her words hit him harder than any earthquake, shattering his world. "No, no!" he shouted into the walkie-talkie. "Don't you say that! Don't you stop—!"

"You have to do it!" The signal began to break up again, pops and crackles threatening to consume her final words. *"You have to live! For Ford!"*

The radio sputtered and died. He smacked it furiously, trying to get her back.

"SANDRA!"

Klaxons blared as a swirling cloud of discharged vapor came gusting around a bend at the far end of the corridor. Red lights flashed in alarm. The radioactive gases rushed toward Joe... and the boundary.

"You have to seal it!" Takashi shouted frantically over the intercom. *"JOE!"*

Joe thought of the unsuspecting city outside the plant. Ford would be at school now, maybe playing at recess... along with dozens of other kids. And thousands of other men, women, and children were going about their business, unaware of the hell that had been unleashed from the damaged reactor, the hell he was trapped in now.

I'm sorry, Sandy... I'm so, so sorry...

Screaming in rage, he drew back his arm and pounded his fist into the emergency control button. A transparent barrier, more than six inches thick, instantly slammed down like the blade of a guillotine, sealing off the contaminated corridor.

The advancing red lights halted right on the other side of the barrier. The screaming sirens faded away, echoing into silence.

Dear God, Joe thought. *What have I done?*

Alone in the control room, Takashi sagged in relief, sinking into his seat as he watched the blinking red icons tail off at the checkpoint. A message flashed upon the screen:

"BARRIER SECURE."

Takashi kept looking at the message, almost afraid to believe it was true. He felt like he'd aged twenty years in the last few minutes. They had come so close to a total catastrophe. If Joe had been just a few seconds slower...

"Radiation is contained," he reported over the comm. He paused before asking the question he was afraid to ask. "Is... is Sandra with you? Joe?"

Joe couldn't answer. He felt destroyed by what he had just done. The finality of shutting the barrier on his wife. The walkie-talkie slipped from his fingers, crashing unnoticed onto the floor. Unable to stand, he slid limply to the ground, his back against the thick plexiglass barrier. He buried his face in his hands.

"Joe?" Takashi continued to harangue him. *"The barrier will only hold so long. We have to close the lead shield, too."*

Joe knew he was right, but he couldn't cope with that right now. He needed a moment, just to try to come to grips with what he had lost, with what his life had just become. He and Sandra had been together since college, even gone into the same industry together. He had always assumed they would grow old together, watching Ford grow up...

A dull pounding reached his ears, coming from the barrier behind him. Dread gripped his heart as he realized what the pounding meant. *Oh, God,* he thought. *I'm not sure I can stand this...*

He didn't want to turn around, but, of course, he had no choice. Lifting his face from his hands, he forced himself to turn slowly toward the barrier and the ghastly sight waiting for him on the other side of the transparent wall. Maybe this was his punishment for failing Sandra and the others. He needed to come face-to-face with what he'd done.

Toyoaki Yamato was there, pressed up frantically against the barrier, pounding with both hands against the unyielding plexiglass. Behind his visor, his face was a portrait of sheer, unadulterated panic. Joe couldn't hear Yamato's screams through the soundproof wall, but that wasn't necessary; the fear and desperation in the man's eyes spoke loud enough. The doomed technician was begging for his life, even though he was already as good as dead.

I'm sorry, Joe thought. *It's too late. There's nothing I can do.*

Part of him envied Yamato. At least his suffering would be over soon. He wouldn't have to live with the consequences of his actions for the rest of his life. He wouldn't have to tell his son that he would never see his mother again. For a moment, Joe was relieved that it wasn't Sandra pounding on the barrier, and felt ashamed for his cowardice, but then the rest of the work crew rounded the corner, catching up with Yamato. The other men threw themselves against the barrier as well, blind animal fear overcoming their reason. Their frenzied faces shrieked behind their masks. Their fists pounded relentlessly at the impenetrable wall between death and survival.

But Sandra didn't try to break through. Instead she merely

slumped in exhaustion on the other side of the wall. Anguished eyes sought out Joe's and they stared at each other hopelessly. Only inches of solid plexiglass divided them, but it might as well have been a continent. Joe tried to speak, to push the words past his throat, but they wouldn't come. His throat tightened. His eyes burned with tears that had yet to spill down his face. He couldn't imagine how they had possibly come to this unthinkable moment. It wasn't fair...

"*Joe,*" Takashi interrupted. *"I'm closing the shield."*

No, Joe thought. *Not yet!* He looked around frantically for the fallen walkie-talkie and snatched it from the floor. Tears began to fall as he held it to his lips. "Sandra? Can you hear me?"

There was so much he needed to say, so much he had to apologize for, but only static answered his agonized entreaties. She shook her head sadly, holding his gaze with her eyes.

"I'm sorry," he sobbed.

She couldn't hear him, but she didn't need to. His pain and anguish and guilt were written all over his face. The fear faded from her eyes as a strange calm appeared to settle over her. He could tell she knew what he did, what he'd had to do, and what it had cost them both. She placed her palm up against the glass. He reached out to place his own hand over hers, only to hear a jarring buzzer inform him that their time was up.

The second barrier engaged. Two solid-lead doors slid in from both sides of the doorway. Joe yanked his hand back just in time. For a few final moments, their eyes met in silent communion. Her lips moved, as though she was trying to comfort him, or perhaps just say goodbye, but he would never know what her last words were.

The doors slammed shut, cutting her off from view... forever.

Goodbye, Joe thought. *May God forgive me.*
He wasn't sure he ever would.

A violent tremor jolted him from his grief. The building quaked all around him. Dust and debris rained down from the ceiling. The floor bucked beneath him.

"The entire plant is collapsing!" Takashi shouted from the comm. *"We have to get out... NOW!"*

Joe placed his hand on the lead door, exactly where he knew Sandra's face must be. It tore him apart to know that she was still there, still alive, less than a foot away. Entombed inside a radioactive deathtrap, facing the end without even her family beside her in her final moments. And it killed him to know that now he had to leave her.

"You have to live!" she had said. *"For Ford!"*

Joe knew she was right. If not for their son, he would have gladly stayed behind to perish with Sandra. At least they'd be together, even if a wall of lead separated them, but he had to think about Ford now. The boy couldn't lose his mother *and* his father. He owed it to Sandra to make it out of this alive... for Ford's sake.

Tearing himself away from the lead doors, he scrambled to his feet and ran for his life.

The control room was empty now. Not even Takashi remained to bear witness to the plant's final moments of operation. Unattended monitors captured real-time video surveillance of the last wave of plant personnel fleeing the complex. Joe could be glimpsed on one monitor, barely making it to the parking lot in time, along with Takashi. Squealing cars and trucks sped out of the gates, trying to put as much distance as possible between themselves and the plant. Power lines snapped and whipped about, spitting showers of sparks. The sky-high transmission towers in the switchyard tottered.

Another screen watched over Reactor Room One, deep in the heart of the abandoned plant. The five-hundred-ton pressure vessel containing the reactor core was shielded by dense layers of steel and concrete, but hot gases continued to leak from the ruptured casing. Silence reigned over the compromised chamber until the massive vessel suddenly toppled over, crashing onto the reinforced concrete floor, as something huge and inconceivable burst up through the floor. A violent discharge of radiation wreaked havoc with the transmission so that the screen caught only a fleeting glimpse of a large, blurry object that vaguely resembled a claw...

Then an immense pulse of energy, indescribably powerful, swept through the entire plant, disrupting every electronic circuit and knocking out all the lights.

The screens in the control room went black.

The Janjira International School was a one-story building boasting traditional Japanese architecture, complete with bamboo shutters on the window. Sitting in class with his fellow students, facing the blackboard, Ford found it hard to concentrate on Miss Okada's language lesson. He couldn't wait for the day to be over so that his dad could finally see the surprise he and Mom had prepared for him. Ford was also hoping for some chocolate cake and ice cream. His mouth watered in anticipation.

Emergency sirens started wailing outside, distracting Ford from his sugary daydreams. The sirens sounded like they were coming from only a few miles away. Frowning, Miss Okada turned away from the chalkboard. "All right, children," she said in Japanese. "Let's practice our safety drills."

Ford figured it was just another duck-and-cover drill as well, until a fearsome metallic groaning penetrated the thin walls of the classroom. Both teacher and students stopped what they were doing and turned their heads toward the window, where the nuclear power plant could be glimpsed not far away. Ford instantly thought of his parents—and how stressed his dad had been that morning.

Did this have something to do with that problem at the plant?

He rushed to the window, even as Miss Okada tried to herd the rest of the class out the door. Boys and girls in matching blue uniforms poured out of the school onto the grassy lawn outside, even as the ominous rumbling grew louder and louder. His teacher called to him, but Ford barely registered her anxious voice. Unable to look away, he stared out the window as...

The entire plant collapsed before his eyes. With a deafening roar, all three containment buildings dropped out of sight, as though suddenly swallowed up by the earth. Billowing clouds of dirt and debris rose up where the towers had once stood. Children, and even a few teachers, screamed as, in a matter of minutes, the looming nuclear power plant ceased to exist.

Mom! Ford thought, all thought of cake and birthdays forgotten. *Dad!*

The roar of the disaster consumed his entire world.

FIVE

PRESENT DAY

A high-pitched hydraulic whine roused Lieutenant Ford Brody from an uneasy slumber. A sliver of light hit his tired brown eyes, causing him to blink and look away. The twenty-five year old Navy officer sat in the cramped-but-spacious hold of a C-17 Globemaster transport plane, surrounded by dozens of troops from other branches of the armed services, all returning from recent tours of duty in Afghanistan. Ford knew he ought to be more excited about finally touching down back home, but, to be honest, he was mostly worn-out, jet-lagged, and even a bit apprehensive.

"Family waiting for you?" Captain Freeman asked, eyeing Ford. A career soldier in his mid-forties, the older man had a seen-it-all air about him. He had been dozing beside Ford for the last several thousand miles.

Ford shrugged. "Hope so."

Freeman nodded. "How long you been away?"

"Fourteen months."

"Take it slow," Freeman advised, gathering up his kit, which was resting at his feet. "It's the one thing they don't train you for."

Tell me about it, Ford thought. The long separation had been hard on everyone.

Daylight flooded the hold as the large cargo doors at the rear of the plane glided open, offering a view of the tarmac beyond. Ford gathered up his own things as he joined the procession of weary, homebound warriors exiting the plane two by two. He quickly lost track of Captain Freeman in the crush of uniformed bodies. He wondered what, if any, kind of reunion the battle-hardened veteran had in store. The call of duty could be hard on one's home life, as Ford was already learning for himself.

Outside the hangar at Travis Air Force Base, a mob of eager friends and family waited impatiently behind a cordon for the first glimpse of their loved ones. The crowd displayed flowers, yellow ribbons, waving flags, and enough handmade signs to stage a political demonstration. The brightly colored signs, often boasting stars, stripes, and generous amounts of glitter, greeted the new arrivals with countless heartfelt variations on the same theme.

"WELCOME HOME, DAD!"

"WELCOME HOME, SIS!"

"WELCOME HOME, SWEETHEART!"

Cheers and applause hailed the first appearance of the troops, followed by tears and squeals of delight as individuals spotted their respective loved ones. Neatly regimented ranks broke apart into a riot of emotional reunions. Spouses leapt into each other's arms, locking lips in public displays of affection. Small children scampered to embrace their parents. Older relatives wept openly at the safe return of long-absent sons, daughters, nephews, nieces, and grand-children. Handcrafted signs, painstakingly prepared, were tossed aside and forgotten in the joy and excitement of the moment. Bouquets of yellow roses were crushed between enthusiastic hugs and kisses.

Lost in a sea of jubilant strangers, Ford looked around anxiously, searching for a familiar face. At first all he saw was other people's reunions, but then:

"Hello, stranger."

Elle emerged from the chaotic mob scene, her sandy blond hair and hazel eyes instantly rendering everyone else insignificant, aside from the mop-headed four-year-old boy clutched in her arms. A rush of emotion overcame Ford at the sight of his wife and son, who had only been flickering images on a computer screen for over a year now. He couldn't help noticing how much bigger Sam was; he'd been barely more than a toddler the last time Ford had laid eyes on him in person. He tried not to think about how much he'd missed during the young boy's growth.

They jostled their way through the crowd toward each other. Beaming and beautiful, Elle put Sam down on the pavement in front of his father. Ford half expected the boy to come charging toward him, as so many of the other children were doing with their parents, but instead Sam looked oddly tentative. He hung back shyly, retreating behind his mother, while Ford stood by helplessly, uncertain what to do. At the moment, defusing a roadside IED seemed simpler and easier than re-connecting with his own child.

Elle broke the awkward silence. "Lots of discussion about who gets the first hug." she explained.

"Where'd you come out on that?" Ford asked.

Elle bent to confer with Sam. "You change your mind, honey?"

Sam stared at Ford wordlessly. Ford knelt down before him, approaching him as delicately as he would an unexploded bomb.

"I've been carrying around that last hug you gave me for a long time," Ford said gently, even as Sam continued to gaze at him as though he didn't quite recognize the uniformed stranger before him. "I could sure use a refill."

The boy came out from behind Elle, but still appeared a little shy. Elle placed a comforting hand on Sam's shoulder, while casting an apologetic look at Ford.

"Let's do this," she suggested. "Why don't I go first and check it out and make sure Daddy still knows what he's doing?"

She came forward and, for the time being, all Ford's fears and worries evaporated as she was there in his arms once more, holding him close, kissing him passionately, and he felt keenly just how much he had missed her during his long months abroad. Sam was squeezed in between them, hesitantly joining in the celebration. The three of them clung to each other, wrapped up tight in the moment, oblivious to the tumultuous scene around them. For the first time since the plane had touched down, Ford truly felt like he was home.

At least for now.

"Welcome Home, Daddy!" read the homemade banner taped to the dining room wall.

The sun had fallen by the time they got back to their modest home in San Francisco. Ford was relieved to see that the house looked much as he remembered, aside from a few new knick-knacks and appliances. Dinner was cartons of ice cream, including Ford's favorite: Rocky Road. Across the table, Sam dug enthusiastically into a big carton of chocolate-chip mint. His earlier shyness had faded somewhat, now that they were all settled back in at home, in familiar surroundings. Maybe Sam had just needed a little time to get used to seeing his dad again?

Ford hoped that was the case. "Sam, you better enjoy this," his mother said. "You're not getting ice cream for dinner every night."

"We aren't?" Ford said through a mouthful of Rocky Road, provoking giggles from Sam. "Why not?"

Elle rolled her eyes. "Sam, how do you have a ten-year-old for a father? How is that mathematically possible?"

After ice cream, it was time to put Sam to bed. His room still had same blue wallpaper, adorned with rockets and blazing comets, he and Elle had picked out four years ago. Pencil markings on a wall charted his growth. Although Elle had been needed to help Sam into his pajamas, Ford had insisted on tucking his son into bed himself. But first he had to clear off a menagerie of toy soldiers, tanks, and dinosaurs from atop the covers. He couldn't help smiling at the toys, which reminded him of the same ones he'd played with as a child—before his mother died and everything went to hell.

Don't think about that now, he scolded himself. *Concentrate on today... and Sam.*

"See this one here?" He plucked a green plastic soldier from the bed-slash-battleground. "That's a lot like Daddy in his uniform, but mine's way cooler. We need to go to the toy store, find you a Navy man. How 'bout that?"

Sam nodded happily, grinning up at Ford, as his dad tucked him in.

"Alright, big man," he said, mussing the boy's hair. "Hit the rack."

Sam cuddled in beneath the covers. "Can you sing the dinosaur song... like Mommy?"

The dinosaur song? Ford was baffled—and acutely aware of long he had been missing from his son's life. "Not sure I know that one."

He looked to Elle for help. She smiled at him from the doorway, letting him fend for himself, just like he'd insisted.

Captain Freeman was right, he decided. *They really don't train us for this.*

He got up to leave. A worried look came over the little boy's face.

"Dad? You'll be here tomorrow, too, right?"

Ford winced at the anxiety in his son's voice.

"Yeah, buddy. I told you. The next two weeks are all yours." He reluctantly retreated toward the hall, where Elle was waiting. "Now get some shut-eye, okay? I'll still be here in the morning."

"You promise?"

Ford leaned in and gave Sam a gentle peck on the forehead. He wished there was more he could to do to reassure his son. He knew what it was like to have a father you barely knew anymore.

"You bet," he promised.

"—so by this point, he's literally buck naked with his jock strap on his forehead, a banana in his teeth, hooting like a monkey—and *that's* when our C.O. steps in—and I swear to God, looks him right in the eye, not skipping a beat, goes: 'At ease, Lieutenant.'"

Elle doubled over, giggling hysterically, as Ford acted out the anecdote for her entertainment. They had the lights on dim in the kitchen and a half-empty bottle of wine rested on the table between them. Ford knew he ought to get some sleep—he had been traveling nonstop for over a day now—but he and Elle had a lot of lost time to make up. She struggled to catch her breath, laughing so hard tears leaked from her eyes. Ford cracked up, too.

He came around the table and pulled her close.

"I missed your laugh," he said, relishing the feel of her against him. "My last roommate honked like a mule."

She melted into him. The familiar scent of her hair stirred his memories.

"I missed you, too," she said.

Their laughter gradually subsided, but he kept holding onto her, unwilling to let her go. Back on tour, while disposing of explosive ordnance, there had been more than a few tense moments when he'd thought he'd never have a chance to hold Elle again. Part of him still couldn't believe that they were really back together again after all that time. Hilarity gave way to intimacy as she rested snugly against him. Just like old times.

He drew her toward him. She resisted at first, eyeing him with a wary expression, but, to his vast relief, she let it go for now. Their lips met as they surrendered to a mutual hunger that had not been satisfied for far too long. The kiss deepened, growing in heat, while they pressed against each other with ever-greater urgency, their hands exploring the tantalizing contours beneath their clothing, their fervent grip and lips anchoring them together. Locked in each other's arms, they began to ease toward the bedroom.

The phone rang.

"Don't," he said. "Not now."

Elle disengaged from the embrace, pulling away, but he

held on to her waist. Her face was flushed. "It could be work."

She was a nurse at San Francisco General Hospital, and she took her responsibilities as seriously as he did his. It was one of the things he loved about her, even when their respective duties pulled them apart. He clung to her playfully, nuzzling her neck, even as she leaned over to answer the phone.

"Hello?" she said into the receiver, fighting back giggles.

"Tell 'em you're busy," he whispered seductively into her ear. "Tell 'em your husband is unbuttoning your shirt as you speak—"

He heard a muffled voice on the other end of the line, but was more interested in exploring the tantalizing contours beneath Elle's clothes. She wriggled deliciously and made a very half-hearted effort to swat away his wandering hands while he nibbled on her ear. She turned her moist, enticing lips away from the phone.

"Ford, stop it—come on—!"

Not a chance, he thought.

The muffled voice spoke again. All at once, her frolicsome manner evaporated. She stopped responding to his caresses and gave her full attention to the phone instead. Barely suppressed giggles were cut off abruptly. Her expression darkened and Ford knew at once that playtime was over. He listened intently, frowning.

"No, this is *Mrs*. Brody," she replied to the unknown caller. "Yes, he's my husband. Hold on a moment."

She covered the phone and turned slowly toward Ford, who braced himself in anticipation. Judging from Elle's reaction, he knew he wasn't going to like this.

"What?" he asked.

"It's the consulate," she said tersely. "Joe... he's been arrested in Japan."

Ford felt like he had just been sucker-punched. Whatever trace of his amorous mood had remained dissolved completely, consumed by an all-too-familiar mixture of resentment and gloom. He should've known that the call was about his father—and his never-ending obsessions.

Jesus Christ, Dad, he thought. *What have you done this time?*

Ford slumped in a kitchen chair, already exhausted at the prospect of having to deal with his dad again. It never ended, year after year, all the way back to terrible day fifteen years ago, when Ford had watched the nuclear power plant vanish from sight, taking his mother with it. Joe Brody had begun to melt down that day as well, and his son was still dealing with the emotional fallout, all these years later.

"Ford?"

Elle held out the phone. He lifted his head to meet her worried gaze. He had no idea whether he could handle this again. He stared at the phone as though it was a ticking time bomb, about to blow up in his face... one more time. What the hell was he supposed to do?

"He's your father," she reminded him.

Ford rummaged unhappily through a bedroom dresser, searching for a clean pair of socks. His duffel bag rested on the bed nearby. He couldn't believe he was doing this. He hadn't even unpacked yet and here he was packing to leave again. He pulled open another drawer, unable to find what he was looking for. He didn't even know where anything was anymore.

"Why was he trespassing in the quarantine zone?" Elle leaned against the wall, watching him pack. She nodded at the dresser. "No, the other drawer."

"Why do you think?" Ford said bitterly. "Lone crusader for the truth, all his crackpot theories."

"Your father's a good man. He just needs help. He lost everything that day."

"So did I. But I got over it."

"I can see that," she said wryly.

Ford paused in his search, realizing how he must sound. A photo of Elle and Sam, residing atop the dresser, reminded him not to take this out on her, and how much this whole situation sucked.

"We've worked so hard for everything we have, Elle. I'm afraid he'll ruin it. Every time I let him close, he tries to drag me back. I can't live in the past. I can't put our family through that."

"He *is* your family, Ford." She came toward him, smiling. "You'll be back in a few days. It's not the end of the world."

He wondered what he had ever done to deserve somebody so patient and understanding. He pulled her close and they kissed, doing their best to make every moment count.

Just a few days, he thought. *That's all.*

SIX

"What is the duration of your stay?" the customs official asked, inspecting Ford's passport.

An endless flight, one connection, and fifteen time zones later, Ford trudged wearily through Narita Airport, toting his carry-on luggage. He'd managed to catch a little sleep on the planes, but the prospect of returning to Japan had stirred up unwanted memories. Bad dreams had followed him all the way across the Pacific.

"One day," he said curtly.

He fully intended to deal with his dad's latest mess and get back on a plane to Frisco as soon as humanly possible. He'd promised Sam two weeks and he'd be damned if he'd let his crazy father cut into that precious time with Sam. More than he already had, that is.

"And the nature of your visit?" the customs official asked.

Ford paused briefly before answering. "Family."

That was good enough for the official, who briskly

stamped Ford's passport. Ford bypassed baggage claim and headed straight for the taxi station outside the airport. The bright sunlight came as shock after leaving Frisco in the middle of the night. He wanted to catch a cab to Tokyo and crash in a cheap hotel, but instead he asked the cabbie to drive him to the police station where his father was still being held.

The drive was both longer and faster than Ford would have preferred. It was late afternoon by the time he found himself sitting in the austere waiting area of a Tokyo police station. Stark institutional walls and sparse furniture rendered the room inhospitable, not that anyone was ever likely to drop by for the amenities. Wanted posters and security alerts were pinned to a bulletin board. Ford tried flipping through some old magazines, only to discover that his Japanese wasn't what it used to be, despite the long-ago efforts of Miss Okada. He glumly watched a parade of cops and perpetrators pass in and out of the station. He would've killed for a cup of black coffee, but that didn't seem to be an option.

A middle-aged couple, their faces drawn, sat stiffly in the seats beside him. They looked about as happy to be here as he was, although he guessed that they hadn't traveled nearly so far. Ford didn't have the energy to try to make conversation with the couple, who appeared caught up in their own troubles anyway. They gripped each other's hands as they waited. He wondered how long they'd been married.

A buzzer sounded and an inner door unlocked. Ford and the couple looked up to see a bedraggled teenager, decked out in Goth regalia, escorted into the waiting room by a duty cop. The boy's Mohawked head was hung in shame and he stared at the floor, unable to meet his parent's gaze. The black mascara around his eyes was smeared, as though he'd been crying. The teen's mother placed a hand over her mouth, stifling a sob.

The father, a sober-looking gentleman in a conservative suit and tie, rose to face his errant son. The older man regarded the teen in silence for a moment, his stony face unreadable, then came forward to hug his son. The boy collapsed against his father, weeping and apologizing for whatever offense had landed him in the hoosegow. His mother, also forgiving, joined her husband in assuring the teen that, no matter what, he was still their son.

Maybe it was just the jet lag and lack of sleep, but Ford was moved by what he witnessed. He watched enviously as the trio departed the station together. *That* was what a family was supposed to look like. Not like…

"Been a while," Joe Brody said.

Ford looked up to see his father standing before him, unkempt and disheveled from a night behind bars. He was rake-thin, having lost weight since the last time Ford had seen him, and there was more grey at his temples than Ford remembered. Stubble carpeted his face. If anything, he looked like he'd been sleeping worse than Ford. Heavy pouches shadowed his puffy, bloodshot eyes.

Caught up in someone else's family drama, Ford hadn't even noticed his dad being led in. Father and son stared at each other awkwardly, both of them searching for a place to begin. It had been a long time since they had known how to talk to each other, or been entirely comfortable in each other's presence. Ford suddenly envied that Goth kid.

Unable to find the right words, Ford just held out his hand to shake.

It was the best he could do.

GODZILLA

* * *

A partial view of downtown Tokyo from one small window was the only selling point of the cramped and cluttered garret Joe Brody currently called home. It was dusk and neon lights filtered in from outside as Ford and his father entered the apartment. Ford glanced around dubiously. This dump was a far cry from the cozy suburban home he had once shared with his parents—in what was now a radioactive ghost town.

"I'm sorry you had to come all this way, Ford," his dad said. Joe stepped over tottering stacks of books, magazines, and newspapers piled high on the floor. A single beat-up futon was littered with dirty laundry. Crusty plates and dishes were heaped in the sink of an adjacent kitchenette. An open doorway revealed an unmade bed. The stuffy atmosphere was badly in need of air freshener. Joe avoided Ford's eyes. "Couldn't you have just given them a credit card?"

I wish, Ford thought. Bailing his dad out wasn't the issue here. It was the fact that Ford had needed to do so in the first place.

He refrained from saying so. The awkwardness between them had not gone away during the short drive here. Joe flipped on a light, igniting a naked bulb hanging from the ceiling, and Ford got a better look at what his father's life had become.

It was a lot to take in. The apartment was more than just a mess. It was a lunatic's hoard of papers, maps, books, notes, photos, Post-its, and graphs occupying every available surface, including the walls. Tangled cables, snaking across the floor, connected a bewildering array of antique computer monitors, old TV sets, battered printers, and used mainframes that looked as though they should have been consigned to a junk heap years ago. There was even a VCR and VHS tapes for Pete's sake. To Ford's eyes, it was a chaotic flurry of random data, accumulated by someone driven round the bend by an obsessive search for answers. Ford dimly remembered how neat and well-ordered his father's home office had once been, before the meltdown, and winced at the disorderly rat's nest before him. Joe Brody had been a respected engineer, a professional, many years ago.

Ford wasn't sure what his father was now.

Joe caught Ford staring silently at the clutter and disarray. He feebly attempted to tidy up, relocating some discarded clothing from the futon to a closet and clearing a path through the heaps of books and magazines. A knee-high stack of newspapers toppled over, spilling onto the floor.

"PhDs don't make much teaching English as a second language," Joe offered by way of explanation for his low-rent accommodation. He waited in vain for Ford to say something, then continued. "How's the bomb business? That must be a growth area these days."

Ford was irked by his dad's remark. "It's called explosive ordinance *disposal*. And my job isn't dropping bombs. It's stopping them."

His gaze was still riveted by the insane accumulation of information pinned and taped to the walls. Looking closer, he spied decades-old news clippings about the meltdown, maps of the quarantine zone, and what appeared to be clandestine spy-photos of tall razor-wire fences and armed sentries on patrol. Ford frowned. He had a pretty good idea who had taken those amateur photos.

"How's Elle doing?" Joe asked, in a transparent attempt to divert Ford's attention from the walls. "Sam must be, what, two already?"

"Almost four." Ford didn't feel like talking about Sam. He made his way across the clutter to a second-hand desk that was practically buried beneath a surplus of scientific tomes. Bookmarks flagged key sections. Notes had been scribbled in the margins. "I thought you were over this stuff." He sorted through the books, looking over the titles and chapter headings. He picked one after another up, trying to make sense of it all. "*Echolocation. Parasitic Communication Patterns.*"

Joe took the book from Ford. "Homework," he said with forced casualness. "I'm studying Bioaccoustics. My new thing."

As though that explains everything, Ford thought, losing patience. He was too tired and fed up to beat around the bush any longer. He turned away from the desk to confront his father.

"Dad, what the hell were you doing?"

"Ah, that trespassing stuff is nonsense, Ford." Joe waved it away with a dismissive gesture. "I was just trying to get to the old house—"

"It's a quarantine zone!"

"Exactly!" Joe's casual pose fell away, revealing what was really driving him. "That's exactly it—there's something happening in there, Ford. I've seen pictures. They didn't quarantine that place because it's dangerous. They've got *something* going on in there. The new readings are exactly like they were on that day, and if I can just get back in before it's too late—"

"DAD!"

Ford cut him off, unable to hear anymore. His dad had been spewing this same wild conspiracy stuff for longer than Ford wanted to remember. His outburst stopped Joe short and the two men stared at each other across the physical residue of

Joe's obsessions. A crestfallen look came over Joe's face as he realized, that his own son thought that he was bat-shit crazy.

His manic energy seeped away. Deflated, he sank into one of the few chairs not covered by scientific journals and reports. He slumped forward, looking defeated.

"You know your mom's still out there," he said weakly, his voice barely above a whisper. "For me, she'll always be there. They evacuated us so quickly I don't even have a picture of her."

Sympathy tugged at Ford's heart, but he had to stay firm.

"This has to stop, Dad. You need to let go."

"I sent her down there, Ford," Joe said plaintively. Fifteen years of anguish poured out of him, as though the disaster had happened only yesterday. "I would do anything, anything to bring her back. That haunts me, and I know it haunts you too"

Ford's resolve melted in the face of his father's inescapable guilt and grief. He couldn't help imagining what would be left of him if something happened to Elle... or Sam. He remembered those disappointed but loving parents back at the police station, embracing their son despite everything, and that customs official asking him what his business in Japan was.

Family, he thought. *Damn it.*

"It's time to come home, Dad," he said, his voice softening. "Come home with me."

The grateful look on his father's face was enough to break Ford's heart. He swallowed hard and wiped at his eyes, obviously touched by his son's offer. Ford prayed that he had finally gotten through to him.

"We'll leave tomorrow," Ford said.

Joe hesitated, just for a moment, but then he nodded. Emotionally exhausted, he could only murmur a quiet, "Yes."

Ford signed in relief. Maybe this could be the start of a whole new beginning for them. He reached out and squeezed his dad's shoulder.

"Let's get some sleep," he said.

At his own insistence, Ford crashed on the futon, letting his father keep his own bed. The flickering screen of a thrift-store TV set cast a phosphor glow over the room as Ford tried to zone out to an old monster movie playing on the late show; sometimes watching vintage movies with the sound down helped him unwind at the end of a long day. His eyelids began to droop as giant prehistoric creatures battled each other amidst balsa-wood sets. He surrendered to sheer exhaustion, and let his eyes close. The brawling monsters could work out their differences without him. He'd done enough for today.

Tomorrow, he thought. *Tomorrow we'll head back home.*

Sleep overcame him, but rest did not. Dreams of Elle and Sam mixed surreally with memories of Afghanistan and that terrible morning, over a decade ago, when the nuclear power plant collapsed before his eyes. If only he could disarm the reactor this time, the same way he could an improvised explosive device, maybe he could somehow save everyone: Mom, Dad, Elle, Sam... Drifting in and out of sleep, he thought he heard a voice whispering urgently in Japanese. The sound of radio distortion intruded on his slumber.

Ford blinked and opened his eyes. The apartment was still dark; the sun had yet to rise, but somebody had switched off the TV at some point. He rested upon the futon, getting his bearings. At first he thought he had just dreamed the voice, but then he heard his father speaking softly in his bedroom. Ford strained his ears to listen in.

"Yes, yes," Joe whispered, switching into English. "The northeast section, that's good. There's never a patrol."

Ford came fully awake. He rose quietly from the futon and crept toward the bedroom. The light of a single lamp spilled into the living room. Ford checked his wristwatch. It would be dawn soon. He peered into the bedroom to see what his father was doing.

The older man was already up and dressed, his dark clothes more suitable for a burglary than a trip to the airport. He whispered into his phone as he furtively packed a selection of files and electronic equipment into a duffle bag. Ford's heart sank. Joe didn't look like he was packing for a trip home.

"Ten minutes," Joe whispered. "*Arigato.*"

He ended the call and put away the phone, only to see Ford staring at him from the doorway. Anger and disappointment warred upon the younger man's features.

I should've known, Ford thought bitterly. "What the hell are you doing?"

Caught red-handed, Joe didn't bother trying to deny anything. "I'm heading out there, Ford—one hour, in and out."

Ford shook his head. "I don't think so."

"You want closure?" Joe challenged him, not backing down. "You want to go home? That's where *I'm* going. Now you can come with me or not, your choice, but I don't have much time left to work this out and I'll be damned if I let it happen again!" He kept on packing, defiantly. "I came back here and I wasted six years staring through that barbed wire thinking it was a military mistake or some horrible design flaw they were trying to cover up. I kept looking at the hard science. *What I knew.* One day I'm tutoring a kid whose studying whale songs. I'm looking at his textbook—'Soundscape

Interpretation,' 'Echolocation.' I'm looking at these graphs and diagrams and I realized that all the data I had been going crazy over before the plant blew wasn't something structural, it wasn't a leaking turbine or a submarine. It was *language*. It was talk. Hard science wasn't the answer—this was biology."

Ford had no idea what his dad was talking about. He watched in dismay as Joe fished a ratty old radiation suit from a pile of crap beside the bed. The suit resembled the ones the workers had used at the plant fifteen years ago, the type his mother had supposedly been wearing when she died. He wondered how the hell Joe had managed to get his hands on it.

"I met a guy runs a cargo boat off-shore," Joe continued, trying to get it all out before Ford could interrupt him. "Every day he goes right past the reactor site. He dropped off a couple monitors on buoys for me." He shook his head at the memory. "Nothing. A year of nothing. *More* than a year." Years of frustration could be heard in Joe's voice. "Two weeks ago—'cause I check this thing like every other day just for the kick in the teeth—two weeks ago, I tune in and, *ohmigod*, there it is. Whatever it is that's in there, whatever it is they're guarding so carefully, it started talking again. And I mean *talking*. I need to get back to the house. I need my old disks if they're still there. The answer's in that data. I need to know that what caused this wasn't just me, Ford. That I'm not who you think I am. I am not crazy. That wasn't just a reactor meltdown. Something's going on there. I need to find the truth and end this. Whatever it takes."

Ford tried to make sense of his father's impassioned outpouring. Was it possible that Joe actually knew what he was talking about? Could you be crazy and still sound that coherent, that lucid, that sensible? Probably, Ford suspected, but one thing at least was clear: this was never going to be over for Joe Brody until he got the answers he was looking for.

Ford shook his head. He couldn't believe he was actually considering what he was considering.

"You got another one of those suits?" he asked.

SEVEN

The trip took longer than Ford liked. It was late afternoon by the time they drew near an eerily deserted coastline. Miles of sagging perimeter fence extended into the choppy waters of a forgotten inlet. Posted signs, many of them showing obvious signs of age and weathering, warned repeatedly of fatal radiation levels. The official notices were in Japanese, but triangular metal signs also bore the international symbol for radiation: an ominous black trefoil against a yellow background. Ford recognized the view from some of the photos back at his father's apartment. They had reached the perimeter of the quarantine zone. Somewhere beyond those fences were the contaminated remains of his childhood.

It didn't feel like much of a homecoming.

A gruff smuggler, who had declined to volunteer his name, piloted a small skiff toward the fence. An outboard motor chugged quietly as it propelled the boat through the water. Ford contemplated the daunting warning signs even as Joe rescued their radiation suits from his duffel bag. Apparently he had purchased them on-line—" from a reputable dealer," Joe had insisted.

Ford shook his head in disbelief. He was starting to wonder which of them was most crazy.

The skiff motored toward a stretch of fence that had sagged beneath the surface of the water, allowing the boat to pass over it unobstructed. The ruins of the abandoned city rose in the distance, visible in the early morning sunlight. No lights shone from the deserted skyline. Seagulls, braving the lingering radiation, perched along wooden pylons like avian sentinels. Ford wondered how secure the "Q-Zone" was if gulls could fly in and out—and a possibly deranged engineer and his idiot son could sneak ashore so easily.

The two men changed into the radiation suits. Ford would have preferred the armored bomb suit he wore on duty; the stiff green radiation suit struck him as worryingly flimsy by comparison. A dosimeter badge was affixed to his sleeve, but this did little to reassure him. Lord knows a suit like this had not saved his mom so many years ago.

The skiff pulled up to a rotting dock that was missing several timbers. Ford and Joe stepped cautiously onto the dock. The muffled tinkle of broken wind chimes, coming from a nearby shack, penetrated Ford's bulky helmet. He guessed a breeze was blowing, although he couldn't feel it through the suit's heavy layers. The used helmet had a musty smell to it.

Joe leaned over to hand the smuggler a wad of yen. The man accepted the currency and, wasting no time, immediately turned the skiff around and put off for less perilous waters. Second thoughts assailed Ford as he watched the boat cruise away, leaving them behind. He resisted a sudden urge to call the boat back until it finally vanished from view. Ford and Joe traded looks through the transparent masks of their helmets.

They were committed now. In theory, the boat would not return until it received their call.

It was a long hike up from the coast, made slower by the heavy suits, which forced them to pause for breaks every half-mile or so. Ford was decades younger than his father, and accustomed to working in full body armor, but even he was exhausted and covered in sweat by the time they arrived at the outskirts of the city. The sun had begun to sink toward the horizon.

One hour, in and out, my ass, Ford thought.

Janjira was nothing like he remembered. Evacuated fifteen years ago, and cut off from the outside world ever since, the once-bustling community had become a ghost town overnight. Abandoned cars and trucks rusted in the empty streets. Weeds sprouted from the pavement, while moss and vines shrouded entire buildings. Mannequins sporting fashions from the late 90s kept silent vigil from shop windows. Newsstands displayed headlines that were over a decade out of date; apparently there was some concern about Y2K. A theater marquee advertised *The Blair Witch Project.*

Ford spied no evidence of vandalism or looting. Everything had been left exactly how it had been the day the reactor melted down, so that only time and decay had overrun the city. Ford found himself hoping they wouldn't have to pass by his old school. His memories of Miss Okada's classroom were fraught enough. He didn't need to see it in ruins.

He figured they had the deserted streets to themselves, until a pack of wild dogs startled the men by padding around a corner. The canines looked mangy and malnourished, their coats dirty and matted, but they seemed to be surviving the Zone's deadly radiation levels. Ford's brow furrowed in confusion as he pulled his dad into a nearby alley to avoid crossing paths with the pack. Minutes passed before Ford's heart stopped racing.

They took a detour around the dogs, then paused to catch their breaths. Ford tried to orient himself, but the rusty street signs, all in Japanese, were of little help. He didn't recognize this neighborhood at all. No surprise, he thought, given that he'd been only nine years old the last time he'd lived in this city. He hoped his father's memories were more reliable.

"Okay, which way?" He glanced around for Joe, who seemed to have wandered off. "Dad?"

A freeway overpass crossed the road before them. Joe paused in the shadow of the concrete supports and extracted a Geiger counter from his pack. Activating the device, he checked the gauge.

Nothing.

Joe smirked behind his faceplate. He tapped the gauge just to make sure it wasn't stuck, but needle still didn't budge. Next he consulted the radiation badge on his forearm. Sure enough, it was still green. Just as he'd expected.

He reached for his helmet.

Ford watched in horror as his father whipped off his protective helmet. Before he could do anything to stop him, Joe tossed the headpiece aside and sucked in a deep breath of the supposedly contaminated air.

"Dad!" he cried out. "What are you doing?"

A horrible thought flashed through Ford's mind. Had Joe come all this way just to kill himself near where Mom had died?

But Joe didn't look particularly suicidal. Instead a look of vindication transfigured his gaunt, careworn face. He pointed triumphantly at the telltale green radiation badge on his arm.

"It's clean, Ford! I *knew* it!" Joe darted forward and showed Ford the readings on his Geiger counter. This was the most excited that Ford had seen his father in years. "The radiation in this place should be lethal... but there's nothing. It's gone. *Something's absorbing it.*"

Ford didn't understand. Everything he'd read or heard about the Q-Zone was that it was supposed to be completely uninhabitable.

He inspected his own green radiation badge and remembered those dogs running through street. He had no idea what could "absorb" all that radiation, but he didn't hear any ominous clacking coming from the Geiger counter. Surely, the counter *and* the radiation badges couldn't be broken?

He warily unzipped his own helmet. He took off the protective mask and held his breath for a long moment before inhaling. He waited for airborne particles to sear his lungs.

Elle is going to kill me for this, he thought ruefully, *if the radiation doesn't get me first.*

"Trust me," Joe said. "It's completely safe."

He certainly sounded confident enough. Ford folded up his helmet and tucked it into his belt, just to be safe. He had to admit it felt good to get the helmet off. A welcome breeze cooled his face.

Joe inspected the street signs. He nodded in recognition.

"It's just left on the next street," he promised.

"The one before or after the rabid pack of dogs?"

* * *

Ford was surprised, but probably shouldn't have been, to discover that his father had held onto the keys to their old house all these years. Rusty hinges squeaked in protest as they entered their former home for the first time in fifteen years. It was dark inside. Vines and bushes had grown over the windows, as though reclaiming the home for nature. Dust, hopefully of the non-radioactive variety, coated the tops of tables and shelves. Cobwebs hung across open doorways. Ford brushed them aside as they worked their way through the murky house. His eyes struggled to adjust to the gloom.

Flashlight beams provided glimpses of long-faded memories. Trophies, souvenirs, a ceramic "lucky cat" figurine, and other knickknacks rested on a shelf, next to a photo of a young Joe Brody in a Navy uniform. A moldy box of breakfast cereal rotted atop the kitchen table. Report cards and art projects were magnetized to the refrigerator, whose contents had long since passed their expiration dates. Dirty dishes had waited in the sink for far too long.

Ford's throat tightened. A rush of emotion overwhelmed him and for a few moments all he could to do was stand frozen amidst the deteriorating wreckage of his past, remembering happier days and how abruptly they all had ended. The last time he'd set foot in this house, his mom had still been alive. He glanced at his father, concerned that the poignant surroundings might be too much for him, but Joe Brody was a man on a mission. He headed straight for his old office without pausing to look around. If this place brought back painful memories for Joe, you wouldn't know it from his determined stride.

Fine, Ford thought. *Probably just as well*.

Nostalgia drew him irresistibly toward his old room. The flashlight beam fell on scattered relics from his boyhood. He smiled wryly at the dusty collection of toys strewn across the floor. One particular toy soldier caught his eye: a miniature Navy man, just like he'd promised Sam.

Maybe this trip wouldn't be a total wild goose chase after all.

He swept the beam across the room. A glass case reflected the light and he spied his old terrarium, which he hadn't thought about in forever. Curiosity, and a flicker of an ancient memory, compelled him to investigate further. Shining the light into the terrarium, he was pleased to see that a dried and crumbling cocoon was split down the middle. As nearly as he could tell, the cocoon was empty, as though its former occupant had finally hatched after all, meltdown or no meltdown.

"Huh," he muttered. *How about that?*

Joe knew what he wanted and he knew where to find them. Old memories and associations lay in wait all around him, poised to strike, but he kept them firmly at bay. Now was no time to wallow in grief and self-pity. He had a job to do—and possibly a disaster to avert.

The beam from his flashlight tracked across his desk, even as he searched his memory for exactly where he'd left certain items fifteen years ago. He remembered pacing irritably across the room, arguing with Takashi on the phone. The light exposed a primitive cordless phone from 1999 and a well-gnawed pencil beside it. *C'mon, c'mon,* he thought impatiently. *Where the hell are you?*

Just when he was about to curse in frustration, the targets of his search turned up: fifteen dusty zip disks scattered across the floor near the desk. He realized belatedly that they must have been knocked off the desk by one of the convulsive tremors or blasts from that morning. And that wasn't all. Lying near the fallen disks were the printouts of that distinctive waveform pattern. His eyes traced the pattern, which had haunted his imagination ever since the meltdown. It was just as he remembered it: small peaks at first, then higher and higher, closer and closer together, until...

Don't think about that now, he thought. *Just get what you came for, while there's still a chance to make people listen.*

He gathered up the disks and printouts, carefully blowing off the dust as he stowed them securely in his pack. Once that was done, he did another sweep of the office just to be certain that he hadn't missed anything. As nearly as he could tell, he had retrieved everything important, except—

An old family portrait, resting atop the desk, stopped him cold. He was held captive by the photo—of Joe, Sandra, and little Ford. Of his family as they once were: happy, loving, untouched by tragedy and estrangement. Before the catastrophe that blew his world apart.

For a moment, the rescued data was forgotten. He lifted the portrait from the desk, gazing at it intently. His hands shook and his eyes threatened to mist over. Lifting his gaze from the portrait, he noticed something bright and shiny over the doorway. Sunset, filtering through the vegetation obscuring the window, was reflected off a homemade banner strung across the arch:

"HAPPY BIRTHDAY, DAD!"

Joe stared numbly at the banner, instantly transported back in time. *"He made you a sign, you know,"* Sandra had said that morning. It all came back to him now. Ford's overlooked banner. The surprise party that never happened.

All the emotions he had been fending off snuck up on him, ambushing him. His elation over finally recovering the disks gave way to a profound welling of regret. Sobered, but still determined to expose the truth, he tore his gaze away from the damning banner and stuffed the family portrait into the bag with the disks and printouts.

It was time to go.

He was sealing up the bag when, unexpectedly, the house came to life. Bells, buzzers, shrieks, and applause suddenly blared from the living room as the TV set turned itself on, breaking the silence with the hysterical din of some hyper-manic Japanese game show. At the same time, the desk lamp in the office crackled and sputtered only a few inches from Joe's face, causing his heart to skip a beat. His dusty old computer booted up noisily.

What the hell?

Outside the office, the hallway lights were flickering, too. Unnerved by activity, Joe hoisted the duffel bag and went to investigate. Was it just a coincidence that this was happening now, around the same time that the cryptic signals had resumed? Joe didn't believe it.

What if it was already too late... again?

He peered out the office door and made eye contact with Ford, who had just stuck his head out of his old bedroom. The two men looked at each other in confusion.

"Did you...?" Ford asked.

Joe shook his head. "No. I have no idea..."

A quick inspection confirmed the truth. Everything electrical in the house had powered up, from the lights and TV to the lucky cat figurine bobbing its paw. The aroma of scented oil from a miniature waterfall drifted from the bathroom, competing with the stale atmosphere of the house. Ceiling fans began to spin, shedding years of accumulated cobwebs. A light bulb popped.

The inane clamor from the TV grated on Joe's nerves, making it hard to think. He moved to switch off the set, but had taken only a few steps when, without warning, the pictures on the wall started rattling. The ceramic cat vibrated off the bookcase and crashed to the floor, shattering into pieces. Just like Joe's coffee cup at the plant fifteen years ago.

For a heart-stopping moment, he thought the tremors had returned already, but then he recognized the thundering *whoomp-whoomp-whoomp* of a helicopter flying low over the house. The chopper's passage shook the rafters and the two men as well. They stared up at the ceiling in surprise, then back at each other. Neither of them knew why a 'copter would be buzzing a house in the middle of the Q-Zone. It made no sense. This entire area was supposed to be a no-fly zone.

Then again, it was supposed to be a radioactive wasteland, too.

Joe decided that he and Ford were pressing their luck by sticking around. After his previous arrest, his old address might be the first house the authorities would search. They needed to get back to the docks with their prizes. In theory, Koruki, the pilot of the skiff, would be waiting for his signal to pick them up. Joe had promised the second half of his payment on their safe return to Tokyo.

But first: Joe took one last look around at the house where his family had once been so happy, where and Sandra had been together.

He suspected he would never set foot in it again.

The fading daylight did not make the return trip through the deserted city any less eerie. Lights flickered in the lifeless storefronts, while snatches of muzak or TV broadcasts escaped open doors and windows. Neon signs cast long, colored shadows on the weed-infested sidewalks. A clock tower started counting off the minutes again, for the first time in who knew how long. Ford didn't like it. He preferred his ghost towns to be a little less animated, especially when he didn't have a clue as to what was turning the lights back on.

I knew this was a bad idea, he thought.

Another helicopter buzzed by overhead, and the two men ducked beneath the tattered awning of a vacant sidewalk café to avoid being spotted. Ford tracked the chopper's progress. It was flying northeast toward the horizon, where he now spotted what appeared to be a large metal structure in the distance. Glowing lights illuminated a towering assemblage of new scaffolding and facilities—right where the nuclear power plant used to be.

He looked to his father in confusion. "Are they rebuilding the plant?"

Joe stared at the distant complex intently, too transfixed by the sight to reply. You could practically see the gears turning behind his eyes as the former engineer tried to absorb this unexpected new development. And yet, Ford observed, his father didn't appear to be *too* surprised to find something happening at the old site, just as he'd theorized earlier. For the first time in years, Ford actually felt like Joe Brody had a better grip on what was going than he did.

How weird was that?

He opened his mouth again, to ask his dad to explain, only to be interrupted by the unmistakable sound of an assault rifle being racked. Ford's mouth went dry.

The men turned around to find a pair of uniformed Japanese soldiers standing behind them, their Howa assault rifles aimed at the trespassers. Neither soldier was wearing a radiation suit, just ordinary camo gear. They shouted at the Americans in a torrent of angry Japanese. Ford couldn't make out what they were saying, but raised his hands in the air.

"What are they saying?" he whispered to Joe.

Belligerent expressions conveyed a lack of hospitality. More choppers thundered past overhead, heading for the mysterious new facility.

"We're screwed," Joe said.

EIGHT

The unmarked security van rumbled down an access road deep in the heart of the Q-Zone. It bounced as it crossed a wooden bridge. The bump jarred the bench beneath Ford, who grunted in response. Things were not going well.

He and Joe sat handcuffed to a steel rail in the back of the van, flanked by two unsmiling Japanese soldiers, who had so far ignored all of Ford's urgent queries as to what was going to happen next. Ford didn't know if the guards didn't speak English and couldn't understand his feeble attempts at Japanese, or if they were just under orders to not engage with the prisoners, but what they had here was a definite failure to communicate. Ford had even tried explaining that he was a U.S. Navy lieutenant, but to no avail. It was clear that this wasn't going to get straightened out right away.

How on Earth was he going to explain this to his superiors? Or Elle?

Night had fallen, throwing the Q-Zone into darkness,

but Ford watched through the rear window as the van drove past numerous military vehicles, heavy equipment, and construction cranes on their way to the massive facility they had spied earlier. The van pulled up to the gates, where a guard conferred with the driver in Japanese. He scoped out the prisoners before waving the van through. Ford guessed that they had arrived at their destination, whatever it was.

Some sort of top-secret base? On top of the old nuclear plant?

Their captors had strongly discouraged the prisoners from conversing with each other. Still, Ford shot a questioning look at Joe.

What the hell have you gotten us into?

A security van passed beneath the elevated steel gantry supporting Serizawa as he and Dr. Graham made their way toward an observation post above the pit. Both scientists wore protective radiation suits, having just toured the restricted level directly above the buried power plant.

"Fifteen years of silence," Graham recounted, shaking her head. "Then two weeks ago, these pulses. As of yesterday, it's up to one an hour and stronger every time. Whelan's practically walking on air, calling it a living fuel cell. All this time absorbing radiation like a sponge... and suddenly it's gone electric."

Serizawa shared his colleague's astonishment. These were truly stunning developments. He only wished he knew whether they boded ill or not. Unlike the esteemed Dr. Whelan, who was the chief scientist in charge of the operation, Serizawa was not entirely convinced that this was cause for celebration. Now in his fifties, he still remembered that devastated mine in the Philippines—and the many lives that had been lost there.

They stepped to a safety rail overlooking a gigantic sinkhole, even larger than the one they had encountered fifteen years ago. Graham signaled Serizawa that it was now safe to remove their safety masks. She gazed in awe at the sight below.

"Nature is spectacular," she observed.

He shook his head. "Nature didn't cause this. We did."

Where the Janjira Nuclear Power Plant had once stood was an enormous pit, more than one hundred meters across. An elaborate multi-story edifice of steel scaffolding and catwalks lined the walls of the sinkhole, descending dozens of levels. Six towering construction cranes were in place around the rim of the pit, bracketing it. Spotlights illuminated the sinkhole. And this entire imposing superstructure, Serizawa knew, had been constructed to monitor a single biological specimen.

The cocoon rested on the floor of the pit, many meters below. Nearly as tall as the pit itself, it was a gnarled, rocky extrusion roughly the size of a fifteen-story building. A bioluminescent red glow came from deep within its thick translucent husk. It was many times larger and denser than the twin egg sacs they had discovered in the Philippines years ago. Its pointed tip curled down towards its base, so that it vaguely resembled a claw or pincer. Its roots were sunken deep into the mangled ruins of the collapsed nuclear power plant buried beneath it.

A complex array of monitoring equipment surrounded the base of the cocoon. Huge cameras, sensors, and scanners probed the cocoon across the entire range of the electromagnetic spectrum. The imposing apparatus, which were at least a story in height, rested upon a ring of grilled metal flooring surrounding the cocoon. Along with Graham, Serizawa watched from above as crews of workers, wearing hazmat suits, scurried about below, attending to the equipment. The flurry of new pulses had the entire base in an uproar, adding new urgency to its operations. Serizawa had gotten on a plane the minute he'd received word from Graham that the cocoon had become active and was manifesting new characteristics. She had just given him a firsthand look at the activities down on the floor of the pit.

"Get ready," she told him. "Here it comes."

All at once, the cocoon flashed brightly. A dazzling burst of light briefly turned night into day.

The van skidded to a stop, throwing Ford and his dad forward. Handcuffs tugged on Ford's wrist, yanking him back; he would've preferred a seatbelt. Numerous voices and footsteps could be heard outside the van. *Something's up,* he guessed. *Now what?*

Their guards whipped open the side door. Gruff words were exchanged in Japanese. Grabbing the prisoners' duffel bag and gear, the soldiers scrambled out of the van and slammed the door shut behind them, leaving Ford and Joe alone in the back of the van. He figured now was their chance to finally talk to each other. Ford hoped to hell his dad knew what this about, because he was totally lost.

"Okay, okay," he said, trying to get a handle on the situation. "So the good news is that we're not going to fry from radiation poisoning." He looked to his dad for confirmation, but Joe seemed lost in a world of his own, staring bleakly at the floor of the van. It dawned on Ford that his father had barely said a word, or even made eye contact with him, since the guards had taken them into custody. "Hey, Dad. You okay?"

Joe didn't react. His lips moved, as though he was talking to himself, but nothing audible emerged. Ford wondered if the strain of the last several hours had been too much for him. What if his dad had finally cracked for good—just as his insane theories were looking less crazy by the moment?

"Hey!" Ford said sharply.

"...dragging you back here." Joe roused a little, at least enough to mumble audibly. He turned anguished eyes toward Ford, his battered spirits in some sort of hellish freefall. Guilt weighed down his voice. "I am, I'm totally insane. It's a replay of fifteen years ago and it's all my fault. Now I'll lose you, too."

Ford tried to snap his father out of whatever sort of post-traumatic depression had gripped him. "See that's the crazy talking. That's not going to help us. No one's losing anyone."

"They're never going to let us out of here, Ford. Why would they? Now they've got the disks..."

"Disks? What disks? What are you talking about, Dad?" Ford leaned anxiously toward his father, desperate to get his dad's full attention. The irony of the moment was not lost on Ford; after years of doing his best to tune out his father's paranoid ramblings, he suddenly wanted more than anything to know exactly what was going through his father's tortured mind. *Look at me. I'm listening now, okay? Help me understand this.*"

"I'm cursed, Ford," the other man said despairingly. "Look what I've done."

Ford wanted to shake him. "**TELL ME WHAT YOU KNOW!**"

Joe flinched, blinking in surprise. The sheer intensity of Ford's demand jolted him back to reality. His eyes came back into focus. He nodded gravely.

"Animals," he began, trying to explain. "All kinds. Any kind. Birds, lizards, whales, insects, millions of creatures are all talking all the time, with sounds we just can't hear. Frequencies we can't process. Bursts of sound so fast or subtle we can't grasp it. Imagine the epic version of that. That's what's on the disks, the sound of some creature screaming."

The control room, nicknamed the "crow's nest," was on the upper level of the installation, overlooking the pit. The tapered tip of the cocoon was almost level with the wide glass windows facing the sinkhole. State-of-the-art scientific equipment was crammed into the control room, along with a dedicated team of scientists and technicians. Monitors displayed readings from an impressive range of scanning devices, including infrared, spectrum analysis, backscatter x-ray, and others that Serizawa couldn't immediately identify. Much of the apparatus bore labels reading "M.U.T.O." A time-code ran across every screen.

"Ishiro," Dr. Gregory Whelan greeted Serizawa as he and Graham entered the control room, after changing out of their radiation gear. The chief scientist was a balding Canadian about the same age as Serizawa. His eyes gleamed with excitement behind a pair of glasses. He had the buoyant attitude of a gambler who had just hit the jackpot. "Good timing. We've just had the luminary precursor. Seem to be due for another pulse."

The lead technician, a man named Jainway, leaned forward to speak into a microphone. "Ten second warning. Ten seconds."

Graham's phone rang and she stepped away to take the call. She nodded apologetically at Serizawa as she took her leave of the control room, called away by some pressing matter. He joined Whelan by the windows, which offered a birds-eye view of the activity down on the floor of the pit. Suited observers manned the extensive assortment of scanners and recording devices aimed at the cocoon. They stared up at the huge, glowing specimen expectantly.

"Six, five, four," Jainway counted down. He was a fit Caucasian in his early forties. A Midwestern American accent testified to the multinational nature of the operation. "Three, two, one..."

The air around the cocoon rippled as it emitted a luminous pulse. The translucent shell of the cocoon convulsed, shaking off a cloud of dust along with bits of outer husk. The spasm caused the entire pit and the attached scaffolding to tremble slightly, which Serizawa found more than a little unsettling. At the same, electric lights flickered throughout the facility. Industrial-sized backup generators, installed for just such occasions, kicked in automatically to override the power drain.

Serizawa nodded in understanding. This was precisely the phenomenon Graham had described to him: a powerful electromagnetic pulse that disrupted all power systems in the vicinity. Powered by the radiation the organism inside the cocoon had been absorbing all these years.

He wondered what else it was capable of.

Joe was talking a mile a minute now. It was as though a dam of depression had been broken by a manic need to make Ford understand. The words spilled out of Joe at a rapid-fire pace, while Ford struggled to keep up.

"... by that point, I had fifteen, twenty days of this signal pattern no one could explain. Pulses, getting stronger, faster, 'til right before the last one—"

The dome light on the ceiling of the van dimmed suddenly. It sputtered erratically, like the lights back in town. The sudden flickering cut Joe off in mid-sentence. Falling silent, he looked up at the light anxiously.

Ford didn't understand. "Dad?"

"*It's the same*," Joe said ominously, his worried gaze fixed on the flickering light.

Something about his father's tone sent a chill down Ford's spine. He tried to keep his dad focused and on track.

"Dad, you said 'right before the last one.'" Ford prompted. "Right before the last one, *what?*"

Joe finally looked away from the sputtering light. He turned his haggard face toward Ford.

"Something responded."

Responded? Ford still wasn't sure what exactly his dad was getting at. Was he actually talking about some kind of animal? All he could tell for sure was that Joe was acting like this was a matter of life and death, and not just from fifteen years ago.

But before Ford could get his dad to elaborate, the van door slid open with a bang. Two armed guards, their granite faces reflecting how hardcore they were, invaded the back of the van. Without a word, they unhooked Joe from the security rail and muscled him none too gently away from the bench. They dragged him toward the open door.

"Hey!" Joe protested in Japanese. Ford could barely make out the gist of it. "Slow down! Where are we going?"

"Whoa!" Ford added, alarmed by the soldiers' rough treatment of his father. He lunged forward as far as his cuffs would allow. "You're gonna hurt him!"

Snarling, one of the soldiers shoved Ford back against the wall. Ford tugged uselessly at his restraints. Still handcuffed to the rail, he could only watch in dismay as the men hustled Joe away from the van. And away from Ford.

"Hey! Hey wait!" he shouted. "Where are you taking him? HEY!"

The soldiers ignored his frantic cries. They slammed the door shut behind them.

With full power restored by the generators, the equipment within the crow's nest monitored the pulse. Glowing screens, tracking emanations all along the electromagnetic spectrum, registered a continuous spike that only gradually diminished in intensity before subsiding altogether.

"That was twelve-point-two seconds," Jainway reported. "We're trending exponentially and—" He rapidly worked his keyboard, collating and translating the latest data from the pulse. "—that's our new curve."

A distinctive waveform appeared on a central display screen. The pattern displayed a series of rising peaks, starting small at first, but quickly increasing in size and frequency. Serizawa examined the display in fascination. The pattern matched no biological phenomenon he was familiar with.

A hand tapped him on the shoulder. He turned to find David Huddleston, the base's head of security, behind him. He was a tall, brusque American who took his duties very seriously.

"Dr. Serizawa," he said. "We arrested two men in the Q-Zone—"

Whelan was annoyed by the interruption. "Can this wait? Have Dr. Graham take a look."

"She did, sir," Huddleston replied. "She sent me."

Whelan glanced around, as though noticing for the first time that Graham was no longer present. Serizawa recalled her being called away during the countdown to the pulse. Intrigued, he gave Huddleston his full attention. He trusted Vivienne's judgment, and wondered what about the trespassers was so significant.

"One says he used to work here," Huddleston said.

At the old nuclear power plant? Serizawa found this provocative enough that he let the security chief escort him downstairs to the antechamber of a utility room that had apparently been converted into a makeshift interrogation room. He found Graham waiting for him outside the utility room, while an armed soldier stood guard at the locked glass door to the larger room beyond. A table held what Serizawa assumed to be the trespassers' confiscated belongings: a duffel bag, a couple of American passports, a vintage Geiger counter, a flashlight, and other odds and ends.

Looking troubled, Graham nodded grimly at Serizawa as he arrived. They peered through the clear glass door as one of Huddleston's subordinates, an American named Fitzgerald, attempted to question the distraught prisoner, whom had been identified as Joseph Brody, a one-time nuclear engineer, formerly employed by the doomed Janjira facility. Serizawa wondered what had brought the man back to this site, some fifteen years later. He noted that Brody was wearing a battered brown radiation suit, minus the hood.

"I want my son," Brody demanded, visibly upset. "I want to see him. I want to know he's alright." He pointed accusingly at the guard posted outside the door. "This guy, he knows where he is. I want my son and I want my bag and my disks and I want to talk to the person who's in charge here. I know what's going on, okay?"

Serizawa listened with interest. Just how much did Brody truly know about what now occupied this site? And what might have caused the disaster so many years ago?

Fitzgerald tried to calm the prisoner. He had a shaved skull and an intimidating manner. "Mr. Brody—"

"You've been telling everybody this place is a death zone," Brody ranted. "All the while you've been hiding something out there! My wife died here! You understand? Something killed my wife and ten other people, and I deserve answers!"

Serizawa recalled that several lives had indeed been lost during the meltdown, although the death toll could have been much, much worse had not all necessary emergency measures been taken in time. Curious, he rifled through the man's possessions, finding a framed family photo, along with over a dozen obsolete zip disks and a collection of graphs and printouts.

"I thought all the data from that day was lost," he whispered to Graham.

She glanced at Brody's collection. "Guess he was doing homework."

Leafing through the confiscated material, Serizawa froze as he came upon a crumpled computer printout of a certain waveform pattern. He recognized the rising series of crests immediately. It was the same curve he had just observed on the monitors upstairs.

Snatching up the printout, he turned excitedly toward Graham—just as the overhead lights flickered once more, even more noticeably this time. The electromagnetic pulses from the cocoon were indeed increasing in intensity.

"See?!" Brody exclaimed, as though in vindication. "There it is again! It knocks out everything electrical for miles!" The foundations beneath their feet rumbled as the lights continued to waver, despite the best efforts of the backup generators. Brody grew louder and more agitated. He shouted fervidly like a prophet of doom. His face grew flushed and the tendons in his neck stood out. "It's what caused this whole thing, and it's happening again. IT'S GONNA SEND US BACK TO THE STONE AGE!"

A technician from the control room rushed into the antechamber. "Dr. Serizawa, they need you upstairs! We have a problem."

Serizawa glanced back and forth between Brody and the confiscated printout. Was it possible that this crazed American engineer knew something they didn't? He stared apprehensively at Brody and their eyes met through the glass door between them. Serizawa wanted to stay and question the man directly, find out what precisely Brody knew about the events of fifteen years ago, and how they related to what was happening today, but the technician from the crow's nest hovered in doorway, waiting anxiously.

He hastily gathered up Brody's possessions and rushed to answer the summons. He shouted back at Huddleston and the guard.

"Keep that man here! I need to talk to him!"

Graham accompanied Serizawa as they raced back to the control room, which was now in a barely controlled frenzy. The elation and excitement of only a few minutes ago had been supplanted by an almost palpable sense of panic. Emergency alerts and warnings flashed urgently on almost every screen and console. Buzzers and sirens sounded. Alarmed technicians shouted over each other.

"Just seconds apart!" Jainway called out.

Another man, whose name Serizawa didn't know, stared

in dismay at the readings before him. "—stronger, broad spectrum!"

Whelan paced back and forth, chewing on his nails. His earlier jubilance had vanished completely, replaced by obvious signs of worry and agitation. The power and intensity of the pulses were exceeding all their expectations and precautions. His historic breakthrough was turning into a disaster.

"Any radiation leakage?" he asked fearfully.

A larger tremor shook the crow's nest as the cocoon emitted an even stronger pulse. Serizawa staggered across the quaking floor to the windows overlooking the pit. Down below, the mammoth cocoon flexed and heaved, causing great hunks of its rocky outer shell to shear off and crash onto the metal grille covering the floor of the pit. Tiny figures, their movements hampered by their cumbersome radiation suits, scrambled for safety as the chunks of the shell tumbled down onto the expensive equipment like a rockslide, smashing portions of the sensor array to pieces. The impact of the fragments slamming into the metal floor echoed off the walls of the pit. As the outer layer of the cocoon disintegrated, more and more of the infernal red glow within it was exposed.

"What the hell is it doing?" Jainway asked.

"Gamma levels still zero," his fellow technician reported, with audible relief. "It's sucked all three reactors dry."

Serizawa held out Brody's printout. "It's done feeding."

Puzzled, Whelan grabbed the document from Serizawa. He peered at it uncomprehendingly. "What's this?"

"Fifteen years ago," Serizawa explained. "It's what caused the meltdown."

Graham had put the pieces together as well. "It was an electromagnetic pulse," she said, chiming in. "That's what it's building to, converting all that radiation."

"We need to shut down," Serizawa said.

Whelan blanched at the prospect. "You're sure this is authentic?"

Serizawa nodded, wishing he'd found out about Joe Brody's findings years ago. The exact connection between the meltdown and the cocoon had always been unclear, but Serizawa now realized that an EMP produced by the larva had shut down the plant's safety systems back in 1999. His grave expression and bearing convinced Whelan to heed his warning.

"Secure the grid!" the scientist ordered. "Wildfire protocols!"

Jainway pressed a button, sounding an alarm. He relayed Whelan's orders into his microphone. "All personnel, clear the first perimeter, immediately!"

Klaxons blared throughout the base. Crimson warning lights flashed and rotated. Outside the crow's nest, the generators were cranked up to full capacity as the six looming construction cranes went into operation. Gears engaged and motors roared as the cranes stretched a net of thick steel cables above the pit.

Just in case anything tried to escape.

NINE

Wailing klaxons penetrated the walls of the security van, causing Ford to start in alarm. He knew emergency warnings when he heard them. All hell was breaking loose somewhere.

Desperate to figure out what was happening, he peered out the rear window of the van. He spotted heavy steel cables winding from the base of a towering construction crane, which had just swung into action. He couldn't make out what the cables were attached to.

Radios squawked outside the van. Ford saws guards rushing past.

"Hey!" he shouted, trying to get their attention. Had everyone forgotten that he was handcuffed inside the van? He yelled over the blaring klaxons. "HEY!"

His shouts went unheeded. Whatever crisis was underway clearly took priority over one inconvenient American trespasser. Ford realized he was on his own, right on top of a buried nuclear power plant. He remembered the radiation helmet tucked in his belt and hastily put it back on. He used his free hand to refasten it to the suit.

Better safe than sorry.

Serizawa watched from the crow's nest as the tech crews on the lower levels of the pit scrambled out of the way as the huge wire "cage" descended, sealing the cocoon inside, even as another layer of the outer shell shook loose, sloughing onto the floor of the pit with tremendous force. Serizawa offered a silent prayer for the workers below, hoping they would not be crushed by the stony fragments, which were as hard and brittle as volcanic rock.

Agitated voices filled the control room. The pulses, coming faster and faster, were growing steadily in strength. Arguments broke out among the panicky scientists and technicians as they debated the correct response to the escalating crisis. Emergency measures were hurriedly deployed, but Serizawa got a definite sense that matters were spiraling out of control. Besieged by critical reports and queries from the staff under his command, Dr. Whelan looked like he wanted to be anywhere else. It appeared now that they had all severely underestimated the forces—and the creature—they had sought to contain. Whelan's dreams of solving the world's energy crisis were turning into a nightmare.

"Grid secure!" Jainway called out as the high-tension netting stretched taut above the quivering cocoon. The technician let out a sigh of relief, which Serizawa feared might be premature. After all, the cage had never been tested.

The announcement quieted the tumult inside the control room. Overlapping voices trailed off as all heads turned toward Whelan, who was pacing back and forth before the windows. Everyone present knew what came next. Jainway's hand hovered above a switch. He looked to Whelan for the go-ahead.

"Say the word," the technician said.

Whelan, for his part, appeared overwhelmed by the responsibility that had fallen on him. He looked in turn to Serizawa, who sympathized with the stricken scientist. This was no easy decision.

"So much we still don't know," Whelan moaned, agonizing over the potential loss to science.

Down in the pit, the cocoon shuddered again, shedding yet another layer of shell. Great chunks of the cocoon rained down on the metal flooring, which began to buckle beneath the avalanche. With each layer, more and more of the unearthly effulgence at the core of the cocoon could be seen, although the organism within remained hidden from view.

But for how much longer?

"Kill it," Serizawa said.

Whelan let Serizawa make the call. He nodded to Jainway, who threw the switch.

Thousands of volts electrified the metal grille at the base of the cocoon. Bright blue flashes crackled across the flooring. The cocoon sizzled and convulsed as the electricity arced across its outer shell, jolting it with bolts of artificial lightning. Smoke rose from its cracking outer shell. Floodlights and fuses blew, throwing the entire pit into darkness. Graham gasped, and Whelan looked away from the window. In theory, whatever was growing inside the cocoon had just been electrocuted.

Serizawa prayed they had not waited too long.

On the monitors, the data feeds all went silent. A hush fell over the control room.

"All readings are flat-lining," Jainway reported.

"Is it dead?" Whelan asked.

Serizawa peered down into the murky pit. As nearly as he could tell, the cocoon remained intact, apart from a single long crack splitting its surface. Shadows filled the gap, making it impossible to discern what lay deeper within the cocoon. The bioluminous glow had been extinguished. No sound or motion could be detected from this height.

Jainway sagged back into his seat, looking drained. He clearly thought the crisis had been averted, as did various other technicians throughout the control room. The electricity appeared to have done the trick, but Serizawa remained on edge. There was too much at stake to take any chances.

"Get a visual," he instructed.

Down in the pit, a work crew cautiously approached the charred cocoon. The metal grid beneath their feet was no longer electrified, but their hazmats suits included rubber boots regardless. Massive fragments of dislodged shell, the size of boulders, were embedded in the floor, forcing the workers to detour around them. Burnt and shattered scientific equipment further obstructed their path. The grilled flooring was dented and cratered, making it difficult to navigate. It was several minutes before they reached the base of the cocoon, which remained dark and inert.

The leader of the team, Koji Tanaka, ignited a handheld flare. An incandescent red glow cast light on the deep, jagged crack running up the blackened exterior of the looming cocoon. He peered up at the crack, but saw only a still, silent darkness. It appeared that the creature was indeed dead, but perhaps there was yet more they could learn by examining its remains?

The team drew nearer to the cocoon. Tanaka was about to report back to the control room, when he thought he spotted a glimmer of movement through the crack. At first he thought it might be just a trick of the light, but, no, *something* was definitely shifting deep within the cocoon. He squinted into shadows, while the rest of his team started shouted and pointing excitedly. They could all see it now: Elusive shapes—no, a *single* shape—stirring inside the cocoon, right before their eyes.

Tanaka's mouth went dry. He began to back away warily.

A deafening howl erupted from the cocoon, echoing off the walls of the pit. Terrified, Tanaka and his team turned and ran frantically for their lives.

They didn't get far.

A bone-rattling shock wave blasted from the cocoon, flinging the fleeing workers across the floor into the ruins and rubble. The concussive force disintegrated what remained of the cocoon, causing it to crumble into dust, even as a tremendous electromagnetic pulse blew through the entire base, shutting everything down. Tumbling through the air, Tanaka was already dead, his organs pulped, before he slammed into a disintegrating pile of debris.

The creature howled again.

The van rattled as though a bomb had gone off nearby. The dome-light in the ceiling, which had been flickering and off, went out completely, leaving Ford trapped in the dark. The blaring klaxons ceased abruptly, while a sudden blackout seemed to hit the entire facility. All the lights outside went dark simultaneously, so that only faint starlight illuminated the scene. The motorized cranes whirred to a stop.

What the—?

Ford was still trying to figure out what was happening, and whether he'd been completely forgotten, when the thunderous howl of some unknown creature rang out over the chaos. That was no machine or siren, Ford realized instantly. The ululating cry was unmistakably coming from something *alive*.

He couldn't believe his ears, and a primordial fear gripped his heart. Bombs and blackouts he understood, and he had seen combat more than once. But the thought of what could have produced that savage wail defied his imagination.

What had his father said before? About some sort of animal...?

Joe found himself alone in the improvised interrogation room. Fitzgerald and the guards had run off, distracted by the crisis, which had apparently caught them completely by surprise. He remembered the feeling.

You should've listened to me, he thought bitterly. *I should've made you listen.*

The lights went out, just as they had at the plant years ago. He heard an electronic lock click as the power shorted. He tried the door and found it unlocked. Cautiously sticking out his head out the door, he glanced around but didn't see any more guards in the vicinity. He wasn't surprised. If history was indeed repeating itself, as he feared, then the people here had a lot bigger problems on their hands than one trespassing engineer.

This was his chance, he realized, to find out the truth at last.

Along with his fellow scientists, Serizawa stared down into the abyss, which was lit only by the intermittent strobing of the emergency lights. The steel-mesh net over the pit remained intact, further obscuring his view of the creature below, which had obviously survived their attempt to electrocute it. Despite the danger posed by the monster, Serizawa marveled at its obvious strength and endurance. They had sent enough voltage through the grid to fry a great white whale, but the creature was still alive and free from its cocoon.

We waited too long, he realized. *It's grown too strong.*

The erratic lighting frustrated him. Straining his eyes, he could make out only the vague impression of some gargantuan form moving below. He caught sporadic glimpses of gigantic red eyes and gleaming fangs. The biologist in him was anxious to see the adult form of the organism, now that it had completed its metamorphosis from the larval stage that had hatched from the Philippine egg sac fifteen years ago, even as he feared for humanity as well.

What exactly had just emerged into the night?

Beside Serizawa, Whelan gasped as the shadowy beast pressed up against the cable netting, testing its cage. The creature heaved upward, shaking the entire pit. Steel scaffolding and support beams began to buckle alarmingly. Tortured metal screamed in protest. The crow's nest bucked beneath Serizawa's beneath feet, and he had to grab onto a window sill to maintain his balance. Graham stumbled against him, her face pale.

"*Evenyone out!*" Whelan shouted. "*Now!*"

His palm slammed down on a panic button.

GREG COX

* * *

A bewildering assemblage of steel gantries and elevated walkways circled the site of the former power plant, overlooking a sinkhole of Biblical proportions. Joe made his way through the unfamiliar complex, heading toward the center, even as a mass evacuation got underway, triggering a distinct sense of *déjà vu*. Hundreds of fleeing workers, many wearing radiation suits similar to his own, rushed past him, descending from metal catwalks and stairways in a desperate exodus. In their haste, nobody noticed an unfamiliar face amidst the crush. Joe jostled through the tide of humanity, like a salmon fighting its way upstream. He alone was heading *toward* the source of the chaos—and the inhuman howl.

I have to see it, he thought. *I have to know what's down there.*

Another deafening wail could be heard above the tumult. He forced his way along the gantries, drawn by the sound of the creature. The terrifying screech was proof that he wasn't crazy after all, that he had been right all along.

He hoped Ford understood that now.

Trapped in the van, Ford found himself forgotten in the midst of an increasingly hellish nightmare. Fleeing workers and emergency crews raced past the van by the dozens, oblivious to the desperate American handcuffed inside the vehicle. The cuffs dug into his wrist as he tried unsuccessfully to wriggle his hand free. He shouted frantically at the people running by.

No one listened or even glanced in his direction. They were all too busy trying to get away from... what?

GODZILLA

* * *

Joe crept along the gantry toward the pit. One level below, a crew of unusually courageous emergency workers warily approached the edge of the giant sinkhole. All at once, some enormous creature, its exact contours obscured by darkness and a net of heavy steel cables, shoved up against its cage. An angry screech conveyed its displeasure at being trapped.

The earsplitting cry convinced the workers to turn and run like hell. Joe didn't blame them; it was a natural response to the gargantuan monster trying to force itself out into the world. He would have run himself if he hadn't spent the last fifteen years looking for answers. This could be his last chance to find out exactly what had destroyed the plant years ago—and why Sandra died.

Luckily for the fleeing mortals, the creature retreated back into the pit after its failed attempt to breach the net. Brody was impressed by the size of the cage, admiring the foresight and ingenuity of the engineers who had designed and implemented the ambitious safety measure. The creature's bellicose howl faded away. It appeared the cage had worked.

Thank God, Joe thought. He wanted desperately to lay eyes on the creature, but that didn't mean he wanted to see it run amok. *That monster's caused enough havoc already.*

Then a giant black appendage rose up through a gap in the cables. Joe's eyes bulged at the sight. At first he thought it was a limb of some sort, but then he realized that it was actually *just a single hooked claw.* His mind reeled at the sheer scale that implied. For the love of God, how big was this thing?

The crooked talon hooked onto the taut steel cables, gripping them. It began pulling downward on the net, exerting tremendous force. The heavy cables stretched and strained at their moorings. The catwalks overlooking the pit started to tip precariously as they were wrenched loose, so that they dangled at alarming angles above the sinkhole and the creature below. All six cranes, each over 150 feet tall, began to tip toward the pit like fishing poles being dragged down by an over-sized catch. Twisting metal squealed as if in agony.

Joe gasped as the gantry quaked beneath him. He stumbled backwards, away from the railing. Suddenly the ingenious steel "cage" didn't seem quite as impressive—or reassuring—as it had been only moments ago. Hearing metal shriek, he spun around and saw the groaning cranes begin to buckle and bend catastrophically. The veteran engineer foresaw the collapse only seconds before it unfolded. One by one, each crane gave way in sequence, crashing down like a row of towering dominoes. More workers raced in terror from the falling cranes, each of which had to weigh at least two hundred tons. The screams of the trapped crane operators were drowned out by the din of warping steel and one earth-shaking impact after another.

Jesus Christ, Joe thought. *It's tearing this whole place down!*

One of the cranes toppled over, falling straight toward Joe. Adrenalin and reflexes kicked in and he dived for safety only a heartbeat before the top of the crane crashed onto the gantry right where he had been standing moments before. It felt like another tremor had struck, rolling Joe across the walkway. Amazed to find himself still alive, he staggered to his feet and looked around.

Several fleeing workers had not been so lucky. They lay crushed beneath the fallen crane. Heads, limbs, and torsos had vanished, buried beneath the heavy piece of construction equipment. Spreading pools of dark arterial blood, looking almost black in the night, seeped out from beneath the mangled steel. Joe could tell at a glance that most of the victims had been killed instantly.

He wondered if they were the lucky ones.

This is insane, Ford thought. *I can't die like this!*

He fought the handcuffs with all his might. His wrist was raw and bleeding, but the cuffs still refused to yield. The perverse absurdity of his situation was enough to drive him nuts. He could disarm a bomb in the middle of a battlefield, but he couldn't get out of a damn van when this entire place was coming down on top of him?

He stopped tugging on cuffs, recognizing the futility of his exertions.

I'm sorry, Elle, Sam, I tried my best. His heart broke at the prospect of never seeing his family again. *I always meant to come home to you.*

A falling crane hit the rear of the van like a giant hammer, shearing off the rear doors and sending the parked vehicle into a spin. Ford cried out, but had no time to react to this heart-stopping shock. Held in place by the cuffs, which yanked viciously on his wrist and arm, he tumbled violently inside the spinning van. His body slammed into the interior wall, knocking the breath from him. Whiplash twisted his back. For an endless moment, his world turned into a bruising carnival ride.

Then, finally, the van came to rest several yards away from its starting point. Dazed, his heart racing, Ford found himself staring out the missing back half of the van, which now faced the heart of the mysterious complex. The facility was apparently constructed around an enormous pit where

Ford guessed the Janjira Nuclear Power Plant had once stood. Compared to the crashing din of moments ago, there was a sudden silence—until he heard what sounded like sturdy steel cables straining against some inconceivable force.

The animal, he realized. *The one Dad tried to tell me about.*

That chilling, mind-boggling realization was enough to snap him out of daze and take stock. It occurred to him that the crashing steel crane might have been a blessing in disguise. Hurriedly checking the security rail, he felt a surge of excitement as he saw that the sturdy steel had been cracked by the accident. It took him a few anxious moments, but he managed to slide the cuffs of the rail, setting him free at last.

Yes! he thought. *That's more like it!*

Wasting no time, he clambered out of the wrecked van by way of its missing back half. His radiation suit was still clumsy and uncomfortable, but, this close to the old reactors, he wasn't about to take it off—even if none of the guards had been wearing them before. He kept the helmet and gas mask in place.

He glanced around the darkened base, trying to get his bearings. The fallen crane lay between him and a steep ridge beyond. Steel catwalks and scaffolding spread across the ridge like overgrown foliage, but he could still dimly glimpse the pit beyond. Metal cables continued to creak and groan. He started toward the scaffolding, wondering how on Earth he was going to find his father in this chaos, when frantic pounding seized his attention. He quickly spotted where it was coming from.

A Japanese crane operator was trapped inside the control booth of the capsized crane. The compartment was partially caved-in, so that there was barely enough room for the man inside, and the exit door was a twisted mass of crumpled metal. It was going to take a blowtorch, or maybe the "Jaws of Life," to extricate the operator from the crushed compartment. The man's face was bloodied and contorted with fear. His fists hammered against the cracked window of the booth. From the looks of things, his legs were probably broken. Frankly, it was a miracle he was still alive.

He locked eyes with Ford, who hesitated, uncertain what to do.

I need to find my father, but...

Ford!

Joe spotted his son from his elevated vantage point atop the quaking gantry. Ford was down below, still wearing the same secondhand radiation suit, and staring at the crushed operator booth of one of the fallen cranes. Joe watched with growing concern as Ford stepped over a tangle of steel cables stretching between the crane and the net above the pit. The cables went taut as the creature tugged again at the bars of its cage, dragging the cables toward the pit. Distracted by some drama below, Ford didn't seem to realize that he was standing in the path of the cables, which were shifting toward him.

"Ford!"

Ford was too far away to hear Joe's shouting over all the other commotion. Frantic, Joe rushed along the wobbling gantry, forcing his way past a stampede of terrified workers. He had to fight not to get carried backwards by the crush of bodies fleeing. Joe waved his hands in the air, yelling at the top of his lungs.

"*Ford!*"

But Ford still couldn't hear him. Unaware of the danger

posed by the moving cables, he appeared intent on rescuing somebody trapped in the crane's demolished control booth. The cables jerked again with another powerful tug from below, which also jolted the gantry beneath Joe. The elevated steel walkway creaked and teetered, tossing Joe from side to side. His elbow smacked painfully into a guardrail, but Joe barely noticed. He sprinted further across the unsteady gantry, even as everyone else scrambled in the opposite direction. The fear-maddened crowd thinned out, clearing his way, as he raced to get within earshot of his son. His eyes widened in horror as the taut cables began to drag the entire crane toward the pit.

"*Ford! Get back now!*"

Ford heard his father shouting. Startled, he looked up to see Joe staring down at him from an elevated walkway. He couldn't quite make out what his dad was yelling, but the utter terror on Joe's face was clear enough. Metal scraped loudly against the pavement, throwing off sparks, as the collapsed crane surged toward Ford. Hundreds of tons of lethal metal and machinery threatened to flatten him like a runaway train.

He dived out of the way, forced to abandon the trapped operator. The crane swept past him, carrying the operator to his doom. Their eyes met briefly before the control booth, along with the rest of the crane, was yanked into the waiting pit. Ford wondered briefly if the man had a family...

Joe kept shouting at him from above. Scrambling to his feet, Ford looked up at his father again—just as the plummeting crane hauled down the entire elevated gantry Joe was standing on. Ford barely had time to register what was happening before the metal scaffolding collapsed, taking Joe with it. Crumpled steel landed in a heap at the edge of the giant sinkhole, atop a jutting concrete ridge.

"DAD!!!"

Ford rushed toward the wreckage, praying that Joe was still alive somewhere in the towering pile of debris. He couldn't lose his father now, not like this! He needed to apologize to his dad for never really listening to him, for thinking he was crazy all these years. Who knew that it was the world that had gone mad—and that Joe Brody was the only person sane enough to see that?

The ruins of the collapsed gantry loomed before him. A thick cloud of dust and pulverized concrete rose from the debris. He was almost there—

Something huge and heavy slammed into the pavement in front of him, blocking his path. A glistening black column suddenly stretched high above his head. Stumbling backwards, it took Ford a second to grasp that what he was seeing was an enormous spiked claw, attached to a limb the size of a redwood.

No, he thought. *It's not possible. No animal can be that big!*

Then another jointed black limb stretched up from the depths of the pit and smacked down on the ground several yards behind Ford.

And another.

And another.

Ford froze in terror. For a moment, all he could hear was his own breathing inside the gas mask and the rapid thumping of his heart. Nothing in his Navy training or combat experience had prepared him for the sight of the colossal creature rising up out of the darkness of the pit like a living mountain. An iridescent black exoskeleton, made of a hard shell-like substance, covered a vaguely insectile behemoth with at least six limbs of varying sizes. Two sturdy hind legs, with "backwards"-jointed ankles, supported the bulk of the creature's weight, while a pair of elongated middle limbs extended from the beast's armored shoulders. A much smaller pair of forearms, resembling those of a praying mantis, protruded from its upper thorax. Glittering red eyes peered out from beneath a flat triangular skull that almost looked like a rattlesnake's. Saliva dripped from a huge hooked beak. The sheer scale of the creature beggared the imagination. It had to be nearly two hundred feet tall.

This was no mere "animal," as his father had predicted. This was a monster.

The beast kept rising higher and higher, straightening to reveal its true, incredible size. Its titanic form blocked out the sky, hiding the stars. Its immense shadow fell across the sprawling base. Ford waited for the monster to squash him like a bug, but it paid no attention to him. Instead it hunched and grunted, heaving as though undergoing some kind of internal convulsion. Its armored back began to buck and bulge violently. For a moment, Ford allowed himself the hope that the monstrous creature was dying for some unknown reason. Perhaps an adverse reaction to the environment or the radiation in the pit? Or maybe the creature was simply too big to survive. Was it possible he was witnessing its death throes?

Please, Ford prayed. *There's no room in this world for a monster like this.*

But then its molting back split open in two long parallel gashes, dozens of feet long. Glistening prongs of flesh emerged from the ruptured carapace, unfurling grotesquely into sleek black wings that reminded Ford of a stealth fighter. Blood pumped into the wings causing them to grow stiff and rigid. Thick veins supported a scaly membrane. They stretched and flexed, wet and shimmering. A hard black sheath, that appeared to be made of the same glossy substance as the creature's exoskeleton, protected the underside of the wings.

No longer hunching, the creature rose up triumphantly, exalting in its metamorphosis. It bloodcurdling screech could probably be heard for miles away. Spreading its newborn wings, it took to the sky.

Awestruck, Ford watched it fly away.

But to where?

TEN

More than a day before:

Sam woke up. Sunlight filtered through the bedroom curtains as he yawned and stretched in bed. It was warm and comfy and he was in no hurry to get up until he remembered that his dad was home and had promised to take him to the toy store today. He sprang out of bed and scampered toward the door in his pajamas. Bare feet expertly dodged the toys strewn across the floor. He smelled pancakes cooking in the kitchen and grinned in anticipation. His mouth watered.

He loved pancakes—and so did his dad.

Yet when he rushed into the kitchen, expecting to find both his parents, he found only his mother cooking over a griddle. Confused, he looked around, but his dad was nowhere to be seen. He noticed that there were only two place settings laid out at the kitchen table.

He knew what that meant.

But he promised, Sam thought. *He said he would still be*

here in the morning when I got up!

His mother heard him come in. She turned away from the stove to greet him. She gazed down at him sadly, forcing a smile. He didn't need to tell her how he felt.

"It's okay, babe," she said gently. "He'll be back soon."

Sam didn't understand. Had the Navy called Dad back already? He was supposed to be home for two weeks this time. Two weeks, not just one night!

His mom turned off the stove to comfort him. She knelt down and hugged him as she tried to explain why Dad was gone again.

"*His* daddy needed help."

Now:

The sun rose over the ruined base. Black smoke rose from the rubble, darkening the sky. The toppled cranes remained where they'd fallen, even though emergency crews had begun the grisly process of carting away the remains (partial and otherwise) of the deceased. Severed steel cables hung in tatters from the edge of the sinkhole. Helicopters circled overhead, observing the devastation below. Survivors were being carried away on stretchers, even as first responders worked overtime to extricate more bodies from the debris. Collapsed gantries and scaffolding had turned the site into an enormous junkyard. Twisted steel beams jutted from the wreckage like abstract grave markers. Sobs and curses filled the air.

Ford wandered directionlessly through the ruins, ignored and forgotten amidst the disaster scene. His face was caked with soot and sweat. He'd discarded his gas mask and helmet hours ago; radiation poisoning had seemed the least of his worries. Every muscle ached and he felt black and blue all over. A loose pair of handcuffs still dangled from one wrist, which stung like the devil. He stumbled clumsily over the rubble, attempting to stay out of the way of the emergency crews. He'd been searching all night for his father without any luck. For all he knew, Joe was still buried beneath the debris.

He spied a crowd of medical personnel tending to another batch of wounded. Unwilling to give up, he pressed his way into the makeshift triage unit. Dozens of casualties occupied gurneys, while the overtaxed doctors, nurses, and medic struggled to cope with the flood of patients. Ford was both appalled and discouraged by the number of victims. He didn't know where to keep looking for his dad. Joe could anywhere.

Or nowhere, anymore.

No, he thought. *Don't even think that.*

He'd already lost his mother on this very same site. He'd be damned if he'd see his father buried here, too. Exhausted and sore, he stubbornly worked his way down row after row of casualties. Ford had seen combat, and the aftermath of suicide bombings, but the widespread suffering on display here still got to him—and left him feeling very afraid. His brain was still trying to come to terms with the reality of the gigantic winged monstrosity he'd witnessed earlier. Bombs and terrorists were one thing. He knew how to protect himself—and others—from them. But a creature like that... how on Earth did you stop it? Was that even possible?

And what was it doing now?

Worried and worn out, he almost walked by his dad without recognizing him, but then he spotted Joe on a gurney, surrounded by harried nurses and medics, fighting to keep the injured man alive. An IV line was set up to administer fluids and medication. Pressure was applied to the most visible wounds. Joe was caked in blood and dirt, his shredded radiation suit almost unrecognizable. The medics were already peeling the suit from him to get at his injuries.

"Dad!"

Ford rushed toward, trying to squeeze past the doctors and nurses, who refused to let him through. He peered anxiously over the shoulders of the busy medics, hoping that he hadn't found his father just in time to see him die. That would be too cruel.

Joe's eyes fluttered at the sound of Ford's voice. He squinted through a fog of pain at his son. Their eyes met, truly seeing each other for perhaps the first time in years.

But was it too late for both of them—and the world?

Not far away, Serizawa also wandered through the ruins. He watched numbly as rows of lifeless bodies were zipped unceremoniously into ugly black body bags. It was like the aftermath of a battle or natural disaster, yet all this carnage and destruction had been caused by a single organism emerging from the cocoon, just as it had burst from its egg sac in the Philippines over a decade ago. History was repeating itself—on an even more apocalyptic scale.

His clothing was torn and rumpled. He and Graham had barely escaped the crow's nest before it had crashed to the ground, but many others had not been so lucky. He watched grimly as Gregory Whelan was zipped into a bag. To his credit, the embattled chief scientist had stayed at his post until the bitter end, waiting until everyone else was evacuated, like a captain going down with his ship. Serizawa recalled ruefully just how excited Whelan had been only hours ago, thinking that he was on the verge of a revolutionary discovery. Little had the man known that the "living fuel cell" in the cocoon would cost him his life.

Goodbye, Gregory. Serizawa bowed his head in respect. *You were a good scientist. Your only mistake was not realizing that certain forces were beyond your control.*

"Dr. Serizawa!"

A deep voice intruded on the moment. Serizawa turned to see a U.S. Navy officer approaching him, accompanied by Graham and a Japan Self-Defense Force captain. A helicopter was revving up behind them, its rotors stirring up the already dusty air.

"Captain Russell Hampton," the American officer introduced himself, shouting to be heard over the 'copter's spinning rotors. He was a tall, fit man wearing military fatigues, at least a decade younger than the scientist. A bald pate crowned his stoic face, which could have been carved from a block of dark brown granite. "Tactical authority of this situation has been accorded to Admiral Stenz, Commander, US Naval Forces, Seventh Fleet, part of a joint task force. I'm told your organization has situational awareness of our unidentified organism?"

Serizawa nodded. For more than six decades, a top-secret international coalition known as Monarch had been covertly studying and monitoring evidence of unknown mega-fauna such as the one that had just hatched from the cocoon. Alas, their practical experience in dealing with living specimens was minimal at best.

"Then I'm going to have to ask you to join me," Hampton said. He glanced around at the surrounding bedlam. "Are there any other personnel you need?"

Serizawa considered the question. There was Graham, of course; that went without saying. But was there anybody else? He joined Hampton in scanning the crowd around them. He noticed that Joe Brody, the power plant engineer, was lying injured on a gurney nearby. A younger American, whom Serizawa's assumed to be Brody's son, Ford, was looking on anxiously as paramedics scrambled to stabilize his father's condition. Serizawa recalled the data that had been confiscated from Brody. Serizawa had made sure that the disks and charts survived the disaster, but, now more than ever, he wanted to know everything the trespassing engineer knew about the nuclear disaster fifteen years ago. He pointed decisively at Brody and son.

"Them."

ELEVEN

The transport chopper roared through the sky toward the *USS Saratoga*, a *Nimitz*-class nuclear-powered super-carrier more than a thousand feet in length. One of the largest warships ever constructed, the *Saratoga* rose twenty stories above the water and was accompanied by a sizable naval strike group composed of smaller frigates, cruisers, an oiler, a supply ship, and other support vessels. Aboard the 'copter, Ford stuck close to his dad while trying to keep up with their rapidly changing situation. One minute, he and Joe had been stuck in the ruins of the base, the next they had been hustled aboard a waiting chopper...

Hang on, Dad, he thought. *Just a few more minutes.*

A medic struggled to keep Joe alive, monitoring the battered engineer's vital signs, but seemed to be fighting a losing battle. Captain Hampton and a pair of civilian scientists looked on as Joe feebly clung to life. Ford still wasn't quite sure why he and his dad were now getting special treatment, after being arrested as trespassers before, but he wasn't about to question this unexpected turn of events. All that mattered was keeping his father alive. They had a second chance to rebuild their fractured relationship, and Ford didn't want to lose that. He wanted his father back.

"You were right," Ford said, squeezing Joe's hand. His eyes welled up. His throat tightened. "I'm sorry."

Joe gazed up at Ford through bloodshot eyes. His voice was weak and raspy as he struggled to speak. Ford leaned in to hear him.

"Whatever it takes," he said faintly. "You have to end this... "

He began to slip away, perhaps for good.

"Dad—"

"Whatever it takes..."

"Dad, stay with me!" Ford exclaimed. "Dad!"

Joe's eyes lost focus, staring somewhere beyond this world. Ford watched helplessly as the medic scrambled to save his failing patient, who was fading fast...

The Saratoga's Combat Direction Center, located below decks, was packed and buzzing. Banks of monitors and work stations, manned by uniformed analysts, were jammed with data feeds. Armed services personnel, sporting the uniforms of several allied nationalities, were crammed into the war room, which reminded Serizawa of the crow's nest back at the base. The overhead lights were kept dim to increase the visibility of the various screens and graphic displays. A backlit table map projected the creature's potential courses, as calculated by the incoming data. As the simulations ran, dotted lines crossed the ocean, branching off in all directions, but with most heading east across the Pacific. Each dotted line was accompanied by a flurry of algorithmic probability data: wind speed, currents, altitude, weather conditions, and so on. Quietly observing the operations, Serizawa was just selfish enough to be relieved that the creature appeared to be winging away from his homeland.

Not that anywhere in the world was truly safe at the moment.

"Okay! Listen up!" Captain Hampton said, taking the floor. To say that his manner was "brisk" would be an understatement. "Quiet please!" He waited, but not for long, for the general chatter and hubbub to die down. "Briefing is up. New faces. New info. From here out, we do not *try* to move quickly, we *will* move quickly." He turned to introduce a figure to his right. "Admiral?"

A senior officer, with cropped white hair and a lean, taciturn face, stepped forward. He gestured at a monitor displaying a blurry image of the creature that had emerged from the cocoon. Hushed voices murmured in awe.

"Good afternoon," the admiral said crisply. "*This* is our needle in a haystack, people. A 'massive unidentified terrestrial organism,' which from this point forward will be referred to as 'MUTO.' The world still thinks this was an earthquake, and it would be preferable if that were to remain so. It was last sighted heading east across the Pacific. However, this... *animal's* electromagnetism has been playing havoc with radar, satellite feeds, you name it, leaving us, for the moment, blind as bats." A frown deepened the well-earned creases on his face. "I emphasize 'for the moment' because I have every confidence in the world that you will find it. *We have to.*"

His remarks concluded, he surrendered the floor and

sought out Serizawa at the back of the room. He extended his hand.

"Doctor Serizawa," the admiral greeted him. "William Stenz. We're glad to have you aboard."

Serizawa accepted Stenz's hand and bowed slightly. He spied Graham beckoning to him from the open hatchway to the command center. He had dispatched her earlier to examine Joe Brody's findings. He nodded back to her in acknowledgment. He was anxious to hear what she had to say.

"Will you excuse me, Admiral?"

Joe Brody's face looked more at peace than it had been for at least fifteen years. His eyes were closed forever, seeing only the next world. Ford could only hope that, whatever had become of his father's tortured spirit, somewhere Joe was gazing on his wife's beloved face once more.

Ford stood by numbly in the *Saratoga*'s well-equipped medical bay as the body bag holding his father's remains was zipped shut. A medic offered him a sympathetic look, but Ford was too stunned to respond. The tears would come in time, he hoped, but right now he just felt drained and lost. San Francisco seemed more than a world away. He wondered how he was going to break this news to Sam. The boy had never really known his grandfather. Would he even understand that now he never would?

"Lieutenant Brody, sir?"

A young petty officer intruded on Ford's grief, as gently as he could. His voice held a distinctly Midwestern accent.

"Would you please come with me?"

* * *

Serizawa and his team had been assigned guest quarters upon the *Saratoga*. Even on a ship as large as the super-carrier, space was at a premium so the cramped cabin was a tight squeeze, but they were making do. Monarch scientists worked beside Navy technicians, monitoring data feeds at various workstations, even as he and Graham each spoke urgently on their respective phones.

"Yes," he reported in Japanese, "the patterns match, but I can't crack the significance."

Joe Brody's antique zip disks, rescued from the M.U.T.O. base, were stacked on a desk beside Serizawa's research materials. Scattered photos and reports held fragments of a history that began years before Serizawa was born: grainy images of a gargantuan creature rising from the sea six decades ago, archive photos of an atomic bomb blast on a remote Pacific atoll, shots from the Philippine mine disaster, reports on the Janjira nuclear plant disaster, and updates on the singular cocoon found on the site afterwards.

It appeared that he and Brody had been colleagues of a sort, pursuing similar lines of investigation all these years.

What a pity, he reflected, *that we never knew each other existed.*

He overheard Graham dealing with the public-relations issue. "Yes, sir," she said into her phone. "Media is reporting an earthquake. The cover's holding for now, but if it—"

A knock at the hatchway interrupted both phone calls. Graham went to answer it.

"Dr. Serizawa?" Petty Officer Thatch stood in the doorway. He had Ford Brody with him, still wearing part of a rundown radiation suit that had seen better days. The man's wrist was chafed, but his handcuffs had been removed en route to the carrier. Serizawa nodded at Thatch that it was all right for him to leave Ford with them. Ford's passport had been found among his belongings; a quick investigation had confirmed that he was a lieutenant in the U.S. Navy, currently on leave. Thatch departed and Graham escorted Ford into the room.

Ford, who looked more than a little shell-shocked, approached the desk warily. His eyes widened as he spotted the photos spread out across the desk, which Serizawa made no effort to conceal. Ford was visibly taken aback by the startling images. Serizawa sympathized; what these pictures displayed would be shocking to the young man, who had just lost his father as well. His entire world had changed overnight.

"Mr. Brody, my condolences," Serizawa said.

Ford stared at them. Pain, anger, and confusion all seemed to simmer inside the unfortunate young man, who was understandably overwhelmed by recent events. Powerful emotions played across Ford's face, while his body language was tense. Serizawa began to fear that the grieving lieutenant would be of little use to their investigation. Judging from his reaction to the photos, Ford was apparently not fully conversant with his father's theories.

Graham tried to secure Ford's cooperation anyway. "We're deeply sorry for your loss, Lieutenant. But I'm afraid we need your help. Your father's data—"

"No, you first," he snapped. His nerves and temper were obviously at the breaking point. "Who are you people?"

Graham shot a questioning look at Serizawa, letting him make the call. He nodded, regarding Ford with sympathy. This man had been through so much already. He deserved to know what his father had given his life for.

"Come in please, Mr. Brody. Come in and we will show you."

Ford stepped deeper into the cabin. Graham shut the door behind him.

Flickering images played upon the wall of the cabin. Hooked into Graham's laptop, a portable digital projector provided relevant visuals as Serizawa attempted to explain.

"In 1954," he began, "the first time a nuclear submarine ever reached the lowest depths, it awakened something."

"The Americans first thought it was the Russians," Graham added. "The Russians thought that it was the Americans. All those nuclear tests in the Pacific? Not tests..."

"They were trying to kill it." Serizawa indicated the ancient film footage from the 1950s. *"Him."*

Ford's jaw dropped. Breaking eye contact with Serizawa, he looked more closely at the projected images of the 1954 A-bomb detonation, the bomb with the cartoon lizard inscribed on its cone, a mushroom cloud rising over the once-tranquil Pacific Ocean, and, finally, impossibly, the grainy silhouette of a titanic beast rising up from the sea, a row of jagged fins dimly visible along its spine.

"An ancient alpha predator," Serizawa explained.

"Millions of years older than mankind," Graham said, "from a time when the Earth was ten times more radioactive than it is today. The animal—and others like it—*consumed* that radiation as a food source. But as radiation levels on the surface naturally subsided, these creatures adapted to live deeper in the oceans, farther underground, absorbing radiation from the planet's core. The organization we work for, Monarch, was established in the wake of this discovery. A multinational organization, formed in secrecy, to search for him, study him, learn everything we could."

Ford stared at the footage. The images were blurry, but the creature's gargantuan proportions and general outline were clear.

"We call him *Godzilla*," Serizawa said.

The name was derived from a legend of the islands: a mythical king of monsters known as *Gojira*. The name had been Americanized by the U.S. Military during their initial attempts to bomb the newly discovered behemoth out of existence.

"The top of a primordial ecosystem," Graham elaborated. "A god for all intents and purposes."

Ford gaped at the images, struggling to process what he was hearing and seeing. *"Monsters..."*

"That is one word for them," Serizawa agreed. He used a handheld remote to call up images of the "cavern" in the Philippines. "Fifteen years ago, we found the fossil of another giant animal in the Philippines. Like Godzilla, but this creature died long ago, *killed* by these..." Close-ups of the MUTO spores appeared on the wall.

"Parasitic organisms," Graham said. "One dormant, but the other hatched. Catalyzed when a mining company unknowingly drilled into its tomb. The hatchling burrowed straight for the nearest source of radiation, your father's power plant in Janjira, and cocooned there. Absorbing the radioactive fuel to gestate, grow."

"Until it hatched like a butterfly into the creature you saw," Serizawa. "We call it a MUTO."

The biology, in fact, was fairly basic, albeit on a monstrous scale. The larval form of various insects and arthropods were basically eating machines, consuming massive amounts of nutrients before creating a cocoon in which to undergo the metamorphosis into their adult stage. Serizawa called up an image of the massive cocoon, which had been discovered fifteen years ago atop the ruins of the Janjira plant, not long after the earlier disaster in the Philippines.

"You're saying you knew about this... *thing*... the whole time?" Ford shook his head, trying to take it all in. "And kept it a secret? Lied to everyone?"

Serizawa remembered a family photo he had found among Ford's effects.

"You have a son, Mr. Brody. Would you tell him there are monsters in the world? Beyond our control? We believed that horror was better kept buried."

"But you let it *feed*?" Ford said. "Why not kill it when you had the chance?"

"It was absorbing radiation from the reactors," Graham said. "Vast doses, like a sponge. We worried killing it might have released that radiation, endangering millions."

Serizawa nodded. "The MUTO *caused* the catastrophe, but also *prevented* it from spreading." Without the cocoon, and the immense pupa developing inside it, the quarantine zone would have indeed been the radioactive wasteland they had let the world believe it was. "That's why Monarch's mission was to contain it, to study its biology. To *understand* it."

But, yes, he thought regretfully, *we waited too long.*

"We knew the creature was having an electrical effect on everything within a close proximity," Graham said. "What we didn't know was that it could harness that same power in an EMP attack."

Footage from Janjira showed the winged creature unleashing its electromagnetic pulse—a heartbeat before the pulse shorted out the monitors.

"Your father did," Graham said. "He predicted it."

"What else did he say?" Serizawa asked. "Anything at all?"

"I—I don't know," Ford confessed, his voice cracking. "I always thought he was crazy, obsessed. *I didn't listen.*" He ran a hand through his hair, overwrought, while he visibly struggled to recall his father's theories. "He said it was some kind of animal call. Like something... talking."

"Talking?" Serizawa sat up straight. Was Ford implying there was more than one signal?

Ford nodded. "Yeah, he was studying something. *Echolocation.*"

Serizawa and Graham stared at each other in shock. Ford clearly had no idea what a bombshell he'd just dropped, but the two scientists immediately grasped the implications. They glanced down at an indistinct snapshot of the majestic creature from the ocean's floor, last seen sixty years ago.

Could they truly be dealing with... him?

"If the MUTO was talking that day," Serizawa reasoned, "your father must have discovered something *talking back.*"

Gripped by a sense of extraordinary urgency, he turned to Graham. "Go back through the data, search for a response call."

She sat down at her laptop, while the projector continued to cycle through the relevant images. Serizawa slumped down into a chair. Ford stared at the wall, trying to make sense of it all. It was a lot to absorb.

"This parasite... it's still out there," he said. "Where's it headed?"

"The MUTO is still young, still growing," Serizawa said. "It will be looking for food."

"Sources of radiation," Graham added, glancing up from her laptop. "We're monitoring all known sites, but if we don't find it soon... "

Her voice trailed off, not needing to say more.

"It killed both my parents," Ford said. "There must be *something* we can do."

Serizawa had his doubts, at least as far as humanity's ability to cope with the threat.

"Nature has an order, Mr. Brody. A power to rebalance."

He stared up at the wall, where Godzilla could be glimpsed once more. The U.S. Army had attempted to destroy the beast with an atomic bomb, but no remains had been found afterwards. Some believed (or hoped) that Godzilla had been completely vaporized by the blast, but that may have been wishful thinking.

"I believe he is that power."

TWELVE

A bugler played taps, but only a small honor guard was in attendance. Standing on the wide rear deck of the *Saratoga*, as the sun slowly sank into the horizon, Ford saluted stoically as his father's body was put to the rest. He had shed the battered radiation suit, but was still wearing rumpled civvies he'd left Joe's apartment in. Serizawa was also present as Joe Brody's flag-draped body slid off the deck into the sea. It disappeared quickly beneath the churning waves.

Goodbye, Dad, Ford thought. *I wish you could go home with me.*

It occurred to him that neither his father nor his mother had a proper grave, but that was not something he wanted to dwell on at the moment. Petty Officer Thatch was waiting off to one side, maintaining a respectful distance while Ford bid farewell to his father, but Ford knew he had to get going if he wanted to make it back to Elle and Sam. He stared for a few more minutes at the endless expanse of ocean that was now

Joe Brody's final resting-place before walking over to Thatch.

It was time to go.

Thatch escorted him across the carrier's expansive flight deck, which was noisy and abuzz with activity. Aside from "the island," a multi-level command center topped by a towering array of radar and communications antenna, the top deck of the Saratoga was a flat expanse used as a runway to land and launch a wide variety of aircraft. There was also room to park a few dozen planes, although the majority of the carrier's eighty-plus aircraft were stored below decks in the hangar bay. A transport chopper was loading off to one side of the runway. Busy seamen worked quickly and efficiently to stow their gear aboard the helicopter as it prepped for take off. Ford quickened his pace, not wanting to be left behind. Thatch shouted to be heard above the clamor.

"Right now we're fifty miles off Hawaii," Thatch explained. "This transport will take you there. You're on a commercial flight back to San Francisco."

Ford was grateful for the arrangements made on his behalf, especially given everything else that was going on. He saluted Thatch as he boarded the chopper and quickly found a seat. He spotted Serizawa watching from the deck a short distance away.

The chopper's rotors were already spinning up. Within moments, the helicopter lifted off from the flight deck, carrying Ford away from the *Saratoga*. In the fading twilight, he made out a faint smudge of land in the distance, which he knew to be the islands of Hawaii. His next stop on his way back to his family. In all the chaos and tragedy of the last forty-eight hours, there'd been no chance to even try to get in touch with Elle back in San Francisco. He wished he was bringing back better news.

Peering down from the chopper, he spied the tiny figure of Dr. Serizawa. The Japanese scientist watched the helicopter depart before turning back to reenter the ship. Ford had left his father's research aboard the ship. With any luck, it would prove useful to the people in charge of figuring out what to do about the giant winged monster on the loose.

If not, the whole world could be in serious trouble.

The TV news was on in the background as Elle and Sam fixed dinner in the kitchen. Although the sound had been muted, a crawl played across the bottom of the screen:

"EARTHQUAKE ROCKS NORTHERN JAPAN – NUCLEAR Q-ZONE SHAKES."

The headline went unnoticed by Elle, who was trying to put up a brave front for Sam despite her growing anxiety. Days had passed since Ford had left for Japan and yet there was still no word from him. Something had obviously gone wrong; otherwise he would have surely checked in by now. All she knew for certain was that his flight to Tokyo had touched down on time and that, according to the local police, he had bailed his dad out of jail at least two days ago.

After that... nothing.

Where are you, Ford? What's happened to you?

Distracted, she dumped some loose scraps and peelings into the sink and ran the garbage disposal. The loud grinding noise drew a frown from Sam, who clapped his hands over his ears.

Neither of them heard her LG mobile phone buzzing on the coffee table, one room away.

"This is Mommy's phone. Leave a message."

Ford swore inwardly as Elle's phone went to voice mail. The sound of his son's voice hit him harder than he had anticipated, but he needed to talk to Elle more than anything. He clutched a borrowed satellite phone as the transport chopper carried him over the Pacific. He raised his voice to be heard over the whirring rotors. It was getting dark outside; barely an hour had passed since he'd buried his father at sea.

"Elle..."

His voice faltered. The conversation he'd been rehearsing instantly flew out of his head, rendering him flustered and at a loss for words.

"I don't know that they're saying on the news. There was an... accident... in Japan. Dad's... gone." His eyes welled up. His throat tightened so he could hardly speak. "Listen. I'm almost to Hawaii. I've got a flight home. I love you both. Tell Sam Daddy's coming home, okay? I'm coming home."

The voice mail beeped, cutting him off. Ford put down the phone. Wiping his eyes, he peered out across the crystal-blue waters below to the Hawaiian Islands directly ahead.

He prayed that Elle would get the message.

Serizawa and Graham huddled before a glowing monitor in the *Saratoga*'s war room as a helpful petty officer uploaded Joe Brody's data onto a display screen. Adapting the antiquated zip disks to the ship's state-of-the-art computer systems had posed a challenge, but, thankfully, not an insurmountable one. The two scientists studied the telltale waveform as it plotted out across the screen. Serizawa tapped his foot impatiently against the floor. This was taking too long.

"Keep scrolling," Graham instructed the technician.

"Near the end, before the final pulse—"

Serizawa's eyes widened. "*There!*" he blurted, pointing at the screen, where, just before the end of the graph, one peak was followed directly by another—as if in reply. Graham gasped out loud. The evidence was undeniable, the conclusion inescapable.

"Something responded," Serizawa said gravely. "He was right."

Graham lowered her voice. "You don't think it could be...?"

He knew she was thinking of the unknown leviathan from sixty years ago, but he was reluctant to jump to conclusions. Perhaps there was another explanation.

"Search for this pattern," he instructed.

Graham regarded him quizzically. "Where?"

"Everywhere," he said.

Another petty officer came up behind them. Serizawa did not know his name, but could tell that he approached with urgent business.

"Doctors," the man said. "You need to see this."

"Terminal A, domestic gates."

Ford rushed through the busy commercial terminal at the Honolulu International Airport. Tourists in floral leis, toting their carry-on luggage, paraded past him as he headed across the crowded concourse to where people were lining up to catch the elevated monorail connecting the various terminals. He needed to hurry if he wanted to catch his flight to San Francisco.

He found a seat on the train and slumped into it, completely worn out. He had barely slept for days now, ever since getting that phone call from Japan about his father, and he was both emotionally and physically exhausted. At this point, he just wanted to get on a plane back to Elle and Sam.

Shifting his weight on the seat, and checking to make sure he still had his boarding pass, he felt something hard and lumpy in his pants pocket. Momentarily puzzled, he reached into his pocket and extracted the object. It was the old toy soldier he'd rescued from his childhood bedroom in Japan. The toy triggered a surge of confused emotions and regrets. He turned it over in his hands. He was glad he had managed to hold onto it—for Sam's sake.

That's one promise I can keep, he thought.

A dense crowd milled about on the platform outside, waiting for another train. Looking up from the toy, Ford contemplated the other weary travelers, who had no idea that they were sharing this world with giant monsters capable of widespread destruction. He envied their blissful ignorance. He found himself pining for the days when his biggest problems were a crazy father, a wife he wasn't always there for, and a strained relationship with his son. He glanced at his watch. It was after nine in San Francisco now. Sam was probably already in bed.

Missing his son more than ever, Ford noticed another little boy, about Sam's age, on the platform outside. The boy peeked out from behind his mother's legs, while his distracted parents coped with their luggage and a map of the airport. Wide eyes stared in fascination at the toy soldier. Ford smiled back at him, amused. His dark mood lifted for a moment.

A chime sounded, warning that Ford's train was about to depart. *"Aloha,"* the recorded voice said cheerily. *"Please stay clear of the automatic doors—"*

Distracted by the announcement, Ford forgot about the boy, until a woman's frantic voice called out abruptly.

"Akio?! Akio!"

On the platform, the boy's parents were looking around anxiously, having obviously misplaced their child. They cried out as they saw that the little boy, whose name was obviously Akio, had darted onto the train when they weren't looking. Drawn by the toy soldier, Akio approached Ford. He pointed a pudgy finger at the miniature Navy man.

"*Ban-ban*," he chirped.

Oh, shit, Ford thought, realizing what was happening. He leapt up to return the boy to his parents, but he was too late. The doors slid shut with a whoosh and the train began to pull away from the platform. Through the windows, Ford saw Akio's parents reacting in consternation. They dashed frantically to the edge of the platform, shouting and throwing out their arms. The father grabbed onto his wife, as though half-afraid that she would rush onto the tracks. She sobbed hysterically.

"Stay there!" he shouted. "I'll bring him back!"

The platform dropped from view as the train glided away on the elevated track. Exiting the terminal, the train cruised above the tarmac, where parked and taxiing jets could be seen through the train's windows. A departing plane took off from a runway as Ford inspected a posted map of the monorail system. According to the map, the train would make a complete circuit of the airport before returning to the station they had just left. He hoped that Akio's parents had heard him and would stay put long enough for him to get the boy back to them. They'd looked Japanese. Did they even speak English? Had they understood what he'd shouted?

Ford looked down at Akio, who had suddenly become his responsibility. He gave the boy a playfully stern expression.

"You're under arrest, bud." He glanced again at his watch,

while keeping one eye on his new charge. "I better not miss my flight."

It was going to be close.

The young petty officer led Serizawa and Graham across the CDC to another work station, where Admiral Stenz awaited them, a grim expression on his weathered features. He wasted no time bringing the two scientists up to speed on the latest development.

"We've lost all comms with a Russian *Borei* in the North Pacific," he said, referring to a class of nuclear submarine. He turned toward the young analyst manning the console. "Martinez?"

An impressive array of data and video screens faced Martinez, an alert young officer in her early twenties. She was focused on various screens displaying what appeared to be night-vision helicopter feeds of a platoon of U.S. Special Forces soldiers trekking through a dense jungle. A spectral green glow tinted a view of dense bamboo groves and underbrush.

"Aye, sir," Martinez reported. "Sparta One is picking up a distress signal northwest of Diamond Head." Disbelief registered on her face as she confirmed the location. "In the midst of Oahu."

Serizawa inhaled sharply. Oahu was no ghost town or remote mining camp. It was the most populous island in Hawaii.

The MUTO and humanity were on a collision course.

* * *

The Green Berets advanced through the nocturnal jungle, kitted out with hazard gas masks and night-vision goggles.

GODZILLA

The dense bamboo forest was lush and fragrant, abloom with wild orchids, hibiscus, and plumeria. Hidden waterfalls cascaded in the background, but any wildlife was unusually silent, as though the local fauna had made themselves scarce. They were only miles away from lively beaches and night life of Waikiki, but, from the looks of things, they might as well as have been deep in the Amazon rain forest. The dense underbrush made for hard slogging, but the soldiers maintained a brisk pace. They hacked their way through the jungle with machetes.

The leader of the team, Captain Bill Cozzone, was a combat veteran who had taken part in a wide variety of missions over the years, ranging from counter-terrorism to humanitarian assistance, but this assignment was a new one. Nothing in his extensive training and experience had involved tracking down a "Massive Unknown Terrestrial Organism," let alone a missing nuclear submarine. He used a Geiger counter to guide them through the jungle. It clicked faster and faster as they zeroed in on their objective. Spotting something ahead, through the green-tinted view of his goggles, he raised his hand to signal a halt.

Whoa, he thought. *There's something you don't see every day.*

The *Alexander Nevsky*, a fourth-generation nuclear submarine, was standing upright among the trees, as though dropped from above. Nearly six hundred feet tall and more than forty feet across, the sub was encrusted with a hardening resinous secretion that dripped slowly down its side. It nose was buried deeply in the earth, amidst smashed and pulverized greenery. In theory, the submarine housed a crew of 130 officers and men. Cozzone found it hard to imagine that any of them could have survived the drop. They were almost certainly crushed to a pulp inside the towering metal shell.

The twelve-man team spread out around the base of the misplaced sub, gazing up at the surreal sight. Cozzone didn't like the look of this. Submarines belonged in the ocean depths, not perched upside-down in the Hawaiian jungle, only a short hop from Diamond Head. This was wrong with a capital W.

"Guardian 3, this is Sparta 1," he reported via radio. "We've located the Russian sub. Break—"

Something stirred above the jungle canopy high overhead. Craning his head back, Cozzone spied the MUTO itself, crouched above the upright sub. Despite his earlier briefing, the soldier was taken aback by the sheer size and freakishness of the winged monstrosity, which looked like a cross between a giant bug and a dinosaur. Its shiny black wings were folded in behind it like an ominous dark cloak. A thick orange secretion oozed from the creature's segmented underside. The photos he'd been shown before had failed to capture how truly monstrous this "organism" was.

Holy mother of—

"Guardian 3, we also have eyes on your bogey."

The command center aboard the *Saratoga* immediately responded. *"Sparta 1, Guardian 3. Six Actual requests a sit-rep, over."*

To Cozzone's relief, the MUTO ignored the stunned Green Berets down on the forest floor. Instead it had torn open the hull of the *Alexander Nevsky* and was gorging on the glowing plutonium core of the nuclear reactor, gobbling down the red-hot fuel rods like a pelican downing a fish. Cozzone was suddenly very thankful that the MUTO supposedly consumed nuclear radiation. Otherwise he and his men would be fried for sure, gas masks or no gas masks.

He tried to convey to Command what he was seeing.

"Guardian 3, tell the Six it's... uh... well, it appears to be eating the reactor."

Of course, Serizawa thought. *Just as it fed on the nuclear fuel at Janjira before.*

A momentary hush fell over the CDC. Admiral Stenz looked at Serizawa, who nodded grimly in confirmation of the Green Berets' on-site assessment of the situation. Stenz absorbed this new intel with admirable calm and efficiency. He stepped briskly to the center of the war room and raised his voice to be heard above the general hubbub.

"Cat's out of the bag, people," he declared. "New protocol is safety, not secrecy. Get me eyes in the air. Notify Coast Guard District Fourteen and Hawaii Civil Defense. There are a million people on that island."

Serizawa recalled the devastation at the M.U.T.O. base and in the Philippines years ago. He could only imagine the consequences of the creature invading a major population center. They were looking at a catastrophe in the making.

"General quarters, please, skipper," the admiral instructed Captain Hampton. "Set condition one."

The order spurred the entire naval strike group into action. Crews reported to battle stations as the carrier's various support ships rotated their huge artillery guns toward the shore. Seeking fresh air, Serizawa stepped out onto the busy flight deck in time to observe the commotion. Flight crews scrambled as several F-35 jet fighters screamed off the runway amidst loud blasts of blistering exhaust. The Lightnings were one-seat, supersonic aircraft capable of reaching the island in seconds. Catapults hurled them into the air at a breathtaking pace.

Covering his ears, Serizawa turned his attention away from the runway to the nearby island. The strike group was positioned off the shore of Oahu in response to the distress signal from the Russian sub. He could see the sparkling lights of Honolulu and Waikiki, as well as the lush green mountains rising up beyond the beaches and resorts. The landmark volcanic cone of Diamond Head dominated the southeastern tip of the island, overlooking the most popular tourist spots. Only a few miles of ocean separated the fleet from the island. Serizawa gazed out over the moonlit waves and the white caps churned up by the coursing battleships. The slumbering Pacific struck him as deceptively placid, hiding an entire undersea ecology with its own unplumbed secrets, such as...

His eyes widened as he spied a large, dark object slicing through the ocean toward the islands. At first he thought that maybe his eyes were deceiving him, that it was just an illusion born of darkness and the restless motion of the waves, but the huge shape began to rise from the water, growing higher and higher with each passing moment, like the fin of some enormous beast.

Serizawa swallowed hard. He remembered the colossal skeleton they'd discovered in the Philippines fifteen years ago, as well as the decades-old photos on his desk below, the ones he'd been studying his entire career. The ominous silhouette of that long-unseen leviathan remained burned into his memory, even though they were taken before he was born.

Could it truly be *him*?

THIRTEEN

Jenny was enjoying her family's vacation in Hawaii. A blond, six-year-old girl from Seattle, she kept close to her parents as they strolled along the beach at Waikiki, along with dozens of other people. Palm trees swayed above the shore. Tiki torches lit up the night while the mouth-watering aroma of roast pig wafted on a balmy breeze from a nearby luau. Hula dancers in grass skirts put on a show for the tourists. A busy beachfront bar offered drinks, both grown-up and otherwise. The rolling surf lapped at the shore, while the white sand was cool and squishy beneath Jenny's bare feet. Rows of multi-story hotels, condos, and resorts faced the water, while thickly forested hills rose up further inland, beyond the shops and nightclubs. Laughter and music filled the warm night air. An ocean breeze had a salty flavor. It was past Jenny's bedtime, but her parents didn't seem to mind. They were on vacation after all.

The festive scene was suddenly disturbed by a flight of fighter jets zooming overhead, heading inland from somewhere out at sea. Sonic booms shook the night. The jets came in so fast and so low that their passage whipped up the sand on the beach. Startled tourists looked up in surprise. Even the hula dancers stopped swaying and stared up at the jets. Contrails of exhaust streaked the night sky. Bartenders stopped serving drinks.

Wow, Jenny thought. *Nobody told me there was going to be an air show!*

The jets were just the beginning. Police helicopters arrived next, swooping in from downtown. SWAT team members, equipped with rifles and body armor, belayed down on ropes from the hovering choppers to the hotel rooftops, staking out sniper positions. They aimed their weapons at the wooded slopes of the Koolau Mountains, almost as though they expected something bad to attack from the hills at any moment. The helicopters buzzed above Waikiki.

Jenny was captivated by all the excitement, until her mom grabbed her and hugged her tight. Her parents exchanged worried looks and whispered anxiously to each other, as did the many others vacationers frozen in place upon the beach. People pointed and stared at the unexpected invasion. Jenny heard someone speculate about "terrorists." Despite her tender years, she felt the mood changing all around her. Grownups were acting confused and scared, which scared her, too.

Suddenly it didn't feel like a fun vacation anymore.

The train glided toward the next terminal along the elevated track, which ran approximately thirty feet above the tarmac below. Rows of jetliners were parked wing to wing away from the runways. Ford lifted Akio onto a seat to await their stop. He wondered what would be faster and more efficient:

getting off at the next stop and trying to catch another train heading in the opposite direction, or staying on this train until its circuit brought it back to their starting place, where, hopefully, the little boy's parents were waiting anxiously for his return? Ford could just imagine how frightened they must be right now. He'd once lost sight of Sam at the mall; it had only been for a few minutes, but he still remembered how panicked he'd been at the time, all the terrifying scenarios that had flashed through his head before Sam had turned up over at the food court, perfectly fine. Those had been some of the longest minutes of his life, including his time on the front. He knew exactly what sort of hell Akio's parents were going through right now. The sooner he got their child back to them, the better.

Akio sat quietly, watching the planes taxi below, until he suddenly sat up and pointed in excitement at a flight of military jet fighters roaring past the airport toward the densely forested hills beyond. Ford held onto him tightly, alarmed by the sight. Those had looked like F-35 Lightnings, probably launched from the *Saratoga* offshore. He could think of no reason why the supersonic fighters would be zooming inland at full speed.

Unless...

Streaking through the sky, the Lightnings flew in formation toward the mountain range overlooking Honolulu. The lead pilot, Captain Douglas Lang, readied himself for combat against an entirely new type of threat. As the jets crested a rocky jungle ridge, the MUTO came into view, crouching above the bamboo trees like the world's biggest praying mantis. Despite being prepped for this mission, Douglas gulped at the sight of the enormous winged monster. It was hard to believe that such a creature actually existed outside of science-fiction movies or comic books. Yet there it was: right in front of them, rippling with some sort of eerie bioluminescence.

It's still just an animal, he reminded himself, keeping his focus on his mission. *And animals can be put down.*

The F-35 was armed with both guns and missiles, which ought to be more than enough to take out the dangerous creature. "Niner-niner," he reported over the radio built into his helmet. He aimed his cross-hairs at the MUTO, but, to his surprise, they bounced and wavered erratically, as though unable to lock onto the target. "What the--?"

The cross-hairs kept sliding off the target. It was like trying to thread a needle with a wobbly piece of thread.

"I'm getting all sorts of guidance errors," he reported. "Switching to manual."

He reached to flip the switch, just as the MUTO reared up on its hind legs and began glowing brighter than before. A rippling aurora charged the air around it, only a heartbeat before it slammed its upper limbs down, generating a visible electromagnetic pulse.

No! The captain's entire cockpit display went black. He fought to maintain control of the plane even though all of its electrical systems had shorted out instantaneously. *This can't be happening. It's just an animal...*

Flaming out, the disabled aircraft spiraled down toward the jungle floor, where the Green Berets scrambled to get out of the way. The crashing fighter jet slammed into the earth with stupendous force. The impact knocked the fleeing soldiers off their feet.

Seconds later, a huge orange fireball billowed up above the trees.

GODZILLA

* * *

All at once, the entire airport lost power.

Agitated voices filled the train as the overhead lights sputtered out, leaving the passengers in darkness. The train slowed to a stop upon the track, stalling between stations. Ford kept a tight grip on Akio as the boy pressed his face up against the window, looking out towards the mountain slopes none too far away. The hellish red glow of rising flames could be seen from the airport, lighting up the night. Confused passengers murmured anxiously as they spied the distant inferno. No one else seemed to know what was happening, but Ford had a likely idea. His memory instantly flashed back to the creature from the pit.

I think we found it, he thought.

Jenny and her family jumped as an explosion went off in the hills. Thick black smoke rose from the dark jungle, followed by bright red flames. Her father swore under his breath while her mother stifled a frightened sob and scooped the little girl up into her arms. All around them, people were acting scared and confused. Nobody seemed to know what to do or even which way to run. Their hotels were even closer to the hills where the explosions were, so there was nowhere to run except into the ocean.

I don't like this, Jenny thought, hugging her mom. *I want to go home.*

Looking away from the menacing flames and smoke up in the hills, she stared out at the sand and surf instead. Her eyes bulged as she spotted something peculiar. The tide appeared to be retreating rapidly from the shore, ebbing back into the bay, as though it, too, was afraid of all the scary noise and commotion on the island. Her brow wrinkled in confusion.

Was it supposed to do that?

She tugged on her dad's arm, calling his attention to the fleeing waters. His sunburnt face went pale at the sight. Her mom turned around and gasped out loud. She thrust Jenny into her daddy's arms and they took off running inland, away from the shore, as fast as they could. Her mom shouted at the other grownups and children on the beach. Jenny had never heard her so scared, not even that time Jenny had accidently stepped out in front of traffic.

"Run!" her mother yelled. "RUN!"

Aboard the *Saratoga*, Serizawa commandeered a pair of binoculars from a passing seaman. His heart racing, he placed the long-distance lenses to his eyes and searched the moonlit sea for the enigmatic shape he had spied before. He quickly relocated the mysterious object, only to discover that the jagged protrusion had been joined by two smaller points on either side. Recognition dawned in his eyes as he grasped what he was seeing: a row of gigantic dorsal fins.

Racing straight toward the fleet.

Warning sirens sounded as observers aboard the various ships spotted the oncoming threat and braced for impact. Serizawa suspected that few aboard the vessels, except perhaps Graham and a handful of others, knew exactly who or what was surging their way, but it was obvious that *something* very large and solid was on a collision course with the *Saratoga* and the other ships. Serizawa grabbed onto a safety rail, not that he expected it would do much good, not if this was indeed what he surmised.

It must be him, the scientist thought. *What else could it be?*

Torn between scientific curiosity and fear for his life, Serizawa prayed that he would at least be allowed to behold the legend in all its majesty before it laid waste to the floating super-carrier. Through the binoculars, he watched as the giant fins came closer and closer.

Then, at the last minute, before the mighty battleship could even attempt to avoid the collision, the fins dipped rapidly beneath the waves, diving beneath the *Saratoga* and the rest of the strike group. The ship pitched back and forth as something impossibly massive passed beneath it. Baffled flight crews shouted to each other in confusion. Only Serizawa understood the awesome force that had just passed them by. Nature had spared them, at least for the moment.

Drained, he lowered the binoculars and let out a sigh of relief. Part of him was actually disappointed that the owner of the fins had not fully revealed himself, but he suspected that that fateful moment would be upon them soon. He turned toward the unsuspecting island only a few miles away. He had visited Oahu before. It was a beautiful island, full of friendly locals and vacationing tourists.

Little did they know what was heading toward them.

FOURTEEN

Piano music tinkled softly in the background as Bob and Barbara McQueen celebrated their fiftieth anniversary in an elegant restaurant on the top floor of their luxury hotel. An open bottle of champagne rested on the table between them as they finished off their entrées. Bob had ordered the surf and turf while Barb had gone for the coconut shrimp. A picture window offered a lovely view of Mamala Bay, but the elderly couple only had eyes for their meals and each other. Bob had vaguely registered some noisy planes zipping by outside, but knew they weren't all that far from the Honolulu airport. Certainly, he had no intention of letting some inconsiderate pilots spoil this romantic dinner. He and Barb had been saving up for this Hawaiian vacation for years.

Caught up in their celebratory meal, the couple completely failed to notice as, less than a mile away, a huge reptilian beast rose up from the bay to tower over Waikiki. Torrents of cascading seawater veiled the monster's form so that only the titanic proportions of the leviathan were revealed. Standing erect on two stout legs, the monster was nearly four hundred feet tall and solidly built, with a broad chest and brawny forearms. A pair of enormous jaws, resembling those of some prehistoric saurian, opened wide, but the creature's roar was drowned out by the urgent wail of a tsunami warning.

Bob lifted his head irritably from his steak. *Now what?*

A massive tidal wave surged onto the shore. Terrified vacationers, including Jenny and her family, ran in panic, seeking higher ground, as the tsunami roared over the beach to flood the crowded streets and buildings beyond. The raging water washed over blocks of bars, night clubs, shops, and restaurants. Telephone poles and power lines snapped one after another, causing a total blackout to envelop Waikiki. Clinging desperately to her daddy and looking back over his shoulder, Jenny stared in fear as the merciless wave chased after them. Her father stumbled in the dark, but kept on running. The wave finally spent itself, only a few blocks behind them, and Jenny thought that maybe they were safe. The roar of the wave died away, only to be supplanted by a series of thunderous impacts, like the slow, ponderous footsteps of a giant, getting closer and closer. *Boom. Boom! BOOM!*

The footsteps were accompanied by a deep, churning rumble that sounded like a giant breathing. Jenny stared wide-eyed into the darkness behind her, seeing only a looming shadow that stood bigger and taller than any of the blacked-out hotels overlooking the beach. A shadow with legs, arms, and a head like a dragon's.

It's a sea monster, Jenny realized. *For real!*

Flares shot up like fireworks from the hotel rooftops.

Flashes of blood-red light offered glimpses of the gigantic creature emerging from the bay and stomping through the flooded streets. The monster was literally too big to take in all at once. Jenny caught only bits and pieces of the colossal whole.

Three rows of jagged fins running down the creature's mountainous back.

Two clawed hands with four fingers each.

An endless, spiny tail that looked as long as a train.

Snipers opened fire from the rooftops. Tracer bullets split the darkness, but the giant sea-monster kept striding forward, squashing cars and trucks and small buildings beneath his mighty tread. His mammoth tail swung back and forth behind him, wiping away bars, boutiques, and coffee shops. Smoke from the gunfire added to the confusion, but the furious barrage had no effect on the monster, which seemed to be heading toward the nearby hills, heedless of whatever structures got in his way. He paid no attention to the insignificant men, women, and children frantically running away from him, or even the SWAT teams trying and failing to repel him. Mere humanity seemed beneath his notice.

Fleeing tourists and locals scrambled to get out of the way of the monster's path of destruction. Jenny's family ducked into an alley and huddled together, clinging to each other in fear, as the lumbering beast passed them by. They stayed there for what felt like forever until, finally, the giant footsteps seemed to recede into the distance. The deafening gunfire gradually died away as well.

Is it over? Jenny wondered. *Please let it be over!*

The family waited several more minutes before cautiously venturing out of the alley and looking around. The electricity was still out all over Waikiki, but numerous small fires blazed inside the ruins of trampled buildings. As the smoke from the guns began to clear, blown away by the wind from the ocean, Jenny and the other survivors gaped in astonishment at the cataclysmic view before them.

The monster was gone, heading northwest toward the hills above Honolulu, but he had left a trail of destruction in his wake. A swath of flattened buildings and vehicles, at least three blocks across, stretched from the sea to the jungle beyond. The invincible creature had cleared a path through the heart of Waikiki, crushing everything in his way. A trolley car had been ground into the pavement. A giant footprint was sunk deep into a luxury golf course. Neither tourist traps nor residential neighborhoods had been spared. Palm trees littered the rubble like broken toothpicks.

Holding onto Jenny, her dad whispered a Bad Word. Throngs of stunned and speechless people staggered into the ravaged streets to gaze in awe at the devastation. Native Hawaiians wept and cursed at the loss of their homes and businesses. Jenny just wanted to go home to Seattle. This vacation wasn't fun anymore.

She had to wonder, though. Where had the monster come from? And where was it going?

The Green Berets staggered away from the burning remains of the crashed F-35. Thick black smoke made Captain Cozzone grateful for his gas mask. A quick head count confirmed that all his men had survived, although the same couldn't be said for the unlucky fighter pilot. Cozzone spared a moment to wish the pilot's soul godspeed and hoped that his sacrifice would not be in vain.

What the hell just happened there? he wondered. *How did that creature bring the plane down?*

Aware that his team was still in danger from the MUTO, he rallied his men, who responded immediately as trained. Rifles at the ready, they shook off the shock of the crash and peered up through the smoke, trying to achieve a fix on their inhuman adversary. The MUTO had not shown any interest in attacking them yet, but Cozzone wasn't about to lower his guard.

A movement in the smoky jungle canopy alerted him to danger. He heard branches and tree trunks shattering loudly as a great black shadow tottered toward them. Diving to one side, he shouted hoarsely at his men.

"Watch out! Incoming!"

The men scrambled for safety as the fourteen-ton Russian submarine came crashing down like a falling redwood. The *Alexander Nevsky*, its reinforced double hull torn open like flimsy tin can, slammed down onto the forest floor, shaking the earth for acres around. Nearly six hundred feet of resin-encrusted sub crushed the verdant undergrowth. Broken branches and trees were strewn around him.

But where was the MUTO?

Cozzone jumped to his feet, armed and ready, while his men did likewise. His night-vision goggles penetrated the murky night, revealing a leveled stretch of jungle leading down to the coast. His heart sank as he spied the flickering lights of the Honolulu Airport in the near distance. Thousands of civilians passed through that airport every hour.

And the MUTO was on its way.

Gasps of relief echoed inside the train as the lights began to flicker to life throughout the airport. It appeared that the power had been restored and the blackout was over. The train even started moving forward again. Ford felt a little better now that he and Akio weren't stuck in the dark anymore. He was still concerned about the battle apparently being raged in the nearby hills, but maybe there was still a chance to get the lost little boy back to his parents. He could only hope that the military could destroy—or at least contain—the winged creature from Japan.

That's not my fight, he thought. The Navy didn't need a bomb-disposal expert for this battle. The best thing he could do was keep Akio safe and get him back to his family. *Thank God that thing hasn't reached San Francisco... yet.*

He looked ahead anxiously, trying to spot the upcoming terminal. Skyward lights came back into service, illuminating a stretch of elevated track ahead. All seemed clear as the train rounded a curve and the reawakened spotlights revealed...

The MUTO, straddling the track directly in front of them!

Pandemonium erupted aboard the train as the other passengers spied the gigantic winged monster directly ahead, but the automated train kept gaining speed, heading straight toward the creature. Fear-crazed passengers rushed toward the opposite end of the train. Ford tried to hold onto Akio, but the panicky stampede tore the boy from his grasp. Akio was swept away by the mob, even as the train sped toward the monster. Ford sprang from his seat and dived after him.

No! he thought. *I can't lose him!*

An Apache helicopter swooped down from the sky, adding to the tumult. The wash from its rotors rattled the train's windows. It soared past the head, right overhead. The attack 'copter's sudden arrival elicited more screams than cheers. Ordinary travellers suddenly found themselves caught in the middle of a battle between the armed forces and a giant insect-thing.

Ford kept his eye on Akio, who was trying to get back to him. Lunging forward, Ford tackled the boy to the floor just as the Apache opened fire on the MUTO. Its 30mm automatic cannon blasted loudly in the night, unleashing a barrage of ammo at the crouching creature, which reacted angrily. Howling in protest, it swiped at the chopper with one of its enormous middle limbs. The elusive 'copter dodged the swipe, but the monster's flailing limb smashed through the front of the train as well the elevated track beneath it.

Horrified screams were drowned by the din of shredded metal and shattered concrete. Tons of debris, mixed with falling bodies, crashed down onto the tarmac, more than two-dozen feet below. The rest of the train continued over the edge of the splintered track, but caught on mangled steel supports and dangled precariously over the rubble below. Gravity seized the survivors who tumbled helplessly out the severed end of the train, screaming all the way, even as the recorded voice kicked in automatically:

"Please watch the gap..."

Ford struggled to hold onto Akio while simultaneously anchoring himself to one on the upright metal poles in the middle of the aisle. Shrieking men and women tumbled past them, nearly knocking Ford loose. Gravity tugged on Akio, briefly yanking him from Ford's grip. Screaming, the boy started to slide away...

No! Ford thought desperately, scrabbling to reach the boy.

He grabbed the boy's wrist and held on tight. He hauled Akio up into his arms and the boy clung to him for his life. Ford wondered how long they could keep from falling, and whether it made any difference with the MUTO several yards away, perched on the other side of the severed tracks, snapping angrily at the buzzing helicopter. Ford stared at the creature, which had already been responsible for his father's death, not to mention his mother's fifteen years ago. Was this same monster going to kill him now—and leave Sam fatherless as well?

Would Sam even miss him?

Ford waited tensely to see what the MUTO was going to do next. The creature tracked the Apache 'copter with its crimson eyes, appearing eager to swipe at it once more, but paused as a series of loud booms, approaching from the east, echoed across the tarmac. The sound instantly captured the MUTO's attention; it hunkered down, as though actually unnerved by the noise. Still hanging onto Akio, Ford shuddered to think what could possibly frighten the giant winged terror.

Maybe an even bigger monster?

The MUTO let out a fearsome howl, then launched itself into the air. Its sudden flight caught the chopper pilot by surprise. The creature's extended wing swiped the Apache, knocking the helicopter from the sky. Spinning out of control, the chopper crashed into a row of parked jetliners. The 'copter and jets alike burst into flame, the blast shaking the dangling train. Billowing fireballs erupted from the wreckage. Ford could feel the heat of the flames even from so many yards away. He choked on the burning jet fuel. The light from the newborn inferno lit up the night, revealing the source of the booming noises that had alarmed the MUTO. Seismic footsteps pounded upon the tarmac, which cracked beneath the tread of two gigantic clawed feet.

Oh my God, Ford thought. He instantly recognized the legendary beast the two scientists had told him about, the one the Navy tried to nuke sixty years ago. *It's really him.*

Godzilla was here.

The fearsome reptile towered above the airport, dwarfing even the MUTO. He was nearly two hundred feet taller than the winged creature and much heftier besides. Striding upright on two legs, he resembled some unknown species of dinosaur, but was at least thirty times larger than even a Tyrannosaurus rex. A rough scaly hide covered his stocky, imposing form. Two muscular forearms ended in viciously clawed hands. Rows of serrated fins ran down his broad back all the way to a thick, spiny tail that was nearly as long as the monster was tall. Ferocious eyes, glaring out from beneath the creature's heavy brow, fixed on the MUTO with predatory intent. Fangs the size of a full-grown man gleamed inside the powerful jaws, which opened wide to let out a bellicose roar that rang out across the entire airport. It was a trumpeting roar with a deep bass reverberation that climbed to a chilling crescendo. Ford had never heard anything like it.

The MUTO accepted the challenge. Howling back at Godzilla, it swooped down from the sky at the legendary king of monsters. Amidst the flames and smoke from the burning jetliners, the primeval creatures collided in combat. Unable to look away, Ford clung to Akio as they gazed up at the titanic clash playing out high above the broken tracks.

Ford felt very small and insignificant.

Sam was curled up on the living room couch, where he'd passed out the night before. A comfy afghan had largely slid off him so that only his bare feet were covered. His sleeping face was lit by the flickering glow of the TV set, where a breaking news story had interrupted regular programming on practically every channel. The volume was turned down low, but the screen was consumed by startling images from

Hawaii, where a fantastic clash between two unbelievable creatures was being captured by dozens of mobile phones from a variety of angles. The destructive battle played out upon the screen in fragmentary bits of chaotic footage, caught on the run by awestruck spectators all across Honolulu.

Hordes of terrified civilians, fleeing the disaster, ran toward the camera, all but blocking the view of a huge winged monster tumbling towards a high-rise hotel, which collapsed upon impact, raining broken glass and masonry onto the panic-filled streets below. An even larger monster, which bore a familial resemblance to the toy dinosaur on the living room carpet, came stomping in for the kill. The huge reptile opened his jaws wide, displaying the flesh-tearing fangs of the ultimate alpha predator. He took a deep breath, sucking in giant-sized mouthful of air, which suddenly rippled within his jaws like a heat-mirage on a summer day.

Sensing danger, the MUTO turned and fled from Godzilla, flapping its wings in a desperate attempt to escape.

Electricity sparked at the back of Godzilla's throat and the super-heated air ignited. A blast of bright blue flame sprayed from his jaws, scorching both the MUTO and the beach below. Palm trees and abandoned cabanas burst into flame. White sand turned black in an instant.

But the MUTO survived.

Screeching in pain, its wings singed and smoking, the smaller monster fled. Abandoning Oahu, it soared out over the open sea, with Godzilla marching relentlessly in pursuit. Cameras on shore caught the fearsome leviathan wading back out into the bay and slowly sinking out of sight.

"Sammy?"

Elle entered the living room, already dressed in her hospital scrubs. She needed to report to work in a few hours and still hadn't managed to find a babysitter. She found the boy still sleeping on the couch, looking so cute it hurt. He had seemed so peaceful last night that she hadn't had the heart to disturb him. Glancing at the TV, she saw a morning news anchor intoning silently behind a desk but she didn't pay attention. She had a job and a child to look after, not to mention an absent husband that was theoretically on his way home. Current affairs would have to go on without her.

She still had some time to kill before she had to head over to the hospital, so she drew the afghan back over Sam to keep him warm. He stirred slightly as she adjusted the blanket. His eyes fluttered briefly, looking past her, and then opened wide. All of a sudden, he was wide awake and staring at the TV behind her.

"Mommy! Look!"

Puzzled, she turned toward the television...

FIFTEEN

The sun rose over the beach at Waikiki, which now resembled a refugee camp more than a vacation spot. Both civilian and military medical tents had been erected along the scorched coastline, while scores of stressed-out first responders coped with the wounded, the homeless, and the traumatized. Most of the major blazes had been extinguished, despite the heaps of rubble blocking the streets, but smoke still rose from scattered small fires between the beach and the airport. Once-luxurious hotels and condos were now just larger mountains of debris, which emergency crews were desperately excavating in hopes of finding trapped survivors beneath the collapsed buildings. The press was already on the scene, interviewing survivors. Rumor had it the president had declared Oahu a disaster area.

For the second time in as many days, Ford found himself wandering through the aftermath of a devastating monster attack, except that this time he had a lost child in his arms.

After being rescued from the damaged monorail, he and Akio had been bussed with numerous other survivors to the beach, which was now the center of the relief efforts. Ford had wanted to search the airport, try to locate Akio's parents, but had been assured that every terminal had been evacuated. In theory, the tents here were his best chance at reconnecting the boy with his family, but Ford was starting to lose hope. The camp was full of desperate people, urgently seeking missing loved ones. Akio's plight was just a drop in the bucket.

He carried the trembling child into one of the larger Red Cross tents. Akio clung to Ford; he had not let go of his rescuer since Godzilla had chased the MUTO away from the airport. Ford found himself feeling oddly grateful for the giant lizard's timely intervention. He wondered where Dr. Serizawa was and what he thought of Godzilla's return.

"Excuse me?" Ford called out, trying to get someone's attention. "This boy's been separated from his parents. I'm—"

But the medics and emergency workers were too busy to deal with him. The canvas tent was crammed with shell-shocked survivors in equally dire straits—or worse. Ford's heart sank as he spied a makeshift morgue where far too many bodies were draped with sheets. He began to wonder if he was fooling himself in thinking that he could bring about a happy reunion in the midst of such widespread carnage and destruction. For all Ford knew, Akio's parents were already dead, killed by rampaging monsters.

Just like dad.

"Akio! Akio!"

A woman's voice cried out frantically. Ford spun around and saw the boy's parents shoving their way through the crowd. Tears of joy streamed down the couple's faces. Although a little worse for wear, neither appeared to be seriously injured.

Akio leapt from Ford's arms and ran straight to his mother and father, who embraced him fervently. Ford couldn't remember the last time he'd seen a family so happy to be reunited; even the loved ones greeting the returning troops in San Francisco paled in comparison. Ford found it hard to believe that mere days had passed since he'd stepped off that plane to meet Elle and Sam at the Air Force base. So much had happened since then, so much death and devastation. His throat tightened as he watched Akio's sobbing mother sweep her child up into her arms. He knew he'd do the same if Sam was here now.

He started forward to speak with Akio's parents, but quickly realized that the weeping couple hadn't even registered his existence. Akio was all that mattered to them right now; the rest of the world had faded into insignificance, which was perfectly understandable. Ford stepped back, not wanting to intrude on the emotional reunion. His role in this particular drama was over. Akio was where he belonged.

Good, Ford thought, overcome with relief. *Take care, bud.*

The family moved off, seeking whatever help or safety could be found these days. Akio glanced back at Ford over his father's shoulder before the family vanished into the crowds and confusion. Ford silently wished them luck. He figured the whole world could all use a little of that with warring monsters on the loose. The entire planet had just become a much more dangerous place.

Mankind was no longer the most dangerous beast alive. Not by a long shot.

Suddenly on his own, in the midst of strangers, Ford now had only had one thing on his mind. Scanning the crowd around him, his eyes zeroed in on a cell phone in the hands of a passing survivor. He rushed up to the man, who was wearing a soot-stained Hawaiian shirt and Bermuda shorts. He was missing one sandal. Numerous small cuts and scratches marred his face. Ford guessed that he probably looked much the same.

"Are you getting service on that thing?" he asked

"No," the man said, shaking his head. "Those things must have taken out every working tower. The pay phones don't even work." He eyed Ford hopefully. "Do you have a car?"

A car wasn't going to do Ford any good. He shook his head and walked away from the other man, already forgetting him. He needed to get hold of Elle and let her know that he was okay and trying to get back to her and Sam.

She must be worried sick.

A contingent of U.S. military personnel, from every branch of the service, entered the tent. Ford hurried up to them. He approached an Army soldier, who had paused to let some injured on stretchers pass in front of him.

"Lieutenant Brody, U.S. Navy," Ford introduced himself. The soldier looked up, seeing only a ragged figure whose torn and filthy civilian clothing had been through the wars. Ford hadn't even shaved for days. "I was here on leave," Ford explained.

The soldier nodded, understanding.

"Excellent timing, Sir." He offered Ford a crisp salute. "Sergeant Morales."

Ford was relieved that Morales, who looked to be about the same age he was, had not challenged Ford's claim. He hoped the friendly soldier could be of assistance.

"I need to get to the mainland," he said.

"Well, see, it really is your lucky day, Sir." Morales grinned at Ford, who didn't get the joke. "General Orders. All branches. Everything not tied down is moving east."

He chuckled wryly as he headed across the tent. "We're all Monster Hunters now."

East, Ford thought. *Across the Pacific... after the creatures?*

"Is that where they're heading?"

The sergeant, although accommodating, was in too much of hurry to answer all Ford's questions. He stepped lively to keep up with the other military personnel. "Our truck's right outside."

Ford hustled after him, even as his mind reeled at the alarming news he'd just received. Whatever relief he'd experienced from reuniting Akio with his parents was instantly dispelled by a growing fear for his own family's safety. His worst fears were coming true.

The giant creatures were heading east... toward the west coast of North America. Toward Elle and Sam.

The observation platform overlooking the *Saratoga*'s flight deck, located on the carrier's upper island, was nicknamed "Vulture's Row." The unnerving parallel with the crow's nest back at the doomed Japanese base was not lost on Serizawa. A briny wind blew against him as he occupied the high balcony, distractedly twisting the stem of his antique pocket watch. The observation platform offered an excellent view of operations down on the flight deck, but he gazed out at the ocean instead, where Godzilla could be seen swimming across the Pacific.

The submerged leviathan was a great dark mass swimming beneath the waves. The peaks of his spiky dorsal fins sliced through the churning foam, directly ahead of the carrier fleet, which had to pour on the speed to keep up with the swiftly moving colossus. The *Saratoga* could manage a maximum speed of more than thirty knots but Godzilla was even faster. Unmanned aerial vehicles, designed for low-altitude surveillance, skimmed above the surface of the water like a flock of seabirds dogging an orca. The *Saratoga* and the rest of the strike group followed behind the undersea monster at what they hoped was a safe distance. To the mounting concern of everyone aboard, Godzilla remained on course for the west coast of the United States.

Which meant the MUTO was heading for America as well.

Frowning, the scientist put his watch away and descended several decks to the CDC, where the war room remained a buzzing hive of activity. Glowing monitors displayed flickering satellite imagery of the flying MUTO as well as live UAV footage of Godzilla swimming beneath the sea. Vivienne Graham stared in fascination at the visuals. Despite the undeniable danger to the human population, she was obviously intrigued by the unique organisms she had tracked and studied for most of her career.

Serizawa knew exactly how she felt.

"Last satellite tracks had the MUTO continuing due east," Petty Officer Martinez reported from her post. She glanced up at an accompanying image of Godzilla. "For the moment, it seems like the big one is following it."

Serizawa corrected her. *"Hunting."*

A theory was coming together in his head, which seemed to be supported by the latest data. Once again, Nature held the key. The monsters' current behavior was consistent with basic biology.

"All vessels maintain current standoff distance," Admiral Stenz ordered, overseeing the operations. He remained in command of the joint forces' response to the crisis. "Map this thing's current course and bearing and start compiling a list of all possible solutions that will allow us to interdict before these... whatever they are... make landfall." His tone and expression were equally grim. "I need options."

The backlit table continued to plot out potential courses for both creatures, constantly updated to reflect the most recent intel. Dotted lines headed for the western seaboard, with possible landfall sites including Vancouver, Seattle, Los Angeles, and San Francisco, as well as locations in Peru, Panama, and Argentina. There were too many possibilities over too great a distance, making it difficult to plan a defense against the monsters' eventual arrival. Serizawa contemplated the ever-changing lines on the map.

Ford Brody is from San Francisco, he recalled. He wondered if the young lieutenant had finally made it home, after burying his father at sea. *I believe he mentioned a wife and child.*

"Sir," Martinez said. "Based on the current tracks, all our models have the targets converging on the US Pacific coast."

Stenz scowled. He turned away from the screens to consult Serizawa.

"Doctor, are we certain this is the same animal from sixty years ago?"

Serizawa suspected as much. "Remains were never found," he reminded the admiral.

"But if the MUTO is his prey," Graham began, calling Serizawa's attention back to the printout of the wave pattern Joe Brody had detected, "this signal shows a call. Why call up a predator?"

Stenz and others present threw out possible explanations, with even Martinez chiming in with something about echoes or audio distortions, but Serizawa no longer had any doubts or questions. There seemed only one obvious conclusion.

"It didn't," he said solemnly. "The predator was only listening. The MUTO was calling *something else*." His reasoning led him to another ominous hypothesis. "The pattern," he addressed Graham urgently. "Focus our search on Nevada."

The intensity of his tone cut through the chatter. Competing voices tapered off as all present gave Serizawa their full attention.

"Nevada?" Captain Hampton asked. "What makes you think—?"

Graham got there first. The blood drained from her face. "You don't think it could be...?"

"Fill me in here," Stenz said impatiently. "Why Nevada?"

"There was another spore," Graham informed him. "Intact. Found in the Philippine mine." She looked at Serizawa, shaking her head in disbelief. "But we examined it, ran every test for years. You confirmed it for yourself. *It was dormant.*"

Serizawa understood her skepticism. He had indeed spent years studying the apparently inert egg sac they had recovered from inside the giant skeleton in the Philippines. Unlike the larva that had burst from the other egg sac and made its way to Japan, the organism in the captured spore had displayed no trace of vitality or growth. It had not been absorbing spilled radiation from a nuclear meltdown. By all indications, it had been an unbroken state of stasis or hibernation. And yet...

"Maybe not anymore," he said.

The horror of this possibility, that they might be dealing with *two* MUTOs, caused a momentary hush to fall over the CDC. Martinez gulped and even Hampton's stoic reserve cracked for a moment.

"The spore," Stenz asked urgently. "Where is it now?"

"It was highly radioactive," Graham said. "It was disposed of... by the Americans."

"*Where?*" Stenz repeated, even more forcefully.

"Where you put your nuclear waste," Serizawa said flatly. He called their attention back to the map table, where two converging dotted lines extended past the west coast of the North America.

Nevada lay directly in their path.

A stone marker, alongside a dusty desert road, pointed to the nearby Nevada National Security Site, about sixty-five miles northeast of Las Vegas. For over forty years, the desolate and cratered terrain beyond had been the site of nearly a thousand nuclear bomb tests. Cacti sprouted amidst the sunbaked dunes and gullies. A military convoy sped past the marker, stirring up a cloud of dust. Air Force helicopters flew overhead, keeping pace with the rumbling troop carriers below. Inside the trucks, tense soldiers geared up in anticipation. An assault force donned radiation suits and gas masks. Heavy weaponry was prepped for battle: assault rifles, machine guns, rocket launchers, grenades, and whatever else might make a dent in a monster. The mood among the soldiers was grim. Everyone on the mission had heard about what had struck Hawaii and had seen some of the on-line footage of the gigantic creatures tearing up Honolulu. They knew they had to be ready for anything.

The convoy quickly reached its destination. The Yucca Mountain Nuclear Waste Depository was the final resting place for more than 70,000 metric tons of spent nuclear fuel and radioactive waste from nuclear power plants and reprocessing operations all over the country. Dug deep into a barren ridge of volcanic rock, surrounded by acres of restricted federal land, the vast repository was designed to contain the highly toxic materials for at least ten thousand years and possibly longer. In theory, it could withstand earthquakes, the elements, even time itself.

Giant prehistoric monsters, on the other hand, had not been taken into account.

The main entrance to the facility consisted of an enormous tunnel that had been bored into the north side of the mountain. Armed guards stationed at the entrance admitted the troops, who deployed with both speed and purpose. The commander of the assault force, Captain Roger Pyle, led his men through a sprawling underground maze of tunnels, branching off into numerous long galleries lined with large sealed compartments. Steel doors, each nearly thirty feet tall, guarded the vaults and their lethal contents, which were routinely sealed inside solid steel canisters. View ports were installed in each door to allow for direct visual inspections.

Moving swiftly but methodically, the soldiers worked their way through the dimly lit tunnels, checking each vault on the go. The precise location of the captured Philippine egg sac was buried amidst layers of official secrecy, misdirection, redactions, and plausible deniability, defying ready access, but Pyle had reason to believe that it was somewhere in this particular gallery, nearly a thousand feet under the mountain. Given the possibility that a second MUTO might be stirring, it had been decided to conduct an immediate search and inspection of the vaults, pronto.

"Move it!" Pyle urged his men. "On the double!"

One after another, view ports were slid open. Flashlights probed the interiors of the vaults, finding only the expected stores of nuclear waste in their airtight casks. So far everything appeared secure, although they had yet to locate the MUTO egg, hatched or otherwise. Pyle had to wonder what the brass was thinking, storing something like that. He would have blown it to pieces years ago.

Then maybe they might not be in the fix they were in.

Pyle hung back, observing the operation, as yet another view port was opened. Instead of the usual darkness, a blinding white light shone in his face. Blinking, he shielded his eyes from the glare and recoiled along with his men. Instantly on guard, soldiers raised their weapons as their comrades warily unsealed the massive hatch. More light flooded the tunnel as the heavy door swung open, revealing a disturbing sight.

Goddamnit, Pyle thought.

The entire vault had been torn open from the inside. An enormous hole, at least three hundred feet in diameter, gaped at the far end of the cavernous chamber, where what appeared to be a newly dug tunnel climbed all the way up to the surface. The blinding light pouring down from above? That was *sunshine,* Pyle realized, coming from outside the buried repository.

Yucca Mountain had been breached—from within.

Already dreading what he'd find, Pyle and his soldiers scrambled up the crude tunnel, which was big enough to accommodate a tank or more. It was a steep climb and he was breathing hard by the time he reached the top, where the passage opened onto a panoramic view of the sprawling desert to the south. Heaps of shattered stone were strewn beneath the tunnel exit, where *something* had obviously burst up through the base of the mountain. Enormous tracks, at least fifty feet across, scarred the arid landscape, leading off to the horizon.

Pyle called sharply for binoculars, which were immediately smacked into his grip by a junior officer. Raising the high-tech lenses to his eyes, he increased the magnification to maximum and scoured the sunlit badlands to the south. Through a haze of uprooted sand and dirt, he glimpsed the distant outline of *another* enormous creature making its way across the desert.

They were too late, he realized. A second MUTO had hatched.

And it was headed straight for Las Vegas.

SIXTEEN

What happened in Vegas now tended to end up on the internet, but Sin City was still going strong. Unconcerned or unaware of the disaster in Hawaii, eager gamblers packed the floor of one of the Strip's many lavish casinos. Rows of men and women sat at slot machines, feeding their salaries to the one-armed bandits. Dice rolled across green felt tabletops to the accompaniment of fervent groans, cheers, and prayers. People gathered around the blackjack and poker tables, spilling their drinks onto the garish carpet. Crystal chandeliers and plenty of neon added to the sensory overload. A color TV, mounted on a wall by the bar, displayed handheld camera footage of the winged MUTO, but was going largely ignored. A skeptical retiree, scowling up at the screen, muttered that the whole thing was a hoax "like global warming," but nobody paid any attention to her. Honolulu was very far away and, anyway, the monsters were somebody else's problem.

Then the lights went out, taking all the glowing neon with it. Strident bells and buzzers went silent, while people looked up from their games with varying degrees of surprise, concern, and annoyance. Roulette wheels slowed to a stop. Cards went unplayed. Piped-in music gave way to anxious muttering, as nervous gamblers scooped up their chips for safekeeping. Cut off by design from the outside world, the casino floor was suddenly a murky, inhospitable cavern. Puzzled staff and visitors waited for some sort of announcement concerning the blackout, but the P.A. system was apparently down too.

All that could heard, coming from somewhere outside the casino, was a piercing, inhuman howl that seemed to be drawing nearer.

Elle paced restlessly around her kitchen, keeping one eye on the TV news in the living room. The horrifying footage was playing continuously and only seemed to get worse every time she saw it. She'd watched every minute over and over, half-hoping, half-dreading that she'd catch a glimpse of Ford amongst the chaos, but so far there had been no sign of him, even though, according to Sam, Ford had called from the Honolulu airport right before the monsters attacked.

"Yes, Ford Brody—Japan to San Francisco," she repeated into the phone at her ear. Pacing in her hospital scrubs, she fought to keep panic at bay. "Look, I know your systems are down," she pleaded to the frazzled-sounding airline representative she'd finally managed to get hold of. So far he hadn't been much help. "What? No, wait! Can I leave my number just in—?"

A click at the other end of the line cut off the call.

"Damn it!" she swore, slamming the phone down onto the kitchen table. The curse came out louder than she intended, startling Sam who was sitting at the table eating a bologna sandwich.

He looked up at her with a worried expression.

She hurried over to comfort him, pulling him close. To be honest, the hug was as much for her benefit as his.

"It's okay," she said, trying to reassure them both. "Daddy's going to be okay."

She wished she could believe that.

Once again, Ford found himself aboard a C-17 Globe-master bound for home. Crammed in among the other soldiers, all of whom were decked out in combat gear, Ford felt out of place in his beaten-up civilian attire. He rubbed his chin, which was badly in need of a shave. He suspected he could use a shower as well. He had been on the move for days now.

Fortunately, his new traveling companion didn't seem to mind his lack of hygiene.

"I'm Queens all the way," Sergeant Tre Morales volunteered, as if his New York accent wasn't proof enough. He proudly shared photos of three generations of Morales. "*Mi familia*. My wife's from San Francisco, but we dragged her over."

Ford felt bad that he didn't have any photos of Elle or Sam on his person. "We're just across the Bridge."

"Kids?" Tre asked.

"I have a son. He's four. Sam."

"I'm having a daughter," Tre said.

Ford appreciated the conversation. He knew he probably ought to be trying to get some sleep, but he was too uneasy knowing that a pair of feuding monsters was heading toward America. He wasn't going to be able to relax until he knew that Sam and Elle were safe.

"You gotta be psyched about that," he said, regarding Tre's upcoming blessed event.

"Oh, yeah. Super-psyched, 'cause we're due next week." Tre grinned, but Ford could hear the genuine tension behind the sergeant's joking tone. "I really wanted to wait until *after* the apocalypse to have kids, so, yeah..."

His voice trailed off.

Ford wanted to reassure Tre, but was still searching for the words when the light coming through the plane's windows suddenly shifted direction. Changing course, the C-17 tilted hard to one side, throwing the seated soldiers against each other. Ford tensed up, concerned with what this might mean. Elle and Sam were waiting for him. The last thing he needed was another complication or detour.

"All right, heads up!" An Air Force loadmaster ducked back into the hold from the cockpit. He spoke loudly enough to rouse any napping soldiers. The stripes on his uniform identified him as a staff sergeant. "We have new orders, new destination. Get geared up!"

Ford frowned. Did this mean they weren't heading to San Francisco after all? Rising from his seat, he approached the loadmaster. The tilting floor beneath him made walking a challenge.

"Hey, Staff Sergeant, what's the word? We're just trying to get home, right?"

The loadmaster shook his head. "Another one of those things just popped up in Nevada, sir. Tore through Vegas, heading for the west coast. We don't stop it now, there might not be a home to get back to."

Ford's blood went cold. *Another* creature? Heading west from Nevada?

Toward California?

Elle was running late by the time she got to work. San Francisco General Hospital was located in the heart of downtown, and treated thousands of patients every day, but she had never seen it this crazy before. Emergency vehicles, including fire trucks and ambulances, packed the loading area out front, while dozens of paramedics were already on hand, preparing for a flood of casualties. It looked like every EMT in town had been called into service. Elle felt a twinge of guilt for not getting here earlier, but she had been trying—and failing—to find out what had happened to Ford in Hawaii.

With Sam in tow, she made her way through the hustle and bustle to the nurses' station on the ground floor. Her supervisor, Laura Watkins, greeted Elle with visible relief. Like the area outside, the E.R. was a madhouse, full of doctors and nurses dashing about and getting ready. The hospital was the only Level 1 Trauma Center serving the 1.5 million residents of the city and surrounding county, so it often took the brunt of any major accidents or disasters.

"There you are!" Laura exclaimed. The head nurse, a fortyish brunette, had coped in her day with everything from earthquakes to multi-car pile-ups, but Elle had never seen her this stressed. "Thank God. What a mess." She didn't waste time chiding Elle for her tardiness. "Okay, where do I need you most? Get that triage unit off its ass. We're just about to start catching overflow from Nevada and no one's even got an estimate yet. I'm gonna be right here, so Sam can stay with me. He'll be fine."

"Thanks, Laura." Elle sat Sam down at the station and handed him a coloring book and crayons. "Honey, I'm sorry, but you need to wait here while Mommy works, okay?"

Sam glanced around, visibly troubled by all the commotion. Even a four-year-old could pick up on the anxiety and agitation in the air. Still, he nodded bravely; this was not the first time Elle had been unable to find a babysitter. She leaned over and planted a firm kiss on his forehead, before reluctantly tearing herself away to get to work. A television screen in the waiting area, intended to occupy bored patients and their loved ones, aired live footage of rampant destruction in some small town further east. It seemed that the carnage was no longer confined to Hawaii. Elle shuddered as she hurried past the televised images of crushed and smoking ruins. Glancing back, she saw Sam staring at the TV, ignoring the coloring book in his lap.

She wished she could turn the TV off, but there was no hiding from the nightmare that had invaded their world. This was no harmless creature feature or childish fantasy.

The monsters were real now.

The penthouse suite at the MGM Grand Hotel was an exercise in opulent luxury, boasting a well-stocked bar with marble accents, a spacious dining area complete with fine linen tablecloths, a king-sized bed, a deluxe Roman spa tub, a full-equipped entertainment center, and a view to die for. Intended for high rollers only, the lavish suite was the height of elegance.

Or at least it had been.

A brigade of firefighters stomped through the suite, searching for survivors. The hotel's entire façade had been ripped away, so that the far wall facing Las Vegas Boulevard no longer existed. Smoke and wind blew in from outside. Emergency helicopters buzzed loudly through the sky. The exhausted firefighters paused before the gaping hole where the wall and picture windows had been. They gazed out in shock and awe at the apocalyptic vista below.

A deep chasm cut across the famed Vegas Strip, where the claws of an enormous beast had gouged the street and sidewalks all the way down to the bedrock. Thousands of displaced and traumatized tourists and casino employees staggered amidst the shattered pavement, while an army of first responders was overwhelmed by the scale of the disaster. Water gushed from ruptured pipes. Flames erupted from the ruins of the Strip's gaudy casinos, hotels, and attractions. New York-New York had been reduced to splinters, its *faux* Statue of Liberty defaced, its replica Empire State Building obliterated. Across the way, on the other side of Tropicana, the mock medieval turrets and battlements of Excalibur had been torn down by a genuine monster, who had wreaked havoc all along the ravaged boulevard. A half-scale copy of the Eiffel Tower had been snapped in two. Mountains of rubble filled the Venetian's canals. The Luxor's great pyramid and matching sphinx were history. It was as though the MUTO was symbolically laying waste to the entire world.

It felt like a prophecy.

The *Saratoga* was speeding across the Pacific, making thirty knots, but the crisis had obviously reached America before the carrier and its attached strike group could. In the briefing room, video feeds captured shocking views of the Las Vegas strip being torn apart by the second MUTO, the one that had just broken loose from the Yucca Mountain facility. Soldiers and scientists crowded before the monitors, gaping at this latest threat. Smoke and static obscured the video feeds, making it difficult at first to compare the new MUTO to the immense winged arthropod that had hatched from the cocoon in Japan, but Serizawa managed to make out its appearance.

Instead of six legs plus a pair of wings, the new MUTO had eight limbs in total: two sturdy hind legs, similar to those on the first creature, *two* sets of elongated middle limbs, and two smaller forearms on its upper thorax. Like the earlier organism, the creature was a chimera that defied ready classification, but, if pressed, Serizawa would have labeled it some manner of gigantic semi-arthropod. Its dark, iridescent exoskeleton, composed of a thick, chitinous material, displayed shades of blue and red. Its backwards-jointed hind legs rested on two squat claws, but its upper limbs ended in hooked talons. A flat, anvil-shaped head boasted glittering red eyes and beak-like jaws.

"You're telling me this is a female?" Admiral Stenz asked. "Which means these things can procreate?"

"I'm afraid so," Serizawa said. Sexual dimorphism would explain why two radically different creatures had hatched from identical egg sacs. Such gender-based variation within a single species was not uncommon in nature. "They've been communicating."

Just as Joe Brody tried to warn us, he thought.

"The female remained completely dormant until the male matured," Graham explained.

"And if they mate?" Stenz asked worriedly. "After that, then what?"

Serizawa did not mince words. "There won't be an after."

Stenz didn't need it spelled out for him. The admiral was

no biologist, but he could grasp the dire implications of the creatures reproducing. Two MUTOs, plus Godzilla, were bad enough, but if they started breeding...

"Let's put *all* options on the table," Stenz said.

Hampton nodded. "Our analysts have drawn up a nuclear option, sir."

"Nuclear?" Graham reacted in shock. "You can't be serious. They're attracted to radiation."

"Exactly," Hampton said. "We get them close and kill them with a blast." He called their attention to the map table, where the two MUTOs were converging toward the western seaboard, with Godzilla in pursuit. Current projections suggested that their ultimate rendezvous was San Francisco. "Their EMPs make remote targeting impossible. But if we rig a warhead with a shielded timer, put it on a boat, and send it twenty miles out... the radiation lures the MUTOs, the MUTOs lure Godzilla, and we detonate with little risk to the city."

Serizawa said nothing, but his expression darkened. He took out his pocket watch and twisted the stem, an old habit that utterly failed to reassure him. To the contrary, it only increased his apprehension and dismay.

"That's assuming everything goes perfectly," Graham said, still skeptical of Hampton's alarming nuclear scenario. "But if it doesn't?"

"If you have another answer, Doctor," Stenz said, "I'm all ears. But conventional arms are only slowing these things down... at best." He weighed his options before reaching a decision. "We'll need presidential approval." He turned to Hampton. "In the meantime, get the warheads prepped and moving to the coast."

Graham looked on speechlessly, visibly aghast, as

Hampton hurried to carry out his assignment. With the decision made, the other scientists and soldiers filed out of the briefing room to get back to their respective stations. Graham departed as well, but Serizawa lingered behind, still toying with the antique watch. Within minutes, only Serizawa and the admiral were left in the cabin.

"You look like you have an opinion on this," Stenz said.

Serizawa placed the watch on the meeting table and slid it over to Stenz, who picked it up. The admiral's puzzled expression made it clear that he wasn't sure where this was going. He examined the watch.

"It's stopped," he noted.

"Yes," Serizawa said. "At 8:15 A.M."

A look of understanding came over Stenz's face. "8:15 A.M. August 6, 1945?"

"Just outside Hiroshima," Serizawa said.

Stenz handed the watch back. He seemed uncertain how to respond. "Quite the collector's piece."

"It was my father's."

And with that, Serizawa exited the room.

SEVENTEEN

The female MUTO's trail of destruction was visible from the air. Acres of American farmland had been devastated by the creature's passage, the gentle geometry of patterned fields left brutalized in the monster's wake. Crushed barns and silos were ground into the clawed earth. Anxious farm animals roamed among the ruins of scattered family farms. Nor were the ensuing small towns and suburbs spared. Highways were flattened. Entire neighborhoods and housing developments were razed to their foundations, their former residents fleeing in panic just ahead of the destruction. The wreckage of abandoned malls and shopping centers, schools and churches, joined a seemingly endless disaster zone that stretched west for as far as the eye could see.

Ford was shaken by what he'd seen from the transport plane. Even with everything he'd witnessed overseas, this struck far too close to home. It felt as though the nightmare that had begun for him in Janjira fifteen years ago was still stalking his family—and the country he'd pledged to defend. And now there were *three* monsters?

"Okay, everybody off!" the loadmaster ordered. "This is as far as we can fly."

The C-17 had touched down on an evacuated airstrip somewhere east of the Sierra Nevada mountain range. The rear doors of the plane opened and the troops disembarked into the harsh sunlight. After being cooped up in the hold of the Globemaster for hours, Ford's eyes needed a moment to adjust.

He spied a small town less than a mile away—and crashed aircraft further in the distance. The loadmaster saw him staring at the smoking wreckage.

"We're well within range of its EMP," Staff Sergeant Hultquist explained. "From here on out, it's by land or not at all."

Ford understood. Dr. Serizawa had explained to him about the MUTO's electromagnetic pulse, the effects of which Ford had personally witnessed in Japan and Honolulu. He deduced that the crashed planes marked the current borders of the second MUTO's field of influence.

He felt glad to be on solid ground.

Along with Morales and the other soldiers, he was crammed into a waiting troop carrier that was part of a larger convoy heading toward the front lines of the conflict. More planes were landing, disgorging yet more personnel, to be transferred into additional carriers. Ford was impressed by the scale of the mobilization. He'd never seen anything like it, not even in Iraq or Afghanistan. The military was pulling out all the stops to deal with the rampaging monsters.

He hoped that would be enough.

The convoy pulled into a small town whose name no longer

mattered. What had once been Main Street, U.S.A. was now a war zone, lined with abandoned cars, charred storefronts, and smoldering debris. A toppled water tower was being cleared away. Broken glass and scraps of newspapers littered the ground. Dry air reeked of smoke and ash. Bloodstains remained on the pavement. No surviving civilians could be seen anywhere; what was left of the town was now a military staging hub. Jeeps and Humvees were parked at every corner. Troops hustled in and out of the few standing buildings, carrying out the duties with a definite air of urgency. Shelling could be heard in the distance.

It was hard to believe that this had once been somebody's hometown.

The carrier braked to a stop and the soldiers piled out of the vehicle. Uncertain where to report to, Ford took a moment to survey his unreal surroundings. He had wanted to return home, but not like this. He glanced around, trying to figure out some way to get from here to San Francisco—and his family.

The pavement began to rumble. Ford experienced a flare of alarm, afraid that one or more of the monsters was approaching, but then he realized that the vibration felt more mechanical than the tread of either Godzilla or a MUTO. He turned to see a wall of smoke approaching from the east. A loud mechanical groan escaped the haze. The noise sounded familiar to Ford, but, tired and disoriented, he couldn't quite place it. The vibration beneath his feet grew steadily stronger.

All along Main Street, busy soldiers halted their efforts to watch. They crowded forward expectantly, while Humvees backed up to clear the way. Ford wondered what was up. The groaning drowned out every other sound and he finally recognized it as the chug of an old-fashioned diesel locomotive, heading into town on a railroad track crossing Main Street.

A train whistle blew. Smoke jetted from the exhaust ports and vents as the train slowed to a stop, its air brakes squealing. The vintage locomotive was impressive, but even more jaw-dropping was the freight behind it. Car after car was loaded with ICBM missiles, lying sideways on open flatbeds. Ford's eyes bulged as he realized that he was looking at an entire nuclear arsenal on the move. There were enough warheads on the train to nuke most of the west coast.

Had it really come to this, that they were seriously considering deploying nuclear weapons on American soil? For a moment, he flashed back to that awful moment in his childhood when he'd watched the atomic power plant melt down before his eyes. The terrifying wail of the warning sirens echoed at the back of his mind.

They tried to nuke Godzilla back in 1954, he recalled. *But he's back, more unstoppable than ever.*

Still, what other options did they have?

An Army Master Sergeant, whose name, "Waltz," was printed in block letters on his fatigues, led a contingent of security troops past Ford toward the train. He assumed they'd been assigned to guard the missiles.

"Alright, guys," Waltz said, addressing the men. "Can't fly them out and the roads are jammed." He nodded at the train before them. "Makes this our best bad option. All goes well—and why wouldn't it?—we'll be in San Francisco in six hours."

San Francisco? Ford contemplated the train. Missiles or no missiles, this could be his ticket home. He *had* to get on that train.

GODZILLA

* * *

"Negative," Waltz said. "Can't do it, sir. That train is a national asset, not Amtrak." A corner storefront, that was still more or less intact, had been converted into an ad hoc operations center. Worried-looking officers studied GCSS-Army maps spread out on top of tables, while aides rushed about, issuing and receiving orders and reports. Radios chattered in the background. TV sets flickered sporadically, providing intermittent news coverage of the unprecedented crisis. Ford was reminded of the frenzied relief efforts back in Waikiki. He hoped that Akio and his family were safe wherever they were now.

"Yeah, copy that," Ford replied. "From the casings on those Minuteman-3 ICBMs, I'd say the digital module has been bypassed and you've prepped them for a full analog retrofit."

"Is my jaw supposed to drop, sir?" Waltz said, unimpressed. "I get it. You're EOD. But I have my crew and we know what we're doing."

Tre came forward to hand Waltz some paperwork. Apparently, he'd been assigned to the security detail on the missile train, even if Ford was still struggling to claim a spot. Ford tried hard not to resent that.

"Aim the pointy end at the monsters, right, sarge?" Tre said. He grinned at Ford as he headed out of the store toward the train. Ford hoped he'd be seeing him again soon.

"When's the last time one of your guys had their fingers in a live bomb, sergeant?" Ford wasn't taking no for an answer. "I'm a damn good EOD... and my family is in that city." He looked Waltz straight in the eyes. "I'm on that train."

It wasn't a question.

* * *

The overflow from Nevada was already flooding the triage unit at San Francisco General. Hospitals up and down the coast were getting hit. Doctors and nurses and EMTs hurried from patient to patient, dealing with burns, head wounds, concussions, broken limbs, and even more serious injuries. Severe cases, who nonetheless still had a chance of survival, were being prepped for surgery. Every bed, cot, seat, and examination room was occupied, while plasma and other vital supplies were beginning to run low. Gurneys full of casualties were lined up in the halls. Elle was busy clamping a leg wound on a scared college student when she heard Laura Watkins calling to her from across the ward.

"Elle!" The embattled head nurse held up a phone. "For you!"

"Tell 'em I'll be right down," Elle said impatiently. Dark arterial blood spurted from the jagged gash on her patient's leg, which was resisting her efforts to halt the bleeding. Answering the phone was the last thing on her mind right now. *If I can just get this slippery artery clamped off...*

"It's your husband!" Laura shouted.

Ford had found a working phone at the rear of the store. As he waited for Elle to pick up the receiver, he kept one eye on the missile train waiting outside. Through the storefront window, he could see troops already boarding. Like the other soldiers, he was now geared up and in uniform. He knew he didn't have much time before he had to join the mission.

He heard a rustle on the other end of the line. "Elle?"

"*Ford!*"

The relief in her voice hit him right in the gut. He turned his face toward the wall, willing himself to stay composed. He had to be strong for her. God only knew what she had been going through.

"*Where are you?*" she asked anxiously, her voice catching in her throat. It sounded like she was crying. "*I've been calling everywhere, are you okay? I can't believe this is happening—*"

"Elle, listen to me."

"*Ford, I'm so scared.*"

"Listen to me, I'm coming to get you guys. I'll be there by dawn, hear me. The military has a plan to get these things, and I'm going to get you out of there."

He hadn't always been there for Elle and Sam, he knew that, but this time he would be. They *were* going to make this work, just like he promised.

"*Okay,*" she replied. "*Please hurry.*"

He stared out the window at the waiting train.

"I'll be at the hospital by sunrise. I'll get you out in a convoy. Okay?" He fought to keep his voice from cracking. "I'm coming to get you, Elle."

A train whistle blew, signaling that he had to go. He clung to the phone as hard as he could. He could definitely hear her crying now. They both knew how much was at stake here—and how precarious their future had become. Nobody was safe as long as the monsters were abroad.

"*I love you,*" she said.

"I love you, too."

She hung on the line, apparently unable to say goodbye, so he hung up for both them. He took a deep breath and wiped the tears from his eyes before heading back outside.

He had a train to catch.

Lugging his gear, he climbed aboard the missile train along with the last remaining troops. He joined Tre on a flatbed car carrying one of the huge ICBMS. Smoke poured from the locomotive's vents as the train got underway, its wheels rattling upon the metal tracks. Sparks flared beneath the wheels as the soldiers left in the town watched the train depart, carrying its lethal load of nuclear warheads. Ford found himself missing the smoother ride of the transport plane.

Within minutes, they had left the nameless town in the dust.

EIGHTEEN

The missile train rolled past mile after mile of devastated scenery, heading west toward California. Trampled towns, farms, factories, and strip malls could be glimpsed from the train as it whipped past them at more than one hundred miles per hour. A drive-in movie theater screen hung in tatters. A used-car lot had been transformed into a junkyard.

Ford tried not to let the apocalyptic landscapes distract him. He had a job to do and it couldn't wait until the train reached its eventual destination, which he gathered was further west, toward the coast. Along with other EODs and a handful of nuclear tech specialists, they had to perform crucial modifications on the missiles and their warheads en route.

Easier said than done.

Working together, he and Tre unhinged the heavy nose cone of a massive ICBM and carefully laid it down on the vibrating bed of the flatbed freight car. Each missile was nearly sixty feet long and weighed close to eighty tons. The rattling of the train added to the challenge, especially when it took a curve, but they succeeded in gaining access to the trunk-sized warhead at the missile's tip. The actual fusion device was packed into a targeted re-entry vehicle, which was connected to an intricate assemblage of sophisticated wires, dials, and electrodes. These electronics were located directly under the missile's payload and above the first- and second-stage rockets.

"Easy there, cowboy," Ford said to Tre.

Ford was already sweating beneath his helmet and fatigues. He had worked on plenty of bombs before and had been trained in manipulating nuclear devices, but he'd never actually handled a nuclear missile. He was acutely aware that the warhead had the explosive power of three hundred thousand tons of TNT. He had to be *very* careful.

Holding his breath, he uncoupled the electronics from the base of the payload before cautiously removing the entire mechanism. Tre passed Ford a mechanical replacement detonator.

"I thought these things all ran by remote control," Tre said.

"The MUTOs fry out everything electronic," Ford explained. "You can't even get in range without stuff going haywire." He patted the new detonator. "This, on the other hand, is old-school clockwork."

The replacement mechanism was all gears and springs, with no electrical components. Ford was impressed by the simplicity of the design. Even the crude roadside bombs he'd disarmed in Afghanistan had been more high-tech. This detonator was bare-bones by comparison. Gears, dials, and a high-torsion mainspring controlled the timing mechanism.

"Takes a lickin', keeps on tickin'," Tre grinned at Ford. "See how the bastards like us now."

He looked away from the missile long enough to spot something off to one side of the tracks. A stunned expression came over his face. "Jesus..."

Ford lifted his eyes from his work to see what the other man was looking at. A veil of trees cleared to reveal a rural highway crammed with bumper-to-bumper traffic for miles on end. Uncertain where safety lay, the confused and panicked refugees were stalled in both directions. Every lane had come to a standstill; unmoving vehicles were packed with displaced civilians fleeing the destruction behind them. Many of the people had gotten out of their cars, some standing on the vehicles' hoods to try to get a better view of just how far ahead the gridlock extended. A desperate exodus was frozen in place.

Ford understood now, more than ever, why they weren't transporting the ICBMs by road.

Heads turned as the missile train went by. Ford wondered what the stranded refugees thought, seeing car after car of heavy-duty ballistic missiles rumble past them. Borrowing a pair of binoculars from Tre, he checked out the bulging eyes and uneasy expressions of the displaced people watching the train go by. His attention was captured by one poor family stuck inside a station wagon, hastily packed with boxes of precious belongings. A young couple viewed the missiles with obvious worry while their little daughter, who looked about Sam's age, clutched her teddy bear. The girl gaped at the train with wide eyes.

Ford wondered if she even knew what a nuclear missile was, or what it was capable of.

The train rolled on, leaving the family—and many, many other families—behind. Ford returned the binoculars to Tre and got back to work. He tried to put the little girl out of his mind.

Those warheads weren't going to retrofit themselves.

"Yes, sir. Yes, sir."

In the CDC aboard the *Saratoga,* Admiral Stenz had a phone to his ear. And not just any phone: the Red Phone. He nodded solemnly, his voice subdued and respectful. "I understand, sir."

Serizawa observed the conversation tensely, twisting the stem of his heirloom pocket watch. He knew exactly what was being discussed, and the dreadful consequences of the choices being made. He looked on as Stenz gravely hung up the phone.

The worried scientist wasn't the only one paying attention. A hush fell over the hectic war room as everyone present waited on the news. Graham was beside Serizawa, wringing her hands anxiously. Captain Hampton stood stiffly at attention. Martinez and the other junior officers looked away from their consoles to see what word would be given.

The admiral nodded his head.

The CDC erupted into flurry of activity. The pregnant stillness of only moments ago gave way to a renewed sense of urgency. Weapons analysts began plotting radial diagrams of concentric circles on the map. The ominous graphics depicted both radioactive fallout patterns and projected casualty figures. Although no one had yet spoken the ghastly words aloud, all involved understood what had just happened.

The order had been given to deploy nuclear arms.

"The president, sir?" Hampton asked finally, compelled to confirm the awful truth.

Stenz nodded. His taciturn face had gone pale. Visibly distressed, he seemed unable to speak for the moment.

Serizawa could not keep silent. "Please don't do this, Admiral."

Stenz regarded the troubled scientist thoughtfully. A pained expression hinted at the admiral's inner conflict.

"Do you have children, doctor?" the admiral said quietly, in a reflective tone. "My father was an ensign on the USS *Indianapolis,* the cruiser that helped transport the Bomb in '45."

Serizawa stiffened, but said nothing.

"He was always very proud of his contribution," the admiral continued, "but all my life he could never talk about the War." Anguished eyes met Serizawa's. "Doctor, I'm a father, too. And I'm sacrificing lives every minute just trying to steer *one* of these things clear of population centers. There are two more on the way—"

On the map table, dotted lines predicted the three monsters' probable collision courses. As the lines redrew themselves yet again, Serizawa saw that they were still converging on the coast of North America.

San Francisco Bay, to be exact.

"That's seven million lives," Stenz said hoarsely. He pleaded with Serizawa. "So please, just tell me. Will it work? Can they be killed?"

Serizawa did not envy the admiral his dilemma or the awful responsibility that had fallen upon him. He weighed Stenz's questions carefully and tried to answer as honestly as he could.

"A direct hit?"

"We're talking dialable yield," Hampton stressed, joining the discussion. "Megatons, not kilotons. Nothing can survive that blast. Makes the bomb from '54 look like a firecracker."

Ah, yes, Serizawa thought ruefully. *Progress.*

"Will it work, Doctor?" Stenz asked again.

"It could," the scientist conceded. "But what then?" He indicated the monitors tracking Godzilla. "What if *he's* been down there all this time? With no interest in our world, but a part of it, a part of the balance. If we kill him, there's no telling what may come."

Stenz listened intently. "Yes? Go on."

"The MUTOs are stronger in a pair, but maybe not enough. He *could* defeat them."

"You're suggesting we let them meet and duke it out?" the admiral asked, sounding dubious. "Then what? Just hope the big one wins and swims back where he came from? And if he loses, are you willing to bet more lives on that?"

Serizawa wasn't certain. He was fully aware of how reckless his proposal must sound, as well as the awesome gravity of the decision before them. He considered all the human lives hanging in the balance. At least seven million, as Stenz had observed, and perhaps billions more. Was he truly prepared to trust humanity's future to a legendary monster?

And ask Stenz to do the same?

He shook his head sadly. "I can only bet my own."

Stenz nodded, appreciating the scientist's candor.

"Me, too, Doctor," he said regretfully. No doubt he had been hoping for a viable alternative to the hellish course of action before him. "That's why I have no choice." He turned away from Serizawa to address Martinez. "Execute our evacuation contingencies for San Francisco Bay. And find me a detonation site at least twenty miles from shore. If these things are attracted to our bombs, let's draw them out and finish this."

Serizawa wondered if that was truly possible.

GODZILLA

* * *

Night had fallen on the rugged Sierra Nevada mountains as the train skirted along high wooded ridges. Darkness cloaked the wilderness through which the tracks ran, but evidence of the female MUTO's destructive migration could still be seen around every curve. Ford and his fellow soldiers spied broken bridges, flattened trees, and suspiciously recent rockslides. The roar of the locomotive drowned out the usual nocturnal sounds you might expect to hear from the woods at this time of night, but Ford suspected that any local wildlife had long since fled from the monstrous invader. As he understood it, the train's route took it straight through "the heart of darkness"— right past the new MUTO. This was a calculated risk, to say the least, but there had been no quicker overland route.

No wonder he hadn't seen a single deer or owl yet.

Tre and the other heavily armed soldiers were on high alert. As the train rolled toward a lonely mountain pass, the nerve-jangling din of battle could be heard up ahead, just beyond the next ridge. Tracer fire lit up the night sky. Ford glimpsed brilliant laser dazzlers and felt the thrum of high-tech sonic weapons. Judging from the distant lights and racket, the train was approaching the "front line" of the conflict, which was still going strong. Even with everything the armed forces were dishing out, the MUTO was obviously not down for the count.

What was it going to take to stop these things?

A loud whoosh startled Ford as a fiery red explosion flared above the pass. Air brakes squealed and the train came to a halt right before the entrance to a narrow railway tunnel bored into the granite face of the mountain. The sudden stop threw Ford and other soldiers off-balance, and even the multi-ton missiles shifted unnervingly, if only for a moment.

A little warning would have been nice, Ford thought, although he couldn't blame the locomotive engineer for hitting the brakes. That explosion had looked way too big, too close. Who knew what was waiting for the train on the other side of that tunnel? Were there even any tracks left?

Master Sergeant Waltz hopped down from the locomotive onto the gravel beside the train. He called out to Tre, who was stationed on the missile car directly behind the locomotive.

"Sergeant, I need you down here... now."

Tre gulped and looked to Ford for sympathy. *Aw, shit* was written all over his face.

The soldier did his duty, however, and quickly joined Waltz down on the ground. A light fog blanketed the earth. Thick groves of pines and sequoias hemmed in the tracks on both sides, while the tunnel entrance ahead was as black as outer space. Ford looked on as Tre donned a large backpack-mounted radio, which Waltz attempted to employ.

"Snake Eyes, this is Bravo," the master sergeant said into the radio. He fiddled impatiently with the knobs. "What's the status at phase line red? Are the tracks clear, over?"

Static growled from the other end of the transmission, along with background noise from a heated battle. Nonstop explosions and shouting crackled from the radio.

"Say again?" a voice answered, barely audible through the interference. *"You're breaking up."*

More soldiers disembarked from the train. They gathered around the radio, frowning. This was not sounding good, for themselves or their mission. Had they reached the end of the line?

Ford was feeling an uncomfortable sense of *déjà vu*.

Hopping down from the missile car, he found himself drawn to the pitch-black tunnel entrance ahead. A flashlight was attached to the barrel of his M4 automatic rifle. For a second, he felt as though he was back on that monorail train in Honolulu, with the original MUTO waiting just around the bend.

The voice from the radio grew louder and more agitated, punctuated by bursts of static:

"... not... time... peat... now! Go, GO NOW!"

An agonized scream came over the radio, followed by a brutal crunching noise. The voice went silent; only static issued from the radio. Waltz and the others stiffened, fearing that they had just heard a comrade die in battle. Tre crossed himself.

Slightly further up the track, Ford peered warily into the mouth of the tunnel. Was it just his imagination or could he faintly make out some sort of the movement inside the tunnel? From what he'd gathered, the second MUTO couldn't possibly fit inside the narrow passage, but *something* appeared to be heading toward them, surging out of the blackness.

He quickly raised his rife and aimed it at the tunnel. The flashlight beam failed to penetrate the darkness. He started to shout a warning, just as a blast of dust and leaves and forest litter exploded from the tunnel, propelled by a luminous electric pulse. The flying dirt and twigs buffeted Ford, driving him backward. His flashlight instantly shorted out and so did all the lights on the train, car after car. The radio on Tre's back went dead, too, killing the static. Startled troops shouted in the dark:

"What the hell was that?"

"What happened?"

"Hey, where are the lights?"

But Ford understood. Instinctively, like a child in a lightning storm, he had started counting to himself under his breath.

"...three-one-thousand, four-one-thousand, five-one-thousand..."

A triumphant howl, echoing from the other side of the mountain, cut him off. The din of the nearby battle ceased, so that only the unsettling screeching of the female MUTO could be heard. There were no more bombs or explosions, no tracers or lasers visible beyond the ridge. Brushing the leaves and twigs from his face, Ford realized what the sudden cessation of hostilities meant.

The battle was over—and the MUTO had won.

That same realization was shared by Waltz and the rest of the troops. The frantic shouts trailed off, replaced by a stunned hush that was finally broken by the master sergeant.

"Corporal," he ordered a nearby communications expert, "get Snake Eyes on the line again. I need to know how close that thing is."

Ford had already counted that out. "Five miles."

Waltz turned toward Ford and squinted at him through the dark. It was hard to make out the master sergeant's features, but Waltz nodded as though impressed. Ford refrained from bragging that this was hardly his first run-in with a MUTO's electromagnetic pulse. He was practically becoming an old hand at this.

Lucky me, he thought.

"Lieutenant," Waltz addressed Ford, sizing him up. He gestured at the deep black cavity of the tunnel entrance. "Wanna join us. We're going in to check that tunnel."

While the train remained parked outside, Ford, Waltz, Tre and another rifleman, Brubaker, cautiously advanced into the stygian blackness of the tunnel. Fallen leaves and gravel crunched beneath their boots. Spare bulbs, screwed into the flashlights on their rifles, restored a degree of visibility. Incandescent beams penetrated the darkness before them. Ford and Tre took point, leading the way.

The men stop short as they suddenly spied two glowing eyes staring back at them. Ford tightened his grip on his rifle and almost fired until the flashlight beams revealed a lone deer, frozen in terror at what lay beyond the tunnel. In a clatter of hooves, the deer dashed past the soldiers, who jumped out of its way.

How about that? Ford thought, gasping in relief. It took a moment for his heart to stop racing. *Guess that fella didn't get the memo to clear out.*

The men moved on until they reached other end of the tunnel. Waltz signaled for alert as he warily stepped out into the open. Ford and the others followed after him, guns at the ready. Ford suspected that the deer had had the right idea, running in the opposite direction.

A long trestle bridge stretched before them, high above a deep gorge carved out by a raging mountain river. Rushing water could be heard, but night and mist hid the bottom of the gorge, as well as the far end of the bridge. The fog made it impossible to tell at a glance if the bridge was still intact all the way across. They would have to check that out and inspect the bridge's supports as well. They needed to know whether the bridge had been damaged by the recent battle and whether it would still support the missile train.

"Master Sergeant," Ford said, taking the initiative. "Why don't you and Brubaker check below?" He nodded at Tre. "Sergeant Morales, you're with me."

Waltz approved Ford's plan of action. He and Brubaker

hopped a side-rail and began to carefully descend a steep path down to the rapids below. Ford and Tre watched them vanish into the mist before turning to face the fog-shrouded span ahead of them. Ford glanced around warily, but couldn't detect any sign of a lurking MUTO. He hoped to God that the monster had moved on after crushing that last wave of troops. He'd already two run-ins with the first MUTO. He could live without encountering the second one as well.

The two men advanced through the fog, discovering obvious signs of damage. Wide gaps stretched between the slats beneath their feet, forcing them to step cautiously. Scorched steel and charred timbers testified that the battle had indeed passed this way. Deep gouges in the tracks looked uncomfortably like claw marks.

A broken slat caught Ford by surprise. Stumbling, he accidentally smacked the barrel of his rifle against an upright safety rail. The impact knocked the flashlight from its holder and it plummeted down through the irregular slats. It spun down into the mist like a falling star.

Damn.

Brubaker jumped as a falling flashlight smacked into the rocky shore of the river, many feet below the bridge. Waltz didn't blame the young rifleman for being scared, given the circumstances, but the master sergeant's face remained stern and unmoving. Chances were, either Brody or Morales had just lost their flashlights for some reason. It was annoying, but if that was the biggest snafu they ran into on this mission he'd count himself lucky. All that mattered now was keeping the missile train going, so that the brass got their nukes—before the MUTO did.

Descending to the bottom of the gorge, they reached the riverbed. White water surged over nearby rapids while the rocks beneath their feet had been worn smooth by flooding waters. Waltz turned back to look in the direction of the bridge, whose iron supports were half hidden by the mist, which was even thicker here down by the river. He scowled as he spotted a dim light flickering further upstream, growing brighter by the second.

What the—?

Flaming wreckage, including mangled helicopters, tanks, jeeps, drones and bodies, came rushing over the rapids. Burning fuel and incendiary gel blazed atop the flowing water, spilling onto the narrow shore. Waltz and Brubaker dived for cover to get out of the way of the blazing debris. They scrambled up the slope to get to safety, dodging the fiery remnants of his fellow soldiers' lost battle.

Something was crashing loudly against the rocks below. Peering over the edge of the bridge, Ford and Tre could make out a red-hot glow through the mist and murk. For a moment, Ford expected to hear the blood-chilling howl of a MUTO but, if this was a monster attack, why weren't Waltz and Brubaker firing their weapons?

Concerned, he whistled once. A tense moment followed before he heard an answering whistle from below. He let out a sigh of relief, as did Tre. It was good to know that the rest of their team had not run into serious trouble . At least, not yet.

Confident that Waltz and Brubaker did not require immediate reinforcements, Ford and Tre continued to make their way across the battle-scarred bridge. The thickening haze and uncertainty made every step a definite test of nerves, but at last the wooded mountain ridge on the far side of the gorge came into view. The two soldiers grinned at each other, encouraged by the sight. Although battered, the bridge was still in one piece. The train could keep going.

Almost giddy with relief, Tre wasted no time notifying the locomotive driver.

"All clear," he said into the radio. "I say again, all clear."

Eager to get on the road, neither man noticed as a craggy mountain peak behind them *began to move...*

In the locomotive's engine room, an Army engineer replaced one last fuse. The monster's EMP had done a number on the train's electronics, but the Missile Express was ready to roll again. He nodded as Morales' "all clear" filtered over the radio. Moments later, Waltz confirmed that the bridges main supports appeared structurally sound.

That's good enough for me, the engineer thought. *Let's get this show back on the road.*

He fired up the diesel engines, which churned to life, sending up plumes of white smoke into the misty mountain air. The whistle blew and the rest of the troops got back on the train and resumed defensive positions around the ICBMs. To be honest, the load of warheads made the engineer nervous. He couldn't wait to get rid of them.

He released the brakes, figuring he could pick up Waltz and the other scouts on the far side of the bridge. The train chugged forward, picking up momentum as it entered the tunnel. Its wheels sparked against the track, providing flashes of light in the blackness of the tunnel.

With any luck, the engineer hoped, it would be a straight shot from here on.

Below the bridge, climbing back up toward the cracks, Waltz thought he saw something stirring high above the trees. He signaled Brubaker and they ducked behind what appeared to be the thick trunk of a towering sequoia. The tree's bark, he noted, was strangely textured, almost though as it was made of some sort of hard shell-like substance. A viscous sap or resin oozed down the side of the tree—which suddenly uprooted itself from the ground. Claws appeared at the base of the tree.

Son of a bitch, Waltz thought. *That's not a tree. It's a leg!*

"MOVE!" he shouted at the top of his lungs. "TAKE COVER!"

The "mountain" detached itself from the ridge and leaned toward the bridge.

"Hit the deck!" Ford shouted to Tre. The men threw themselves on the tracks and rolled over onto their backs. They froze, holding their breaths, as the female MUTO crouched over the bridge. Ford couldn't help comparing it to the winged monster he'd encountered in Japan and Honolulu. The new creature was even larger and more massive than the first MUTO. Inhuman red eyes searched the night. Bioluminous sensors pulsed along its snout, as if it was sniffing the air for... what?

Us, Ford thought. *Maybe it's looking for us.*

The men lay still upon the tracks, not moving a muscle. Ford allowed himself to hope that maybe they would escape the colossal beast's attention. The first MUTO had ignored him back in Japan after all. In the foggy night, they might be too small and insignificant to notice. All they had to do was keep quiet.

Then Tre's radio began to sputter, perhaps affected by the MUTO's electrical aura. Static crackled loudly. Terrified, Tre tried to turn the radio off, but the switch had no effect.

"Shit, shit," he cursed. "Come on, come on—"

The MUTO'S hideous face dipped in closer, attracted by the noise. Its crimson eyes narrowed in concentration. Drool dripped from its beak, which was big enough to swallow both men whole in a single gulp, and still have room for a nuclear missile or two.

Unable to silence the radio, Tre struggled to undo the straps of the backpack, but his frantic efforts threatened to expose the two men even more than the squawking radio. Ford grabbed onto the backpack to hold it still. He raised a finger to his lips. His eyes locked onto the other man's, conveying an urgent message.

Don't move.

Tre stopped wriggling and kept perfectly still. Sweat drenched his face, though, and his naked fear matched Ford's own. Endless moments passed as the soldiers lay flat on their backs atop the bridge, waiting to see if they personally had reached the end of the line. The sheer unfairness of it all tore at Ford's soul. He couldn't believe that he'd survived the attacks in Japan and Hawaii, and finally made it back to America, only to be done in by yet *another* goddamn monster, only a few hundred miles away from Elle and Sam. He'd come so close to making it back to them.

But then the MUTO seemed to lose their scent or perhaps just its interest. Lifting its head, it reared up on its hind legs, blotting out the sky. Ford spied a large glowing nodule clinging to the underside of the creature's abdomen, only yards above the two soldiers. The sight jogged his memory and he recalled some of the old photos Dr. Serizawa had showed him back on the *Saratoga*. The luminous nodule bore disturbing resemblance to the giant egg sacs that had been found in the Philippines years ago. The ones that MUTOs had hatched from.

Holy crap, he thought. *They're breeding.*

The MUTO began to move off, heading west toward the coast, but then the tracks began to rattle, signaling the approach of an oncoming train. Ford realized with horror that the missile train was coming through the tunnel and had no idea that the MUTO was on the other side.

He prayed that the monster would hurry on its way, but no such luck. Attracted by the vibrating of the tracks, the MUTO wheeled about and trundled into the fog to meet the train. Obscured by the mist, it hunched over the tracks, eight monstrous limbs lying in wait. Its maw opened wide.

No! Ford thought. He leapt to his feet and sprinted toward the tunnel exit, shouting and waving his arms. "STOP THE TRAIN!"

But a savage howl drowned out his cries. Moments later, gunfire erupted in the fog and Ford saw muzzles flashes going off like crazy. The battle had been joined and, horribly, Ford had no doubt which side was fighting for their lives. If the best efforts of the U.S. military had been unable to halt the MUTO's destructive rampage so far, what chance did the train's pitiful defenders have?

Only Godzilla had proven a match for the MUTOs so far.

The besieged train came roaring out of the fog, even as its gargantuan attacker grabbed at it with its claws and fangs. Multiple limbs greedily snatched up the eighty-ton ICBMs as though they were sticks of candy. Armed soldiers, valiantly attempting to defend the missiles, were swept aside by the monster's claws, their torn bodies plunging into the flaming waters far below. Automatic-weapon fire had no effect on the voracious creature, whose obsidian shell repelled everything the doomed troopers threw at it. The MUTO's prismatic aura rippled the air around it.

Ford and Tre ran from the oncoming train and the monster attacking it. Desperate to get off the bridge, they sprinted for the western end of the span and safety. Their boots pounded on the tracks as they threw caution to the winds. Ford leapt over gaps in the slats, racing to reach the far end of the bridge in time. Tre tried to keep up with him, but was weighed down by the bulky radio unit on his back. Huffing and puffing, he fell badly behind. Glancing behind him, Ford saw the besieged train bearing down on them faster than they could run.

They weren't going to make it.

"GET DOWN!" he shouted back at Tre.

But it was too late. A gigantic limb obliterated the track right where Tre was. The soldier disappeared along with a wide stretch of track, even as train came barreling across the broken bridge toward the gap... and Ford.

The entire bridge began to disintegrate beneath his feet. With no time to think, he leapt from the crumbling structure and plunged toward the churning river. The entire train, complete with its remaining cargo of ICBMs plummeted after him, cascading over the edge of the severed tracks. Ford fell through the fog and hit the cold water feet first, sinking beneath the foam. He kicked his way to the surface long enough to snatch a breath of air before the current dragged him under again and carried him away. Tons of train and missiles rained down behind him, sounding like an avalanche.

And yet, above the din, he could still hear the MUTO's shrieking howl.

NINETEEN

The lights of San Francisco could be seen from the *Saratoga*, which continued to trail Godzilla at a safe distance. The monster's immense dorsal fins sliced through the churning waves toward the coast, where a row of Navy LCS vessels had formed a blockade miles offshore. The Littoral Combat Ships, which were expressly designed for operations close to shore, were somewhat smaller, swifter and shallower than conventional frigates or destroyers, but still packed plenty of punch. Each vessel was armed with both 57mm guns and a full complement of surface-to-air missiles.

But would that be enough to deter Godzilla?

The warships held their fire as the fins approached. Searchlights lit up the night. In the *Saratoga*'s war room, Serizawa and the others watched tensely in anticipation, waiting for Godzilla to rise up and reveal himself. Nobody expected the giant reptile to simply turn around in the face of the blockade, not with the male MUTO reportedly flying toward the city. The minutes ticked down toward a likely confrontation that Serizawa still had serious reservations about. He understood that Admiral Stenz and the U.S. military could hardly be expected to let such a formidable threat come ashore unopposed, but Serizawa remained unconvinced that challenging Godzilla was a good idea, and not just because of the many valiant lives that might be thrown away in a futile attempt to turn back an unstoppable force of nature. With the MUTOs still abroad, it might well be that obstructing Godzilla, if that was even possible, was not in the world's best interests.

We may be making a dreadful mistake, he thought.

But then, just when the conflict appeared inevitable, the great fins suddenly descended, sinking beneath the frothing waves until they vanished from view. The *Saratoga* pitched as turbulence upset the waters ahead. Serizawa held on to the corner of a computerized workstation to keep his balance. Graham gasped in relief. Stenz frowned, but also looked relieved to a degree. Serizawa guessed that the admiral also had profoundly mixed feelings about throwing the combat ships up against Godzilla.

Glowing green sonar screens tracked the leviathan until his mammoth form dissolved into a thousand tiny pixels, broken up by static, and eventually disappeared from the screens altogether. Serizawa assumed that Godzilla had simply chosen to dive under the blockade, as he'd done with the fleet two days ago. That he was still heading for San Francisco Bay went without saying.

Perhaps it is just as well, he thought, although his heart went out to the innocent men, women, and children in the city. They had not asked for their home to become a meeting-place for monsters, and Serizawa had no illusions that Godzilla cared anything for the insignificant human lives between him and his prey. *We are all just collateral damage now.*

Captain Hampton rushed up to Stenz, clutching a printout. "The warhead transport just went missing," he reported urgently. "The next closest, we'd have to fly in, but with the MUTOs' sphere of influence, there's no way we get one here in time."

Stenz's face turned ashen. "Get Air Force recovery teams out there. Find a weapon we can use!"

The rising sun gradually roused Ford from unconsciousness. His eyelids fluttered, blinking against the early morning light. As he slowly woke from restless dreams of flames and falling, he became aware of a gentle lapping sound nearby. Opening his eyes, he was greeted by the idyllic sight of a solitary doe drinking peacefully from the waters of a muddy river delta. The deer turned its head towards Ford and for a moment their eyes met in silent communion, man and nature sharing the world in peace.

Then a loud noise overhead shattered the moment. Startled, the doe bounded off—past the smoking wreckage of a tank.

Flying low, two Air Force helicopters came in over a mountain ridge. A large heavy-lift Super Stallion was accompanied by a smaller escort chopper. The low-lying delta was strewn with the mangled remains of numerous vehicles and equipment washed down from further upstream. Crushed cars and trucks, both civilian and military, mixed with broken timbers, twisted steel beams, heavy artillery, and other debris less readily identifiable. The tranquil riverbed had become a junkyard and perhaps a graveyard as well.

Charred and pulverized human remains could be glimpsed amidst the piled wreckage. Ford avoided looking at them, not wanting to spot Tre or Waltz or any of his other comrades among the dead.

Despite a pounding headache, he lifted his gaze to see at least a half-dozen Airmen abseil down from the hovering escort chopper. Dropping nimbly onto the ground, they spread out and started methodically scouring the ruins a bit further upstream. They moved briskly, intent on their mission.

Thank God, Ford thought.

He assumed the men were searching for survivors. Sitting up weakly, he tried to call out to the rescue team, who didn't appear to have spotted him yet. His throat was parched and he felt completely wasted, worn out not just by his punishing trip down the river, but by the accumulated stress and exhaustion of the last few days. He could barely remember when he wasn't about to killed by monsters or trying to make his way halfway across the world. A hoarse whisper escaped his cracked lips, but went unheard beneath the noisy rotors of the choppers. The rescue team kept on searching, not even looking in his direction.

Help, Ford thought. *Over here.*

Terrified that he might be overlooked and left behind, he forced himself to his feet and began to stagger through the ruins toward the searchers. A wave of dizziness assailed him and the violated landscape seemed to spin around him. He lurched clumsily from side to side, bumping into demolished vehicles and freight cars, which he occasionally grabbed onto for support. Soaked to the skin, he was cold and trembling and aching all over. Somewhere down the river, he'd lost his helmet and goggles along with his rifle. Muddy water dripped from his hair and down his neck. His mouth tasted of blood and silt. His boots squished with every slow, unsteady step.

Elle, he thought. *Gotta keep going for Elle and Sam.*

A filthy teddy bear, missing one arm, lay half-buried in the muck, next to the charred skeleton of an overturned station wagon. Something about this particular wreck jabbed at his heart, making him wince, but he was too groggy and debilitated to identify the memory, which quickly slipped away. He stumbled past the wagon, leaving the lost toy behind. His heavy boots dragged through the mud and splashed through puddles of icy mountain water. Random pieces of debris threatened to trip him.

He caught glimpses of the search team up ahead. The men were rooting through the wreckage several yards away, still oblivious to Ford's presence. As far as he could tell, they hadn't found any other survivors yet. Ford wondered if he was the only one left from the missile train. He tried again to call out, but could barely muster more than a squeak. Darkness encroached on his vision and he feared he was on the verge of passing out again.

I'm right here. Look this way.

His distress went unnoticed as one of the searchers found something among a heap of shattered steel trestles, railway cars, and other debris.

"We've got a live one!" he shouted excitedly. "Let's move!"

In response, lines were lowered from the choppers and hooked into winches. Exhausted and out breath, Ford watched as the surrounding wreckage slid way to reveal not an injured survivor, but an intact nuclear warhead partially submerged in the mud. The missile's massive booster rockets had been destroyed, but the cone-shaped re-entry vehicle bearing its lethal payload appeared to be still in one piece.

That's what they came for. Ford's hopes for rescue faded. The searchers weren't looking for survivors at all. *They're after a working nuke.*

Defeated and at the end of his rope, Ford slumped against the bottom chassis of a blackened Jeep that was lying sideways next to the river. He slid to the ground and watched numbly as the ten-foot-long re-entry vehicle was loaded aboard the larger of the helicopters. Once that was completed, the airmen took turns being hoisted back up into the smaller escort chopper. Just before he departed, the final man took one last look around. His eyes widened as he spotted Ford sagging upon the ground, next to the trashed Jeep.

"Hold it!" the airmen yelled. "We have a man down!"

The entire ward had become a triage unit. Doctors and nurses, just like Sam's mom, were super-busy trying to take care of all the hurt people who kept pouring into the hospital, some of them from as far as Nevada. All the blood and confusion scared Sam, who wanted his mommy, but he stayed at the nurse's desk like he had been told. A new coloring book rested on his lap, ignored and forgotten, while he stared in horrified fascination at the TV set on the wall.

"Military personnel are assisting in the evacuations," a government lady said on the TV. *"We're urging civilians who have not already left to stay off the roads and make their way immediately to shelter."*

A group of soldiers marched through the ward. Their helmets and uniforms looked a lot like the ones his dad wore. Sam looked away from the TV hopefully.

"Daddy?"

He hopped off his seat and tottered after them.

GODZILLA

* * *

Elle was at her wit's end. Just when she thought they couldn't possibly cope with one more patient, another batch of casualties arrived from the disaster zone, all requiring immediate attention. She'd been running herself ragged for nearly twenty-four hours now, with only short breaks for food and naps. She hadn't even had a chance to go home yet. Poor Sam had practically been living at the nurse's station. The only good thing about the ongoing crisis was that she wasn't worrying *every* second about Ford and whatever danger he might be in at this very moment.

She glanced anxiously at her wristwatch. Ford had said he'd be here by now and yet there was no sign of him. And no word either.

"Ford, where are you?"

More National Guardsmen invaded the ward. To her dismay, they started rounding up children and critical patients and herding them toward the exits. She hurried toward them.

"Wait, wait!" she protested. "These patients are my responsibility. Where are you taking them?"

A Guardsman took a moment to a moment to answer her. "Across the bridges," he said gruffly. "Critical and children only."

Elle was caught off-guard. They were evacuating the hospital now? Did that mean the monsters were that close already?

Laura Watkins joined them, escorting another group of children. "The shelters are going to fill up fast, Elle," she said. "Trust me, they'll be much safer outside the city." The older nurse revealed that she had been assigned to go along with the children and supervise their care at the emergency centers outside the city. "I can take Sam, too."

Take Sam? Away from her?

Elle realized that Laura was offering as a friend, but she shook her head vehemently.

"No," she said. "No way. My father-in-law's dead. I have no idea where my husband is. The phones aren't working, the roads are closed..." Elle couldn't imagine not knowing where her son was, too. "I'm as spread out and freaked out right now as I can handle. Sam's staying with me."

She glanced over at the nurse's station, expecting to see the boy where he belonged.

But Sam was gone.

Sam followed the soldiers through the hospital lobby to outside, where he was surprised and scared by the chaotic scene before him. Soldiers were busily loading patients, many in wheelchairs, into a fleet of bright orange school buses, while harried nurses and paramedics struggled to care for the displaced patients, many of whom looked too sick or hurt to travel. Empty gurneys were rushed back indoors to get still more patients before it was too late. Announcements blared from loudspeakers:

"This is not a test. A mandatory evacuation has been issued by the Federal Emergency Management Agency for the San Francisco Bay Area..."

Confused and disoriented by all the frantic activity, Sam lost sight of the soldiers he'd been trailing. The little boy wandered randomly toward the buses, overlooked in the general tumult. He wasn't sure where he was supposed to go now. Back to the nurse's desk?

A thunderous racket overhead made him tilt his head back. He stared upward as two military helicopters—a big one and a smaller one—thundered across the cloudy sky. A great big bomb, carried in a sling, dangled from cables beneath the larger chopper. All the grownups around him reacted in shock and fear to the sight of the bomb. Sam heard one of the soldiers call it a "warhead."

Bloodied, muddied, and dazed, Ford rode with the Air Force response team aboard the escort chopper. A heavy wool blanket was slung around his shoulders. Fresh water and black coffee, in that order, had helped restore him to a degree, but he still felt like death warmed over. He figured he was lucky he was alive at all, considering.

Tre and the others hadn't made it.

Tucked in among the airmen, Ford watched as the heavy-lift transport chopper peeled away from its escort, flying toward San Francisco Bay with the recovered warhead. Ford wondered if it was one of the bombs he'd replaced the detonator on.

"Where are they taking it?" he asked, referring to the warhead.

"Twenty miles out to sea," an airman explained. "Convergence point. We're going to lure them there. Three birds, one stone!"

The escort 'copter banked away toward Sausalito to the north. Ford shuddered beneath the blanket as the chopper bearing the 300-kiloton warhead made its way toward San Francisco.

His home. His family.

TWENTY

A makeshift command center had been established on a mountain overlook to the north of the Golden Gate Bridge. The scenic location offered a workable view of San Francisco Bay and the city proper. Mobile trailers and temporary structures were swarming with military personnel, who hustled to make sure everything was in readiness for the next, and possibly final, stage of the defense operations. Sunlight filtered through gray clouds. An overcast sky threatened to rain.

Airlifted to the site, Serizawa and Graham accompanied Admiral Stenz, Captain Hampton, and key personnel from the *Saratoga* as they hurried across the grounds to their new tactical operations center. Hampton updated the admiral on the move.

"We only found one warhead, sir," he reported, "but it's intact and already prepped with a manual timer and detonation mechanism. Should be immune to those things."

Stenz nodded. "Where is it right now?"

"En route, sir. There's a transport vessel waiting in the bay. The warhead should be there any minute."

Serizawa paused to look south, where he spied a heavy-lift military helicopter carrying the nuclear warhead toward the bay. The sight of the chopper's lethal cargo filled his soul with dread. His fingers found the antique watch in his pocket. He thought of mushroom clouds rising over a devastated atoll in the Pacific.

History, he feared, was repeating itself.

The Air Force helicopter touched down in the foothills overlooking the bay. As Ford exited the chopper, civilian relief workers rushed up to treat his injuries. He brushed them off impatiently, anxious to get to Elle and Sam somehow. It was maddening to be so close, to actually be within sight of the city, and still be separated from his family.

Hang, on Elle, he thought. *I'm almost there.*

He surveyed his surroundings. A parking lot in the hills was jammed with vehicles: some military, but also plenty of school buses and ambulances. Hundreds of anxious people milled about an emergency staging area and shelter, hastily assembled on the outskirts of the city north of the Golden Gate Bridge. Trying to make sense of the situation, he buttonholed a passing relief worker bearing an armload of first aid supplies.

"Is the city evacuated?" Ford asked.

The other man shook his head. "Only schools and hospitals. Everyone else is still inside."

Including Elle and Sam? Or were they among those evacuated? Ford flashed back to that nightmarish morning fifteen years ago when he and the other children had been hurriedly evacuated from Miss Okada's classroom. He knew exactly how scared Sam must be right now, but he had no way of knowing where his family was. For all he knew, Sam was on one of those crowded buses in the parking lot.

He ran toward the vehicles, desperate to find out.

"Hey!" the puzzled relief worker said. "Where are you going?"

The USNS *Yakima*, a fast combat support ship, was docked at Fisherman's Wharf. A skycrane helicopter hovered above the ship as the recovered nuclear warhead was lowered via winches onto the *Yakima*'s deck. Office workers being evacuated from nearby buildings glanced nervously at the nuclear warhead as they were hustled into waiting vans and buses. Jeff Lewis, one of the missile techs assigned to the operation, didn't blame the spectators for looking askance at the warhead. To be honest, it made him uncomfortable, too. Nuclear bombs belonged in silos or submarines, not heading out into San Francisco Bay.

But what other choice did they have? Nothing else seemed to be stopping the monsters.

Running out of the hospital, Elle searched frantically for her son.

A full-scale evacuation was underway in front of San Francisco General. EMTs and orderlies assisted in loading critical patients into waiting ambulances, monitoring vitals as they did so. Many of the patients could not walk on their own and had to be wheeled to the vehicles and physically lifted inside. Moving them at all would be a bad idea under most circumstances, but these were definitely not normal conditions. Better to transport them now than leave them helpless in the path of the creatures that were reportedly converging on the city. Unlike more able-bodied people, these patients wouldn't be able to make their own escape.

Meanwhile, at the other end of the loading and unloading area, National Guard troops were ushering more children onto school buses. Could Sam have accidentally been swept up in the mass evacuation? Standing atop the front steps of the hospital, she peered at the buses, hoping she wasn't already too late. Panic threatened as one bus after another drove away from the hospital, heading toward God knew where. What if Sam was already on one of those buses? How on Earth would she ever find him again?

No, I can't lose him, too!

Then, through the bustling confusion, she glimpsed Sam tottering about in the chaos, looking lost and confused. Numerous strangers jostled the little boy, too caught up in the overall emergency to pay attention to a single unattended child on the verge of tears. Sam looked about anxiously, searching for a familiar face. Elle's heart nearly burst from her chest.

"SAM!"

Her voice reached him through the hubbub. Turning toward her, he spied his mother at the top of the steps. His face lit up in relief.

"Mommy!"

He ran toward her with his tiny arms outstretched.

"No!" she cried out, afraid of losing him in the crowd again. "Wait there!"

But it was no use. Desperate for his mother, Sam raced for the steps and was almost immediately swallowed up by swirling maelstrom of soldiers, paramedics, evacuees, stretchers, IVs, and gurneys. Rushing down the steps, shoving her way through the hectic mass exodus, Elle tried to keep him in sight, but too many much larger bodies got in the way. People were practically stampeding toward the buses and ambulances now, desperate not to be left behind. Any pretense at a calm and orderly evacuation was devolving into bedlam.

Hang on, baby, I'm coming!

Sam couldn't get to his mommy. Big people rushed past him on all sides, blocking him and spinning him around until he didn't know which way to go. He looked for Mommy, but he couldn't see her anymore. There were too many people all around, all in too big of a hurry to notice him. A swinging elbow knocked him down and he fell onto the pavement. Rushing feet stomped past him and, unable to get back up, he curled up into a ball, afraid that the crowd was going to stomp all over him. Boots and shoes smacked against the ground, only inches away from him. Terrified, tears pouring down his face, he screamed for his mommy.

And all at once she was there, her comforting arms scooping him up from the pavement and holding him close. A flood of grownups swept past them on either side, ignoring the rescue, but Sam wasn't afraid anymore. His mother had found him.

"It's okay, I got you," she cooed, hugging him tightly. "I got you."

Thank God, Elle thought.

She had gotten to him just in time. Things were getting seriously crazy out here now that the last of the buses were beginning to pull away. A few more moments and Sam might have actually been trampled in the rush. She hefted him in her arms and squeezed him with all her strength. She never wanted to let go of him again.

And yet, glancing around, she saw that there was only one school bus left. Her heart was torn in two as she spotted Laura herding the children from their ward onto the bus, which, in theory, would take them out of harm's way. If Sam stayed behind with her, he would be trapped in a city that was looking at a disaster of unimaginable proportions. Conflicted, Elle found herself faced with two equally ghastly prospects: letting Sam out of her sight or risking his life by keeping him with her. It was agonizing dilemma, but, deep down inside, she understood that, if he stayed, she would not be able to protect him from the horrors in store.

The monsters were coming—and she knew what she had to do.

"Wait!" she shouted, running toward the last bus with Sam in her arms. "Wait!"

She reached the bus and tried to put him down on the bus's steps. He clung to her, just as unwilling to let go as she was. Laura stepped forward to help Sam onto the bus. The older nurse held out her hand, but Sam turned away from her, wanting his mother instead.

"Sammy," Elle said, her heart breaking. "You remember Laura, mommy's work-friend? You need to go with her, okay?"

His eyes welled with tears. Panic filled his voice. "No, mommy, no!"

She was briefly tempted to climb into the bus with him, but then she remembered all the injured patients back in the triage unit. *Someone* had to stay to look after them. She suddenly appreciated, more than ever, the dilemma Ford confronted every time his duty called him away from his family. Fighting back tears of her own, she fought to keep up a brave face. For Sam's sake.

"Mommy has to stay and help people. But I'll see you soon, I promise."

She pulled him tightly to her chest, just for a moment, then reluctantly let go. Peeling his tiny arms away from her was harder than clamping any bleeding artery. She felt like her own heart was being shredded by a monster's claws. What if this was the last time she ever held her baby boy?

Laura tried again to take Sam from her. Her expression made it clear that she understood just how excruciating this farewell was for Elle. She gave the young mother a reassuring nod that testified to years of perfecting a good bedside manner.

"It's okay," she said, corralling Sam and taking his hand. "C'mon, Sammy."

Laura led the boy up into the bus, where the driver was getting visibly impatient behind the wheel. She paused at the top of the steps to look back at Elle, who doing her best not to fall apart until the bus left. She didn't want Sam to see how scared she was.

"I'll keep him safe, Elle," Laura said.

Elle knew she could count on Laura to keep her promise. Even so, as the door slid shut and the bus began to drive off, carrying Sam away, it took all of Elle's strength and resolve not to change her mind and chase after the bus, screaming and shouting for it turn around and bring her boy back to her. He was only four years old. He needed his mother.

But he needed to get away, too. Before the monsters came.

GODZILLA

Rain began to drizzle from the sky as she watched the bus join the procession heading for the Bridge. She waited, frozen in place, until she couldn't see Sam's bus anymore.

Then she turned and headed back to work.

At least Sam will be safe, she thought. *If any of us are.*

TWENTY-ONE

The tac-ops command center occupied a large state-of-the-art mobile trailer that had been tricked out with sophisticated communications and monitoring equipment. Networked screens lined the interior of the trailer to provide Admiral Stenz and his staff with real-time data, video, and satellite feeds. Large windows at the rear of the trailer offered a direct view of the bay and San Francisco. Analysts and technicians were already at their stations as Stenz strode into the trailer.

"Sit rep!" he demanded. "Where are our targets?"

"The male was spotted thirty miles west," a civilian analyst reported, "off the Farallon Islands."

"We're showing seismic activity to the east, near Livermore," Martinez added. "Should be the female, closing in."

Stenz nodded. "And the big one?"

The analysts shook their heads. The admiral glanced at the sonar screens from the ships offshore. They remained blank.

"Last contact was five hours ago," Martinez said, "maintaining a bearing of zero-five-three degrees and descending past ten thousand feet. Nothing since."

Five hours, Stenz thought. That was more than enough time for the submerged leviathan to reach the strait leading into the bay. Frowning, he turned his attention to another bank of monitors, where live satellite and CCTV feeds showed the Golden Gate Bridge. The outbound lanes, leading away from the city, were jammed bumper-to-bumper with school buses packed with kids. *Damn it. Why aren't those children to safety yet?*

"There are still buses on that bridge," he said. "Deploy everything we have. If they come at the bay, at least we'll slow them down."

But for how long?

"Everyone stay in your seats!" the bus driver hollered from behind the wheel. He honked his horn and shouted impatiently at the long line of buses in front of them on the bridge. "Come on, what's the holdup?"

Sam's bus, the last in the procession, was barely moving. Restless kids, most of them older than him, were getting loud and rowdy. Younger children were crying or refusing to stay in their seats, while the teenagers, who were working way too hard to hide how scared they were, joked and roughhoused with each other. Sam sat huddled in the back, wanting his mother, but trying to be brave. He peered out of the rain-streaked windows at the huge steel cables of the bridge and the foggy waters of the bay. Mommy's friend Laura was up near the front of the bus, struggling to maintain order. Sam wasn't entirely sure where the bus was taking them, but he hoped they got there soon—and that Mommy would come get him as soon as she could.

Horns blasted loudly across the bridge, but the caravan of buses remained snarled in traffic. The vehicles crept forward, their drivers jostling for inches. Inside Sam's bus, somebody started throwing spit wads at the other kids. A paper airplane flew by Sam's head. A teenager complained that he was starving. Sam tried to ignore the ruckus. He wished everybody would just calm down.

The TV had said a monster was coming. A monster named Godzilla.

The roadway started to rumble beneath them and everyone got very quiet very fast. It felt a little like an earthquake, but then Sam spotted a convoy of army tanks and Stryker vehicles rolling onto the bridge's vacant inbound lanes. The intimidating armored vehicles took up defensive positions on the bridge. Their big guns swiveled to face the ocean, which was hidden from view by a thick bank of fog. Sam remembered the toy soldiers and tanks he'd played with on the floor at home.

The dinosaur always wins, he remembered.

Sam gazed out the window, both scared and excited to see what the guns were aiming for. Drizzle streaked the windows, making them harder to see through. He wished there was some way he could wipe them clean from the inside. He pressed his nose up against the window.

THWACK!

Without warning, a seagull smacked headfirst into the window, startling Sam, who shrieked in alarm as more and more birds slammed into the bus, leaving bloody smears on the glass. The entire bus started freaking out as a whole flock of panicked gulls came flying inland out of the fog. Squawking loudly, they flapped frantically toward the city, as though desperately trying to escape... what?

He's coming, Sam realized. *The monster from TV.*

Eyes wide, he glimpsed a huge shadowy form approaching through the fog and rain.

A rear guard of Navy LCS vessels ringed the entrance to the Golden Gate strait leading to the bay beyond. Sailors manned the ship's powerful Mark-100 57mm naval guns. The approaching creature had simply dived beneath the earlier blockade further out at sea, but no one knew if he would resort to the same tactic again. This time a confrontation was all but inevitable.

Along with his fellow sailors, Ensign Mark Pierce waited tensely. They understood too well that this was the Navy's last chance to keep the sea monster from making landfall—and that so far the beast had proved unstoppable.

Here he comes, Pierce thought. *God help us all.*

Computer-controlled, the fifteen-ton guns pivoted to take aim at the emerging shape as it began to rise high above the water. Peering through the mist, Pierce made out a tall, upright form ridged with jagged spikes or fins. The shape kept rising higher and higher until it towered above the surface of the sea like a newborn volcano. Pierce estimated that it had to be at least two hundred feet tall.

Jesus, I knew this thing was supposed to be big, but...

The shape grew higher and closer with every moment. The guns waited for the creature to fully reveal itself so they could target its head and chest. Great torrents of water cascaded off the sides of the creature until Pierce realized that what he'd assumed must be the head was just the pointed top of a large scaly appendage that swayed ominously back and forth above the water. The horrifying truth hit him like a thunderbolt.

That's not the monster! That's just the tip of his tail!

Two nearby ships suddenly keeled up from below, capsizing as the rest of Godzilla's colossal body rose up from the strait behind them. Violent waves slammed against Pierce's ship, causing it to pitch sharply. The startled seaman was thrown across the deck. Landing on his back, he stared up in shock at the titanic beast.

Walking upright on two prodigious legs, the giant reptile was nearly four hundred feet tall. His ponderous footsteps echoed through the fog as he waded toward the Golden Gate Bridge.

Godzilla's appearance shattered the traffic jam on the bridge. Buses lurched forward, honking and ramming each other as they rushed to get off the bridge before the monster reached it. Tanks and Strykers opened fire all at once, unleashing a deafening barrage full of smoke and fire. Geysers of water sprayed high into the air where the explosive rounds struck the waves. Scorching salvos of advanced anti-tank ammo blistered Godzilla's hard, scaly hide, causing him to flinch and roar in pain. He swatted furiously at the projectiles, as though they were a swarm of angry bees. The rounds chipped away at the armored plates protecting his mammoth form, but, weathering the inferno, he kept on coming.

Sam watched from the bus in both fear and fascination. Godzilla was not just a dinosaur. He was a *giant* dinosaur, and he was heading straight for the bridge, despite the army's attack. The bus driver swore and leaned on his horn, alerting the other drivers that he was coming through no matter what. He hit the gas and the bus surged forward, tossing the kids back into their seats. Nurse Laura had to grab onto a seatback to keep from falling. Sam's gaze swung back and forth between the far end of the bridge and the monster getting closer and closer. The nearer the Godzilla got, the bigger he looked.

And the smaller Sam felt.

Roaring furiously, Godzilla waded into the military's fiery assault, which was obviously not going to slow him down for long. Sam held his breath, terrified that his bus was not going to make it across in time. He stared at Godzilla's giant fangs and hoped that being eaten by a monster wouldn't hurt too much.

"C'mon, c'mon!" the bus driver exclaimed. A gap opened up briefly in the traffic and he floored the accelerator so that the bus shot forward and cleared the bridge. Everyone was too scared to cheer, but Nurse Laura gasped in relief, sinking into an empty seat next to Sam. He had never seen a grownup look so scared before. She was pale and shaking.

We made it, he realized. *We didn't die.*

Turning around in his seat, Sam gaped as, braving the heavy artillery, Godzilla reached the Golden Gate Bridge and tore right through it as though it was made of cardboard. The magnificent orange towers collapsed and thick steel cables, each nearly a yard in diameter, snapped like rubber bands as the monster smashed through the bridge midway across its span. The concrete roadway, with its six lanes, crumbled to pieces. Tanks and soldiers, along with ruptured cables and great slabs of bridge, spilled into the strait, falling hundreds of feet into the foaming water below where they disappeared beneath the waves and fog. The tanks and Strykers had done their part, Sam realized, slowing Godzilla long enough for the buses to make it to safety, but they couldn't save themselves. Godzilla was just too strong.

Maybe nothing could stop him.

Godzilla waded into the bay, his gargantuan contours still partly veiled by the thick fog and rain. Snapped steel cables and mangled pieces of the bridge trailed from him like torn vines. He lifted his head toward the sky, as though sensing something. He snarled in anticipation.

Seconds later, a squadron of F-35 fighter jets screamed in over the bay. They homed in on Godzilla, letting loose with an onslaught of armor-piercing rounds and guided missiles. The high-tech weapons pocked his armored hide and pierced whole dorsal fins, inflicting more significant damage than the land-based forces had. Godzilla reeled in pain, obviously feeling the injuries. His clawed forearms slashed uselessly at the planes, which were careful to stay above his reach. They strafed him, then circled around for another run.

The fighters actually managed to halt Godzilla's forward progress, at least for the moment. As Sam watched from the back of the bus, the battle-scarred monster lumbered onto Alcatraz Island, just a few miles past the wrecked bridge, where he towered above the abandoned prison, which Sam had once toured with his parents. The visitor's center was crushed beneath his huge clawed feet.

The F-35s pursued him, but Godzilla did not retreat. His jaws opened wide and a full-throated roar rang out over the bay. Sam shuddered as the buses sped north toward the hills beyond the bridge. The Air Force had hurt Godzilla, but the little boy knew that the battle wasn't over yet.

The dinosaur always wins...

* * *

GODZILLA

The *Yakima* sped through the choppy waters of the bay, heading for the open sea beyond. As Pierce understood it, the idea was to try to lure the MUTOs and Godzilla out into the ocean before detonating the warhead. Along with the rest of the technical crew, Pierce hurriedly prepped the primitive mechanical timer on the bomb, which was lashed down to the deck of the ship. He used a DIP switch to manually enter the launch codes, while hoping that the winged MUTO, wherever it was, wouldn't come swooping down from the sky before he was finished. He could hear the Air Force fighters pounding away at Godzilla across the bay. The monster's roar, audible even above the plane's unleashed firepower, sent a chill down Pierce's spine.

"Six, niner, bravo, zulu," he said, trying to keep his voice and hands steady.

Another technician, Schultz, confirmed the code sequence. "Six, niner, bravo, zulu."

That's it then, Pierce thought. Despite the rain and fog, his mouth suddenly felt as dry as the Mojave. He traded disbelieving looks with Schultz. *We're really doing this.*

Swallowing hard, he set the timer.

Schultz signaled to another man, who nodded and fired a flare into the sky. It rocketed upward, trailing a stream of bright red fire. Pierce watched the flare ascend before looking back at the ticking timer. The countdown had begun.

Three hours and counting.

TWENTY-TWO

The flare was visible at the mobile command center overlooking the bay. Spotters immediately reported it to Tac-Ops, where Martinez started the timer countdown on a digital wall display above the main monitor:

3:00:00. 02:59:59. 02:59:58...

Everyone in the trailer felt the weight of the moment. The countdown made the unthinkable decision more real somehow. Standing gravely behind the tense military personnel, Serizawa wound his watch. He and Stenz exchanged somber looks, both of them fully aware of the magnitude of what was to come and the responsibility they both bore.

God help us all, he thought.

"Our fighters have been engaging the big one," Captain Hampton noted, "and getting some effect with guns and ATGMs, but it won't hold him long."

Stenz glanced at a separate monitor tracking the progress of the MUTOs. They were already beginning to sputter worryingly. Visual snow and static interfered with the displays. "How long before we lose power to the city?"

"Satellites and drones are losing signal, sir," Martinez reported. "They're close."

"Send more birds and tell them to use extreme caution," Stenz ordered. "I want eyes."

Another squadron of F-35s roared past overhead, zooming toward the fogbound bay. The roar of the jets briefly competed with the chatter in the trailer. Serizawa lifted his eyes toward the ceiling, visualizing the fighters on their way to confront Godzilla. At least, he reflected, that mighty predator did not generate a disruptive electromagnetic aura like the MUTOs. The aircraft *might* have a chance against Godzilla.

But he doubted it.

"Yes," the relief worker confirmed. "Sam Brody was checked into the Oakland Coliseum shelter an hour ago. His bus was sent on a ferry to the overflow facility there. But I have no record of Elle Brody. She never left the city."

Exhausted and out of breath, Ford stood before a table where harried evacuation workers sorted through lists of incoming civilians. All around him, mobs of displaced persons filled the overcrowded refugee camp. More buses and ambulances were arriving every minute, bringing still more evacuees from the city. A steady drizzle rained down on him as a seemingly endless row of parked vehicles unloaded old people, hospital patients, and children. Most of them looked positively shell-shocked, as though they'd never been chased from their homes by giant prehistoric monsters before. Ford knew exactly how they felt; a few days ago, he would've never believed such creatures existed either.

"Can you check again?" he asked anxiously. "Please? I told her to wait for me, but I didn't make it..."

"I'm sorry," the worker said, shaking her head. "They're trying to get everybody downtown into the subway shelters."

The thought of Elle trapped underground during the crisis was agonizing. At least he knew Sam was safe, for the time being, but what about Elle? All three monsters, and possibly an armed nuclear warhead were aimed right at her.

I have to do something, he thought. *I promised.*

"Lieutenant Brody?"

He turned to see an officer standing at attention. He hoped this meant he was being drafted back into the battle. Rejoining the fight was his best chance to save the city.

And Elle.

* * *

The Golden Gate Bridge, which had spanned the strait for more than seventy-five years, was no more. The iconic bridge was smashed right through the middle, so that only amputated stumps of roadway jutted from its opposite ends. Severed steel cables dangled limply from the ruins, which swayed ominously, on the verge of further collapse. Crumbling slabs of concrete shook loose and plunged into the waters below, which had already claimed the armored divisions sent to defend the bridge. Fallen warriors floated atop the waves.

Holy crap, Pierce thought, viewing the apocalyptic scene from the deck of the *Yakima* as the Navy transport ship sailed toward the wreckage, past Alcatraz, bearing the ticking nuclear warhead. Despite everything he'd been briefed on, and had glimpsed on TV, it was still hard to accept that a single living creature could be responsible for so much destruction. The bridge looked like it had been taken down by a war or terrorist attack, not torn to pieces by some sort of overgrown lizard. *How is this even possible?*

Then Alcatraz came into view and it all made sense.

Godzilla loomed like a mountain above the island, slashing and snarling at the F-35 fighter jets harassing him. Pierce and his fellow technicians gawked at their first sight of the gargantuan sea monster in the flesh. This wasn't just an animal, Pierce realized. This was a *dragon*, and as big as a skyscraper. The bridge hadn't stood a chance.

At the moment, the jets seemed to have the monster contained, but then the F-35s broke off from circling Godzilla and zoomed off in a tight "V" formation, seemingly abandoning the fight. They disappeared into the stormy gray clouds overhead, heading inland toward the city.

Huh? Pierce thought. "Where are they going?"

Static burst from the shipboard radio. Sparks flared as it suddenly shorted out with a pop and a hiss. Pierce gulped. He knew what the electrical disruptions meant.

A MUTO was on its way.

In the Tac-Ops trailer, the feeds from Alcatraz abruptly went to static.

"Boxcar, this is Guardian 3, over!" Martinez barked into her radio. "Boxcar, this is Guardian 3. Do you copy, over?"

Interference whined over every channel, frustrating her efforts. And that wasn't all; every feed from San Francisco began to flicker alarmingly, reminding Serizawa of the electrical disturbances and blackouts that had preceded the male MUTO's cataclysmic escape from the secret base in Japan. Analysts feverishly worked their keyboards and controls, trying to compensate for the interference, but with little success. Serizawa joined Admiral Stenz and Captain Hampton, who were intent on the wavering feeds from the F-35s zooming inland through the dense clouds between Alcatraz and the city. The scientist understood that the planes were trying to outrace the MUTO's crippling electromagnetic emissions. Stenz muttered unhappily under his breath. The MUTO's approach had forced the jets to abandon their assault on Godzilla. The defense effort was losing ground on every front.

"*CAG, my nose is cold,*" a Lightning pilot reported over the radio. "*I just lost radar. Do you copy?*"

On the flickering screens, a monstrous shadow darkened the murky sky above the planes. Just for a moment, the fierce male came winging down from the sky like the stealth aircraft it somewhat resembled. Serizawa and the others caught only a glimpse of the creature's inhuman red eyes, snapping beak and outstretched claws before the video feeds distorted beyond clarity. The fighter pilot shouted through the static.

"*Engage, eng—!*"

A blinding electromagnetic pulse lit up the screens, before knocking them out completely.

The doomed pilots had lost their race for life.

The evacuation was still underway at the hospital. A cold rain sprinkled on Elle as she helped the orderlies load more patients into a waiting ambulance. With the children and most critical patients already shipped out, they were now concentrating on the remainder of the patients, the one with less dire injuries or conditions. Like the poor guy on the stretcher in front of her, who had chosen the worst possible time to have a routine knee operation. More ambulances waited in the open plaza outside the hospital. The ambulance's engine idled, its driver impatient to get on his way, as Elle slammed shut the rear doors of the vehicle and signaled the driver that he could go. The ambulance started to pull away from the curb... and its engine died.

Are you kidding me? Elle thought. *Of all times!*

Then she noticed that the other ambulances had come to a stop, too, and the lights were going out in the buildings nearby. Even the traffic lights had gone dead. She and the other hospital workers looked at each other in confusion, trying to figure out what had caused the blackout. Elle knew in her heart that they had all just run out of time.

There was a whooshing sound overhead. Somebody screamed and pointed at the sky. Elle looked up in time to see an F-35 fighter plane spinning out of control and diving toward downtown. A second later, it crashed to earth only a block away from where Elle was standing with an explosive boom that caused her to stumble backwards. A billowing fireball rose up from the blazing wreckage. Elle felt the heat of the flames against her face. Her heart was pounding.

This is it, she realized. *It's begun.*

The *Yakima* was in trouble. Every electrical system, from navigation to communications, had shorted out at the same time. Pierce and his crewmates scrambled about the deck, trying cope with the emergency and complete their mission, despite the blackout.

"We lost power!" Schultz shouted.

I can see that, Pierce thought impatiently. "Check the warhead!"

They raced toward the bomb. The re-entry vehicle's nose cone had been screwed back on, but a latched transparent window allowed them to view the mechanical detonator attached to the payload, which was still ticking away, its lathe gears unaffected by the EMP that had taken out the ship's electronics. Pierce wiped his brow in relief.

"Still running," Shultz shouted to the others.

Maybe they could still carry out their mission, Pierce hoped, until he heard the *Yakima*'s four powerful turbine engines die. Suddenly, the ship was dead in the water, carried along only by momentum and the current. Pierce's blood froze as he grasped the full horror of their situation.

We're stuck here, he realized, *with a ticking nuclear warhead.*

He looked out across the bay at the skyline of San Francisco, which had gone completely dark. No city lights shone through the mist and rain. The entire area had obviously fallen within the MUTOs' sphere of influence, which meant that one or more of the creatures had to be in vicinity. Creatures that fed on radioactive materials like that installed in the warhead, which had been intended to serve as a bait to lure them back out to sea, but now was not going anywhere.

Oh crap, he thought. *This just keeps getting worse.*

He glanced up at the clouds, half-expecting to see a pair of monstrous black wings, but instead he saw a disabled F-35 spiraling down toward the bay. The fighter slammed into the water and exploded into flame. Stunned, Pierce was still trying to catch his breath when *another* jet crashed into the bay.

And another... and another...

An entire squadron rained down from the skies.

GODZILLA

"Take cover!" Pierce shouted as the missile techs scrambled for shelter. More planes slammed into the water, narrowly missing the stalled transport ship. One after another, they exploded on impact, filling the foggy air with smoke and flames. Multiple impacts stirred up the waves, causing the ship to pitch from side to side. Pierce was thrown against the side of the warhead. The smell of burning jet fuel invaded his nose and throat. He choked on the thick black fumes.

This is insane, he thought. *This can't be happening!*

Miraculously, however, none of the falling F-35s struck the *Yakima*. The rain of fighter jets felt like it went on forever, but was actually over in a few minutes. All at once, the planes stopped falling and an eerie calm fell on the deck, broken only by the crackling flames upon the water. Pierce and the others cautiously emerged from hiding. Dazed, they stood upon the deck and watched the burning wreckage sink beneath the waves. The unlucky pilots joined the scores of soldiers who had been lost upon the bridge. The bay was claiming more than its share of dead today.

And that's before *the warhead goes off,* Pierce thought. He peered up at the brooding gray clouds above them. *Is that it? Is it over?*

A menacing shadow fell over the deck of the transport ship as the male MUTO, his hooked jaws opened wide, dived from the clouds, surrounded by yet another deluge of crashing F-35s. Its dark wings spread out behind it, its six clawed limbs reaching out hungrily, the male attacked the *Yakima*, instantly plunging the entire ship underwater. Nearly fifty thousand tons of displaced seawater splashed into the air, dousing some of the burning aircraft sinking slowly nearby. The water sprayed like a geyser before crashing back down onto the churning foam.

There were no survivors.

The turbulent waters began to settle, just for a moment, before the male erupted from the waves and took to the sky once more. The ten-foot-long re-entry vehicle was clenched between its jaws as the creature soared high above the bay, then swooped down toward the city ahead.

Bearing its ticking prize, the male flew over San Francisco.

TWENTY-THREE

Panic spread through the Tac-Ops center. Screens shorted and went black. Frantic analysts and technicians struggled to restore contact with the city. Paper maps were spread out atop a portable chart table, charting blast radiuses and fallout patterns from a new ground zero. This was beyond a worst-case scenario. This was a potential catastrophe beyond anticipation.

"Fifty-four minutes and counting!" an analyst called out.

Admiral Stenz stared in horror at the digital clock on the wall. The mechanical device continued to count down the minutes and seconds to detonation. They had less than an hour before the warhead exploded—and now that winged monster was carrying it into the city.

"It's right in the middle of downtown, sir," Hampton reported, confirming their latest visual reconnaissance of the male's flight path. He started to elaborate, but Stenz cut him off.

"*How many?*" the admiral demanded.

"At least a hundred thousand," Hampton said. "But we put

in a shielded detonator. Nothing can stop it remotely."

In other words, we can't deactivate the damn bomb from here, Stenz thought. Their precautions against the MUTOs' electromagnetic auras were coming back to bite them. But who could have expected that the male would hijack the warhead and bring it inland?

I should've, that's who.

But there would time enough to crucify himself later. Right now their top priority, even beyond containing the monsters, was that ticking nuclear warhead. If they couldn't defuse it remotely, then somebody was going to need to get the job done on-site.

"Both bridges are down," Martinez informed him, as though reading his mind. "All roads into the city are jammed with cars, and we're seeing electrical disturbances as high as thirty-thousand feet."

The feverish activity in Tac-Ops slowed as the seeming hopelessness of their efforts sank in. Time was running out and so were their options. The odds against them felt insurmountable, but Stenz refused to give up. Failure in this instance was more than unacceptable. It was inconceivable.

Almost a hundred thousand people.

"Find a way to get men in there," he ordered. "We need to disarm that warhead." He turned to Serizawa, who had been keeping his own council during the escalating crisis. The scientist stood quietly off to the side with his colleague, Graham. "Your alpha predator, Doctor. 'Godzilla.' You really think he has a chance?"

Serizawa turned toward the rear of the trailer, where large plate-glass windows looked out over the fogbound bay and the imperiled city beyond. Even from this distance, the male could be glimpsed soaring over San Francisco, pursued by Godzilla, who was wading majestically toward the blacked-out waterfront. No longer detained by tanks or jet fighters, the invincible leviathan was closing in on his primordial prey, driven by a powerful biological instinct.

"The arrogance of Man is thinking Nature is in our control, and not the other way around." Serizawa turned solemnly toward the others and nodded gravely. "Let them fight."

Elle ran for her life, along with everyone else still downtown. Thousands of terrified men, women, and children ran through the streets. Panicked people crowded toward a BART subway entrance, seeking shelter from the titanic monsters that had invaded the city. Billowing plumes of smoke and fire rose to meet the falling rain. Abandoned vehicles clotted the streets. Elle squeezed between an unmoving taxi and a delivery van as she tried to make it to the stairs leading down to the subway. The frantic mob carried her along; she couldn't have changed direction if she'd wanted to. She glanced wildly around her, afraid that the disaster would find her before she could reach safety. She had waited for Ford as long as she could, but obviously they had run out of time. Skyscrapers and office buildings blocked her view, but wide concrete canyons offered fleeting glimpses of the madness that had come to her city.

A giant winged monster, looking something like a huge alien insect, perched atop two adjacent high-rises, straddling them as though there were stilts. Despite her terror, Elle couldn't look away. It was one thing to see a blurry image on TV or the internet; it was something else altogether to actually see a creature that big with your own eyes and be confronted with the escapable fact that such monsters truly existed.

According to the news reports, this was the male "MUTO" and there was a female running amok as well. The creature lifted its head. An ear-piercing howl issued from its jaws.

The ground rumbled in response, throwing Elle to the ground. She threw her hands out in time to keep her face from hitting the wet pavement. Rushing feet pounded past her, and she grasped just how scared Sam must have been when he'd nearly been trampled outside the hospital. She struggled to get to her feet even as the tremors increased in intensity. Through the crush of weaving bodies around her, she gaped in horror as, up the hill in Chinatown, an entire intersection bucked as though it was the epicenter of a quake.

Pavement cracked, wide fissures splitting the asphalt. Steam spewed from broken pipes. Several blocks away, the trembling intersection sank beneath ground level, briefly forming a deep crater, before erupting upward with explosive force. Chunks of cement and blacktop went flying as *another* monster, even larger than the first, surfaced from beneath the city. Eight giant limbs, each sporting vicious claws, pulled the grotesque body up onto the demolished pavement. The female screeched back at the male.

Oh, God, no, Elle thought. *Not the other one, too!*

More bodies shoved past her, obstructing her view of Chinatown and the new creature. She clambered awkwardly to her feet and rejoined the frenzied mob fleeing the creatures. The subway entrance beckoned her and she stumbled down the steps toward the gloomy, unlit station. National Guard members began to herd her through the entrance as they prepared to shut the emergency doors behind them. Elle didn't like the idea of being locked underground in the dark, but it was better than staying out in the open in a city overrun with giant monsters.

GODZILLA

Just as she reached the bottom of the steps, a fierce roar trumpeted across the city. The riveting growl was even louder and more intimidating than the strident howls of the MUTOs. Despite her desperate quest for shelter, Elle turned toward the source of the bellowing roar, as did all the Guards and awestruck citizens around her. Eyes bulged and jaws dropped as Elle and the others stared up the stairs at the riveting sight above. *Oh my God*, Elle thought.

Godzilla rose from the bay and stepped onto the land. His thunderous tread shook the earth as he stomped through industrial shipyards and piers. Office buildings and warehouses were reduced to splinters beneath him. A cable car was crushed beneath a great, clawed foot. His tail whipped behind him, toppling entire buildings. Smoke and flames and billowing clouds of dust and pulverized concrete obscured some details of his appearance, but his overwhelming size and power rendered Elle speechless and made her feel like a minuscule insect by comparison. Godzilla's pitiless eyes fixed on the MUTOs, his ancestral foes. A furious roar shattered windows across the city and left Elle's ears ringing. Everyone around stared up at the raging behemoth in awe and terror.

A giant now strode the earth, terrible in his wrath.

Elle had only a moment to absorb this humbling realization before the Guards pulled her all the way into the station and slammed the corrugated steel doors shut behind her. Impenetrable blackness replaced her view of Godzilla, but his footsteps still shook the station. Petrified people clung to each other in the dark, but Elle was alone with her fears.

She could only pray that, somewhere, the rest of her family was safe.

* * *

General alarm sirens wailed from loudspeakers at the refugee camp in the hills. Holding Sam's hand, Ford frowned as groups of soldiers rushed past them. An announcement issued from the speakers:

"All U.S. Military and Emergency Response personnel, report immediately for duty—"

Ford didn't like the sound of that. Stepping away from Laura Watkins and the other children from the school bus, he called out to the troops.

"Hey! What's happening?!"

"All hands on deck!" an Army soldier shouted back at him. "Those things dragged the nuke downtown! It goes off, so does the city!"

"They need a crew down on the ground to disarm it!" another soldier said.

Ford couldn't believe his ears. He remembered the warhead the helicopters had rescued from the wreckage in the mountains. The plan had been to lure all three monsters out to sea, then detonate the warhead. How the hell had it ended up downtown—where Elle was?

Sam picked up on the heightened anxiety in the air. "Daddy?"

Damn it. Ford hated what he was about to say, but there was no other choice. "Sam, buddy, you need to wait here with these nice people."

Understanding, Laura came forward to take the little boy's hand. "It's okay, Sam—"

"NO!" Sam yelped. Fear contorted his childish features. "DADDY, WAIT!" He broke away from the nurse and rushed frantically toward his father. "I want to stay with you!"

His son's plea hit Ford right in the gut. He couldn't remember Sam ever saying that before, which only made what he had to do that much harder. His throat tightened and his eyes misted over as he knelt down to face the tearful child, while keeping one eye on the departing troops. Ford didn't have long, but he owed his son more than just another abrupt disappearance. There had been too many of those already.

"Alright, squid, listen I—" He realized that this was no time to be glib. He dug deeper, speaking from his heart. "I'm going back to find your mom. That's why I need you to stay here, where it's safe. Can you do that for me?"

Sam absorbed his father's words. It took him a moment, but he wiped his eyes and nodded. He was only four, but he seemed to understand. They both knew how important Elle was. Ford felt incredibly proud of his little boy—and grateful for his courage.

"Daddy loves you so much. You and Mommy are all I've got in this world. I love you more than anything. So I need you to be a brave boy, okay?" Ford's voice cracked as he thought of his own father, who had sacrificed everything to save him so many years ago. Joe Brody had lost the love of his life and the mother of his child. Ford wasn't about to let history repeat itself. "No matter what happens, just know—" He choked up, tears leaking from his eyes. "I'm gonna do everything I can."

Sam responded by throwing his arms around his dad and hugging him tightly. Caught by surprise, and moved more than he would have ever thought possible, Ford squeezed the little boy back for as long as he could spare, which, sadly, wasn't very long at all. More soldiers ran past them, answering the general alarm, and Ford reluctantly let go of his son. Ford started to stand up, then remembered something. He fished a small item from his pocket and placed it in Sam's hand. The boy's eyes widened as he saw what it was.

A toy Navy man, as promised.

He looked up at his dad and their eyes met, truly seeing each other for perhaps the first time. And possibly the last. Wiping his eyes, Ford climbed to his feet and sprinted off after the other troops, while Laura Watkins came forward to comfort Sam. Ford felt confident the boy was in good hands.

Now he just had to save Elle, too.

TWENTY-FOUR

Chinatown was ground zero. Concentric circles spread out on the paper map from the current known location of the stolen ICBM. Stenz grimly contemplated the chart as his analysts pored over what data they could access with the power down. He listened as they formulated a desperate, last-ditch attempt to get troops in place to disarm the warhead before it took out the whole city.

"Thirty thousand feet should be right above the sphere of influence," an analyst estimated.

A more skeptical analyst shook his head. "Even if they survive the jump, we're talking a Hail Mary."

Stenz understood the odds against them, but didn't see any other choice. They could hardly stand by and watch the clock tick down to a thermonuclear explosion in the center of San Francisco. A hundred thousand lives were at risk. If there was even a chance of disarming the warhead, they had to take it, or there wouldn't be a city left to defend.

Racing footsteps rushed past the trailer. Through the windows at the rear of the command center, Stenz saw dozens of soldiers reporting for duty. He took a deep breath and went out to address them. They needed to know what was at stake and how much was expected of them.

He didn't envy them the daunting task ahead.

Captain Hampton presented the plan to Admiral Stenz and the troops inside the command center, which was now crammed with fresh volunteers like Ford. Video feeds from the city showed nothing but static. Computers tried and failed to reboot. Paper charts and satellite photos were mounted behind Hampton, while the admiral stood off to one side. Milling among the other soldiers, Ford spotted Doctors Serizawa and Graham with the brass. He listened attentively.

"The male delivered the warhead here, at the center of downtown," Hampton said, pointing to a table map of the city. An "X" marked the last known location of the nuclear weapon. "Putting more than a hundred thousand citizens in the blast radius. We can't stop it remotely."

Low mutters and whispered remarks rippled among the gathered soldiers. Ford wondered how many of the troops had friends or family in San Francisco. Everyone seemed appropriately disturbed by the prospect of the warhead going off in the city, on top of the unprecedented threat posed by Godzilla and the MUTOs. On top of the nuclear blast, the city also faced the danger of lingering radiation as well. He was gratified that none of his comrades-in-arms even suggested sacrificing the city to get rid of the monsters.

An Army Captain, who identified himself as Quinn, took over the presentation.

"An analog initiator has been installed. And the MUTOs are frying electronics within a five-mile bubble. Approaching overhead is not an option." He placed a transparent plastic dome over the "X" on the map to represent the MUTOs sphere of influence. "That's why we'll be conducting a HALO jump insertion. Jump altitude is thirty thousand feet. Skate just over the top and drop here and here." He indicated two spots atop the plastic dome. "And if you don't eat a skyscraper, we'll rally here and find the bomb."

A bomb technician raised his hand. "Doctor Serizawa, any guesses where to look?"

"Underground," the scientist said. "If the MUTOs have spawned, they'll be building a nest."

"In which case," Graham added, "the bomb going off would only be the beginning. Its fallout would catalyze their eggs. We'd have hundreds of them, annihilating everything."

A hush fell over the command center as that nightmarish possibility sank in. Ford tried to imagine hundreds of creatures like the ones he'd encountered before. He couldn't imagine how civilization—or even humanity—could even survive an onslaught of that magnitude. Sam's future would be utterly wiped out, along with that of every other human being on the planet.

Stenz addressed Quinn. "Captain, once you find the warhead, how long to defuse it?"

"Without having seen the analog mod, sir, I couldn't say, but—"

"Sixty seconds," Ford interrupted. "If I can access it."

All eyes turned toward Ford. Captain Hampton nodded, acknowledging him. "Lieutenant Brody was the only EOD to survive the train attack."

"I retrofitted that device myself," Ford said.

Quinn deferred to Ford's expertise. "Then we'll say sixty seconds, sir, if he can access it. If for whatever reason we can't defuse the device, we go to Plan B." He indicated a pier on the map. "The waterfront should be no more than one click downhill. We get it to the pier, onto a boat, and as far away from the city as possible before it detonates."

Let's hope it doesn't come to that, Ford thought.

"Lieutenant," Hampton said to Ford. "To be clear, we have no extraction plan. If you don't walk out, you don't come back at all."

Ford nodded, as did the other men around him.

"My wife is in the city, sir. I'll do whatever it takes."

That's what Dad asked me to do, Ford recalled, *with his dying breath. I'm not going to let him down... or the rest of my family.*

Serizawa smiled in approval. Ford liked to think Joe Brody would have done the same.

Admiral Stenz watched the men file out, on their way to their mission. With any luck, they would defuse the warhead before it went off, or at least get it safely away from the city. But even if the bomb squad succeeded, that was hardly the end of their worries.

"So they take care of the bomb," he murmured. "Who takes care of the monsters?"

He looked for Serizawa and found that the scientist had stepped outside the command center. Serizawa was gazing out across the water at the city with a pensive expression on his face. The admiral could guess who and what Serizawa was thinking about.

Godzilla.

GODZILLA

* * *

In no time at all, Ford was getting suited up for the HALO jump. Along with a durable green jump suit and a packed parachute, he had also been supplied with a helmet, oxygen mask, gloves, new boots, a heavy-duty altimeter, and a bulging combat pack. As he and dozens of other soldiers prepared to board the C-17 that would drop them from a high altitude into the city, he watched a violent electrical storm brewing over San Francisco. Thunder and lightning added to the tumult battering the city and wasn't going to make the coming jump any safer. Just bad timing, he wondered, or were the MUTOs peculiar auras stirring up the atmosphere somehow? He was no scientist, like those doctors on the *Saratoga*, but he suspected the latter.

"Lieutenant Brody!"

A voice from behind him shouted over the revving plane engines. He turned to see Dr. Serizawa hurrying across the tarmac toward him. Ford had noticed the Japanese scientist with Admiral Stenz earlier. Serizawa must have had spotted him among the troops listening to the admiral's pep talk.

"I believe this belongs to you," the scientist said.

He handed Ford a photo that must have been confiscated from Joe back in Japan. It was a family portrait of the Brody family in happier days. Joe, Sandra, and little Ford beamed at the camera. Ford couldn't believe how young and happy they all looked.

Little did we know...

A bittersweet tide of emotion washed over Ford, who didn't know what to say. He stared at the photo seeing not just the unsuspecting family from long ago, but also, superimposed over the portrait, he and Elle and Sam. A second generation of Brodys facing the same catastrophic forces.

"Time to load up!" an Air Force loadmaster shouted. "Move it out!"

Ford accepted the photo gratefully and tucked it into a Velcro pocket on his jump suit. He nodded at Serizawa, too choked up to speak, and turned toward the waiting aircraft. His fellow soldiers were already boarding the plane. They had to move quickly if they wanted to get to that warhead in time.

Assuming they could get past the monsters, that is.

"Lieutenant!" Serizawa called again. "He would be proud!"

I hope so, Ford thought. He glanced back at Serizawa. Ford hoped he could be half as determined as his father had been. Joe Brody had never given up trying to find the truth and warn the world. Ford wasn't going to let his dad's sacrifices be in vain.

He boarded the plane.

The sun was setting as the C-17 approached the city at an altitude of 35,000 feet, which was believed to be safely above the MUTOs' sphere of influence. Seated in the cargo bay with the other troops, Ford assumed the brass had some evidence to support that assumption. Even so, he caught himself holding his breath as the plane came over the city. Crashing the Globemaster into the middle of downtown wasn't going to do anyone any good.

The low bass hum of the plane's engines continued uninterrupted, at least for the present. Ford chose to take that as a good sign as he peered out a window at their destination. Thick black smoke and heavy cloud cover largely hid the city below, but he could dimly make out immense shapes grappling in the haze. It appeared that the monsters were already locked in mortal combat. They charged at each other like divine beasts out of myth and legend.

Good, Ford thought. *Maybe they'll keep each other occupied while we deal with the warhead.*

He removed the family portrait from his pocket and contemplated it one last time. The Brodys as they once were, as he and Elle and Sam could still be, if they survived the perilous hours ahead. It felt as though, one way or another, the unbearable trial that had tested his family for fifteen years was finally coming to a close. He hoped that, against all odds, they could still arrive at a happy ending somewhere down the line.

Glancing around, he saw that the other HALO jumpers were each preparing themselves in their own way. Photos of loved ones were cherished and heads were bowed in prayer or meditation. Everyone appeared deep in thought, searching for the courage and will to do what needed to be done, as well as remembering why exactly it mattered so very much. Across from Ford, a redheaded young soldier prayed softly to himself, reading aloud from a pocket Bible:

"... now as we leave one another, remember the comrades who are not with us today. 'And He will send His angels with great trumpets.'"

The loadmaster's booming voice roused everyone from their private thoughts.

"One minute, one more time!" he announced. "No comms at all down below. Use your flares to stay together!"

The rear bay doors opened and a ferocious rush of air drowned out any further discussion. Row by row, the HALO jumpers rose from their seats and headed briskly toward the ramp. The first in line ignited their flares and leapt out of the plane.

Here we go, Ford thought.

Ford returned the photo to his pocket and got his oxygen mask in place. HALO stood for High Altitude, Low Opening, which made the breathing apparatus a must. Joining the line, he made his way toward the ramp. Despite his resolve, he felt more than a flicker of trepidation. He was a Navy bomb disposal tech, not a Special Forces guy. He didn't have a lot of experience with HALO jumps.

He didn't hesitate when his turn came, however. Sucking down a deep breath of O2, he threw himself out of the plane... for Elle's sake.

The roaring in his ears went away, and the world went strangely quiet. All that could be heard was the thin air whistling faintly above the clouds. He extended his arms and legs to slow his fall, as he'd been instructed, while accelerating toward terminal velocity. Dozens of paratroopers free-fell through the darkening sky. Blood-red smoke trailed from the blazing flares strapped to their ankles as they descended toward the embattled city like falling angels, minus the trumpets. Lightning flashed in the turbulent clouds and smoke below. Thunder rumbled, but Ford had no idea if it was coming from the storm or the clashing monsters or some dreadful combination thereof. His own flare ignited as he plunged into the clouds.

Falling at nearly 125 miles per hour, he passed quickly through the clammy mist, somehow managing to avoid being electrocuted by a random bolt of lightning. The downtown area—or what was left of it—came into view. The devastation was staggering. Despite what he'd already witnessed overseas, Ford was shocked by what he saw.

A giant sinkhole, much like the one in Japan, had swallowed Chinatown. A wide path of destruction, like the one in Hawaii, had torn across The Embarcadero to Telegraph Hill, where Godzilla and the male MUTO could be glimpsed fighting amidst crumbling high-rises and residential buildings. Clouds of smoke and dust billowed up from the war zone. Fires blazed within the demolished buildings. As in Honolulu, Godzilla had the advantage of size over the other monster, but the male appeared in no hurry to retreat this time. The winged creature was standing its ground, with the surrounding neighborhoods paying the price. Angry snarls and screeches were punctuated by crashing buildings. Thunderclaps, reverberating overhead, provided a percussive soundtrack to the cataclysmic tussle, whose outcome seemed far from certain. It was survival of the fittest—on a grandiose scale.

Ford dropped between rows of buildings that blocked his view of the battling monsters. He tugged on his ripcord and was yanked upward as his main canopy deployed. A square, "ram-air" parafoil inflated above him and he used the steering toggles to come in for a landing on a rubble-strewn street somewhere in the ruins of the Financial District. He touched down with an awkward stutter-step onto the cracked and broken pavement, without actually falling or breaking anything, and stumbled to a halt.

Whew, he thought. *Made it.*

He was relieved to be back on solid ground again. Tugging off his oxygen mask, he took a deep breath of real air, which smelled of smoke and ash. He glanced around warily, but did not spy any monsters in his immediate vicinity. Smashed skyscrapers jutting up from the ravaged streets suggested that the monsters had already passed through this district, leaving little intact. Night had fallen so that only the glow from scattered fires illuminated the darkened city. From the sound of things, however, the beasts were still raging several blocks away. It dawned on him that he'd had yet to see the female MUTO, the one that had attacked the missile train. He had to assume that it was abroad as well.

Better keep my eyes out for that bitch, he thought.

Shedding his 'chute, which was draped over the rubble, he hastily rescued a rifle and flashlight from his gear bag and fitted the light to the barrel of his gun. A gust of wind blew aside the voluminous nylon canopy, exposing charred human bodies lying amidst the debris, half-buried beneath fallen chunks of masonry. A blackened arm stretched lifelessly from beneath a mass of crumbling concrete and rebar.

More collateral damage, Ford realized, of the timeless feud between Godzilla and the MUTOs. He winced at the sight, wondering briefly whom the burned bodies had belonged to and what families would mourn them, but he also knew that the death rate would skyrocket unless he and his comrades completed their mission and disarmed the stolen warhead. He had to keep moving.

Anxious to reconnect with the others, Ford looked up and down the damaged and deserted streets. The unsettling darkness failed to mask the extreme damage done to his hometown. Once known as "The Wall Street of the West," the Financial District now looked as though the Big One had finally hit. Gleaming towers of glass and steel, built to withstand all but the most powerful earthquakes, were now smoking husks. A toppled skyscraper leaned precarious against its neighbor. Broken glass, mangled steel beams, and crumbling blocks on concrete littered the streets and sidewalks. Elevated sky-bridges had crashed to earth. The Transamerica Pyramid, once the tallest structure in the city, was missing its tip and several of its upper stories. Abandoned cars, trucks, and buses had been crushed by falling debris.

Ford stared aghast at the devastation. The monsters had done all this—in less than an hour?

A titanic roar jolted him back to the crisis at hand. Ford spotted more soldiers running up a street one block over. He hustled after them, readying his gear on the run. A rifle hadn't done him much good against the female up in the mountains, but he sure as hell wasn't going to go up against the creatures unarmed. Better to go down fighting if he had to.

Panting, he caught up with several other soldiers. An EOD specialist named Bennett was busily assembling a device that resembled a Geiger counter, while the other soldiers conferred tersely, comparing notes on what they'd seen on the way down. Ford figured that some of them were still coming to grips with laying eyes on the monsters for the first time.

Bennett finished assembling the tracking device. It started clacking immediately, especially when he pointed it up toward Chinatown, where the warhead was reported to be.

"We're moving up the hill," their jumpmaster said gruffly. "Keep it spread out. Move out!"

The soldiers took only a moment to get their bearings before jogging up Grant Avenue. Within minutes, they passed through the ruins of the "Dragon Gate" at the southern entrance to Chinatown. Fallen ceramic tiles shattered beneath their boots, while the head of one of the gateway's two guardian dragons stared up from the rubble. Advancing into the heart of Chinatown, they hurried past trampled shops, temples, banks, and restaurants. An upended cable car lay on its side, squashed bodies spilling out of it. A street lamp crafted to resemble a bright red pagoda leaned precariously over the obliterated avenue. Colorful flags and banners lay trampled on the ground. As they neared the crest of the hill, the infernal orange glow of an unseen fire could be seen through a dense wall of smoke. The veiled flames, and the clacking of the tracking device, drew the troops on.

Getting warmer, Ford thought. *Let's hope we don't run into any company.*

One by one, the soldiers warily entered the haze. Ford found his visibility cut almost to zero and relied on the flashlight mounted on his rifle to pierce the smoke. He aimed the beam at the ground before him to keep his footing, but then his flashlight dimmed. He smacked it with his palm, hoping to restore it, but the beam kept flickering. By now, Ford knew that meant.

A MUTO was near.

He wasn't the only soldier experiencing technical difficulties or aware of their significance. He spied other flashlights sputtering in the smoke. Alert troops hefted their weapons and took cover behind wrecked and overturned cars. Ford darted behind a crushed SUV. The jump master, Quinn, whistled and put a finger to his lips, signaling quiet.

Damn right, Ford thought. The last thing they wanted to do was attract a monster's attention.

But while the rest of them kept quiet, the tracking device was clacking louder than ever. Ford flinched at the racket as Bennett aimed the device straight ahead at the smoke and flames. He nodded at Quinn, who got the message.

The warhead was close.

The wall of smoke thinned out, revealing the female crouched above the giant sinkhole Ford had spotted from above. An involuntary shudder went through Ford; the last time he'd seen this creature, it had been tearing apart the bridge and locomotive in the mountains, sending Tre and Waltz and the others to their deaths. It hadn't gotten any less terrifying in the interim. Its six lower limbs straddled the pit, while its smaller forearms were still large enough to qualify as enormous. Drool dripped from its beak. Its bony carapace caught the glare from the fires. Lightning flashed overhead; Ford wondered again if the MUTO was somehow causing it.

Hunkered down behind the available cover, the troops shared frustrated looks. The warhead was apparently down in the sinkhole somewhere, but how were they supposed to get past the female to reach it? Ford glanced at his ticking wristwatch. Time was running out.

Now what?

Ford was stumped, uncertain how to proceed, when booming footsteps shook the night. The thunderous tread triggered immediate flashbacks to Honolulu Airport—and his first sight of an even more colossal monster than the MUTO guarding the pit. The ground shook beneath Ford. Looking back, he already knew what he was going to see.

Godzilla lumbered toward them, cresting the hill behind them. His eyes narrowed as he spied the female. He dropped into a defensive crouch, like a fighter preparing for battle. He threw back his head and roared loud enough that Ford's heavy-duty helmet provided no protection at all. There was no mistaking the primordial fury in that roar; Ford realized in horror that he and the other soldiers were stuck between the two monsters.

The female responded to the challenge with a defiant howl of its own. It sprang from the sinkhole and skittered across the ruins to face Godzilla. Endangered troopers dashed out of the way of her great, clawed limbs. Ford saw a hind leg crashing down toward him and dived for safety only seconds before it flattened the crumpled SUV he had been hiding behind. Rolling across the broken pavement, he saw the MUTO slam into Godzilla with extreme force. Grappling furiously, they tumbled down the hill, disappearing into the smoke and fog.

This is our chance, Ford realized.

The soldiers sprinted toward the unguarded sinkhole, peering down over its rim. The size and depth of the pit was even more impressive up close; it was possibly even bigger than the sinkhole that had swallowed the nuclear power plant in Japan. At least a block of homes and buildings appeared to have fallen into the pit. Ford did not relish climbing the crumbling, debris-strewn slope in search of the missing warhead. Fires burned down in the stygian depths of the abyss. Smoke rose from below.

Bennett employed his tracker. Rapid clacking pointed the troops toward an open fissure leading down into the side of the sinkhole. A hellish orange glow emanated from what looked like small cave opening. Ford felt the heat of burning wreckage as the soldiers cautiously ventured through the entrance and found themselves inside an uprooted Victorian row house, hanging upside-down from its foundations. An inverted staircase looked like something out of an M.C. Escher drawing. Tinny music issued from an antique music box lying sideways on the ceiling. Ford felt as though he'd stepped through the looking-glass into some sort of surreal fever-dream.

This just keeps getting weirder and weirder, he thought. *I can barely remember what normal is anymore.*

The troops hurried through the capsized house and out an open doorway. Leaving the bizarre setting behind, they found themselves faced with an infernal vista that could have easily passed for the lower pits of Hell. A huge cavernous burrow had been carved out beneath Chinatown, littered with debris from the ransacked city above. Bits and pieces of the city were strewn about randomly. An overturned gasoline tanker was partially buried in the rubble. A bronze dragon guarded heaps of broken refuse. A church steeple lay on its side.

They descended to the floor of the cavern. Thankfully, their flashlights were working better now that the female had charged off to fight Godzilla. Bright white beams soon located a huge organic shape hanging like a stalactite from the ceiling above them. It took Ford and the others a moment to realize that they had found what they were searching for: the nuclear warhead was encased inside layers of a hardened, translucent secretion. The outermost layers of the shell were still wet and viscous. They oozed slowly down the sides of the trapped weapon.

Ford gazed up at the suspended warhead. He could only assume that the male had brought his prize to the female, perhaps as some sort of courtship ritual. No doubt Serizawa and Graham would have a theory to explain how it all worked, but Ford didn't care about that right now. All that mattered was disarming the bomb before the detonator went off.

At least we've found it, he thought hopefully. *Perhaps we still have a chance.*

A tremor shook the cavern, causing dust and gravel to rain down on them. It felt like an earthquake, but Ford knew better. The earth was shaking because of the titanic conflict being waged above. Godzilla had hunted the MUTOs halfway around the world, but now the chase was over and the final battle was underway.

With a nuclear warhead added to the mix.

TWENTY-FIVE

Godzilla clashed with the female in the blazing ruins of the Financial District. Sky-high smoke and flames provided an apocalyptic backdrop to their savage combat, which was being fought furiously amidst the demolished skyscrapers. Godzilla snapped and slashed at the female, who locked her jaws onto his scaly shoulder. The mighty saurian towered at least fifty feet above the vicious, multi-legged parasite and was significantly heavier and stronger as well, but female did not back off. Grimacing in pain, Godzilla tore himself free from the MUTO's fangs and spun away from her. His spiked tail whipped around to lash the female, who was sent tumbling down Broadway, carving out another swath of destruction. Her flailing arms and legs smashed through buildings large and small. Flames and explosions erupted in her wake.

Sensing victory, Godzilla closed in for the kill. The desperate female hurriedly righted herself and swung one of her clawed middle arms at Godzilla, but he dodged the attack and charged forward to pin her against a high-rise office building. The MUTO thrashed and screeched as Godzilla pummeled her with his fists and snapped at her twisting head and thorax. His jaws were going for her skull when the entire building suddenly collapsed under the force of the struggle. A mountain of sundered steel and concrete caved in on thefemale, burying her beneath the debris.

Snarling, Godzilla loomed above his fallen foe. He raised his right foot over the female, preparing to squash her into the ground, when the male came swooping down from the sky to defend his mate. The winged MUTO barreled into Godzilla, knocking him off his feet. Locked in combat, the monsters rolled across the district, grinding landmark buildings into dust. Their growls and screeches were matched by the rumble of disintegrating hotels, banks, and museums.

The earth shook all the way up to Chinatown.

The seismic shocks were coming fast and furious, causing the entire cavern to tremble and heaps of debris to shift in an unsettling manner, but Ford and the other soldiers redoubled their efforts to liberate the ticking warhead from the hard, resin-like substance it was encased in. They had already managed to break the weapon loose from the ceiling and lower it to the floor of the cavern; now they were chipping away at the sticky secretion with the butts of their rifles. Concentrating on the tip of the re-entry vehicle, they managed to expose enough of the casing that, grunting with effort, they could begin to pry off the nose cone.

Here it comes, Ford thought. *Almost there...*

To his surprise, the remaining secretion began to pulse with light. *Did we trigger that with our hammering,* Ford wondered, *or was it the tremors?* The cool effulgence grew in intensity and began to spread throughout the cavern. The soldiers backed away momentarily, caught off-guard by the unexpected bioluminescence. The glow rippled upward to light up the entire cavern. Ford glanced at the ceiling, where the wavering light now appeared to be concentrated, and gasped in shock.

No longer hidden in darkness, thousands of bulging egg sacs hung from the ceiling, which was positively encrusted with the pulsing organisms. Ford recalled the photos Serizawa had shown him upon the *Saratoga* as well as the egg he had briefly glimpsed on the underside of the female MUTO in the mountains. As nearly as he could tell, these new sacs were identical to the ones found in the Philippines fifteen years ago. The ones that had eventually spawned the two MUTOs.

They've already mated, he realized, *and this is their nest.*

The fertilized eggs continued to flash, as though reacting to their food source being disturbed. Something had to be done about the eggs, Ford knew, but first they needed to deal with the warhead or nothing else mattered.

The nose cone came loose, clattering onto the floor of the nest. The soldiers huddled around the exposed warhead and detonator. Flashlight beams penetrated the small window above the timing mechanism. The intricate gears continued to turn and engage, ticking down to Armageddon. Moving carefully, despite the urgency of the situation, the men took hold of the warhead by a set of metal handholds and eased it out of the cone-shaped reentry vehicle.

Easy does it, Ford thought.

Godzilla was outnumbered two to one. Acting in tandem, the MUTOs circled their relentless foe, who was undaunted by the odds against him. His eyes narrowed in anticipation of the parasites' attack. His nostrils flared and he bared his fangs. He roared defiantly, challenging the MUTOs. He had not come all this way to shrink from the battle.

The MUTOs were prey. Dangerous prey, but prey regardless. They had to be destroyed.

Howling in unison, the MUTOs pounced on him from above and below.

A tremor shook the subway platform, causing dust and debris to rain down from the ceiling. Trapped underground, while giant monsters overran the city above, Elle and throng of other frightened people backed away fearfully from the thunderous impact. A baby cried in the arms of a young couple who huddled together fearfully, protecting the child with their own bodies.

Alone and scared, Elle didn't know whether to envy them for being together or to be thankful that Sam was hopefully far from the embattled city by now. Probably a little bit of both.

She squinted at her phone. There were no new messages from Ford, not that she was likely to get a signal down here. She hoped to God that he was safe and on his way to find her. But would there still be a city left by the time he got here? It sounded like armies were clashing up above.

The lights flickered overhead and her phone died. People gasped and looked up in alarm as the lights sputtered and died, throwing them all into the dark. Panicked people screamed. Blackness swallowed them, so that all that was left was fear—and the earth-shaking sound of monsters destroying the city.

Be careful, Ford, she thought. *Wherever you are.*

The soldiers lowered the heavy warhead onto the floor of the nest. Divorced from its massive rocket boosters, the warhead was still at least ten feet long and five across. On closer inspection, it was obvious that the casing had been badly damaged during its travails. Bennett tried to pry open the access panel to the timer, but the metal was warped and refused to budge. Quinn and a few of the others added their strength to his, but it was no use. The latch was jammed.

"It's sealed shut," Bennett said. "We need time to get this open!"

"We don't have time," another soldier objected. "Let's haul it out of here!"

Ford shoved his way to the front of the huddle and knelt down beside the warhead. He extracted a kit from a Velcro pocket on his flight suit. He unsealed the kit to expose a set of intricate tools, including screw drivers, crimpers, surgical scissors, forceps, tweezers, and a dental mirror. They were similar to the tools he had used to disarm any number of explosive devices in Iraq and Afghanistan. He had never used them on a nuclear bomb before, but...

"I can do it!" he insisted. "Just give me some light!"

Flashlight beams converged on the latch, providing a steady white light that Ford vastly preferred to the rippling glow of the agitated egg sacs. He tried to tune out the pulsing bioluminescence, and the rumble of the warring monsters, to concentrate on the task at hand. The warhead was the primary threat now. Everything else, even Godzilla, was secondary.

I can do this, he thought. *I have to do this.*

* * *

GODZILLA

The city trembled as Godzilla dropped to one knee, besieged by the MUTOs. The parasites' combined assault was enough to stagger even the mighty leviathan. The male dived at him from above, gouging Godzilla's dorsal fins with his claws. Broken shards of fin rained down onto the pulverized streets, adding to the heaped debris, even as the female sprang at Godzilla, slashing at his throat with her talons, which sliced through his scaly armor to the vulnerable flesh below. Blood seeped through the bony plates. The female howled triumphantly.

Godzilla reeled beneath the joint attack, but did not fall. His maw opened wide and, choking and gasping, he exhaled a gust of rippling, super-heated vapor. A spark ignited at the back of his throat and a searing blast of blue-white fire sprayed from his jaws.

Taking the full force of the Godzilla's volcanic breath, the female screeched in agony and collapsed in a heap of twitching arms and legs. Her chitinous exoskeleton was scorched and blackened in places. Ichor leaked from cracks in her shell. Eight limbs vibrated spastically. She wasn't dead, but she had been hurt and stunned by the blistering incendiary attack. Unable to defend herself, at least for the moment, she was ripe for the kill.

Godzilla climbed back to his feet, like a mountain thrusting up from the earth, and glared at the downed female. He opened his jaws once more, intending to incinerate her completely, but as his fiery breath flared up the male flew in low overhead and clapped his iridescent black wings together. A luminous pulse rippled through the air and snuffed the bioelectric spark in Godzilla's throat. The draconic flames belching from his jaws sputtered and died out.

Godzilla blinked in confusion. Smoke billowed from his

nostrils. He tried again to summon his most powerful weapon, but felt only an irritating tickle within his gullet. The spark refused to ignite. The flames would not come.

Frustrated, he glared at the soaring male, whom had interfered with his kill. He snarled and gnashed his fangs. His tail whipped back and forth in anger.

The male had done this to him. The male would suffer.

Flashlight bulbs exploded inside the nest, so that only the glow of smoldering wreckage and the strobe-like luminosity of the hanging egg sacs lit up the underground burrow. Startled soldiers swore profanely.

"Another EMP!" Bennett exclaimed.

"Bulb just blew," another EOD specialist blurted. "I'm out."

Still trying to get at the bomb's sealed timer, Ford squinted at the jammed latch, which was stubbornly resisting his efforts to get it open. The dimming light only made his task harder. He could barely see what he was doing.

"I need more light," he said.

In charge of the operation, Quinn made a command decision. "Time for Plan B. Let's get this thing out of here! Come on, come on!"

Ford understood the man's reasoning. If they couldn't disarm the bomb, then maybe they could still get it out to sea before the warhead detonated. He stepped back and let six burly soldiers hoist the warhead by the handles on each side. Grunting in effort, they toted it back the way they'd come, retracing their path up the rubble-covered slope to the inverted doorway of the topsy-turvy Victorian home. Gathering up his tools, Ford hurried after them, only to pause on the threshold of the buried house. He glanced back over his shoulder at the multitude of pulsing egg sacs encrusting the ceiling. There had to be dozens of the eggs, each capable of hatching yet another MUTO.

The enormity of the threat was not lost on Ford. Two MUTOs were bad enough, but an entire swarm of them?

Uh-uh, Ford thought. *Not a chance.*

He signaled the other men to go on without him. One way or another, he had to end this.

Godzilla and the male faced off amidst the burning skyscrapers. They eyed each other warily, each seeking an advantage or opening. The MUTO glided between the surviving high-rises, keeping just out of reach of Godzilla's outstretched forearms and claws. Baring his fangs, Godzilla dared the male to get closer.

But the standoff gave the female a chance to recover from Godzilla's fire breath. Singed and smoking, she rose up on her hind legs and lunged at Godzilla. Hatred burned in her crimson eyes. She screeched in rage, out for revenge.

The male attacked simultaneously.

The upended gasoline tanker was right where Ford had seen it before, partially buried in debris on the floor of the sinkhole. Ford clambered up the exposed underbelly of tanker to reach the pipe valve and hammered at it with the butt of his rifle. He was beyond exhausted, but adrenaline and fear for his family kept him going. A couple of solid whacks bent the valve. Encouraged, Ford pounded it again—and the valve snapped off altogether.

Fuel gushed from the pipe, the gasoline smell invading

Ford's nose and mouth. The fuel spilled down the belly of the tanker onto the floor of the pit, where numerous small fires still smoldered. The gas washed over the bronze dragon and the other debris, streaming toward the flames.

Ford wasn't going to stick around for the fireworks. Leaping down from the tanker, he landed roughly on the loose debris, twisting his ankle. Despite the pain, he sprinted out of the cavern, making tracks for the surface. His boots pounded against the ceiling of the upside-down Victorian.

This was going to be close.

The MUTOs pressed their attack, ganging up on Godzilla. He staggered backwards down a wide, wrecked boulevard, inflicting yet more damage to the city with every faltering step. His jagged fins scraped against a red granite building, shredding its elegant façade. Gasping for breath, he choked on the swirling smoke and ash and the volatile gases filling his lungs. He tried to burn it all away, but his hot breath caught in his throat, scalding it. Boiling blood and saliva trickled down his gullet.

The male strafed him from above, clawing at Godzilla's head and shoulders. A half-dozen talons went for his eyes, and Godzilla barely managed to keep them at bay with his snapping jaws. The female sank her fangs into his neck, holding back his muscular forearms with six arms of her own. Godzilla roared in pain, wanting to fry her to ashes, but could muster only a faint crackle of electricity in his throat, which wasn't enough to ignite the fire. His tail lashed the air, striking only a historic clock tower, which was knocked off its foundations. The tower crashed into an adjacent building, which collapsed onto the block beyond, the wholesale destruction going unnoticed by any of the battling monsters.

Bricks and mortar cascaded down onto the battered streets and sidewalks. Flames burst from ruptured fuel lines.

Godzilla was losing ground. Cold reptilian blood streamed from deep bites and claw marks in his scaly hide. The frenzied battle reopened the wounds he had sustained from the planes and tanks. Blood loss sapped his indomitable strength. Weakening, he dropped to one knee, crushing a covered bus stop and an ornamental fountain beneath it. His jaws snapped impotently, unable to latch onto either foe. He growled feebly, grimacing in pain, as the male's claws carved another chunk out of his fins. A beaked jaw pecked at his skull, while the female's fangs embedded themselves deeper into his throat. Down on one knee, it was all Godzilla could do to keep semi-upright. The MUTOs had him on the defensive.

He was fighting for his life—and he was losing.

Breathing hard, his heart pounding, Ford had just made it out of the pit when he heard the gasoline-flooded sinkhole burst into flames. A tremendous whoosh of heat and light came rushing up from the underground nest. Ford kept on running, desperate to put plenty of distance between himself and the newborn inferno, but his boot caught on a fallen street sign, slowing his escape.

Damn it!

He yanked his boot loose a moment too late. The pit exploded in flames behind him, throwing burning debris in all directions. The force of the explosion flipped Ford and sent him flying away from the blast. An enormous fireball erupted from the butchered heart of Chinatown.

Thick black smoke enveloped Ford and everything went dark.

TWENTY-SIX

The fireball rose high into the stormy sky. The billowing conflagration was visible all the way down to the ravaged Financial District, where a primeval battle for survival was playing out on a Brobdingnagian scale. The explosion caught the monsters' attention, interrupting their elemental fight to the death.

The female started in shock, sensing the danger to her nest. Her limbs drew back spasmodically. Her red eyes rolled in their sockets. Instantly forgetting about Godzilla, she yanked her fangs from his neck and bounded away from him. Landing heavily on the razed street, she scurried away from the fight, heading back uphill toward Chinatown. A keening wail betrayed her distress... and fury.

Intent on her burning nest, she rushed right past the troops bearing the warhead, ignoring the minuscule soldiers as they hauled the bomb downhill through the Financial District toward the bay. A collective shudder went through the men as the nightmarish arthropod briefly crossed their path, but they did not question their good fortune when she left them alone. Leaving Chinatown behind, they hustled as quickly as they could with their ticking burden, making it another block before a gigantic clawed foot slammed down from the sky directly in front of them. They tilted their heads back in order to take in the awe-inspiring owner of the foot.

No longer outnumbered, Godzilla rose to his feet and roared ferociously at the sky. Blood poured from deep gashes on his throat, but he was free of the female's biting jaws at last. He bared his fangs at the flying male, taunting him, and swung his tail back and forth. Scarred fins shed loose chunks of scale and bone. Godzilla raised his clawed fists and waited for his remaining foe.

The enraged male took the bait. It dived at its enemy, but this time Godzilla was ready for him. Unencumbered by a second foe, he lunged forward and caught the MUTO's left wing in his jaws. He bit down hard, shredding its hard protective sheath and the veiny membrane beneath. His fangs punched through the scales covering the underside of the wing.

The male screeched and spat, flapping wildly in a frantic attempt to free his wing. His entire body bucked and twisted, but Godzilla just bit down harder, clenching his jaws to keep his prey from escaping. Broken scales, the size of roof tiles, fell from Godzilla's jaws onto the rubble below. The wing crunched beneath his fangs. Ichor spurted into his mouth.

Godzilla tasted victory.

Desperate and dying, the male tore himself free, leaving a huge segment of wing behind. The shredded segment twitched between Godzilla's jaws for a moment or two before going limp and lifeless. He spit the chewed-up wing parts onto the street and growled menacingly at the crippled parasite.

Who was winning now?

Screeching in agony, the male fluttered erratically above the ruins. Barely able to stay aloft, the MUTO was mortally wounded, but Godzilla wasn't done with him yet. With the last of his strength, Godzilla charged at the injured creature. Battered and bleeding, he drove the male through a fifty-story skyscraper two blocks away, destroying the building. Thousands of tons of glass and steel and concrete caved in around the monsters, entombing them in a mountain of fresh debris. The male's dying howl was lost in the deafening roar of the skyscraper's collapse. A tremendous cloud of smoke and dust rose to hide the destruction.

The city streets shuddered.

Another tremor, even stronger than before, shook the blacked-out subway station. Dust and debris fell from the ceiling and the subway entrance caved in. Trapped in the dark with dozens of equally panicked strangers, Elle screamed as the impact knocked her off her feet.

Sparks sprayed from the bottom of the damaged warhead as the soldiers dragged down it down an evacuated pier at Fisherman's Wharf. A tour boat offering "See the bay" cruises was tied up in a slip. Cursive writing on its prow identified the boat as the *Angel of the Bay*. Commandeering the vessel, the troops lugged the warhead up the gangway.

Quinn raced ahead of his men to reach the helm. Prying open the ignition panel, he struggled to hot-wire the vessel, while keeping one eye on the bomb and the burning city behind them. The monsters appeared occupied at the moment, but it was only a matter of time before one of the MUTOs started tracking the recovered warhead. Quinn wanted to be well out to sea before that happened.

He realized that the odds that he and his men would be able to get away from the bomb before it exploded were shrinking by the minute, but he couldn't think about that now. Their lives would be a small price to pay if they saved San Francisco from going the way of Hiroshima. That would still leave the rampaging monsters to deal with, but someone else was going to have to get that job done. Just keeping the warhead from destroying the city was good enough for him.

He trusted that every one of his men felt the same.

The pier rattled and shook. Looking up, Quinn spotted the female charging onto the hilltop where Chinatown had once been. Lieutenant Ford's work, no doubt. The eight-legged creature was silhouetted against the blazing fire consuming her nest. Quinn smiled grimly. He hoped the murderous monster choked on the fumes.

So much for your babies, bitch.

Now they just needed to get the bomb clear of the city. Sweating, he revved the engines, which fired up noisily. The ship's lights came on.

All right, Quinn thought. *That's more like it!*

An anguished wail roused Ford from unconsciousness. At first he thought maybe it was just the ringing in his ears, left over from the explosion, but then his eyes fluttered open to see the female towering above him, howling over the destruction of her nest. Her charred carapace had seen better days, but she still looked perfectly capable of wiping Ford out with one flick of a claw.

Like the MUTO, Ford was in bad shape. His flight suit was torn and scorched. Soot caked his face and his hair and eyebrows were singed. Blood seeped from countless cuts and scrapes, some serious. Nothing seemed broken, but his already-battered body felt as though it had been dragged for miles behind a locomotive. His mouth tasted of blood and ash and a couple of his teeth were loose. Every muscle ached and his head was throbbing. The ringing in ears melded with the wail of the angry MUTO.

Ford held his breath, hoping to escape the monster's notice. A racking cough threatened to escape his chest, but he clenched his jaws to hold it in. He had survived the female's attack on the missile train. Maybe he could do so again, or had his luck finally run out?

The MUTO's glowing sensors twitched and her huge anvil-shaped head began to swing toward Ford. Sprawled helplessly amidst the rubble of a demolished street, he figured he was a goner. He could only pray that he was buying time for Quinn and the others to get the warhead out of the city. His biggest regret was that he hadn't managed to reunite his family one last time.

Goodbye, Elle. I'm sorry I didn't make it back to you.

He braced himself for the end, hoping it would be quick at least, but then the female paused and turned her attention downhill instead, where the deck lights of a tour boat could be glimpsed through the smoky haze. Pivoting atop her mammoth limbs, she lumbered downhill toward the waterfront. Ford guessed that she was going after the other soldiers—and the warhead.

Forgotten by the MUTO, Ford let out a gasp that turned

into a violent coughing jag. He spat blood onto the fractured pavement and debris. His head spun and it would have been easy to slip back into unconsciousness, leaving the fight to others, but instead, wincing in pain, he climbed awkwardly to his feet and limped downhill after the monster. Blood soaked through clothes, making them stick to his skin. Bruised ribs ached in protest. He wasn't sure what he could do in his current condition, especially against a furious three-hundred-foot-tall insect monster, but he knew one thing for sure. The city—and Elle—were still in danger.

And he had a mission to fulfill.

Crap, Quinn thought. *She's coming for us.*

The pier shook as the female charged down the hill toward the wharf. The warhead landed with a thud on the deck of the tour boat and a soldier raced to unhitch the dock-line binding the vessel to the slip. Quinn's hand hovered impatiently on the throttle as he watched the monster close in on them.

Could the female swim? Quinn had no idea, but maybe there was still a chance they could leave the MUTO behind before it reclaimed the warhead. As the line came free, he thought, *Let's get the hell out of here!*

He revved the throttle—and the engine died.

Quinn cursed and slammed the helm with his fist. A shadow fell over the boat, blocking the light from the fires, and he looked up to see the female looming over the wharf. A pulsing electromagnetic aura emanated from her immense form. The EMP had killed the engines, but not, unfortunately, the warhead counting down on the deck. The soldiers on the boat stared up in horror at the MUTO.

We're screwed, Quinn realized.

GREG COX

* * *

Despite his injuries, Ford hurried toward the wharf as fast as he could manage. At least it was downhill all the way; in his current state, he wasn't sure he could manage a steep climb. Gravity was on his side for once, which was about the only advantage he had going for him. He stumbled through the ruins of the Financial District, overwhelmed by the devastation surrounding him, which made the ghost town back in the Q-Zone seem like a vacation spot by comparison. The air was thick with dust and ash, irritating Ford's eyes and throat. Charred paper from busted-out offices wafted down from above like snow. Lightning streaked the cloudy night sky. Dawn was still hours away. Ford wondered if the city would be around to greet it.

A loud, rhythmic rasping could be heard over the crackling of the flames and the noisy settling of the collapsed buildings. Puzzled by the unnerving sound, it took Ford a moment to realize that it was the *breathing* of an enormous beast, coming from far too close at hand. He slowed to stop and looked around. The suffocating cloud of dust began to settle and he squinted through the haze, searching for the source of the labored breathing. His eyes bulged as he spotted Godzilla lying beneath the ruins of a collapsed skyscraper.

The toppled monster looked as bad as Ford felt. His scaly body was scarred and bleeding, raw muscle and sinew showing through his armored plates in places. An ugly gash stretched across his neck. Stalactite-like fangs were cracked and chipped. Blood and bile dripped from his sagging jaws. His tremendous tail twitched feebly beneath the debris. Ford felt a twinge of sympathy for the injured behemoth, which had inadvertently saved him from the other monsters at least twice. The MUTOs had obviously done a number on him.

You and me both, Ford thought.

For a long moment, man and beast locked eyes across the desolate ruins. Two weary warriors, injured on the same battleground. A severed black wing, protruding from the rubble, gave Ford hope that Godzilla had killed at least the male MUTO. Ford nodded in approval, grateful for the destruction of the creature that had killed his parents and so many others. According to Dr. Serizawa, he recalled, Godzilla had left humanity alone for ages until the MUTOs lured him up from the depths.

Bursts of gunfire down at the wharf jolted Ford from his reverie. Leaving Godzilla behind, he sprinted toward the action, tracking bloody boot prints behind him.

Looks like my war's not over yet.

Racing downhill on adrenaline, he saw Quinn and the others opening fire on the female from the deck of a commandeered tour boat. The men unloaded their M4s at the MUTO in a final, defiant blaze of glory. Muzzles flashed and bullets flew, chipping away at the monster's scorched black carapace. Smoke filled the air between the troops and the female, but Ford spied the warhead resting on the deck of the boat, which appeared dead in the water. He hoped Bennett had managed to disarm it already, but suspected that was just wishful thinking.

The countdown was still on.

The female reared backwards on her hind legs, momentarily taken aback by the troops' firepower. Then, screeching furiously, she lashed out with an upper middle arm and swept all the annoying humans from the boat with a single motion. A hooked talon sheared off the roof of the cabin.

Ford froze, stunned by the speed with which Quinn and

Bennett and the rest had been wiped out. For a moment, he thought he was on his own until two more soldiers emerged from defensive positions along the wharf. They signaled Ford to make for the boat—and the warhead—while they provided cover.

"Go, go!" they hollered.

The men opened fire on the female from behind, getting her attention. She whirled about to confront them, murder in her blood-red eyes. Spittle sprayed from her snapping beak. Ford feared for the other men's safety, but took advantage of the distraction they were heroically providing. Sprinting down to the waterfront, he raced across the dock and leapt onto the stranded tour boat. Ignoring the blood splattered across the deck, he hurried to the helm, which was now roofless and exposed to the elements. He tried to gun the engine, but to no avail; the MUTO's disruptive sphere of influence was still in effect. Frustrated, he scrambled back down the deck and attempted to drag the warhead below and out of sight of the MUTO, but the bomb was far too heavy for just one man to manage. It wasn't going anywhere.

Ford put his rifle aside. Desperate to get the warhead away from the city and the MUTO, in that order, he grabbed a pole and tried to shove off from the dock. It took all his remaining strength, but the boat only drifted a few yards out into the bay before ending up dead in the water again. It floated listlessly upon the surf, not remotely far enough away from the city to make the slightest difference. Shell casings rolled noisily across the pitching deck. Ford glanced anxiously at his watch. The mushroom cloud was less than fifteen minutes away.

Now what was he supposed to?

The gunfire halted abruptly, which told Ford that his remaining comrades had probably not survived their assault on the female. The boat rotated slowly in the water, so that the waterfront came into view before him.

And so did the female.

She leaned out over the boat, which was still easily within her grasp. The glowing sensors on her snout twitched. Drool dripped from her maw as she gazed greedily at the warhead. Her clawed forearms flexed in anticipation.

Does she know I'm the one that torched her nest, Ford wondered, *or is she just after the warhead?*

Not that it really mattered. He reached instinctively for his rifle, only to find it lying out of reach on the deck a few yards away. He slumped against a railing, exhausted and defeated. He'd fought the good fight, but there was nowhere left to run and nothing left to do. The boat was dead, the bomb was live, and the monster had him cornered at last. This time there was no bridge to dive off.

So long, Elle, Sam, he thought again. *You'll never know how much I loved you.*

The female lowered her jaws toward him, so that Ford found himself face to ugly face with the giant MUTO. Her breath was hot and smelled of ozone. Sticky orange pus oozed from her burns. With nothing to lose, he formed a gun with his fingers and pointed it right between the female's eyes. A wry smile lifted the corners of his lips.

"Pow," he mouthed.

The female snorted. She drew back a clawed arm to dispose of this final nuisance. Ford readied himself for the fatal blow, then experienced a sudden surge of hope as he spotted something above and behind the MUTO.

Something big.

The female's slavering maw opened wide, but her hostile screech was drowned out by a louder, more commanding roar that rang out across the waterfront and perhaps even the entire city. Ford gazed in awe at his unexpected savior.

Godzilla, King of the Monsters, loomed behind the MUTO. His scaly hide torn and battered, his dorsal fins cracked or broken off completely, he swayed unsteadily upon his mammoth legs like a twelfth-round boxer making his final stand. His endless tail was braced against the ground behind him, helping to keep him upright. He looked almost as spent as Ford, but an indomitable fury still blazed within his fierce eyes. He wasn't done yet.

Startled, the female whipped around to face her enemy. A furious howl issued from her throat, but was abruptly cut off—by a blast of volcanic blue fire.

Godzilla's fiery breath staggered the MUTO. With a single swipe of his arm, he decapitated the other creature whose lower limps crumpled beneath her as she crashed lifelessly onto the pier, crushing it beneath her weight. Her head went flying into the bay, where it sank from sight. Dislodged docks and pilings splashed into the bay. Water splashed onto the creature's headless remains.

Ford's jaw dropped. He couldn't believe it.

The MUTO was dead.

Almost immediately, the lights began to come back on in what was left of the city. Streetlights flared to life and the bright lights of Fisherman's Wharf returned despite the lack of any tourists to enjoy them. With both MUTOs deceased, their sphere of influence had popped like a soap bubble.

Thanks to Godzilla.

TWENTY-SEVEN

Serizawa started as, abruptly, the power came back on in the Tac-Ops trailer. Dead video screens awoke and fresh data began feeding into the mobile command center. Startled analysts and technicians looked at each other in confusion, but Serizawa understood.

He did it, he realized. *Godzilla destroyed the MUTOs... as Nature intended.*

He and Graham exchanged looks of relief until he realized that the countdown clock on the wall was still ticking down to a thermonuclear explosion. Concentric circles, spreading out on illuminated maps and simulations, confirmed that the warhead was now down by the waterfront, which put the entire city still squarely within the blast zone.

But at least Admiral Stenz and his forces were no longer blinded and crippled by the MUTO's electromagnetic pulses. Perhaps there was still hope.

Stenz appeared to think so. He nodded urgently at Captain Hampton.

"Go," he ordered. "Go!"

Seconds later, Serizawa heard a helicopter taking off outside.

Ford watched in wonder as, block by block, the surviving street lamps came on across the city. The comforting glow of the lamps combatted the harsh black smoke from the fires. On the waterfront, standing victorious over his fallen foe, Godzilla tottered and dropped onto a massive knee. His weight squashed the headless body of the female, which spurted a gooey ichor over the crumbling piers. Godzilla's shoulders slumped in exhaustion. Ford guessed that it had taken the very last of the great reptile's strength to dispose of the final MUTO once and for all. Godzilla's labored breathing could be heard across the water. The monster's eyelids drooped. He appeared utterly spent.

Ford knew just how he felt.

He slumped against boat's exposed helm, all too aware that the armed warhead rendered the MUTOs' defeat academic. It was possible, he supposed, that Godzilla might survive the blast, as he had back in '54, but San Francisco was doomed regardless. Ford prayed that somehow, against the odds, Elle had managed to make it out of the city after all. With any luck, she and Sam would survive.

Dropping to his own knees, he was on the verge of passing out when the boat's engines suddenly revved to life. A fresh jolt of adrenaline rushed through Ford as he scrambled to his feet and jammed the throttle.

The boat shot away from the docks and out into the bay.

Losing blood and strength, Ford clung to the helm and fought to stay conscious. Within minutes, the mangled remains of the Golden Gate Bridge came into the view. Ford steered the boat toward the strait and the open sea beyond. He could barely stand and felt light-headed, but he kept bearing down on the throttle.

Hang on, he ordered himself. *Just a little bit further...*

In the command trailer, all eyes were locked onto the screen monitoring the warhead. The radial circles denoting the blast zone were swiftly shifting across the map. The warhead was on the move again, but was it going fast enough? Time was running out.

Serizawa twisted the stem of his pocket watch.

A resounding crash echoed across the bay. Glancing behind him, Ford saw Godzilla collapse onto the wharf. Blocks of world-famous waterfront were crushed beneath the monster's sprawled form. For a moment, Ford thought Godzilla was dead, but then he saw the fallen giant's chest heaving ponderously. The huge saurian was wheezing audibly with every breath.

Ford looked away from the debilitated monster, turning his gaze back toward the strait ahead. Godzilla had done his part, ridding the world of the MUTOs. Now Ford had to make sure that the goliath's victory was not a Pyrrhic one and that the remainder of San Francisco would not be consumed by thermonuclear fire, like that atoll in the South Pacific so many years ago.

His vision began to blur. Ford shook his head to clear it, but he knew he was nearing his limit if he hadn't already passed it before now. Fresh blood pooled at his feet. He felt chilled and dizzy. Given all he'd been through the last few days, it was a wonder that he was still standing at all, but none of that would matter if he didn't complete this final mission. He wondered if this was how his dad had felt right before the Janjira plant melted down.

Probably not, he thought. Unlike Joe, he had no doubts or unanswered questions to torment him. Everything was very simple now; Ford knew exactly what he had to do. He glanced back at the bomb on the deck and peered at his watch to see how much time he had left, but the digital display blurred and wavered before his eyes. It was getting harder and harder to focus.

No matter, he decided. *Just keep going as long as you can. Either it will be enough... or it won't.*

A peculiar calm descended on him. The world and its cares began to recede from his consciousness, becoming fuzzy and dream-like. The surreal image of the sundered Bridge appeared before him and he sped the tour boat beneath the jarring gap in its span. Leaving the bay behind, he navigated the boat through the floating debris out into the wide open waters of the Pacific Ocean.

Keep going, he thought.

His rubbery legs gave out beneath him and he eased himself down onto the deck, guiding the wheel with just his fingertips. It didn't really matter where he went now, just so long as it was away from the mainland... and his family. Darkness encroached on his vision and the sound began to drain away from the world as well. A comforting stillness, very different from the tumult he'd been enduring for days now, beckoned to him, offering him peace and quiet at last. All he had to do was let go.

He wondered if he would see his Mom and Dad again.

But a loud, whirring noise intruded on his hard won serenity. He frowned as the noise grew louder and more insistent, dragging him back into the world. His eyes, which had closed without him even noticing, flickered. He tilted his head back in annoyance.

What the hell?

Bizarrely, a voice called out to him, so faintly that it might just be a dream:

"... uuuu..."

Ford stirred, annoyed by the disturbance. A glaring white light shone into his eyes, forcing him to look away. He listened again for the unlikely voice. Had he actually heard something or had he just imagined it?

"... uuuuten..."

There it was again! Squinting into the glare, he saw a blurry object sweeping through the light. He tried to focus, but the blur wouldn't stay put. It was there and gone, there and gone, there and gone. Like the tip of a helicopter rotor!

"LIEUTENANT!"

The voice shouted over the spinning rotors. The chopper's backwash whipped up the air above the deck, scattering the splintered remains of the truncated cabin. Hundreds of empty shell casings danced atop the deck. Blinking in confusion, Ford dimly glimpsed a figure leaning out the chopper's side-door, a megaphone before his lips.

"LIEUTENANT!"

The rescue 'copter kept pace above the boat. Gloved hands seized Ford and looped his arms into a vest. Only half-conscious, he vaguely registered being lifted from the bloody deck of the boat into the light. Skilled hands hoisted him aboard the chopper, which immediately swung around and sped back toward the bay as fast as humanly possible. Slumped in the crew compartment behind the cockpit, he stared numbly back at the ocean.

The last thing he saw, before passing out, was a tremendous flash of light miles behind them. Night briefly turned into day.

A mushroom cloud rose above the Pacific.

TWENTY-EIGHT

Dawn found the devastated city on the road to recovery.

Fire crews worked tirelessly to douse fires, leaving blackened husks behind. Rescue workers helped shell-shocked citizens from the subway tunnels under the city. Volunteers scoured the wreckage for survivors. Emergency vehicles, their sirens blaring, braved the surviving streets. Helicopters airlifted casualties to neighboring hospitals. There was already talk of a website and televised concert to raise money for disaster relief. The president was supposed to be on his way.

Down by the waterfront, crowds of people began to gather near the prostrate body of Godzilla, coming to see the great beast for themselves. National Guards kept the onlookers at a distance, while TV journalists and camera crews reported live from the scene. Wandering amidst the other pilgrims, Serizawa overheard snatches of the reporters' spiels.

"In a city spared from fallout by prevailing winds, many feel another force of nature protected them today..."

"Gathering here to witness the fallen creature in what may well be its death throes..."

Serizawa contemplated the downed leviathan, feeling privileged to be able to behold Godzilla in the flesh, after devoting much of his life to merely studying reports of such creatures. Even sprawled atop the demolished piers, appearing barely alive, the formidable mega-saurian was humbling to behold. Serizawa found it hard to believe that such as Godzilla could truly expire from his injuries, and yet there was a skeleton buried in the Philippines that proved that even the mightiest of predators was mortal. Death, too, was part of Nature's grand design.

Was he truly witnessing the passing of a legend?

Blocks away, volunteers were excavating a buried BART station. A neighboring building had collapsed on top of the subway entrance, all but entombing it. Collapsed and flooded tunnels had made reaching the station a challenge. It was unclear whether there were any survivors left below, but the crew hauled away the heavy wreckage, just in case. The leader of the crew was growing increasingly skeptical of their chances of rescuing anyone, but then, over the grunting of the workers and the incessant wailing of the sirens, he thought he heard something.

"QUIET!" he shouted.

A hush fell over the site. Straining his ears, he heard it again: a babble of voices calling faintly from beneath the rubble. The crew reacted immediately, clearing away the debris as fast as they could. Hope and excitement lent strength to their efforts. A huge chunk of fallen masonry was rolled out of the way, leaving only a layer of smaller rubble behind.

A hand thrust up from the ruins, reaching for the light.

GODZILLA

* * *

News footage from the city played on the Jumbotron screen at Oakland Coliseum across the bay from San Francisco. A caption along the bottom of the screen identified Godzilla as the "King of Monsters."

Sounds about right, Ford thought.

He and Sam wandered through the crowded stadium, which had been repurposed to serve as an emergency relief center for thousands of injured and displaced survivors. Ford cradled Sam in his arm while limping on a crutch. His twisted ankle had swollen up badly, but Ford couldn't sit still, not until he found out what had happened to Elle. A grateful Admiral Stenz had offered to see that Ford and Sam got whatever care they needed, but Ford had insisted on being transported to the Coliseum so he could look for Elle. This was where they were bringing the bulk of the refugees, so this was where he needed to be. Bruised and bandaged, he searched the teeming stadium, looking in vain for his missing wife.

The bomb didn't go off downtown, he reminded himself. *She could have survived.*

He circled back to the Coliseum's main entrance, where a fresh crop of survivors appeared to have arrived. Dozens of dazed men and women staggered into the stadium, while others had to be transported by stretchers, gurneys, or wheelchairs. Thick layers of dirt and ash coated the new arrivals, obscuring their identities. Ford peered past the blood and soot masking the strangers. What if he missed Elle because he didn't recognize her right away?

He was hardly the only person desperately searching for a lost loved one. A ragged mob of survivors waited behind cordons, anxiously scanning the faces of the survivors. A lucky few had their prayers answered. Calling out the names of friends and family, they pushed their way through the crowds to be reunited with husbands, wives, children, parents, or whoever else they had been worried sick about. Tears of joy streamed from faces, people hugged each other deliriously. It was like the "Welcome Home!" reception at the Air Force base a few days ago, only twice as heart-rending. Until this moment, none of these people had even known if the other was still alive.

Ford was happy for them, but he envied them as well. He gazed down at Sam, who looked crushed by the fact that his mom did not appear to be among the arriving refugees. The naked anxiety and disappointment on his son's face tore at Ford's heart. Sam's tiny fingers clutched the toy soldier he had rescued from Japan. Father and son had both come through the crisis intact, more or less, and found their way back to each other, but there was still a gaping hole in their family.

Where are you, Elle?

His ankle killing him, Ford turned away from the cordon, looking for someplace he and Sam could rest until the next batch of the survivors arrived. He began to limp toward a first-aid station, hoping to secure them a spare cot. He couldn't remember the last time he'd had a decent night's sleep.

"MOMMY!"

Sam's jubilant cry electrified Ford. He spun around, almost afraid to hope.

The boy leapt from Ford's arms and charged into the crowd. Ford was briefly alarmed, afraid that he would lose Sam in the crush, but then Elle emerged from the mob, dirty and disheveled, but walking on her own two legs. Sam sprang into her arms and she hugged him close, laughing and crying at the same time. Lifting her eyes, she spotted Ford limping toward them. A radiant smile shone through the soot and dust soiling her beautiful face.

Ford had never seen anything so beautiful.

Crutch or no crutch, he couldn't get to her fast enough. They crashed together, squeezing Sam between them, as they embraced beneath the open roof of the stadium. The sun beamed down on them, warming them with its light. The storm had passed and they were together again.

A family.

"He's moving! He's moving!"

The cry echoed throughout the crowd keeping vigil over Godzilla. Dusk was falling and the mob of spectators had grown and multiplied over the day. Debris tumbled onto the pier as the monster's chest heaved and he drew a vigorous breath. A ripple ran down his tail, shaking loose the dust and ash that had accumulated on it. His nostrils twitched.

He's waking, Serizawa realized.

The crowd drew back in both fear and wonder. Many of the spectators turned and fled, having suddenly reconsidered the wisdom of coming to see the unpredictable monster, while others remained rooted in place, transfixed by the unbelievable sight before them. Serizawa nodded solemnly to himself. Godzilla was Nature incarnate, eternally resilient and unstoppable. He would not succumb so easily. The monster's eyes opened, meeting Serizawa's, and, for a moment, they seemed to understand each other.

Your work here is done, the scientist thought. *The world is in balance once more.*

The moment passed and Godzilla shook his colossal head, as though clearing the cobwebs from his skull. National

Guards hurriedly tried to disperse the crowds, who needed little encouragement to get out of the stirring behemoth's way. People fled up the hill, away from the waterfront, leaving the shore to Godzilla, who stretched his enormous limbs and flexed his claws. Serizawa let the crowd carry him to safety, but his gaze remained fixed on the breathtaking spectacle before him.

Slowly, surely, Godzilla rose to his feet. Scarred but no longer bleeding, he stood like a mountain above the city he had claimed from the voracious MUTOs. His enemies were dead and rotting, but he had survived to tower over the world like the legend he was. Nature, red in tooth and claw, had created him to be the ultimate predator and he had claimed that title beyond any doubt. Where humanity and all its technology had failed, he alone had saved the planet from being overrun by a plague of giant parasites.

But would he now leave humanity in peace?

All across the ravaged city, helpless humans held their breath as Godzilla paused between the city and the sea. They watched from rooftops, balconies, hills, and helicopters as the revived leviathan trudged slowly toward the bay. The earth trembled beneath his cataclysmic tread as it receded from the mainland, wading into the water:

BOOM! Boom! Boom...

Cheers erupted in the Coliseum as the Jumbotron carried live coverage of Godzilla striding back to sea. Glancing up at the screen, Ford wasn't sure if the hordes of refugees were actually cheering the victorious monster or just his departure.

Probably hefty amounts of both, he guessed.

And, honestly, he didn't care. While everyone else stared

raptly at the giant TV screen, Ford turned away to concentrate on what really mattered: Elle and Sam. He'd seen enough monsters to last a lifetime. From now on, his family was getting his full attention. They were going to make it work after all, just like he'd promised.

He figured his dad would approve.

The sun was setting over the Pacific as Godzilla sank beneath the ocean, returning to the depths. His jagged fins remained above the waves for a moment, slicing through the foam, but they too gradually vanished from sight. The churning waters settled until no hint of the mighty leviathan remained. All was as it was before.

Nature was at peace.

ABOUT THE AUTHOR

Greg Cox is the *New York Times* bestselling author of numerous novels and short stories. He has written the official novelizations of such films as *Man of Steel*, *The Dark Knight Rises*, *Ghost Rider*, *Daredevil*, and the first three *Underworld* movies, as well as novelizations of various DC Comics miniseries.

In addition, he has written books and stories based on such popular series as *Alias*, *The Avengers*, *Buffy the Vampire Slayer*, *CSI: Crime Scene Investigation*, *Farscape*, *The 4400*, *The Green Hornet*, *Iron Man*, *Leverage*, *Riese: Kingdom Falling*, *Roswell*, *Spider-Man*, *Star Trek*, *Terminator*, *Warehouse 13*, *Xena: Warrior Princess*, *X-Men*, and *Zorro*. He has received two Scribe Awards from the International Association of Media Tie-In Writers. He lives in Oxford, Pennsylvania.

His official website is: www.gregcox-author.com.

ACKNOWLEDGMENTS

As my sister recently reminded me, an Aurora plastic model of Godzilla (with Glo-in-the-Dark fins!) stood guard atop the dresser in my bedroom pretty much the whole time we were growing up, which just shows how long Godzilla has been a source of fascination to me. I honestly can't remember what my first Godzilla movie was. Maybe the American version of the original 1954 classic, with Raymond Burr, or one of the later ones with Mothra and Rodan and the rest. But I have many fond memories of watching Godzilla tear apart Tokyo on TV and the occasional drive-in movie screen, so it was a thrill to be able to recapture that excitement again—and I have a lot of people to thank for that opportunity.

My dad, for making sure I was properly exposed to classic Japanese monster movies in the first place.

My editors, Steve Saffel and Jaime Levine, and the rest of the gang at Titan, including Cath Trechman, Nick Landau, and Alice Nightingale, for signing me up yet again.

GREG COX

My agent, Russ Galen, for ably negotiating on my behalf.

Josh Anderson at Warner Bros., along with Shane Thompson, Jill Benscoter and Spencer Douglas for making sure I had all the materials I needed to write the book. Thank you also to Jamie Kampel from Legendary Pcitures.

Gareth Edwards and the team at Legendary for bringing the King of the Monsters back to the big screen in a big way.

Author Christopher Bennett, for letting me tap into his encyclopedic knowledge of classic kaiju.

And, as always, Karen Palinko for putting up with me while I obsessed over a giant radioactive lizard for weeks on end, and our family of four-legged distractions, Lyla, Sophie, and Henry, just because. Henry sadly left us during the writing of this book, but was a big part of our lives for over twelve years.

We'll miss you, you little goofball.

BOOK TWO

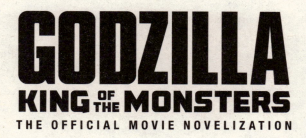
THE OFFICIAL MOVIE NOVELIZATION

NOVELIZATION BY **GREG KEYES**

BASED UPON THE SCREENPLAY BY **MICHAEL DOUGHERTY & ZACH SHIELDS**
STORY BY **MAX BORENSTEIN AND MICHAEL DOUGHERTY & ZACH SHIELDS**
BASED ON THE CHARACTERS "GODZILLA," "KING GHIDORAH," "MOTHRA"
AND "RODAN" OWNED AND CREATED BY TOHO CO., LTD.

To Gwen Campbell

Turning and turning in the widening gyre
The falcon cannot hear the falconer;
Things fall apart; the centre cannot hold;
Mere anarchy is loosed upon the world,
The blood-dimmed tide is loosed, and everywhere
The ceremony of innocence is drowned;
The best lack all conviction, while the worst
Are full of passionate intensity.

Surely some revelation is at hand;
Surely the Second Coming is at hand.
The Second Coming! Hardly are those words out
When a vast image out of *Spiritus Mundi*
Troubles my sight: somewhere in sands of the desert
A shape with lion body and the head of a man,
A gaze blank and pitiless as the sun,
Is moving its slow thighs, while all about it
Reel shadows of the indignant desert birds.
The darkness drops again; but now I know
That twenty centuries of stony sleep
Were vexed to nightmare by a rocking cradle,
And what rough beast, its hour come round at last,
Slouches towards Bethlehem to be born?

The Second Coming
William Butler Yeats

PROLOGUE

THE DEPTHS

He woke, and he prowled his territory.

He was in no hurry. He wasn't hungry, only smelling, seeing – listening.

The depths were not silent.

The deepest sound was time; the steady, slow grind of the earth, the slipping of stone under stone. He heard this not with his ears but through his bones. It was loudest in the hot places where he fed and rested, but it was everywhere, the background against which all other sounds existed. Sometimes it grew sharper when the earth cracked, and the heat came out, bearing sustenance.

Quicker were the songs of the tides, which were nowhere the same. He knew each contour of the continents by the sound of their tides, moving in and out like breath. Even in deep ocean, no two trenches or seamounts sounded the same as the surface swelled and sank above them.

Smaller and swifter still, the clicks, the low and high calls of the great swimmers, the high-pitched pipping of the smaller ones, the grunts, whistles, chirps of *life*.

The sea was never silent.

But it had been quieter, before strange sounds invaded the ocean; the churning and banging and screeching of unliving things that left the smell of oil behind them. The great swimmers could no longer hear each other well. Sometimes they lost their way, could not find each other. Over the ages, the sounds of the sea had changed, but never so much, and never so quickly.

Now there was a new song. It pulsed through the deeps, faint, but unmistakable. The voice of something in his territory that should not be there.

ONE

As usual, Emma woke before the alarm sounded. Her restless mind rarely allowed her the benefit of a full night's sleep, and today was shaping up to be an exciting one. She'd put in a long night, but it had been worth it. She stayed in bed a few more minutes, going over her plans for the day.

She rose, showered, brushed her teeth, combed out her long auburn hair, dressed. She turned on the television, flipped through a few channels, but didn't hear anything she didn't already know. She paused, however, when she came to the BWN. It showed a senate hearing. Serizawa and Graham were there, looking beleaguered. She remembered a similar inquiry, five years ago, with her in the hot seat. She didn't envy the two scientists.

"Top brass at the mysterious Monarch organization will face another intense grilling as the government continues to push for extermination of the Titans," the anchor was saying, "and rumors persist that Monarch may be hiding even more creatures discovered since the attacks of 2014, a historic tragedy that changed the world as we know it forever. The day the world discovered that monsters are real..."

Some people had known there were monsters in the world for many years. Generations. But mostly the monsters slept or lurked in remote corners of the planet. They kept to themselves. They were watched, and in some cases contained – by Monarch. But five years ago, when a monster broke free from containment in Japan and charted a path of destruction from Japan, through Honolulu and finally San Francisco, the fact that monsters were real became very public knowledge. The world learned of Godzilla.

Thousands died in a few days. Once great cities lay in ruins. When it was over, two MUTOs – Massive Unidentified Terrestrial Organisms – lay dead, killed by Godzilla. And when the fight was over the wounded Godzilla dragged himself into the ocean and vanished.

A few months later he reappeared to fight another MUTO, this time in more remote places with less damage and fewer collateral deaths. Then he once more returned to the deeps.

For five years, humanity had lived in fear of another attack. The housing market crashed as the value of waterfront property plummeted. Schoolchildren drilled to evacuate in case of a monster attack.

As the monsters' existence came to light, so did Monarch. Scientists from the organization were called before various government bodies and questioned at length about their intentions and methods. In the years since the attacks, intelligence agencies and investigative reporters had come to believe that Godzilla and the MUTOs weren't the only monsters out there. That there might be more. Many more.

Emma turned her gaze from the screen and down to a hard black plastic case on the floor.

It's going to work, she thought. *I know it will.* But if she was sure, why was she so nervous?

She turned the TV off, and heard a piercing noise from the next room.

"Maddie?" she said.

Madison pushed some of the schoolbooks on the kitchen table aside to make room for her sticker-plastered laptop, put in her earbuds and scrolled through her email as the Pixies' "Wave of Mutilation" began hammering at her eardrums.

As usual, more than half of the emails were from Dad. That wasn't all that surprising; she didn't have many friends and even less family, outside of Mom and Dad. Neither did Dad, at least not anymore, which probably explained why he wrote her at least once a day, and often more, despite the fact that it had been a long time since she'd answered him. She hadn't even opened the most recent ones.

She wasn't entirely sure why. There was Mom, of course, and what she would think. And she had her own misgivings. But he was so persistent, and she did miss him, a lot. She had a clear picture of him in her mind, sending the mail, checking for her response and finding nothing. The look of disappointment on his face.

Mom might not understand, but Maddie was sure he was different now. Maybe not all the way back to his old self, but better, way better.

She let out a breath and clicked on the most recent mail.

Hey Madison, it read, *haven't heard from you guys in a few months. Hope you're having fun. Here are a few pics of the wolves I've been studying. Aren't they cute?*

Of course, she loved the wolves. He knew that. Like everything wild and pure, they appealed to her in a way so deep and strong she couldn't explain it out loud. And the pups were really cute. But she was also a little jealous of them. Dad was always out in the wilderness, in Colorado. With the wolves. And although she knew it was more complicated than that, it still left a hollow in her gut that boiled down to this: why could he be there for the wolves, but not for her?

But of course, when he was around, the tug-of-war always started again, with her as the rope.

Among the pictures was one selfie. Dad had a little more gray in his brown hair than when she had last seen him. He was attempting to look silly and doing a pretty good job of it. It made her think of better times, the games they had played together. He was trying to reconnect with her. So maybe she should try, too.

She hit reply and placed her fingers on the keyboard, trying to think how to start.

Maybe just the basics.

Sorry I haven't written back, she began. *I miss you. But there's something I want to talk to you about.*

Again she paused, glancing nervously at her mother's room. How much should she tell him? Nothing, if Mom had anything to say about it. Dad wasn't supposed to be involved in any of this anymore. But it was so big, what was happening, so important. He shouldn't be completely out of the loop.

I'm getting worried about Mom— she began.

And then the smoke detector started its shrill beeping.

"Oh, shit, shit, shit," she yelped, bolting up. She had forgotten. Why hadn't she smelled it?

But she did now, as smoke boiled up from the pan of burning bacon, filling the tiny kitchen with a gray haze and the smell of ruined porky goodness. She yanked it off the stove, but it was way too late. The rashers were now just strips of charcoal.

Out of the corner of her eye, she saw Mom enter the kitchen. Of course.

Shit, again, she thought. This place was way too small to get away with anything.

"Maddie?" Mom said.

Her mother – Dr. Emma Russell – was a paleobiologist. These days, that was one of the coolest jobs around. But paleobiology was a lot like detective work, or forensics – deducing the big picture from the little things.

Which meant it was hard to pull anything over on her.

"Good morning!" she blurted as she scrambled to turn off the smoke alarm. "Mom! Hi! I made us breakfast."

"Oh, God," Mom said, and hurried to help her with the mess.

"It's eggs, toast, and what was once… bacon."

Her mom smiled. "And which do you recommend?"

"The toast and eggs," she said, with a chuckle.

"Thank you," Mom said, turning to the counter and sitting down. She glanced at the open laptop.

Maddie reached over and pushed it closed, trying to look casual.

Okay, she thought, *that didn't look suspicious at all*.

"Coffee?" she asked, pouring a cup.

"What were you working on?" her mom asked.

"Nothing," Madison lied, putting the plates on the table. "Just looking up recipes."

Before she even finished the sentence, she saw her mother didn't buy it. Of course she didn't.

She sat and poked at her eggs, trying to find the right spin on it.

"Dad's been emailing me," she admitted, finally.

Alarm and consternation flitted across her mother's face, quickly replaced by a carefully neutral expression. She was trying not to freak out. And as usual, doing a pretty good job, at least on the outside. And she was still listening, which was good.

"He looks good," Maddie said. "Healthy."

"Have you responded?" Mom asked.

"Not yet," she said. She took a bite of her eggs. Now Mom was trying to find the tactful response. It was strange; they were so tight on most things. They didn't argue a lot, and it was very seldom things got awkward between them.

But the subject of Dad never failed to make them both uncomfortable.

"Honey," her mother began, "I just don't want to see you get hurt."

"I know."

"Especially with everything that's going on right now."

But that was just the thing. A lot was going on, and maybe Dad should know. He deserved to know. But she knew she couldn't say that to Mom.

"Mom, *I know*," she said instead. "Really."

For a moment her mother was silent.

"Listen," she said finally, in a softer voice. "I know things haven't been easy for you, but we're gonna get through this. Together."

She thought of Dad, in Colorado, with the wolves. And years ago, when everything had seemed fine – and wasn't. It was hard to trust that kind of promise. No one knew for sure what was going to happen even in the next few minutes, much less a year from now, or more. Not even her mother.

"You're sure he's gonna be okay?" she pressed.

"He's in the safest place he can be right now," her mother assured her. Then she perked up a little.

"Hey, wanna hear some good news? I finished it."

For a split second, Madison didn't know what she meant. But then she saw the metal case. The ORCA.

"Really?"

Her mother nodded, unable to suppress a beam of pride. And why shouldn't she be proud? She had been working her ass off on it for years. She even remembered her and Dad tinkering with it a little, way back when. But these past few months the ORCA had seen more of Mom than she had. But that was okay. This was exciting. This was everything, really. It was going to change the world.

"You think it's going to work?" she asked.

Mom stood up and lifted the case.

"It's going to work," she said.

A low, grating rumble shivered the room. The lights went out, flickered back on, dimmed, and came back up again. A high-pitched shriek cut through the nearly subsonic growl. It sounded like nothing Maddie had ever heard before – and living with Mom, she had heard some awfully weird things.

Mom went to the window, frowning, eyes wide and lips pulled tight. Maddie joined her.

"It's going to be okay," Maddie said.

Mom put her arm around her.

Her two-way radio crackled on.

"Dr. Russell," a man's voice said. "We need you in containment."

Her mother seemed a little disoriented, but then she looked at Madison and her composure returned.

"On my way," she said. She put on her jacket and picked up her boots.

Maddie grabbed her own muddy boots. She already had her hoodie on. Good to go.

Mom shot her a questioning glance.

"You're kidding," Maddie said. "Of course I'm going."

Mom's only answer was a proud smile. Then she picked up the ORCA and they went outside.

Inside, their quarters could have been anywhere. Her mom had tried to make them as "normal" as possible. But once you went outside – or even looked out the window – the illusion was broken. Their apartment was a temporary barracks, a neat little prefab house, L-shaped, with solar panels on the roof. It sat on a forested hill looking down on a compound of similar structures – a sort of fancy trailer court surrounded by a chain-link fence. A couple of watchtowers kept vigil over the compound, and satellite dishes maintained their connection with the rest of the world, at least as much contact as Monarch protocols allowed.

Outside, the cool damp air smelled of decay, freshly turned earth, tropical flowers, bruised leaves, and something faintly metallic. Council trees with thickly buttressed trunks rose up through a lower canopy of tropical evergreens and climbing vines, their little piece of the highland rainforest that filled the valley and spread into the surrounding mountains. Monkeys, gibbons, more birds than she could identify even with the help of the Internet variously flew, climbed or swung through the dense branches. And insects – so many strange, fascinating species. Once she had seen a walking stick half a foot long. She'd thought that was impressive, at the time.

But as amazing as all that was, the "site" was much cooler.

Surrounded by lush, green mountains, from the camp it looked something like a mountain itself, although on second look it was too regular. Beneath an encrustation of climbing vines, lianas, ferns, and creepers, a gigantic four-sided pyramid rose in steps, eight in all. It resembled the Great Pyramid of Cholula in Mexico and the ziggurats of ancient Mesopotamia, but it also shared some features with the hundreds of ancient temples scattered around China and Southeast Asia. But the archaeologists said this one was different. From what they said, it was far older than any of the better-known ruins. Dr. Lille, one of the epigraphers on the team, once told Maddie the glyphs on its carved surfaces no more resembled ancient Chinese than they did Mayan hieroglyphs – yet they reminded her of both, and also of the Indus valley script and undeciphered glyphs of Easter Island.

"Perhaps a prototype of all of them," Lille had said, in her musical French accent. "When I have deciphered them, perhaps we shall see."

There had once been more to the site. The rainforest around the pyramid concealed the ruins of an impressive city before whatever catastrophe befell it, thousands of years ago. Now little remained of the other structures; mounds of stone blocks, strange faces of broken statues peering from the underbrush with empty eyes, the occasional low wall that still sketched the foundations of once imposing buildings. The world at large had forgotten the place. The locals knew about it of course, but they rarely admitted it; not because it was taboo, or they were afraid of it, but because they were protective of it, and suspicious of the intentions of outsiders.

Monarch had discovered it through sophisticated satellite imaging rather than through word of mouth.

But the site was more than an archaeological dig. What mattered most was deep within the pyramid.

Which was where they were headed. And where the weird sounds were coming from.

She and Mom climbed into a jeep as the guards opened the gate. A woman – Renata – on one of the watchtowers waved at her, and she waved back. She had a daughter about her age back home.

They drove through the gate, down the bumpy packed-dirt trail to the temple.

Up close you could see the unique features of the pyramid. Comparable structures around the world were usually solid, filled-in bases for temple structures on top. Some might contain relatively small burial or treasure chambers. The Temple of the Moth was different: it was largely hollow, supported by stone columns; it had multiple interior levels and entrances.

Like their living compound, it was surrounded by a fence and watchtowers.

They left the jeep outside of the fence and went on foot. Another set of guards let them through, then closed the gate behind them.

They climbed the broad central stair, through the center doorway.

TWO

From Dr. Chen's notes:

Who smote Azhi Dahaka, three-jawed and triple-headed, six-eyed, with a thousand perceptions, and of mighty strength, a deception-demon of the Daevas, evil to our settlements, and wicked, whom the evil spirit Angra Mainyu made as the most mighty deception-demon, and for the murder of our settlements, and to slay the homes of Asha!

—*The Avesta*, Yt. 9.8. Book of Zoroastrian scripture compiled from oral sources sometime between AD 300–600.

The stone within the temple was ornately carved in enigmatic glyphs and bas-reliefs of humans and beasts that hinted at ancient, mythic stories lost in time, but struggling to be known again. Statues of women in ornate headdresses held up the roof, their expressions knowing and serene. It seemed to Maddie they shared a mystery, but that each also held a secret all her own.

Dr. Mancini, the entomologist, met them in the corridors. He was a little younger than Mom, around forty. He had dark hair and a receding hairline and kind of a nice, slightly silly smile, if he chose to show it off. When he really got talking about insects, he could be pretty interesting. He had a passion and an appreciation for them. But that had only happened once or twice, mostly when he was talking to another adult in the room. He didn't have kids, and sometimes she thought he didn't think much of them.

"What the hell happened?" her mom asked Mancini.

"No idea," Dr. Mancini said. "She was sleeping like a baby until an hour ago and then boom, her radiation levels went through the roof. Almost like something triggered it."

Mancini looked over at Maddie.

"Are you sure she safe's in here?" he asked.

That ticked Maddie off. It always did when somebody looked at her and saw nothing but a helpless twelve-year-old.

"She's sure," Madison said.

Mancini looked suitably rebuked, but only for an instant. He had bigger things on his mind. Or at least one bigger thing.

"Thanks, Tim," her mom told Mancini as they approached some double doors. "You know, I can take it from here. Why don't you get some rest?"

"No way," Mancini said. "Sleep or no sleep, I'm not missing this."

Her mom didn't like that answer, Madison could tell, but after a pause she nodded.

As they went deeper into the temple, Maddie paused to admire a stone carving some guys in hazmat suits were photographing. It was beautiful, and she wondered what ancient artist had carved it. It was stylized, but clearly represented a moth. A very special one.

After the pause, she followed the others through the entry hallway.

The chamber inside was stone, like the rest of the temple, but the stuff filling it up was modern, state of the art. Overhead illumination had been wired to the low ceiling. Desks with computers, diagnostic equipment, and multiple displays butted up against the wall, leaving some of the corridor free for the approach to a much larger central chamber. On the screens, EEG and EKG machines presented their continuous reports, radiation profiles shifted and reconfigured, sonar images and just *mounds* of data. Scientists and techs in Monarch apparel excitedly scurried about their jobs. When she had last been here, it had been a lot – quieter.

Was it happening? Finally?

"Sedatives?" her mother asked Mancini.

"No effect," he said. "This thing wants to be born."

A high-pitched chittering drowned out every other sound. Madison jerked her gaze to the central chamber, which she could see through the decontamination lock at the end of the corridor.

It was a big room, with bigger-than-life statues of women looking down upon a very large altar stone. Their arms were behind their backs, supporting the walls; they leaned forward a little, and their carven expressions were – encouraging, Maddie thought. Like when a preschool teacher was trying to get a five-year-old to pronounce a new word the right way. Sunlight shone down from openings in the pyramid's apex;

climbing vines had invaded the chamber, draping everything in green. Birds fluttered through the shaft of light.

Everything seemed to be waiting for what lay on the altar.

And that was something fantastic.

Some of Maddie's earliest memories were of the backyard behind their small house in Boston. There, she had discovered a world as complex as any jungle on earth, a community of strange creatures that could hold her fascination for the best part of a lazy summer day. The butterflies and moths that drank from flowers; the dragonflies, veined wings glistening in the sun; the spiders, some stalking their prey, others waiting in their webs for it to blunder along. Rainbow-colored beetles so metallic in appearance they seemed more like robots than living things. Ants, building their colonies, their empires. It was like a world from the distant past, before vertebrates inherited the world – with only the occasional squirrel, bird, or human being to disturb that fancy. Giants stalking through their world.

Insects had fascinated her the most because of the way they transformed throughout their lives. It seemed so mysterious that they could have such completely different forms in the same life. Kittens, puppies, chicks were just littler versions of their parents. But cicadas laid eggs that hatched into worms, worms that burrowed into the earth for seventeen years before transforming into something with legs and a triple-segmented body, until finally that too split from its skin and spread its wings.

What rested on the ancient altar brought all that mystery back to her, amplified – and sort of inverted. In her backyard, insect eggs had been tiny. To them, she was a giant of unfathomable size. Now the situation was reversed.

It looked a lot like the silken egg sacs spiders wove; a

roundish thing with a skirt of threads attaching it to the stone, so it appeared dome-shaped. Of course, no egg sac she'd ever seen had been big enough to contain a double-decker bus. Inside, light flickered – bioluminescence, like that of a firefly – revealing the squirming shape within. Something alive. Becoming. Something trying to get out.

The sac was completely surrounded by metal catwalks, giving access to her mom and the other scientists who studied it; a larger platform looked down on it from above. Maddie knew not all of that was about science. Some of the equipment was in case things went wrong. A containment field could be switched on if the hatchling became violent. And her mother had also mentioned a kill switch, if things went *very* wrong. Added to that was a team of military types in hazmat suits, armed with shock rifles.

But hopefully none of that would be needed. Dr. Chen had once told her the creature's name meant "giver of life." Everything would be fine.

Nevertheless, Madison's heart was racing. She and Mom had been talking about this for so long, now that the moment was actually here it seemed unreal.

The voices of the other people in the room sounded distant to Madison. She was completely focused on the movement within the sac, which was intensifying, as was the oscillating radiance.

"Mom," she said. "I think it's happening…"

She wasn't afraid, she realized. She had thought she might be. After all, a Titan was being born – a thing like Godzilla and the MUTOs, a creature capable of crushing a city into ruins. But instead all she felt was awe at what she was witnessing, like the time she had observed a butterfly emerge from its chrysalis. But this was on such a different scale. How long had this egg been waiting? Centuries, the scientists thought, or even thousands, maybe *millions* of years. And she was here to see it happen.

"Her time has come..." her mom said.

The guards moved from the edges of the room, surrounding the sac, shock rifles ready. Maddie watched them, puzzled. What did they think they were doing?

With a final terrific jerk from the creature within, the sac split open and the pupa lifted out of it, towering up into the light, high above the protective goddesses who had been looking down on it. The birds scattered. In the control room, there was a collective gasp.

It – no, she *looked very grub-like,* Maddie thought, as the Titan's head lifted still higher, revealing the many caterpillar-like prolegs on her underbelly. But that didn't capture her majesty. Nor was it completely accurate. She was shaped like a grub or a caterpillar, but armor-plated with chiton, or something similar. Light shimmered from the colorful markings on her thick body. She was so magnificent Madison forgot to breathe for a moment.

The Titan screeched triumphantly, celebrating her own birth.

This was no dumb beast, Maddie realized. She could see intelligence in those strange eyes, as this ancient goddess, this Titan, struggled to orient herself, to take in where she was, and why.

Her mother felt it too and pulled Maddie close. They had been waiting for this moment, building it up – yet it didn't disappoint. The reality was way more amazing than anything Maddie had imagined. The pulsing, moving patterns, a bit like deep-ocean jellyfish she had seen once in the New England Aquarium, but more complex. They didn't seem random; they seemed to *mean* something, however weird that might be to say aloud.

"Meet Titanus Mosura," Dr. Mancini said. "Or as we like to call her—"

"Mothra," Madison finished.

"Incredible," her mother said.

Dr. Mancini pushed a switch and the containment field came on, a glowing blue net, but then it sputtered, faded to red, and flickered out.

"What's happening?" her mother asked Mancini.

"Something's really wrong here," Mancini said. "The containment systems are failing – perimeter alarms are going off – the whole network is going insane."

"What do you mean?" her mother said. "How's that possible?

"Emma, I think someone else is doing this," Mancini shot back.

Mothra's scream shook the building. Not a triumphant sound this time, but a warning cry.

It was terrifying how everything had gone wrong so quickly.

Her mom grabbed the radio.

"Containment teams, stand down," she said. "I repeat, stand down, you're scaring—"

Her command came too late. Mothra was in full panic now, smashing equipment and slamming into the walls. One of the guards fired his shock rifle and the rest quickly followed. If the weapons had any effect at all, it was only to focus the Titan's fear and anger on them. She swung her body, knocking guards from the catwalks, crushing the scaffolding, battering the cage of equipment surrounding her. And something was spraying from her, wrapping around the teal-clad figures, encasing them. *Silk*, Maddie thought, her mind in a fog of anxiety. *She's like a silkworm...*

It wasn't just Mothra who was losing it. Everyone was now in a panic. She saw Dr. Mancini open a panel and reach toward a button. *The kill switch*, she thought. Mancini was going to destroy Mothra.

Her mom grabbed Mancini's wrist.

"No," she said.

"Dr. Russell," he said, "I'm sorry but you know the protocols. We have to terminate—"

"No," she said. "I'll handle this." Her tone left no room for argument.

She grabbed her metal briefcase and ran for the door to the containment area.

"Emma, we don't know if it will work," Mancini shouted after her.

Oh, shit, she's going in there, Madison realized. Into the chamber with Mothra. She was going to try to use the ORCA.

"Mom, no!" she said.

"Madison, stay here. It's going to work."

She watched with mounting fear as her mother went through the decontamination chamber. Disinfecting mist obscured her for a moment, and then she emerged in Mothra's temple.

The Titan shrieked as she approached, unwilling to trust anyone now. Her mother looked tiny as she approached the vast larva towering above her. But she moved with purpose. Laying the plastic case on the ground like an offering before an ancient deity. She opened it, never taking her eyes off the immense, raging pupa.

The ORCA unfolded; several screens expanded beyond the case, along with the speakers and amplifier. If it worked like her mom believed it would, it would change the world. This would be the test. But if it didn't work or didn't work right – Maddie didn't want to think about it.

Mothra grew even more agitated as her mom set up the machine. The Titan probably thought the ORCA was some sort of weapon, like the shock rifles. She could hardly be blamed, considering the greeting her birth had been met with.

But that wouldn't be of any comfort if Mothra attacked her mother, which was exactly what she looked like she was doing, rearing up to her full height, like a cobra about to strike down on her.

The ORCA came to life; a strange throbbing filled the chamber.

Mothra jerked as if stung and then shot webs at Maddie's mother. She dodged them, but something snapped in Maddie. She'd been trying to stay cool, to at least look calm. But without even thinking about what she was doing, she bolted toward Dr. Mancini, grabbed his keycard, and ran through the decontamination chamber after her mother. She heard Dr. Mancini shout after her, but he was no more going to stop her than he had her mother. She didn't have a plan, but she did have a conviction. Mothra was not – should not be – their enemy. She sensed that with every fiber of her being. Mothra was on their side. She was just confused.

She ran up to her mother and embraced her as she worked desperately at the controls of the ORCA. Mothra reared up in fury.

Alpha Frequency found, appeared on the display.

Her mother gathered her in her arms as Mothra struck down at them.

The ORCA began to sing. Mothra stopped, just short of crushing them.

Thum, thum, thum. It sounded like a heartbeat.

Mothra appeared to calm, became entranced. Her bioluminescent display became slower, less erratic. She began to sway, very slightly. Once again she resembled a cobra – no longer poised to strike, but mesmerized by a snake charmer.

As the Titan quieted, so did everyone else. Through the glass, Maddie saw Mancini and the other scientists staring, as enthralled as Mothra.

It was working.

Madison felt the thrumming of the ORCA all the way to her bones. As she joined her mother she felt a profound connection to this entrancing creature. She couldn't say what it was, exactly. It was just an understanding, a feeling that she knew Mothra, that she had somehow been here before. And that this was exactly where she should be now.

The now peaceful behemoth leaned down, examining her and her mom. Maybe wondering what these little things were, the way Maddie had once marveled over a weird green bug with red spots. As if in a dream, Madison reached out her hand toward Mothra's head. Her eyes were like blue diamonds, each larger than Maddie's head. What would it be like, when they touched?

Mothra exhaled, and her breath pushed them back like a strong, warm wind. Her breath smelled like hay and rotten eggs. They both laughed softly as the last of the tension dissolved.

An explosion shook the entire chamber, followed by the deadly rattle of gunfire. Mothra jerked back, as startled as Maddie.

At first she thought the containment guards had lost their minds, but when she looked she saw strangers had invaded the temple. They swarmed through the control center, shooting the Monarch personnel. She saw Mancini, one minute alive, the next just a crumpled corpse. She saw Li fall, and Costas...

This isn't happening, she thought, desperately. They weren't killing everyone. Why would they?

But the murder continued before her horrified gaze, until the invaders had no one left to shoot – except for her and her mother.

Then one of them – the leader, she thought – turned his gaze on them. His eyes were empty, cold, like the eyes of a shark. Her mother pulled her close.

But then the man was no longer looking at them. His attention shifted to Mothra, and the faintest of smiles touched his lips. As the ORCA continued its rhythmic song, Mothra roared so loudly Madison thought the very stone would crack.

THREE

From Dr. Chen's notes:

> *The minokawa-bird is as large as the Island of Negros or Bohol. He has a beak of steel, and his claws too are of steel. His eyes are mirrors, and each single feather is a sharp sword. He lives outside the sky, at the eastern horizon, ready to seize the moon when she reaches there from her journey under the earth.*
>
> *The moon makes eight holes in the eastern horizon to come out of, and eight holes in the western horizon to go into, because every day the big bird tries to catch her, and she is afraid. The exact moment he tries to swallow her is just when she is about to come in through one of the holes in the east to shine on us again. If the minokawa should swallow the moon, and swallow the sun too, he would then come down to earth and gulp down men also. But when the moon is in the belly of the big bird,*

and the sky is dark, then all the Bagobo scream and cry, and beat agongs, because they fear they will all "get dead." Soon this racket makes the minokawa-bird look down and "open his mouth to hear the sound." Then the moon jumps out of the bird's mouth and runs away.

All the old men know about the minokawa-bird in the ulit stories.

—A myth of the Bagobo people of the Southern Philippines.

Senate Hearing Chamber, Washington D.C., United States

Ishiro Serizawa was no stranger to hearings. He'd been involved in a number of them.

Some were more important than others. Today he found himself gazing at the seal of the United States on the wall behind the senators assembled for the meeting on their elevated platform, the barrier of dark wood panels that separated the interrogators from those interrogated. This hearing was one of the important ones. Tensions between Monarch and the government had been growing now for five years. They were close to coming to a head. The committee chair was Claire Godine. She was smart, powerful, assertive. As a senator from Hawai'i, a state both the MUTOs and Godzilla had made very destructive tracks through, she was no fan of Titans. Or Monarch.

Presently, she and the rest of the committee were regarding Monarch's Head of Tech, Sam Coleman, as he filled the presentation screen with a montage of Titans.

"What we are witnessing here, Senators," Sam said, "is the

return of an ancient and forgotten superspecies. Godzilla, the MUTOs, Kong. We believe that these 'Titans' and others like them provide an essential balance to our world. And while some may pose a threat, Monarch is uniquely prepared to determine which of these Titans are here to threaten us, and which of these Titans are here to protect us."

"Thank you for the fifth-grade history lesson, Mr. Coleman," Senator Godine said. "But we still haven't heard one good reason why Monarch shouldn't fall under military jurisdiction or why these creatures shouldn't be exterminated."

Coleman walked back to his seat. Serizawa glanced over at Admiral Stenz, who was also looking sidelong at him. They had worked together five years ago. He thought Stenz respected him. But his military mind was – limited, in some situations. Serizawa knew where a lot of the push to kill the creatures came from.

"Monarch was tasked with finding and destroying these radioactive monsters," Godine went on. "But you either can't or won't tell us how many there are, or why they're showing up. So, maybe it's time for the military to put them down."

"Killing them would be a mistake," Serizawa said. "They returned because of us. It was our atomic testing that awoke Godzilla. Other creatures like the MUTOs from strip mining and seismic surveys. But these are *not* monsters, they are animals, rising to reclaim a world that was once theirs."

"It almost sounds like you're protecting them, Dr. Serizawa," the Senator said. "As if you admire them."

"I admire all forms of life," Serizawa replied. He stood up. "Senators, if you hope to survive, we must find ways to coexist with Titans. With Godzilla."

"A sort of symbiotic relationship, if you will," Dr. Vivienne

Graham – his friend and protégé of many years – added, from the seat to his left. "Like the lion and the mouse."

Serizawa settled back into his seat.

"Or the scorpion and the frog," Godine said. "So you'd want to make Godzilla our pet?"

"No," Serizawa said. "We would be *his*."

Everyone laughed at that. As if he had been joking.

From the corner of his eye he saw Vivienne pull out her phone. As the laughter died down, she tapped him on the shoulder. When he turned she showed him the message on the little screen. He knew she wouldn't do that unless it was something urgent.

And it was.

Sam was still desperately tried to salvage the hearing.

"Uh, no, uh, no actually," he said. "That's not what Dr. Serizawa meant. No one is implying that we would be Godzilla's – or anyone's…"

"Sorry, we need to go," Vivienne interrupted. Serizawa stood up as she did. They quickly made their way toward the exit.

"Dr. Serizawa, Dr. Graham," Godine called after them. "This hearing is not adjourned. Dr. Serizawa! I hope you understand the consequences of walking out that door."

He ignored her.

Sam watched Serizawa and Graham leave, embarrassed and wondering what the hell was going on. He turned back to the committee. He clicked on an icon in his presentation.

"Uh, you know what, Senators?" he said. "While I confer with my colleagues here, I'm gonna set you up with a very brief and pretty fun documentary on Titan reproduction. I think this is the one where the genitals are blurred out but if not, you can leave a comment with my assistant."

As images of the MUTOs came up, he hurried after Graham and Serizawa.

Jebel Barkal, Sudan
Monarch Outpost 75

"So, there you go, Sergeant Nez," Esmail said. "Jebel Barkal. The place where the world began."

Master Sergeant Margaret Nez tilted her head a little to the side and squinted her eyes against the hot Sudanese sun. The place where the world began didn't look like much, just a little mountain, maybe a hundred meters high, flat on top. It wouldn't look that out of place in her New Mexican birthplace. Well, except for the pyramids scattered around it. Smaller and narrower than the pyramids she'd seen in Egypt.

"Is it?" she said.

"So my ancestors said," Esmail replied, "and the Ancient Egyptians believed so too. In the beginning the world was covered in water, and then this mountain, Jebel Barkal, rose up out of it. Then the god Atum was born, and things got busy after that."

"Uh-huh," Nez said.

Esmail was a local, a zoologist, and an employee of Monarch. He'd met her at the dusty little airport in Merowe and driven her here, proudly displaying his knowledge of the various empires that had ruled this place in ancient times. How there were more pyramids in Sudan than in Egypt, and so forth. She judged him to be around the same age as her daughter, early twenties. She was glad he spoke English. Her

Arabic was pretty decent, but the Sudanese dialect of Arabic was... challenging.

"Your people have similar legends, yes?" Esmail said.

"My people?" she said.

"Native Americans. You're Navajo?"

"Diné," she corrected. "Yeah. Our story is we came out of a hole in the ground. Got chased around by monsters for a while until these two brothers killed them all." She shrugged. "I grew up on the Checkerboard Rez. My folks didn't talk about that stuff much."

"But you believe in monsters, don't you?" Esmail said.

"After Godzilla flattened San Francisco, who doesn't?" she said. "I take it there's one right here, someplace, or we wouldn't be here."

"So you were briefed?" Esmail asked.

She nodded. "The army had to clear me before they loaned me out to Monarch. But they were light on details. So what is it? Another big lizard? A bug thing?"

"Mokele-Mbembe," he said.

"Sir?"

"Mokele-Mbembe," he repeated. "The name comes from a legendary creature in the tales of the people of Zimbabwe. The name means 'One who Stops the Flow of Rivers.'"

"Okay," she said. "So is it a lizard, or a bug, or..."

"Closer to a snake, I guess," he said. "Or maybe an elephant. You'll see."

"Okay." She shifted her rucksack, so it dug into a different part of her shoulder.

He noticed.

"I'm sorry," he said. "I get excited. You'd like to put your things down and have a cold drink, I'm sure."

"That'd be nice," she said.

"Come along."

A sturdy-looking fence had been set up around the ancient cemetery. The gate guards saluted her after checking her I.D. Inside of the fence, rows of temporary barracks had been set up. Nez didn't see any place to hide a monster, though. Maybe inside one of the pyramids, although they weren't all that big. There were other ruins, too – ancient palaces and temples, all mostly leveled by wind and time.

Esmail pulled up to one of the larger prefab buildings. Guards met them at the door, saluted, and let her through.

"Colonel Freer will be back tomorrow," he explained. "We can really get into your duties and such then. But in the meantime, I've been cleared to show you the big boy. I'll walk you to your quarters, and we'll meet in the canteen at, let's say 1100?"

She nodded.

Her quarters were spare, but serviceable. It had a real bed and not a cot, which amused her a little bit. Monarch wasn't a military organization, and it showed in the details as well as the big picture. Most of the military equipment and personnel came from the government.

She washed her face and took a quick spit-bath, changed her shirt and ran a comb through her short – still mostly black – hair. Then she went to meet Esmail.

He took her across the compound to another building. Inside that was a cylindrical pit, with walls of cut and fitted stone. In the floodlights it looked like a gigantic deep well, but with a stairway spiraling down its walls.

"This was under one of the structures," he said. "About two meters below and capped with stone. Shall we go down?"

She nodded, and they continued. The harsh light picked out inscriptions on the stone, pictographs, or perhaps hieroglyphs.

"Most of the structures upstairs are anywhere from about twenty-three hundred years old to about three thousand," Esmail explained. "This stuff down here is... older. The archaeologists think it could be more like fifteen or twenty, which is nuts, because human civilization isn't supposed to stretch back that far."

They reached the bottom of the shaft, which opened into a low stone chamber buttressed by columns carved to resemble strange, inhuman figures.

One side of the structure was collapsed, and further in, that rubble had been dug out and shored up with much more modern hardware. The result was an immense cavern.

Lying in it was something equally huge.

It was too big to take in all at once. She strained to pick out details in the dim light, to factor out the containment rigging from the thing it contained.

It was coiled up like a snake. But something big lay in the middle of the coils, suggesting that what she was looking at wasn't a snake, but something with a massive, snake-like tail. The coils hid most of the details of the central body and head, but the wicked-looking curve of a horn stuck up from it, pulsing with a very faint green light.

She hadn't exactly told Esmail the truth. Her parents hadn't talked about the stories of her people, the Diné, very much, but a lot of the older people in her family did. They spoke often of the *Naayéé*, the ancient alien god-giants who had once plagued their ancestors. *Tsé nináhálééh*, the Rock Monster Eagle, *Yé'iitsoh*, the Big Giant, *Shash na'alkaahi*, the Tracking Bear Monster. *Déélgééd* the Horned Monster.

She didn't get the shivers. But her belly felt like it was full of caterpillars.

"Maybe this guy is why we never heard of those earlier civilizations," she murmured.

"Yeah," Esmail said. "Maybe."

Jonah pushed the dead body of a Monarch tech from his chair, checked to make sure the seat wasn't bloody. No sense in staining his clothes. It was clean, so he sat down. The dead man was still signed in, so it was no trouble to find the other containment sites. He copied them out. Just in case the data he'd come by five years before was obsolete.

There were more of them than he'd thought. That was good – the more the better.

He was just finishing up when Asher arrived.

"Colonel," Asher said.

"Are Dr. Russell and her daughter secure?" he asked.

"Yes, sir. We've got them in the Osprey. We're ready any time you are."

"Good." He noticed Asher staring at the man he'd pushed out of the chair. "Something bothering you?"

"No, sir," he said.

"We're at war," Jonah said. "There are casualties in war."

"I don't question that," Asher said.

Jonah smiled, a really genuine smile he almost never brought out.

"Yes, you do," he said, softly. "You're young, yet. You still care for… these. After all, they are our species. Evolution built us to care for them. But evolution isn't always right, is it?"

Asher swallowed and tried to smile.

"Well there was the dodo," he said. "And the platypus – that doesn't seem quite right."

"You know what I mean," Jonah said.

"I do, yeah," Asher said. "Look, what you did for me – nobody ever did anything like that for me before. I'm with you all the way to the end, no matter what. I'll kill a thousand more like this if you tell me it's necessary. I'm just not necessarily going to *like* it."

"I know that," Jonah told him. "But we've got it all right here in our hands, now. We can do everything we've dreamed of. It's not the time for hesitation."

"Yes, sir," Asher said. "I understand that."

Jonah nodded. "We've got the passcodes and Monarch gear?"

"Waiting on you, sir."

"Let's go, then," Jonah said. "I'm done with this place."

The metallic scent of blood mingled with that of pine and juniper. Overhead, a few vultures had already caught on, and were beginning their slow, patient surveillance. The songbirds had fallen silent, except for the crows and jays hacking out warnings to their kin.

The pack was feeding.

Mark had watched them take the elk down, albeit from a good distance. How long they had been running it he didn't know, but by the time he located them the beast was too tired to put up a fight. A single wolf wouldn't have had much of a chance against an adult elk like this one, but wolves worked together. They communicated, coordinated, and executed. They followed their Alpha. And now they feasted on their prey while their pups played.

Crouched behind a fallen tree, taking in that primal scene, under the wide blue sky with trees and mountains towering around him, Mark felt as he imagined the first human to behold these splendid creatures had. The admiration for them. The sense of kinship. The affinity between man and wolf had been so strong that some wolves had joined human packs, back in the day, and eventually became dogs.

And some humans had joined wolf packs.

He clicked more pictures, wondering if Maddie would like them, if there was any sense in sending her any more. She hadn't answered any of his emails in a long time.

He couldn't blame her. She had been so young, and when she needed him most he'd fallen apart. He had been no good to her, to Emma, to anyone. But it still hurt. She was his Maddie, his daughter.

His only child.

She was almost his only tether to that other world, the world of cities and airplanes and the swarming masses. The connection felt weaker every day. Soon he would have no reason to ever go back there.

He took out his digital recorder and set up a shotgun mike. He was here to work, after all, not just take in the sights. Funding went away if you never produced any results, especially when the people funding you were already a little dubious of your research. But he was sure he was on to something. Pack predators used a variety of sounds to communicate in obvious ways, depending on the species. Some of his earlier work had been with killer whales and dolphins, where much of that communication was outside of the range of human hearing. He was convinced that other pack hunters like wolves also relied on sub-vocal signals to maintain pack cohesion. To help them sense the Alpha and read his intentions.

But to prove that, he needed data.

The magnified sounds of the wolves came in through his headphones—the snarls and sharp barks, the sound of flesh tearing, the whimper of a pup.

But then he started adjusting through all of that, tuning out the extraneous sound, zeroing in on the literal heart of the beast, until all he heard was a rhythmic *thub, thub, thub.*

For a moment Mark knew true bliss. He was where he belonged, doing what he was supposed to be doing, and any doubts he had were swept away as by a mountain stream.

A faint growl and scuff of leaves brought him out of it. He looked over his shoulder. The Alpha, Okami, was about three meters behind him. His fangs were bared, and the ruff of his neck stood up.

Crap.

Mark slowly pulled out the .45 from its holster and pointed it at the beast.

Their gazes locked; Okami growled and showed all his teeth. The moment hung there. Mark felt the beat of his own heart. And although his microphone wasn't pointed at the Alpha, he thought he could feel Okami's pulse matching his own. He'd felt connected to the imposing creature since he'd first seen him, and now, in this moment of life and death, the bond was stronger than ever. Okami led his pack and protected them. He knew what human beings were capable of. He wasn't the one out of line here.

Mark broke eye contact; wolves saw that as a threat. He bowed lower, holstered the gun, and reached out toward the wolf, submissively.

Okami growled again, but softer. The standing hair on his neck relaxed a little. He took a step toward Mark.

But then his head jerked up, and he bounded away, toward his pack.

Mark watched him go, taking deep, long breaths, feeling the flush of reaction. What had just happened?

But then he heard a distant *thut*. A familiar sound, not

natural but mechanical. Rotors beating in the air above. A helicopter.

He scanned the sky and saw it. No, not a helicopter. An Osprey. It looked almost like a plane with stubby wings, except that at the end of each wing it sported cylindrical engines and rotors like a helicopter.

The wolves darted away. Within seconds they all vanished. That was it for his fieldwork today. Maybe for several days. Because the damned thing wasn't just passing over. It was landing. The wolves wouldn't like that at all.

The buzzards, on the other hand, would be pleased. They would get more than their usual share of the leftovers.

The Osprey dropped lower.

What the hell? he thought. *What did they think they were doing? Who did they think they were?*

Then he saw the marking on the machine's stabilizer, four lines – a cross with two ends closed off, so it resembled an hourglass on its side. Or a highly stylized butterfly.

Monarch. These were monster hunters. What could they want with him? He didn't work for Monarch anymore. Hadn't for years.

But he knew the answer to that even as he asked it. Or was afraid he did. Maybe he was being paranoid; maybe they were just bringing Maddie for a visit. If that was the case, he could forgive them scaring off the wolves.

The craft touched down on a relatively even spot. The motors cut and the rotors began to slow. He watched as three people debarked. None of them were Maddie.

He knew two of them – Dr. Ishiro Serizawa and Dr. Vivienne Graham. They were both important players in Monarch. Serizawa had been obsessed with Godzilla, chasing signs of the reptilian monster for decades. Hoping to get a glimpse of it years ago, he'd gotten his wish, when not just he but everyone else on the planet got a good look at the rampaging beast. A lot of people had gotten such a good look they never saw anything else again.

Graham had been Serizawa's protégé for a long time, but last he'd heard she had been assigned to some project in Antarctica. He had worked with both of them, along with Emma, prior to the Godzilla thing.

The third guy he didn't know from Adam.

They didn't look like they were bringing good news.

FOUR

From Dr. Chen's notes:

*I was among my cubs
on a meadow beside a brook.
This was the way
I continued to live
on and on until*

*One day downstream
noises were heard
I looked and saw
an evil monster bear
a vile demon bear,
with his lower fangs
jutting out beyond
his upper jaw,
with his upper fangs*

jutting out beyond
his lower jaw,
and with his inner gums
exposed.
The evil monster bear
the vile demon bear
came this way.
As soon as
he caught sight of me,
he glared at me
with his eyes wide open.
Then he attacked me.

—*Song of Wolf Goddess*
Ainu traditional song

Mark had bought the cabin not long after the 2014 attacks. He'd thought the three of them could make a life here. Off the grid. The place had everything they needed. They could homeschool Maddie, and she could grow up without further terror. Far from the coasts. From Godzilla and whatever other monsters might drag their prehistoric asses out of the sea.

Emma had had other ideas. She didn't want to quit Monarch; in fact, she just threw herself into her work that much more. He'd tried to talk her into at least letting him bring Maddie up here while she was in China.

But that was never going to happen.

He'd thought he was buying for three, so the cabin was a little bigger than he needed, but it gave him room to sprawl out comfortably.

Now it felt... crowded.

He rarely had visitors, and when he did they didn't stay long, and that was to his liking. Today he had not one, but three. Normally that would be irritating – except that he was far too distracted by what they had come to tell him. As he listened to their story, he realized that an overcrowded house was the very least of his worries.

He focused on the picture as they spoke, the photo of his daughter and him on a fishing trip. Maddie. It had been a good day, all of it, from the long drive out to the campfire that night.

This was not a good day. What his visitors were telling him seemed impossible, a fiction they were selling for some bent reason.

But, of course, they had video.

"The feed cuts out here," Dr. Graham said in her soft British accent. "The survivors haven't been able to give us much more than what the footage allows. Only that Emma and Madison were the only ones taken."

Yeah, he thought. *But they killed everyone else in sight*.

He couldn't say anything. He just stared at the picture. Wishing he could go back to that moment, keep her with him out here, where it was safe, far from the coast and the hell away from Monarch.

"I'm sorry, Mark," Serizawa said.

Mark looked back at the video feed on the laptop. The temple in the Yunnan Province of China. The monster. The gunmen. If his life had gone differently he might have been in Yunnan, too.

"I never should have... I should have been there for her," he said. "Who did this?"

"We don't know yet," Dr. Graham said. "We believe they

were after this." Graham zoomed the image on the laptop in to Emma, facing the... whatever it was. The black case open in front of her. The ORCA.

He hadn't caught that on the first viewing. He'd thought it was just some random piece of equipment, a radiation sensor or something.

"You didn't..."

"The ORCA," the third person said. The one he didn't know. Nervous-looking fellow with a wispy beard and wide, blue eyes.

"We think it's why they need Emma," the guy went on. "She believed if we could somehow replicate the bio-sonar the Titans use to communicate—"

"I know what the hell it is," Mark broke in, his shock, fear, and guilt now joined by anger. "I helped build the prototype."

He looked at Graham. "Who is he?"

"Uh, Sam Coleman," the man said. "Head of Technology. I joined Monarch shortly after you left – I'm a big fan of your wife's work... and you... the whole... That came out so weird. I'm sorry."

Mark turned back to Serizawa.

"Emma and I destroyed the prototype," Mark told him.

"And then Emma decided to rebuild it after San Francisco," Graham said. "She went home to Boston, spent years developing it. She thought it could help—"

"Help what?" Mark snapped. "Play God?"

"No," the Englishwoman said. "Help prevent another attack."

"The ORCA was a grad-school science project," Mark said. "It was meant to keep whales away from the shoreline, not so you could talk to your little creatures out there. Listen to me – they'll think it's one of them. You use the wrong frequency on any one of 'em, and you're gonna be responsible for a thousand San Franciscos."

"Which is why we need to get it back," Serizawa said. "Emma always said no one knew the ORCA better than you."

"It shouldn't even exist," Mark said.

"That may be, Mark," Coleman replied, "but it's fallen into the wrong hands. And right now the ORCA is the only thing keeping Emma and Madison alive."

Mark turned away from them and stared out the window. What was Emma up to? What did she think she was going to do with the ORCA? Have a conversation with monsters? Talk out a peace treaty with Godzilla?

But the question now wasn't what her plans had been, was it? It was what her captors meant to do.

"Mark, please," Dr. Graham said. "We know you're hurting. But if we find the ORCA we'll find your family. I promise."

Mark looked around his little cabin. He could think of a dozen reasons why he didn't want anything to do with Monarch ever again. But there were two reasons why he must, and they were all that mattered now.

The Osprey was a tiltrotor aircraft, which was a fancy way of saying that it could land, take off, and hover like a helicopter but also fly like a prop plane by switching the propellers from overhead to facing front. Helicopters were pretty lousy at long-distance travel; they got terrible gas mileage. But they were great at coming and going from tight places. The Osprey was a solution to that problem.

They had been in plane mode for a while now. The

mountains of Colorado gave way to the checkerboard Kansas farmland and then wetter, greener country as they moved further east. Night came, and he dozed, fitfully. When he woke they were cruising over a whole lot of water, with the occasional scatter of mist-shrouded islands. He'd tried at first to reckon where they were going based on direction and landmarks and sneaking looks at the instruments, but finally decided it didn't matter. It wasn't like he was going to try to get back to Colorado anytime soon.

The wolves wouldn't miss him. He needed them, not the other way around. Which seemed to sum up all of his relationships.

It was not a smooth ride. The craft bumped and bucked through an agitated sky. Up front, he noticed Serizawa checking his phone and flipping the old pocket watch he carried everywhere. Just like old times. Mark remembered Serizawa had gotten the watch from his father, who had also been with Monarch. And he remembered a joke about that watch.

He was in the back, left to himself, which was fine by him. He figured these guys had told him as much as they planned to for the moment; now all he could do was parse out the information he had.

He was pretty sure if the ORCA was turned on, he could track it – if they were in range of the signal. From what he could make out of Emma's latest version of the machine, its speakers were probably not that much stronger than their first model. If the bad guys amplified the output, the range would increase, making detecting it easier. So there was that – Monarch could start listening, and he could probably help tell them how.

But it all came back to what the terrorists or whatever wanted, didn't it? What did they intend to use the ORCA for?

He kept replaying the video of Emma and Maddie in his mind. Had she been communicating with that maggot-thing, or had the sound of the ORCA merely calmed it down?

The bad guys had taken Emma so she could work the machine for them, that much was clear. But why take Maddie? Once he detached a father's wishful thinking from the question, that was just as obvious.

They wanted Maddie in case Emma was brave. What if Emma wouldn't show them how to work it, even if they threatened her life? Anyone who knew his ex – or anything about her – would know she wouldn't cooperate with terrorists, even if her own life was at stake.

No. They needed Maddie to motivate Emma. Maybe a threat would be enough. Maybe they would have to hurt her before Emma gave in. Hurt his little girl...

No, scratch that. It was worse. Madison wasn't a little girl anymore. She was a strong, hard-headed, smart young woman. She would push back against the bad guys. They would punish her until she stopped.

He couldn't bear the thought, and yet his mind kept coming back to it. It was like a roadblock in his brain that kept him from progressing.

He saw Graham get up and head his way. She settled into the seat next to him.

"How are you holding up?" she asked, softly.

He just stared at her. He didn't want to make conversation right now. He didn't want company.

"You could yell at us more if it will make you feel any better," she said.

He smiled a little. He had liked Vivienne, back in the day. He knew that whatever else was going on, she was worried about Emma and Maddie, too.

"It *is* good to see you, Vivienne," he said. He found that he meant it. She was an effortlessly comforting person.

Her lips turned up a generous, sympathetic smile.

"I know you were a good friend to Emma after the divorce."

"When's the last time you spoke to Emma?" she asked.

"About three years ago. After San Francisco, we went back home to Boston... tried to put the pieces back together. Emma dealt with it by doubling down on saving the world and I – I started drinking. I can't tell you how much I hate myself for letting Maddie see me that way."

Vivienne didn't remark on that, but her gaze brimmed with sympathy.

Mark noticed Coleman approaching, too. Opening up to Vivienne was one thing but he had no interest in airing out his heart around a stranger. And there came Serizawa, too. Was everyone going to come back?

"Uh... you mind if we cut in here?" Coleman asked.

Mark shrugged.

"It's just... you're going to want to see this," Coleman explained.

Coleman plopped down across from him and handed him a tablet.

Emma's research on the ORCA. Blueprints, 3-D models of what must be monster vocal cords, sonic snapshots, audio graphs, sequence builders... She'd been busy. This thing was a long way from their little science project, but at its most basic it was pretty much what he remembered. Except for some of the audio profiles. Those got pretty weird.

"Emma combined the bioacoustics of different Titans to create the ORCA's signal," Coleman said. "A sort of baseline frequency that all the creatures respond to – attracting them, repelling them, even, at times, calming them down. It's pretty remarkable, actually."

"The problem," Vivienne said, "is that we don't know which Titans she combined. But if you can identify those frequencies, we'll be able to track the ORCA. And find Emma and Madison."

So pretty much as he'd thought.

Mark continued through the data, to a set of – X-rays. Of monsters. More than a few. They were all over the place; some had primarily exoskeletons with some interior buttressing. Others were more like Godzilla, vertebrates. To his zoologist's eye, no two of them looked like the same species.

"Jesus," he said. "How many of these things are there?"

"Seventeen," Serizawa said. "And counting, after Godzilla."

He absorbed that. Seventeen more monsters like Godzilla? Seventeen creatures that could level a city just by taking a stroll through it?

"Seventeen?" he said.

Coleman pulled up a map of the world with various locations marked. Some he recognized – Skull Island, for instance. But most of these were totally new to him. He noticed one off the Gulf Coast of Mexico. Another near Atlanta. Was something under Stone Mountain?

But the one he focused in on was the one in the Yunnan Province in China, where Emma and Maddie had been taken.

"Most of them were discovered in deep hibernation," Vivienne said, "while others we've *contained* at top secret sites around the globe: Cambodia, Mexico, Skull Island. We even found one in Wyoming. They're everywhere."

Wyoming. So even his plan to stay high, dry, and monster-free in Colorado had been wrongheaded. These things were everywhere.

"Why don't you kill them?" Mark asked.

"The government wants to," Serizawa said. "But Emma and I believe some are… benevolent."

Not this again.

"Don't kid yourself," Mark told him.

Hadn't they learned anything? They had kept watch over one latent monster, years before, thinking they could contain it. They hadn't, and the result had been catastrophic. It had trashed the Monarch base there, cut a swath through Hawai'i and totaled San Francisco. Now they had *seventeen* they were trying to keep sedated or whatever? It was insane.

Something in the cabin began beeping.

"Uh, hey," Sam said. "Look at that. We're here."

Where was *here*? Mark got up and went into the cockpit for a better view.

The otherwise open sea was broken ahead by the cloud-shrouded mountains of an island. It seemed like a small one, but he couldn't see all of it. Just offshore, an oil platform stood out of the water on four thick red pylons. Several cranes stuck out from the deck and the derrick towered up on one side. He wasn't sure about the rest of it, but he could easily identify a landing pad and spare living quarters.

The props had rotated, and the Osprey was back in helicopter mode. They began to drop toward the landing pad on the rig.

It was funny, he'd been expecting something a little grander from Monarch. They had big plans, and a knack for getting the funds to pull them off. He supposed an oil rig wouldn't attract a lot of unwanted attention, but it was a little underwhelming.

Were they going down too fast? It seemed like they were going down too fast. The pad was coming up with breathtaking speed, and the pilot seemed to have no interest in slowing down.

Or something had gone very wrong with the Osprey.

He braced for impact.

FIVE

From Dr. Chen's notes:

> *When Gilgamesh reached Mount Mashu,*
> *Which each day guards the rise of the sun*
> *Whose two peaks support the heavens,*
> *Whose lower flanks reach to the Netherworld,*
> *There were Scorpion-men guarding its gate.*
> *Fearful dread they stir, their glance is death,*
> *Their terrifying radiance engulfs the mountains.*
>
> —*The Epic of Gilgamesh*
> Tablet I X, 1300–1000 BCE

They were still dropping like a rock; Mark flinched, but the impact didn't come. Instead, the landing pad on the oil rig opened, revealing a hole that went down – *way* down.

Or rather, a shaft, one comfortably large enough for the Osprey, and which functioned as the central space of a vast underwater building. Every ten or fifteen meters they passed a railed-off floor, many of which were bustling with people going about their workdays. Pipes of various sizes ran up the sides of the shaft. What they carried he didn't know, but he was now damn certain it wasn't oil. Scaffolding, ladders, and elevators festooned the surfaces of the tunnel. He figured this whole thing must go down into the rocky core of the island he'd seen.

It was a big, busy place, and they were still going down.

"Well," Mark said, "this is new."

"Yeah," Coleman said. The pride in his voice was unmistakable. "We call it Castle Bravo. Our new flagship facility, built to track and study Godzilla on his own turf."

Godzilla? That brought Mark up short. Godzilla had popped up since San Francisco. A few months later, he'd taken off on another global romp, chasing another bug-thing, this time starting in Guam. He'd found out later that Emma had been involved in that, although thankfully Maddie hadn't been along that time, at least not for the worst of it. Godzilla had been beaten up pretty badly, as he understood it. The glowing spines on his back had been completely shattered before he crawled back into the sea. Since then, there hadn't been a public sighting.

"I thought he was missing," Mark said.

"Well, only if you don't know where to look," Coleman replied.

That landed like a punch. He had hoped Godzilla was dead. He had almost believed it. At least then he would have some smidgen of justice. But no, the damn thing was still alive. And these people are okay with that. *Studying* him.

The Osprey continued on, slowing dramatically. Peering down, Mark saw the shaft ended in water, and what looked like a submarine or two. The Osprey came to a hover and then shifted horizontally, entering an impressively large Osprey bay. There the aircraft settled. Her engines went offline.

"This is our stop," Sam said.

Mark debarked, keeping his head low. The props were slowing but not stopped, their chopping echoing in the hollows of the underwater fortress. He smelled salt water, and the new car smell of metal and plastic.

A group of men and women in camouflage were waiting for them. *A greeting party, that was always nice*, he thought.

Their leader was unmistakable, a tough-looking woman with a clean-shaven head and the birds of a colonel.

"Dr. Russell," Sam said. "This is Colonel Foster. She heads up G-Team."

"A pleasure," Foster said, offering her hand. They shook.

"I take it you aren't part of the scientific mission here," Mark said.

"No," a man with a black, close-cropped beard said. "We're more the ass-kicking part of the situation."

The Colonel nodded at the man. "Now you've met Chief Warrant Officer Barnes," she said. "This is Master Sergeant Hendricks, Staff Sergeant Martinez, and First Lieutenant Griffin."

He shook hands with each of them; it felt sort of like an audition. And maybe it was. When they found who had Emma and Maddie, it was going to be these people going in after them. He eyed them the way he would wolves, looking for clues to their character.

They tended toward young. Barnes looked the oldest, probably early thirties. Hendricks was a brown-eyed boy that didn't look old enough to be in the military. Square-jawed Martinez seemed affable enough, but Mark sensed toughness below the surface. Griffin, dark-eyed and broad-cheeked, radiated competence, but maybe a little cockiness as well.

"Dr. Graham and I have some catching up to do with Colonel Foster," Serizawa said.

"I'll be okay," Mark said.

"Sam, why don't you give Dr. Russell a tour of Castle Bravo. I'd like him to be aware of our capabilities."

Mark flinched. After all those months with just the wolves, he was having a hard time with so much company. And Coleman – he was hard to take even in little doses.

"I can just show myself around, if that's okay," Mark said.

"No, it's no trouble," Coleman said. "Give us some get-to-know-you time."

"Awesome," Mark said.

Jebel Barkal

Colonel Freer got in the next day. He was short, fit, red-headed, ten years her junior. He had her into the office for a sit-down.

"You've got an excellent record, Nez," he said. "Almost too good. Anything I should know?"

"You should never play poker with me, sir," she said. "Or horseshoes."

"Solid information," he said. "So, you met the troops?"

"Yes, sir. They seem like a good bunch. Although Weems—"

"Yeah," Freer said. "We'll talk about Weems later. I just

want to make sure you understand our situation here."

"Yes, sir."

"As in any normal situation, you answer to me. And I answer to the Monarch chain of command. Until I don't."

"Sir?"

"I take orders from Dr. Kearns – we're here for him. But if the brass says boo, we look for ghosts. Any civilian order is superseded by our upper command."

"I understand that, sir."

"Good. Then understand this. You saw that thing downstairs?"

"Yes, sir."

"If anything goes wrong, anything – if it looks like it's going to escape or even sneeze too hard – we terminate it. Period. Now, the civilians here aren't aware of this command. And they will not be."

"No, they will not, sir."

"Okay," he said. "Is there anything you need from me?"

"No, sir."

"Good," he said. "Let me know if you do."

Nez woke around 0330 to a red alert. She got the Monarch briefing from Kearns about Yunnan, and immediately doubled the patrol, leading a squad herself on an inspection of the perimeter. By that time the sky was starting to gray in the east. Venus stood a little above the horizon.

She could tell the squad was nervous. One of them, Larson, finally spoke up.

"What's going on, Sarge?"

"The Monarch site in Yunnan Province in China was compromised early this morning," she said. "We just got word."

"Compromised, Sarge?"

"Someone invaded the containment unit, kidnapped a Monarch scientist and her kid, killed everyone else and released the Titan," she clarified.

"Oh, shit, Sarge," Larson said.

"Yeah," she said. "Oh, shit. Who are those people?"

She motioned toward an encampment near the mountain itself.

"Pilgrims, Ma'am," Larson said. "Some big shot is buried over there by the rock. People come in little groups like that to pay their respects, or whatever."

"Not today," she said. "I want a new perimeter, half a klick out from the fence. Nobody in here except for us."

"You think they'll hit us, too?"

"We don't who *they* are, Larson, or what they want, so we have no idea. But we're going to be prepared."

Castle Bravo

As Mark suspected, the base was mostly housed in the sunken bedrock of the island, but a good bit of it jutted out into the sea. Some of the corridors were stone on one wall, and reinforced glass on the other, allowing some spectacular views of the surrounding ocean.

But these views, he saw, weren't always about observation for the sake of observation. As its name suggested, the underwater base was also a fortress, with good visibility of all approaches. There were portals in the stone with raised metal sleeves he was willing to bet contained guns or cannons of some kind.

The first stop on the tour was the submarine bay.

Well, that's more than one or two submarines, Mark thought.

Coming down the shaft, it hadn't been possible to see how big the submarine bay was, and even the better view from the Osprey pad hadn't given a full appreciation. He counted seven submarines, a whole slew of smaller submersibles, and dock space for a lot more.

"You could stage a war from here," he said.

"Most of these are research vessels," Coleman said. "We're still looking for Titans. Emma – I mean Dr. Russell – thinks there could be a dozen more, at least."

"Yeah," Mark said. "That's just great."

"If they're out there, shouldn't we know?" Coleman asked. "I mean, even if you think they're all really just monsters, better to be prepared."

"Monarch has been chasing these things since the forties," Mark said. "As far as I can tell, nothing they learned prepared us in the slightest for what happened in 2014. The opposite, in fact."

"Maybe. But we're trying to change that. Emma's trying to change that."

"Emma is fooling with something she shouldn't be."

Sam looked suddenly more nervous. He coughed, and pointed out one of the subs.

"So that's the Naglfar," he said. "Fun fact about her—"

"What?" Mark said.

"Excuse me?"

"That look. When I said Emma doesn't know what the hell she's doing."

"It's just – I thought you probably knew."

"Knew what?"

"Five years ago, when Jinshin-Mushi attacked. Emma

used your prototype ORCA to beat her."

"That's not possible—" Mark began. But then he stopped. She'd told him she'd destroyed it. But he hadn't actually seen her do it. When she started talking about building a new one, that was when the split between them became a chasm. But the cracks must have begun earlier.

Coleman was watching him, waiting for him to finish.

"No," he said. "That wasn't in the news, and she didn't choose to tell me that."

It had been right in the middle of their divorce proceedings. There hadn't been much talk about anything between them at that point except custody issues.

"Anything else you know about my ex-wife that I don't?" Mark said.

"Ah, no," Coleman. "That'll do. You want to see Level Two? That's this way. Really interesting stuff there. You're a zoologist, right?"

Coleman was right; Level Two was interesting, in a horrific way.

"What the hell is that?" Mark asked, staring at the nightmarish thing in front of him.

It looked reptilian, like Godzilla, but that's where the resemblance ended. Instead of a protruding snout, its face was flat, eyes facing forward, like a human being, but the nostrils were set above its eyes, something like a whale, which it was roughly the size of. The skull continued back, forming a bony shield over its neck.

It was also undeniably dead. He couldn't see the whole body, because all sorts of lifts and scaffolding had been placed around it, but what he could see of it looked – bad. Something had torn through its armored flesh, leaving a long, jagged rift from below its neck to its abdomen. Part of its skull was showing, where the scales looked as if they had been torched off.

"That's Margygr," he said. "She was dead when we found her in the Arctic. Some other Titan messed her up pretty good."

Margygr wasn't the only Titan in the room. As Sam led him through, he saw plenty of them. In some cases, there were just bones. Few of them were whole. The only ones he recognized were the remains of the MUTOs and Jinshin-Mushi.

"You're dissecting them," Mark said.

"That and lots of other things," Coleman said. "You would really have to ask some of these guys. I'm a techie, not a biologist. But the mission is to understand them, how their ecosystem works, sequence their DNA—"

"Their DNA?" Mark said. "Are you planning on cloning the goddamn things?"

"Well not cloning, exactly. But there are a lot of useful traits that might be inserted into other sequences. I mean that's in the future…" he trailed off as he saw Mark's expression.

"Are you talking about genetically modifying animals with monster DNA? People?"

"Um… no?" Sam replied.

"Jesus," Mark said.

"Okay, but look. What I'm saying is we have tons more information on these things than when you were around. Since Godzilla showed up five years ago, things have become really fascinating—"

"Just – shut up, okay?" Mark said. "Fascinating? Godzilla is not fascinating, he…" He stopped, took a deep breath, closed his eyes for a moment, opened them again.

"I don't care about this," he said, waving his hand at the room. "I want my daughter back, that's it. Once that's done,

I'm washing my hands of all this – again. Forever. I am not and will not be a part of this. You can't recruit me. Is that clear?"

Sam paused, then nodded.

"It is," he said. "What *do* you want to see?"

"Emma's office," Mark replied.

"That's on the same level as command," Coleman said. "Where we're headed now. I can show you after the meeting."

"Meeting?"

"We've got ten minutes," Coleman said. "I guess the tour is over."

There was a time when Mark would have felt comfortable in a situation room crammed with strangers, even if it was in an underwater house of horrors. Not happy, maybe, just comfortable.

But now... this was a part of the life he'd left behind. The trap he had escaped. He wanted his cabin, his wolves, the freedom of the forest. Solitude.

But more than that, he wanted Maddie and Emma back, so he would deal. He tried to focus on the unfamiliar faces, to remember the hurried introductions. The members of G-Team he'd met in the hangar were all present, along with a lot more of them.

As Vivienne began the briefing the chatter in the room died away.

"As you know," she said, "at approximately 0700 hours, our containment site in China's Yunnan rainforest was raided."

The master screen displayed a waterfall in a mountain rainforest. The scale fooled him for an instant. He saw what appeared to be a silkworm or some similar larva wrapping itself in otherworldly, iridescent thread. But then it all came into focus. It was the monster from the video he had seen earlier. The one his daughter had been reaching toward. The waterfall was enormous; the silk casing larger than a double-decker bus.

"The specimen, code-named Mothra, escaped, only to cocoon itself later under a nearby waterfall, while Dr. Russell and her daughter Madison were taken hostage."

Emma's file photo and personal data flashed across the screen, including her marital status, which was listed as "separated."

An ache he thought he'd put away was suddenly there again, as bad as ever. Uninvited images flashed through his head – their first kiss, an argument about nothing, fingers lacing together, her in their bed, still asleep in the morning light.

All gone. Lost to him forever. Because the file wasn't up to date. The separation was now legally permanent.

"This is the man responsible—"

Mark found himself staring at the face of the man who had taken his daughter. Older guy with gray hair and a hawk-nose. Looked like he had been eating nails every day for the last forty years. No one he knew, but his steely gaze was... not encouraging.

"Alan Jonah," Vivienne said, "a former British army colonel turned ecoterrorist obsessed with restoring the natural order. And to fund his operations he began trafficking in a new and dangerous market – Titan DNA."

"What the hell's someone gonna do with a giant worm?" Staff Sergeant Martinez wanted to know.

Young. Cocky. Mark was willing to bet he had never seen a live Titan up close and personal. Maybe none of them had.

"You kidding, Martinez?"

That was Dr. Stanton, another new face for Mark. He was a biophysicist, and he sounded impatient. Mark guessed he thought the meeting was a waste of time he could be spending doing something more productive.

"What can't you do with it?" Stanton continued. "Pharmaceuticals, bioweapons, food – hell, there isn't a country or a company on the planet that doesn't wanna get its hands on one of these suckers. I mean, remember, this one is just a larva. That's a baby. After it cocoons? Something *else* is gonna crawl out. Something *bigger. Meaner*—"

"We don't know that, Rick."

Mark didn't know her, either. She had dark, penetrating eyes and black hair cut in bangs. She wasn't dressed like military, so probably another scientist.

"Oh yeah?" Stanton said. "Just wait for it, Chen."

Chen, Mark thought. *File that away, too.*

Colonel Foster spoke into the following silence.

"Our Intel indicates Jonah wants to capture the specimen *alive*, which means he and his mercs won't be far behind. At 0500, we'll ship out to launch a joint military operation—"

This was idiotic, Mark thought, *and it was time for someone to say so*. It looked like it would have to be him. Hell, they really *did* need him.

"I wouldn't bother," he said.

That got their attention. Everyone shut up and stared at him.

"Excuse me?" Foster said.

"Sounds like a duck hunt to me," he said.

"Mark," Coleman said. "Why don't we let Colonel Foster finish—"

"A decoy," Mark said. "A diversion. Look, they've already

got Emma and the ORCA. Why would they want just this one when they've got the keys to your entire magic kingdom of horrors back here? I think that they want you to go after this Mothra, so they can go after a real prize. Something bigger."

"Mark," Serizawa said, "this is not the first specimen they've captured. They know what they are doing—"

"That's not just a specimen. I've got an ex-wife and a daughter out there. In case you forgot."

"No, no one has forgotten that, Mark," Coleman said. "But to remind you, you were brought on here to help track the ORCA and to advise—"

"I advise you to kill these things," Mark snapped. "All of them." He pointed at the screen, which now depicted Godzilla. "Especially him. You want to make sure these things don't fall into the wrong hands? You kill them, and the ORCA is useless."

"Emma wouldn't have wanted that," Dr. Chen said. "Even to save her life."

So Chen was on a first-name basis with his ex-wife? Okay.

"Well it wouldn't be the first time Emma put all of this before herself," he retorted, "or her family. Would it?"

Barnes watched the guy storm off, wondering exactly who he was other than the husband of a kidnapped scientist. He wasn't with the Monarch team. He wasn't government. But when he talked, they listened.

Maybe because he made sense. Why did this Jonah dude need the worm when he had all those other monsters to pick from? Or if he did want Mothra, why hadn't he just taken it when he broke into the containment facility? Because the worm squirmed away? That was seriously bad planning – or like Mark said, the setup for a duck hunt.

Still, the guy clearly had a big Godzilla-shaped chip on his shoulder.

"Dude hates Titans," he said.

Sam Coleman overheard.

"Yeah, well," he said. "You would too if you were him."

SIX

From Dr. Chen's notes:

When it is stormy weather the thunderbird flies through the skies. He is of monstrous size. When he opens and shut his eyes, he makes the lightning. The flapping of his wings makes the thunder and the great winds. Thunderbird keeps his meat in a dark hole under the glacier at the foot of the Olympic glacial field. This is his home. When he moves about in there, he makes the noise there under the ice.

—Legend of the Hoh people of the Pacific Northwest

Even knowing what level Emma's office was on, it still took Mark a while to find it, but not nearly long enough to cool off. These people held the fate of the world in their hands. They were making decisions that threatened billions of people who didn't even know they were in danger.

He paused when he saw her name on the door, a little surprised. She was still Emma Russell – still using her married name. His name.

Of course, with Emma, that didn't necessarily mean anything other than that she had been too preoccupied with her pet monsters to do the paperwork to change it back. There was no point reading anything into it.

Still.

He began searching the place, at first methodically, but as he went on he became more and more agitated, flinging drawers open, pushing through blueprints, more X-rays of monsters. All useless. It was only when he finally admitted to himself he didn't even know what he was looking for that he stopped, slumping into her chair. He felt exhausted, even though he hadn't really done anything. For the first time in a long time, he felt like he needed a drink, and hated himself for it.

He'd hoped something would jump out at him, the solution, the key. Something to tell him where this Jonah guy might take her. One of the containment sites, sure, but which one? Maybe he could at least look at the files of the "Titans," to work out which one might look most valuable to a DNA prospector.

Wait. If Jonah is after DNA, why did he need the ORCA, or Emma? Most of these monsters were contained, in stasis. As long as Jonah was willing to murder Monarch personnel – and clearly, he was – he could easily get samples without waking the donors up. They didn't need a whole wide-awake monster to get DNA.

Maybe he was overthinking it. Maybe Jonah wanted the

ORCA in case one did wake up and got touchy about being sampled. Emma could calm it down.

Or maybe this Jonah guy was changing his game. Foster had said he was an ecoterrorist obsessed with the "natural order," whatever that was supposed to mean. What would a man like that want to do? Control a Titan to sink whaling ships or destroy offshore oil rigs?

If so, he was going to be disappointed. *Control* was not a word that applied to Titans, with or without the ORCA.

Wearily, he glanced at Emma's computer screen, scanning the folders.

Plenty about monsters, a file on Permian Faunal Discrepancies – but the one that caught his attention was a folder simply labeled "Boston."

He took a breath, torn. What had Emma kept from Boston? At this point, he felt like he was close to a breakdown. Whatever was in that file might push him over the edge.

What the hell. He clicked on the file.

Moving images appeared. He heard a laugh he hadn't heard in a long time.

It was the time they had dressed as a family of bears. Not for any special occasion, just something the kids had wanted to do. They had put on faux-fur coats and smeared their faces with makeup, made claws from tinfoil. They were finishing him – Mark – up, but he kept moving.

"Dad," Andrew said, "you gotta sit still."

"Sorry Andrew, my nose is itching," the image of himself on the screen said. It didn't seem real, although he remembered all of this. But it felt like he was watching an entirely different person who just happened to have his face.

Andrew had been, what, eight then? Maddie had been four.

"My name isn't Andrew!" his son said. "It's Onikuma. I've come to eat your horses!"

Yeah, now he remembered. Andrew had been obsessed with *yokai* – Japanese spirits, demons, and cryptids. His favorite was Onikuma, the demon-bear. Not surprising, given he and Emma were both monster hunters back then.

Andrew had written a short movie about Onikuma he wanted to film.

The old Mark – the one on the screen – chuckled, and suddenly Emma's musical laugh was there, too, coming from behind the camera.

"An intruder!" Mark said. "Get her!"

The chase began, as he and the kids ran after Emma, out the door, where they finally caught and tackled her, pulling her down. The camera, no longer in her hand, came to rest so it showed them all there, laughing, tangled, together. Mom, dad, son, daughter. The townhouse they shared in Boston in the background.

Andrew.

Life had been so full then. So complete. But now one of the pieces was missing, and none of them would ever be whole again.

Yunnan Province, China

Houston Brooks rolled out of his cot, suppressing a groan. At seventy-one the everyday of fieldwork was tougher than it had been when he was younger. But he was still happy to be out here again. Looking back on it, it was hard to believe he had ever planned on retiring. What would he have done, play golf? Not really his thing.

He dressed and stepped out of his tent and assessed the camp.

Mothra had relocated far enough from the Yunnan containment center that it required setting up a separate camp; they'd had to do it in a hurry, too, so what they got were tents, and a lot of them. After the slaughter at Outpost 61, Monarch was armed for bear, so in addition to scientists and technicians, there was a good deal of military in their bunch. They had landed late the evening before. He had been so busy setting everything up he hadn't had a chance to observe the object of their mission closely. He aimed to straighten that out now.

Before he could start off, he saw Dr. Ling approaching. They had never met, but there couldn't be any mistaking who she was.

"Dr. Brooks," she said, offering her hand. "So nice to meet you."

"And you, Dr. Ling."

"You know me?" she asked.

He smiled. "I knew your mother. You're her spitting image."

"Yes," she said. "So I'm told."

"Have you been up to the cocoon?" he asked.

"Yes, as soon as I arrived," she said. "I couldn't wait. But it was quite dark. I'd like to have a better look."

"Come on, then," he said. They began walking up the steep, gravelly trail.

"Have you been to Yunnan before?" Ling asked.

"I have, in fact," he said. "There are some pretty amazing cave systems around here. Some of them are more than seven hundred thousand years old, but the rock they formed in goes back to the Carboniferous and Permian periods, hundreds of millions of years ago. And they go deep."

"That's right," she said. "Your chief interest is in geology, isn't it?"

"Yes," he said. "I started out that way, anyway. But over my years with Monarch I've acquired other... let's say, sets of knowledge."

"Of course," she said. "You're quite famous."

"In a small circle," he said.

"And modest."

"Of course," he said, smiling. "That goes without saying."

They were at the waterfall now, an impressive – and quite beautiful – cataract. Mothra was in the hollow behind it, snugged against a wall. Cerulean light rippled within her chrysalis and shimmered through the falling water.

They skirted around, through the fine, cold cloud of spray. The mineral smell of limestone mingled with the various, sweeter scents of the rainforest, and – despite the rush of the water – it felt quiet.

Once beyond the falls, he brushed the water from his eyes.

"So beautiful," Ling said.

He had to agree. The pulsing of the bioluminescent cocoon, the morning light through the falls. Truly enchanting. But he had learned over the years that some of the most beautiful things in nature could also hide the deadliest. He'd had a real education in that on Skull Island.

"Myth is our compass," Ling whispered, in Chinese.

"How is that?" he answered, in the same language.

"Oh," she said. "You speak Mandarin?"

"A little," he said. "But I think I take your meaning. Before we found any Titans, there were rumors of them in legends and tales. Almost every culture had stories of worlds beneath the ground, netherworlds filled with monsters. We now know some of those weren't just stories. What does our compass tell us about Mothra?"

"Oh," she shrugged. "It's difficult to put it all together.

There are tales of giant worms, of course, from many times and places. I ran across a creation story from Nauru Island in Micronesia in which a caterpillar or grub named Rigi pushed up the sky and died from the effort. The creator – who was a spider, by the way – wrapped him in silk and placed him in the sky as a constellation. In a different tale, Rigi is a butterfly, who separated the sea from land by flying over it. Same god, two different forms, you see? There is a small island in Indonesia where they speak of a goddess named Mosura, a protector who transforms, embodies life – a sort of guardian angel. That's where we got her name. But there are similar tales of destructive beings in the same vein."

"We thought Kong was a monster at first," Brooks said. "But he turned out to be the protector of the island. Do you have a feeling one way or another about this species? If you had to guess?"

"I watched the video with Dr. Russell and her daughter," Ling said. "If I add that to what the legends say – I have a good feeling about her."

He looked back at the cocoon, trying to work out how big the *imago* would be. Hopefully by tomorrow they would have the equipment set up to image what was within. But it was going to be *big*.

"I hope you're right about that," he said.

Antartica

Maddie gazed out the window of the Osprey, but there wasn't much to see in the Antarctic night. It was still better than looking at the men in the aircraft. The thugs who had shot and killed everyone at the Yunnan control center. Now they joked and chuckled and talked about things they had eaten that grossed them out. It wasn't that they didn't seem to think they had done anything wrong; it was as if they hadn't done anything at all.

She was never going to forget the smell of that much blood. The looks of surprise or fear or agony or – nothing, frozen on the faces of the dead. The whimpering of those still alive, before one of these guys finished them off. And they were people she *knew*. Maybe that shouldn't make a difference, but it did. Tana had helped her with her calculus and taught her how to count to ten in Chuukese. Dr. Mancini had had coffee at their kitchen table. Ben, one of the techs – one day he'd had the hell scared out of him when a monkey came up behind him and took his earbuds. She must have laughed for ten minutes, and once he got over the embarrassment, he'd laughed too.

He'd had that same look of shock and fright when the bullets struck him, and nothing about any of it seemed funny. The thought of her laughter that day now made her feel like vomiting. But she'd already done that, back in Yunnan, walking through the carnage. There was nothing in her stomach left to come up.

Maddie didn't know what death was like for the dead, but she knew what it was like for the living. It was a big hole in the heart that could never be filled. Those people, they'd had mothers and fathers, wives, husbands. Brothers. Sisters. Lots of unfillable holes.

Mom had told her to try not to think about it. They had to get through this and freaking out wasn't going to help anything. Or bring anyone back from the dead. But that was tough, really tough.

She closed her eyes, trying to put those dead faces away.

Remembering Mothra, instead. The feeling of connection. How important it all seemed. Maybe if she had actually made contact – if these guys hadn't come busting in – she might have figured it out.

One thing Mom was right about. Mothra wasn't a monster. She hoped the big pupa was okay.

She caught motion from the corner of her eye. A man lifting his rifle, checking it out. The rest were doing the same. The engines of the Osprey sounded different; it felt like they were descending.

She forced herself to look at them. They were all now dressed in white Monarch snowsuits. That, along with the Osprey they stole from the Yunnan base, would help them pass as a Monarch team on their next little adventure.

As her glance shifted from face to face, she wondered: if she hadn't known they were killers, would she guess they were by their expressions, their demeanor?

Probably. Certainly, their leader, Jonah, gave off that vibe.

Her mother was nervous, too, she could tell. Who wouldn't be? Since Jonah and his men showed up, the two of them hadn't been able to speak alone. She hoped they got a chance to, soon.

Antarctic winds buffeted the Osprey; it pitched and wobbled as it descended. Outside, under the light of moon and stars, an icy landscape stretched off as far as she could see. Except ahead, where ice and rock rose in a low mound over a concrete and metal façade, more or less the same color as the ice.

The Antarctic base. Under different circumstances she would be excited to be here. Dr. Graham – Vivienne – had talked about it often. The beautiful simplicity of the landscape, the surprising amount of life on the shore – the silence.

And, of course, what was inside. Although she had been

less forthcoming about that; Maddie's mother had a high security clearance, but Maddie didn't.

"Outpost thirty-two," one of the pilots said, speaking to the people at the base. "This is Raptor Five on approach with reinforcements and supplies requesting permission to land. Serizawa has all sites on high alert so transmitting emergency codes now."

"Copy that, Raptor Five," a voice on the radio said. "Codes are good. Nice to have you back."

No, it won't be, Maddie thought. The ruse had worked. The Monarch staff at the base thought the good guys had arrived. They were wrong. She thought that maybe if she could get to the radio, warn them...

But then what?

Weapons clattered as the mercenaries locked and loaded their weapons. All business. Just another day at the office. In the floodlights, Madison saw men and women from the base emerging to greet them.

Go back! she thought. But she couldn't say it out loud. She was starting to feel even sicker.

The Osprey touched down. The doors opened, and Jonah and his men began to debark.

For a moment, there was silence, except for the wind.

When the gunfire started, she and her mother huddled together.

"I'm scared," she said.

"I know," her mother said. "Me too."

A few moments later, the gunfire stopped. Jonah reappeared.

"Okay," he told them. "Let's go."

* * *

The walk to the facility was a nightmare of wind, hard slanting snow, and more dead bodies. She shivered through the parka Jonah had given her, and not just because it was cold.

"Eyes straight ahead," her mother told her. "Deep breaths. Just like we talked about."

She nodded, incrementally. She remembered the talk. It seemed a long time ago, another lifetime.

Inside, they crowded onto an elevator and began to descend. Jonah, wiping blood from his face, flashed her a little smile. Like they were friends, and he was trying to buck her up. It was strange and terrible, and she did her best to stare straight through him, as if he wasn't there at all. But since she couldn't quite manage that, she scratched her eye with her middle finger and felt a little satisfaction that he understood her.

After what felt like an epoch or two, the elevator doors opened – revealing a wonderland, a vast cavern of ice. Catwalks and scientific equipment surrounded an ice face hundreds of feet high.

"Mother of God," one of Jonah's men said. His name was Asher. He was sort of Jonah's right-hand man.

"She had nothing to do with this," Jonah replied.

Maddie saw it too. Inside the ice. Tangles of serpentine coils and gigantic claws, a silhouette that was far larger than Mothra, maybe bigger than Godzilla himself. Or maybe it was several Titans jumbled together. She could make out at least two dragon-like heads.

"Monster Zero," she whispered. It's what Vivienne and Mom had called it.

It suddenly struck her that she didn't know if Vivienne was still running things down here. Was she here now? Had Jonah's goons killed her, too?

She hoped not. That would be too much. After her folks

split up, Vivienne... it had been good to have her around. Almost like an aunt, or something.

Another thing to try not to think about.

Her mother led them into a tunnel that had been cut through the ice and insulated with what she figured was plastic of some kind. It reminded her of a hamster tube, though obviously bigger. Inside it was warmer; she felt air circulating. It wasn't just a single tube-corridor but a maze of them, a whole hamster city in the ice, allowing access to different parts of Monster Zero. They worked their way up, past offices and workspaces, until they reached the heart of the place – the biolab.

From her position Maddie could see one of the horned heads. The rest of the creature was obscured by layers of ice.

The mercenaries were hard men, but they hung back from the thing in the ice. Her mother walked to it, placed her hand against the frozen surface.

"Any survivors?" Jonah asked Asher.

"No," Asher said. "They tried to launch an emergency beacon, but we cut them off in time."

"They'll figure it out," Jonah said. "Fire up the drills."

Jonah looked over at the ORCA, and her mom.

"Do you have everything you need?" he asked.

Her mother barely seemed to hear him. She was too caught up in it all. But she nodded.

"Good," Jonah said. "Let's get started."

Her mother began connecting the ORCA to the biolab's diagnostic equipment. Jonah's men started up several massive drills mounted on robotic arms that hung from the ceiling. The hardware descended and began boring into the wall of ice. Maddie stepped over and placed her hand against the frozen surface, just as her mother had.

How had a creature so immense been iced over like this? Mammoths had been found, frozen in the Arctic. But they were usually on their side – they died first and were then covered in ice.

From what she could make out, Monster Zero had been standing, in a very lifelike pose. It seemed impossible that the ice had accumulated on him over time; he must have been frozen really quickly. Maybe he'd fallen into a pool of icy water. A pool hundreds of feet deep that dropped below freezing as he struggled to get out. If that could happen.

How long ago had this happened? Antarctica hadn't been frozen forever, but it had been that way for a long time, like fifteen million years? Was it even possible that Monster Zero was still living?

She got her answer an instant later, when she heard a sharp beep from the diagnostic signal. It jumped from flat line to active. The waves were brief, shallow, inconsistent – but they were there.

Monster Zero was alive.

SEVEN

From Dr. Chen's notes:

His face is that of a lion, his body is covered in sharp scales, he has the claws of a vulture and the horns of a wild bull. When he looks at someone, it is the look of death. Humbaba's roar is a flood, his mouth is death and his breath is fire! He can hear a hundred leagues away any rustling in his forest! Who would go down into his forest!

—The Epic of Gilgamesh
Tablet III

Mark pulled up the security camera footage again, hoping to find some clue, some breadcrumb that might lead him to Maddie and Emma, but if it was there, he wasn't seeing it.

Despite his horror that Emma had finished the ORCA, he couldn't help but be impressed that she had made the damn thing work. He played the tape once more, this time focusing on pulling up the sounds, trying to figure out exactly how she had tuned in to the monster. What frequency to look for to help them spot the ORCA when it was used again.

It was all too messy. But maybe if he could isolate the ORCA sounds.

He reviewed the footage again, just listening this time.

When Emma first turned the ORCA on there wasn't anything, no reaction from Mothra. But she'd done something...

He ran it back and heard it one more time. This time he got it.

"You bypassed the low-end harmonics," he murmured. "Pretty smart, girl."

He smiled at the image of her on the screen, remembering their early years together, dreaming about this thing. She could be stubborn when she got hold of something. He realized looking back on it, when they'd agreed to stop work on the project, that it had really been his idea. She'd never wanted to abandon it.

Now she had perfected it. Despite everything, he was proud of her for that.

But it was still a bad idea to use it. She'd been lucky so far. But he felt in his gut that luck wasn't going to hold.

Then the gunshots rang out, the anarchists appeared, and Mark snapped back to reality. The monitor almost seemed to shake from the explosions it was portraying.

No, the monitor *was* shaking. The whole facility was.

Colonel Foster's voice blared from the loudspeakers.

"All personnel report to battle stations," she said. "Code red. This is not a drill. Code red, I repeat, code red!"

By the time she finished, Mark was on his feet and headed out the door.

When he reached the command center, he saw the whole station was on lockdown. Their beautiful under-the-sea view was now hidden behind thick, ugly blast doors. Were they expecting torpedoes, or something? Was Jonah attacking Castle Bravo?

Barnes, Martinez, Griffin, and the rest of G-Team were already there, standing in loose ranks but at ease. Stanton was there too, and Dr. Chen. Mark went over to her station.

"What's happening?" he asked.

"Something's wrong," she replied. "He's never been this close before."

"Who's *he*?" he demanded.

"Who do you think?" she said.

"He's taking out our observation drones," Vivienne said.

Mark saw what she meant, as screen after screen was swallowed by static. There was a sudden flurry of motion on one, something large, moving *fast* – and then it too cut out. Meanwhile, on radar, they were tracking something *big*.

Right. Of course. Their favorite specimen had turned on them. Huge surprise, there.

"Trajectory?" Serizawa demanded.

"Straight at us," Stanton informed him. "Twelve hundred meters and closing."

"G-Team!" Colonel Foster barked. "Barnes, Martinez, Hendricks – I want you on those CROWS now!"

"You heard the boss lady," Barnes said. "Let's move!"

As G-Team scrambled into the remote turrets, gigantic guns sprang up all over the base and began adjusting range.

"Dr. Stanton, do you have his bioacoustics?" Serizawa asked.

In response, Stanton fiddled with his equipment, and a deep thudding sound filled the room. It was similar to what Emma had isolated from Mothra.

Godzilla's deep heartbeat.

"Acoustics coming up," Stanton said. "Okay, he's closing! We're at eight hundred meters."

"His movements are erratic," Vivienne said. "Heart and breathing elevated—"

"He's definitely not happy about something," Stanton said.

"How are they getting all this?" Mark asked Chen.

"Emma isolated Godzilla's bioacoustics. It allows us to track him, even to get his vitals."

Another low rumble shook the base.

"Circling now," Stanton said. "Closing in. Two hundred meters. "

One of the few monitors still working began to brighten with a light that Mark knew all too well. The monster's radioactive aura.

"Colonel?" Serizawa said.

"All teams in position," Foster commanded. "Weapons hot, ready to engage on my command."

The unnerving beat of Godzilla's heart grew in volume.

"Hold your fire," Serizawa said. "We don't know he will attack."

"Well, he will if you keep those guns on him," Mark said. "I want him dead more than anybody, but unless this is a fight you know you can win, for God's sake stand down."

He waited for the blowback. But if this base had been here for a while, why was Godzilla just now bothering to come take it apart? Unless something in the equation had changed.

He was an apex predator, and he sensed a threat of some kind. By deploying the guns, they were proving to him he was right. And if they thought those guns were going to *stop* him – they should know better.

The floor bucked under Mark's feet. The base, huge as it was, anchored in bedrock, shuddered like a flimsy shack in a hurricane.

"Stand down," Serizawa said.

Foster looked at him. She took a step forward.

"You can't be serious," she said.

Serizawa turned to her. "I am," he said. "Stand down."

Foster paused, frowning. Then she reached slowly up and touched her earpiece.

"Stand down," she said. "I say again, safe your weapons, do not engage."

"Listen," Chen said, after a moment. "His heart rate – it's slowing."

He heard. Pulling in the guns had helped. Godzilla was calming down a little. But not enough. What if Serizawa was right, or at least partly right? What if Godzilla was more than just a monster? Maybe he didn't only recognize active threats, but passive ones, too?

"Open the shields," Mark said. He felt more than saw everyone in the room staring at him.

"Yeah, sure," Stanton said. "Let's bring him in for a beer. Are you out of your goddamn mind?"

"Let him know we're not a threat," Mark said. "Open the shields."

Mark looked to Serizawa. The scientist's brow creased.

"Do it," Serizawa said.

Colonel Foster clearly didn't like that notion any more than the stand-down order, but she grudgingly complied.

She pulled a switch, and the blast doors began to rumble up, revealing the deep sea beyond.

And what was in it. A huge shape emerging, still mostly light and shadow in the murk, but Mark could see those glowing dorsal spines that could only belong to Godzilla.

They'd grown back, obviously.

He was about a hundred meters out, waiting, watching in the dark. Facing them, his spines slowly brightening, then going dark, leaving only shadow, then lighting up again.

It was breathtaking, and for a moment everyone was too stunned to say anything, although Mark noticed Martinez crossing himself.

Sergeant Hendricks broke the silence.

"What's with the light show?" he asked.

"It's an intimidation display," Vivienne said. "Like a gorilla pounding its chest."

"Consider us very intimidated," Coleman said.

"I don't think it's for us," Dr. Chen said.

Mark didn't think so, either. After his encounter with the military a few years back, Godzilla might have gotten it into his reptilian brain that the little termites under his feet had weapons that could hurt him, at least a little bit. But if Vivienne was right – and she probably was – he wouldn't be responding to them like this. This was more how a predator would respond to a rival for his territory.

Was something else out there? Mothra was still in her cocoon. Was yet another monster on the loose?

He took a step closer. All of his hatred for the beast was still there, but oddly muted. He had never understood how Emma had felt about these things, not after what happened. But now – maybe he appreciated a little of her awe for the creature. But it was more than that. He had a bone-deep feeling that this monster, this Titan – this was his link to Maddie and Emma. Somehow, Godzilla was going to help him find them.

He continued forward.

"What are you doing, dude?" Stanton said.

Mark ignored him. He closed his eyes, listening, reaching out to the glass. Because there was something new out there. A low, heavy growl transmitted through the water, along with deep clicks that reminded him of whale sonar.

And there was something else, something he felt rather than heard. But it was so mixed with anger, hatred, regret – he didn't want to know what it was. He didn't care.

Then Godzilla's spines faded to black, and they couldn't see anything but the murky waters. The odd noises diminished and then stopped altogether.

Mark could almost hear the collective sigh of relief.

Until Godzilla was suddenly there again charging at the window, incredibly fast, filling their view. There was no way the glass would stop him...

And then he blew past again and was gone. According to the tracking monitors, this time for real. They watched the signal recede.

More chest-pounding, Mark thought – *or maybe just a straight-up threat*.

Stanton peeked up from behind his workstation.

"Can we maybe close the shield now?" he said.

As Mark's breathing began to even out, he had an idea. Whatever else he was, Godzilla was a predator. Like a wolf, or a killer whale. So he would have some things in common with them.

"Show me his territorial routes," he told Stanton.

"What – why?" Stanton asked.

"Cause I wanna start a boat tour," Mark snapped. "Just show me!"

"Okay, coming up!" Stanton said.

He pulled up a map of Earth, with Godzilla's recorded paths highlighted. It was clear they weren't random. There was some variation, but in general the big lizard followed the same track within a given cycle of time.

"Care to tell us what you're looking for?" Colonel Foster asked.

"When an animal leaves its hunting ground it's usually because it is threatened by something," Mark said.

The map said it all; Godzilla had recently deviated significantly from his usual walkabout. Something new had entered his territory, and recently. Something Godzilla hadn't seen yet, maybe. But he knew it was out there.

Maybe it wasn't another Titan Godzilla was reacting to. Maybe it was something that *sounded* like one.

"Run a course projection," Vivienne said.

Stanton went back to work. Potential paths began arcing across the map.

"We gotta go after him," Mark said. "He's looking for something out there. It could be the ORCA."

There was nervous silence as the others absorbed that possibility.

"Dr. Stanton," Serizawa said. "What's your projection?"

Stanton finally looked up.

"All paths have him landing in the same place," Stanton said. "Antarctica."

The satellite map zoomed in on the frozen continent to where the projected routes converged at a point in East Antarctica, on the coast of the Indian Ocean.

"Good, then!" Mark said. "Let's go! Let's go find them! Let's—"

He looked around at their anxious expressions.

"Wait... What's in Antarctica?"

"Barnes," Colonel Foster said, "Contact the *Argo*."

Once he was sure the operation was going well, Jonah chose one of the office spaces around the lab, and lay down on the floor. He had been awake for more than forty-eight hours, and it was beginning to tell. They had a little time now, but soon he would need all of his wits about him.

He dozed. He wasn't sure for how long. When he woke, Asher was in the room, sitting at the desk.

"I could have found you a cot," Asher said.

Jonah levered himself up. "I've plenty of experience sleeping on the ground," he said. "How are things proceeding?"

"On schedule," Asher said, suppressing a smile. "When they get here, we'll be ready for them."

"Better if we're done before they get here," Jonah said. "But it's always best to be prepared. Why are you grinning like that?"

Asher brought up something from behind the desk. A twenty-five-year-old Laphroaig.

"Found it in one of the offices," he said. He placed two tumblers on the table.

"Well," Jonah said. "Someone had good taste."

Asher poured a little in each glass and offered him one. He took it, brought it up to his nose, smelled the peat and smoke, the salt of the seaweed of the North Atlantic.

"To Monster Zero," Asher said.

"To the higher cause," Jonah replied. They drank.

"Takes me back," Jonah said. "I was younger than you when I first had this. I had been a few years in Her Majesty's army. Took a leave to Islay, where they make this stuff. Beautiful place. I actually believed then, you know. All the bullshit. The justifications, the outright lies." He took another drink.

"What changed your mind?" Asher asked. "Lindy? You've never said."

"Lindy? No. Maybe that was the tipping point, but no. I had already reached my conclusion. I just needed a push to live my purpose."

"To that," Asher said. They drank again.

"You remember when I brought you in?" Jonah said. "What we were doing?"

"Yeah. The chemical plant in China was my first. Then the thing in the DRC, the big game hunters. God, did those guys deserve everything they got."

"Little things," Jonah said. "Chipping away at the walls to a fortress we were never going to be able to destroy. But all that changed when the Titans appeared. When those bloody MUTOs went careening across the world. We got our hands in it five years ago, but our dear Dr. Russell shut it down. Just as well. I was still thinking too small, even then. But now – now I finally know how to do it."

"I'm glad to be a part of it," Asher said. "There is a better world ahead."

"Yes, there is," Jonah said. He took another sip.

"People look at that thing in the ice, and they think it's a monster." He shook his head. "They're not the monsters. We are. The whole bloody human race."

* * *

The USS *Argo* was a flying wing, a boomerang-shaped vehicle with five powerful jet engines situated behind the "V" where the wings met in the back. The command cabin lay in the front of a ridge in the center of the craft that ran from the cockpit at the nose back to the engines. But there was plenty of space in the wings. Barnes supervised the loading of the gear they'd need in Antarctica, and double-checked the status of their on-board arms.

"So we're finally going on a monster hunt," Hendricks said.

"Is that what you heard?" Barnes asked. "Because what I got out of the briefing is that we're chasing after a suitcase."

"And a bunch of bad guys," Hendricks said. "And a monster, right? It's a containment center."

"Yeah," Barnes said. "We're gonna make sure we keep whatever it is contained."

"But if it does get out, we'll torch it, right?"

Barnes caught Hendricks's gaze.

"Hey," he said. "I know you lost your dad in Honolulu. I'm sorry about that. But don't get out ahead of us, understand? You do the job as the Colonel calls it. By the numbers. Or you stay here."

"You know me," Hendricks replied. "I'm no loose cannon. I just want to be clear about our options if things go wrong."

"The Colonel will break all that down before we get there. It's a long way to Antarctica, even in this thing."

When Barnes got back to the command cabin, Griffin was settling behind the controls.

"You ready to fly this bad boy?" he asked her.

"The week before you were born," she said. "Are we all ready to go?"

"As soon as the PhDs are on board," he said. He nodded at a monitor.

"Looks like that's them now."

"Chief?" Griffin said.

"Yeah?"

She pointed out of the cockpit, toward the sky.

"I'm gonna knock a hole in that."

Ten minutes later, she did, and the *Argo* was on its way, accompanied by a squadron of F-35s.

"Damn, we're impressive," he told Griffin.

Gathered around a set of digital displays, they got a further briefing.

"The specimen at this site has been kept entirely off-book," Vivienne said. "And since it's a more recent discovery our data is limited, but it seems to be another apex predator."

"Emma called it 'Monster Zero'," Serizawa said.

An X-ray of the thing was on screen. It was all horns, claws and teeth, with a good bit of snake thrown in. He tried to imagine what it looked like with skin on. It was not a pretty image.

It also explained the collective gasp when Godzilla's path converged on this place. Even as Titans went, this looked like a bad one.

"It may have been a rival Alpha to Godzilla," Vivienne said, "battling for dominance over the other Titans."

Mark nodded; that made sense. It was also terrifying. A monster that could rival Godzilla? No thanks.

"Dr. Chen?" Serizawa asked.

"I've been scouring through thousands of years of myths and legends," Chen said, "but it's almost as if people were scared to even write about it."

"As if it was *meant* to be forgotten," Serizawa mused.

Mark looked over as Stanton entered.

"So, I hate to crash the party," Stanton said, "but I got some bad news."

"You can just say 'news'," Barnes said. "It's always bad."

"We lost Godzilla," Stanton continued. "Dropped off the scan near Venezuela."

"Dropped off?" Mark asked.

But Stanton seemed excited.

"I'm telling you," Stanton said. "Dr. Brooks was right – it's the Hollow Earth. That's how he moves so fast using these underwater tunnels like wormholes – just, like, zipping around—" He jerked his hand inventively through the air.

Mark remembered Brooks. He'd been with Monarch since the seventies, had been involved in the Skull Island situation. And yeah, he'd had this crackpot theory that the Earth was like Swiss cheese, full of gigantic subterranean chambers, where monsters hid.

Mark hadn't believed it. Godzilla was big, but so was the ocean. Humans had only explored the tiniest fraction of the deep sea. In the crushing black deeps that marked the boundaries between continental plates, you could hide any number of Godzilla-sized beasts. They were big, but not *that* big.

But it sounded like Stanton was a believer. Maybe he knew something Mark didn't.

"Everyone look sharp," Colonel Foster cut in. "We're approaching the base."

Madison watched Jonah's men work with mounting anxiety.

The drilling continued, but now the mercenaries were placing explosives in the holes.

They were going to blast Monster Zero free. But then what?

What would it do when it woke up with explosions going off everywhere? Mothra had freaked out over a few guys with guns. And Mothra had been a baby compared to this thing. Its standing height was estimated at five hundred and twenty-one feet. Godzilla only stood three hundred and fifty-five feet. If it really was an apex predator, like Mom thought, it would probably react like one. Of course, she imagined Jonah planned to set off the charges remotely, but still...

"They're here," Asher said, looking up from the radar screen.

Monarch must have figured out what had happened and sent more troops. But Jonah didn't seem worried.

"Keep them busy," he told Asher.

Asher signaled some of the others, and they quickly left the cave.

Another fight coming up, Madison thought. *Please let it stop.*

But she knew it wasn't likely to stop anytime soon.

EIGHT

From Dr. Chen's notes:

Lord of the dwelling, he subdued the demon who roared aloud, six-eyed and triple-headed.

—*Rigveda* 10.99.6
Sanskrit hymns, 1500–1200 BCE

Suddenly the clouds arose; the sea surged, and from it arose a three-headed dragon.

—*Two Ivans*, A Russian folk tale

As they neared the frozen continent, Mark, Serizawa, Vivienne, Coleman, Chen, Stanford, and Foster and her G-Team filed into the hangar and onto an Osprey. Once they were aboard, settled, and through the checklist, the hangar door opened below them. The Osprey was suspended by clamps above the void below.

"Hang on," Griffin said.

Mark heard a clang as the clamps detached.

Then they were falling. Griffin nosed the craft sharply down.

For an awful moment, Mark thought she intended to nose-dive all the way to the surface, but then she pulled up; their airfoil caught the wind with a sharp bump, and the engines kicked in.

The *Argo* rumbled by above, with its escort of fighters.

She had just been trying to get clear of the bigger ship. If she hadn't nosed down – if the Osprey had lifted *up* – they would have slammed into the underside of the *Argo* or jumped up into the blue-white flame of her jet engines.

Or both.

He turned his attention to what he could see of the Antarctic. It was night, so that wasn't much. Looking upward he had a glimpse of the bright southern stars, but then they descended through a thin layer of clouds. Snow whirled past the windows in flurries.

He'd always wanted to see Antarctica. He'd even applied for a grant to study the hunting behavior of orcas along the continental shelf, but that had fallen through. Now he was finally here, for all the wrong reasons. It was a nightmare... What was down here? What was Monster Zero? Vivienne had said it might be *worse* than Godzilla. Mark struggled to imagine anything that could possibly fit that description.

Antarctica hadn't always been covered in ice. Two hundred and fifty million years ago, in the Permian period, it had been part of Pangea, the supercontinent, cozied up against what would one day be Australia, South America, and Africa.

The working theory about Godzilla was that he'd been around back then – or at least his species had – stomping through the late Permian until the massive extinction at the end of the period. Ninety percent of everything had died, most likely due to an asteroid similar to the one that had wiped out the dinosaurs. It also left the radiation levels on the Earth's surface too meager to provide the massive reptile with enough sustenance. So he retreated to the depths, where he could subsist on radiation leaking up from the Earth's core. Other Titans of the period had also gone into hibernation, or what have you.

A few crackpots subscribed to a different theory – that the Titans evolved underground, in huge hollows in the Earth, and return there in times of need.

Either way, when the first A-bombs were unleashed, and nuclear subs started nosing around, Godzilla and the other Titans began to take notice. There was "food" up there again. And so now here we were.

Eventually continental drift pulled Pangea apart, and what would become Antarctica ended up at the South Pole; but the world was still warm, much warmer than in the present. For millions of years, dinosaurs continued to prowl the forests and swamps of a green Antarctic, adapting to the months-long night and cooler conditions.

The world continued to cool, and Antarctica with it. The forests and the dinosaurs died, and the ice came, blanketing the continent in glaciers.

What else had that ice covered over?

G-Team was gearing up, checking their weapons. They must be getting close.

Hendricks brought up a ground scan for them.

"Shows signs of heavy contact," Hendricks said. "Appear to be casualties."

He switched to a map depicting the network of tunnels beneath the ice – and the one huge cavern they all led to.

Vivienne indicated a bit of the central chamber. "If Jonah is looking to extract genetic samples they'll be here – in the biolabs."

Right, he thought. But it still nagged him. Why did they need Emma and the ORCA to extract DNA samples from a frozen monster?

Maybe they didn't need the ORCA for Monster Zero. Maybe it was for the next few monsters on the list, the ones that were more likely to wake up. In which case, would Emma even be with them? Or would they have her and Maddie secure someplace else?

The warren of tunnels was dauntingly vast. It might take days to search the whole thing.

"All right, two minutes," Chief Warrant Officer Barnes said. "Check your equipment and stand by the door!"

It seemed like much longer than two minutes to Mark, but eventually the Osprey did touch down and G-Team pounded out onto the ice. He had been instructed to stay in the vehicle with the other scientists until they got the all-clear, but he found it hard to stay still. He kept casting about for something – anything – he could do to help. He got it. They were trained for combat and he wasn't. If there was a fight, he might get in the way more than he could help. But it didn't feel right, sitting in the Osprey when Maddie and Emma might be out there.

And at least he could watch their movements on-screen.

G-Team was equipped with helmet cams and the feed was on display in the Osprey.

Feeling helpless, he watched the jittery images as G-Team moved into the base.

"Come on Ash," Jonah said. "Make it snappy."

The charges were all set; Asher was rigging a remote detonator, but now suddenly the alarms were going off and lights were flashing. Someone else must have arrived, another team from Monarch.

Her mom grabbed Maddie as Jonah pulled them into the tunnels.

Barnes didn't like anything about this place. Begin with the coldest, nastiest continent on the planet. Add a mess of tight tunnels – *carved through the ice* – sprinkle all of that with corpses, drop in a monster that time forgot and a bunch of anarchist terrorists that could be around any one of these curves or bends, and what it added up to was not his idea of a party.

On the other hand, he'd known two of the people they lost in Yunnan, and he didn't mind the idea of popping open a cold bottle of payback.

"Remember," Foster cautioned, "eyes wide. We've got friendlies in here."

A few minutes later, the Colonel signaled for them to halt. They had reached a major branch in the tunnels. Foster indicated for him to take Green team down the left one. That was Martinez, Dukes, Kim, Johnson, Li, D'Aguilar, Rahn, and him. Foster took Gold team to the right.

Splitting up made him a little nervous, but it was Foster's call.

Martinez took point as they entered the tunnel.

Mark watched anxiously as Foster divided the team. He followed each on their head-cam feeds.

Both teams were soon picking their way through corpses. All of those Mark could make out were in Monarch staff clothing. Jonah and his men must have taken the base completely by surprise. He was having trouble breathing, terrified that at any moment he might see Emma and Maddie among the dead.

"It's a massacre..." Hendricks said.

"Hendricks, keep your shit together," Foster snapped. "We've got a lot of tunnels to get through."

Hendricks flinched at a noise. Foster signaled a halt.

Mark heard a muffled explosion, and then all the helmet cams were a blur of confusion, swinging every which way. Foster stabilized first. Her camera showed that the tunnel had collapsed behind them.

Foster swung back, and now they were shooting as mercenaries came swarming from everywhere. But through Foster's cam – through all of the fighting and confusion – he saw two very familiar faces in the distance.

Emma and Maddie. They were being hustled along by the guy from the video, Jonah, down another tunnel.

Foster and her team were unable to pursue; they were pinned down. By the looks of things, some of them were already dead.

The hell with this, he thought.

In the next heartbeat he was out of the Osprey, sprinting across the ice toward the base.

"Mark!" Serizawa yelled after him.

Inside, Mark stopped long enough to pick up a pistol dropped by one of the dead Monarch guards. He didn't have a lot of experience with guns, but he knew the basics and was willing to train on the run. He only hoped some of G-Team had survived the ambush, and that there was a fight left to join.

I should have known better, Serizawa thought. If he had been in Mark's position – if his own son Ren were the one in there – he would probably have done the same thing. Mark had lost a lot, too much, and he shouldn't have been put in this position. If Serizawa had had any other choice, he wouldn't have. But it had been the right decision to bring the zoologist in. It was Mark's insights that had brought them this far. But if Mark or his family didn't survive this…

Serizawa found he was playing with his father's watch again.

Mark had made his decision. There wasn't anything Serizawa could do about it now. He had to concentrate on the problem at hand.

Monster Zero.

Serizawa turned his attention back to the camera feeds, trying to get some sense of what was going on, but the sheer chaos of combat aside, the signal was starting to break up. Did Jonah and his anarchists have a jamming device? Maybe. But he knew there was a likelier explanation.

"Guys," Chen said. "I'm getting an EKG reading."

So. Not a jamming device.

* * *

Mark sprinted through the tunnels, hoping he was going the right way. Gunfire rang out now and then, hollow echoes bouncing around the tunnel.

He came to a branch; the light looked a little different to the left. He went that way.

He emerged into what could only be the big central chamber, but the thing he focused on – what he saw first – was Emma and Maddie. They were above him, moving along a catwalk right up against a wall of ice. Jonah and some other guy were with them.

He scrambled up a ladder and onto the catwalk in front of them, pointing the pistol at the guy in front.

"Let them go!" he said.

Jonah, Emma, and Maddie stared at him with shocked expressions. The other man with Jonah didn't hesitate; he jerked his own gun up. The moment seemed to hang like a drop of water on the lip of a faucet, but at the same time Mark's heart felt like it was about to beat itself from his chest—

A shot exploded above him. The man pitched back and crumpled to the floor. Something fell from his left hand onto the catwalk between them.

"Ash!" Jonah yelled, dropping into a crouch.

Mark swung around and saw Colonel Foster on a catwalk above, trying to cover Jonah. But from her position the terrorist was probably now under cover of the catwalk, so Mark pointed his pistol at Jonah, too.

Mark glanced down at the thing on the catwalk. It looked like a remote detonator.

They hadn't been taking DNA samples. They had been planting charges. But why?

For the first time, his angle widened, and he saw the thing

in the ice, towering behind them. Monster Zero – a pure nightmare.

Oh, shit. Were they planning to blast it free? Was it still alive, under all that ice? Why? Did Jonah think he could *control* it?

"Mark!" Emma yelled.

He had Jonah covered. It was time to get this done, before more terrorists showed up and they were outnumbered again.

"Madison," Mark shouted. "Let's go!"

"Dad?" Maddie said. Panic nearly overwhelmed him. His little girl, in the middle of all of this – the gunfire, the murder. He had to get her out. But she was confused; of course she was. She was used to not having him around, and yet here he was in freaking Antarctica. But he had to break through that, make her understand. Quickly.

"Let's go!" Mark repeated. "Emma, Maddie, come on!"

To his relief, Maddie took a couple of steps toward him. They were getting out of this, the three of them.

"Madison, walk to me! Walk to me now. Come on, honey."

He glanced past her at Jonah, who was still down, out of reach of Foster's rifle.

Emma was still back there, too. She hadn't moved.

"Emma," he said. "What are you doing? Let's go. Come on!"

"Maddie," Emma said.

"Dad," Maddie said.

Emma looked Mark in the eye, then back to their daughter.

"Madison," she said, firmly.

Maddie stopped. Something in her expression changed. Her gaze wandered; she couldn't quite meet his eyes. Then she stepped back, behind her mother. What did they know that he didn't? What card was Jonah still holding that he couldn't see?

He glanced at Foster. She looked as confused as he was.

Emma walked forward and picked up the detonator the anarchist had dropped. Then her gaze fastened on his, and he saw that familiar, diamond-hard resolve in her eyes.

"I'm sorry," Emma told him. "Run!"

She pressed the detonator.

A chain of explosions ran through the massive ice wall. Cracks spread with lightning speed. The bright metallic scent of ozone filled his nasal cavity and he watched with disbelief as Emma grabbed Madison and pulled her toward a cargo elevator. Jonah stepped in, too.

Madison kept her face turned toward him, though.

"No, wait!" Madison shouted. "We can't leave him! Dad! Dad!"

"Maddie!" he screamed.

He started forward, but Jonah shot at him. He knew logically that he couldn't dodge a bullet, but his reflexes didn't, so he threw himself to the side. By the time he recovered, Maddie, Emma, and Jonah were on the elevator, going up.

He looked around wildly, fresh out of ideas. Then he saw the second elevator. He raced toward it, dodging chunks of the ice wall that was now coming down like an avalanche.

He made it to the platform, hit the button, and started up. They only had a few seconds on him. He could make it.

Barnes squeezed off another round and moved up as Martinez laid down cover fire. Foster was back in touch and was somewhere up ahead, although the connection was iffy and getting worse. But they had a rendezvous point.

The problem was, they were pinned down. They could retreat, but moving forward was difficult. The enemy had used explosives to create a makeshift barrier out of ice and structural junk.

He crouched behind a transformer just as bullets began spanging into it. He caught a movement from the corner of his eye, someone in a snow parka trying to flank him.

Yeah, no. He fired, swinging his weapon in an arc. The figure in white stumbled and fell behind a pile of ice. He wasn't sure if he'd hit him or not.

A hail of bullets struck all around him.

He'd lost three. That left Martinez, Johnson, D'Aguilar, Li. Not enough to break through here. In fact...

Gunfire stuttered, and another figure whipped by, headed for the same flanking position. This one made it for sure; Barnes didn't get a shot off.

"I'm coming up, chief," Martinez said.

"No," Barnes said. "Stay back."

"They're gonna move up on you."

He knew that. The only smart thing to do was retreat. But there might not be a way out behind them; he'd heard a lot of explosions in that direction, too.

A sudden barrage of gunfire started up ahead of him. He braced himself; this was it, they were coming. Time to take as many of the assholes out as possible.

A head and rifle popped up on his flank. He fired and had the satisfaction of seeing the man's wind-goggles shatter. Then he turned to face whoever was coming from ahead.

The shots continued, but he realized there weren't any rounds kicking up near him. Who were they shooting at?

He leaned out and saw someone charging toward him.

He stood and shot him, then swung his weapon wildly, looking for the next.

But there wasn't a next.

Everything was quiet now. He blinked, wondering what had happened.

"Barnes," a familiar voice shouted from behind the barricade. "It's Hendricks. Don't fire."

Now he saw a hand waving from behind the rubble, followed by Hendricks's familiar face.

They'd come in from behind the enemy.

"What took so long?" he asked.

"We were on a coffee break," Hendricks said.

Just then, everything shook. He thought it was another ambush, but it felt bigger than that.

Way bigger.

"Come on," Hendricks yelled.

"Yeah, that sounds good," Barnes replied.

By the time they got to Foster, the whole damn place was coming down. Gigantic chunks of ice were crashing all around them, and the floor beneath their feet was crumbling. He saw two freight elevators ahead; one was already going up, but the other was waiting for them, and Foster led them toward it.

But then it started up, too.

"Well, shit," he said. "This sucks."

Mark looked down from the elevator and saw what was left of G-Team. More ice was falling, and soon the whole billion-ton chamber would collapse, and then they would be buried.

There wasn't another elevator. There was nothing he could do for them. If he went back down, he would give Jonah too big a lead. And he would probably die, along with the commandos. It was G-Team or his family, wasn't it?

"Dammit!"

He hit the down button. The elevator reversed course.

It's probably already too late anyway, he thought. *For them and for me.*

"Come on!" he shouted as the doors opened.

The soldiers piled in as the cavern came apart.

Maddie was still in a daze when the elevator brought them above ground, and she was hustled along to board the Osprey. The gunfire, the splintering ice. Her dad…

She glared at Jonah, but he didn't notice. In fact, he looked – hurt. It had all been a sort of blur, but now she remembered the way he'd held Asher, the look on his face.

So even Jonah could care about someone. Amazing.

She didn't give a shit. Jonah had tried to kill her father.

But he'd missed, right? She had seen him climb onto the other elevator. But she couldn't be sure. What if he had a bullet hole in him, like everyone else Jonah met?

And the elevator hadn't arrived, even though it had only been a few seconds behind them. She kept looking back, even as she was pushed into the Osprey. Jonah's remaining men were scrambling aboard, and her mother began fiddling with the ORCA. She started strapping in as the craft, in helicopter mode, began to leave the ground.

"Why is Dad here?" she asked.

"I don't know, honey—" her mom began.

"We can't leave him!" she said.

But rather than responding to her, her mother looked over at Jonah.

"What are you waiting for?" Jonah demanded. "Wake it up."

Her mother gave Maddie another glance. Then she stood

up and walked toward the back of the plane, holding the ORCA, looking out the open hatch.

What was she doing? Dad was out there. Yes, they were divorced, but didn't she understand how much he meant to her? Why was it always like this? Why did she have to choose?

The ORCA began throbbing a deep, slow rhythm.

NINE

From the field notes of Dr. Ling:

It is said he came from another place, the sky maybe. A star. That he was a younger son and would not inherit territory, and so he came here to find his own. Long ago. He had three heads, each on a long neck. Each head was like a death adder, with horns you know, but the horns were bigger. But he wasn't a snake; he had legs, and wings like a bat. His color was like that of the sun near the horizon. He was very, very large. Like a mountain. And he brought storms wherever he went. His breath was lightning, and his eyes were flashes in a storm cloud. He was similar to the Ancestor Gods — but also unlike them. He fought with them, sometimes. We don't talk about him much. When we do we just call him Mandandare Aqenomba "Three Heads." But he had a name. We still remember it. Each mother and father whispers it to their children, when they are old enough. Once.

> —Told by Basau of the remote Taza
> people of Highland New Guinea

When they reached the surface of the ice it had already begun to shiver and fracture. Mark and G-Team sprinted toward the Osprey, leaping and sliding as cracks appeared, until all they could do was make one final leap from a surface that was already falling.

They landed on solid ice and collapsed in a pile, as behind them the din of a glacier's worth of frozen water collapsed into a sinkhole that took most of the base down with it.

Maddie? But they'd been ahead of him.

Casting about, Mark saw an Osprey lifting off – not the one they'd come in. Maddie was there, he was sure of it. Emma had gotten her out, and even though that meant his daughter was again slipping away from him, the fact that she was still alive and escaping this frozen hell brought the greatest relief he'd ever felt. Whatever this was all about, his daughter was safe, at least for now.

Before he could begin to think what to do about that, a deep, eerie moan rose from the sinkhole, accompanied by a blast of hot air.

Things were about to get worse. Much worse. Monster Zero's time in the deep freeze was over.

Steam and fog boiled up from the pit, and in that cloud, a massive, serpentine head.

It was all dragon. Bigger than an Osprey, and covered in dull, golden scales. Long, twisting horns swept back and fanned from the skull. Devilish eyes burned in the crevice beneath its bony brow, and sharp fangs gleamed in the jaws of a snout that seemed equal parts snake and demonic horse. A forked tongue flicked in and out, tasting the air.

Then another head snaked up, and a third. As he stared, paralyzed by terror, huge leathery wings unfolded, shaking off millennia of ice, blotting out the sky. The monster's whole body crackled with golden bio-electricity. Twin tails lashed through the freezing winds.

A three-headed dragon. Something from ancient mythology come to life. A hydra. He remembered Chen saying something about myths…

"You gotta be fucking kidding me," Barnes said. He had signed up with Monarch not long after San Francisco. He had wanted to fight monsters – he'd known what he was doing. But this was just piling it on. First the firefight with the anarchy dudes, then half of Antarctica getting sucked into a hole.

Now a freaking dragon. With three heads, no less.

It was clear of the hole now. Its spiked tail swept through one of the few structures still standing. Then all three heads seemed to notice them at once.

"Open fire!" Hendricks yelled.

Their rifles spat; tracers streaked through the frigid air at a monster so big they couldn't miss, but that barely registered their efforts. Probably felt like they were throwing pebbles at it. Barnes figured they would fall back, but Hendricks looked like he was digging in. That was crazy, but it might buy a little time for Colonel Foster and Mark to get back to the Osprey.

His estimation of Mark had risen considerably. He'd come back for them, knowing the asshole who had his little girl would probably get away. He figured it was time to return the favor.

"Chief," Hendricks said. "We've got this. Get back to the Osprey."

"Hendricks—"

"Seriously, chief, one more gun's not gonna help. The Osprey has missiles. We can slow him down, but you have to hurry."

"Okay," Barnes said. The monster reared above them. The son-of-a-bitch almost looked like he thought this was funny.

He raced with the others toward the Osprey as Hendricks and his team unloaded their peashooters at the prehistoric nightmare. They were probably toast, but the way he saw it, odds were none of them were getting out of this little situation.

They reached the craft, got Mark in, and then climbed in after him. Barnes looked back out at Hendricks and his squad, still firing at the Titan. Griffin got the Osprey started; her rotors began to turn.

Monster Zero looked more curious than hurt as his heads turned to the squad. Lightning crackled along his scaled hide, more every second, like he was charging up.

"Aw, sh—" he heard Hendricks say, in his earjack.

Beams of golden energy crackled from all three maws, straight onto the commandos. He saw them outlined for a second, shadows dancing, and then they were gone.

But that wasn't all of it.

The lightning or whatever the hell it was surged through the ice, spreading out as it did so. It reached the Osprey just before her engines came up to speed. Sparks and raw electricity arced all over the ship, and behind his eyes everything went white. A terrible spasm jolted through him, like the worst cramp he'd ever had, but in every muscle of his body. The worst of it only lasted a few seconds, but when it was over, his heart was still doing weird shit in his chest, like it was a three-legged jackrabbit trying to outrun the hounds.

The engines had stopped powering up. The Osprey was dead on the ground.

Colonel Foster recovered first.

"This is Raptor One to *Argo*," she said into her transmitter. "Requesting immediate emergency extract. I say again, urgent extract!"

Oh, hell yes, Barnes quietly agreed. They did not have anything like the firepower they needed to deal with this thing.

"Griffin!" Sam yelled. "Get us the hell out of here!"

Madison watched in awe as Monster Zero rose from the sinkhole. But it wasn't the same feeling as when she'd first seen Mothra. This was different. Terrifying. This was no mere animal either; she could see the fierce intelligence in each set of eyes. But there was also cruelty there, and more than anything, rage. This was not a Titan they were going to coexist with peacefully, ever.

It was difficult to make out what was going on below. She saw the flashes of someone shooting at Monster Zero, from the edge of the sinkhole. Nearby another Osprey was powering up, and in the light of the floods she saw her father, climbing aboard. Jonah hadn't killed him. He had escaped the explosion.

But he wasn't safe.

The dragon heads reared up, and spat golden lightning at

them. It spidered and spread through the ice and lit up the Osprey like a sparkler. Then the craft went dark. Its rotors stopped turning.

Monster Zero stooped forward to examine the damaged aircraft.

"No!" she yelled. "Dad!"

She'd been watching everything from the sidelines, doing what she was told, trusting her mother's judgment. Trying to be a good daughter to her, support her. But this was too much. She'd had a choice, back in the base. She could have gone with him; now she thought maybe she'd chosen wrong. She wasn't just going to watch her father die.

She grabbed the ORCA and yanked it away from her mother, then ran to the open bay of the Osprey, working the controls, changing the frequency to a piercing, head-drilling shriek. Monster Zero heard it, too. All three heads howled in agony, the crippled Osprey forgotten.

Take that, asshole, she thought. It was working!

But of course, her mother was trying to take the machine away from her.

"Honey, let go!" she said. She tried to wrestle it away, but Maddie fought, continuing to broadcast. Monster Zero turned toward them, identifying the sound causing his pain. He started to flash and flicker, as he had before he fried the soldiers.

"Madison," her mother shouted. "You have to let go—"

Then Jonah was there. His fingers bit into her like steel, and between him and her mom, they forced the ORCA from her. Panting, she watched as her mother began powering the ORCA down.

With the noise gone, Monster Zero lost interest in them and turned away, his charge fading. They were far from him now as the Osprey picked up speed. And from her dad. Her mom tried to put a hand on her, but she jerked away, continuing to watch the downed Osprey until Jonah's men closed the bay doors.

Mark knew the source of the monster's pain, and he saw Maddie in the open bay of the other Osprey, holding the ORCA. He felt a swell of pride for his girl, quickly followed by fear. If she didn't stop, the beast would electrocute her as it had Hendricks and the rest.

But then the noise stopped, and Monster Zero broke off his attack. The Osprey with his child and ex-wife vanished into the Antarctic sky.

At least Maddie was safe – for now.

The Osprey suddenly rocked half-over.

Monster Zero had renewed his interest in them. One of his heads loomed in the side window. A second head struck them from the front. Then the roof began to buckle in. Windows shattered as the Osprey's frame bent.

It was taking its time, Mark realized. Monster Zero could have breathed on them again or crushed them in an instant. Godzilla clocked in at ninety thousand tons, and this horror looked bigger than the big G.

No, it was killing them slowly, savoring their terror.

Quick or slow, their fate was sealed. Stanton was praying; Sam was bracing for the inevitable.

The one still point was Chen. She looked completely serene, ready to accept whatever happened. He didn't understand it, but watching her, his breathing evened out and grew deeper; the drum of his heart lessened in tempo.

The metal stopped protesting; the pressure came off as all

three heads rose up on their snaky necks, sniffing, smelling something. It vented a peculiar hiss. Monster Zero sounded almost... afraid.

Mark followed the beast's six-eyed gaze.

Blue light shimmered below the frozen surface, building in strength as the ice buckled, melted, cracked. The Osprey rattled about like a penny on a drumhead. The ice sheet exploded upward, followed by a tremendous form, dorsal spines crackling with blue energy.

Godzilla.

The huge lizard faced Monster Zero, opened his jaws, and roared.

Monster Zero shrieked back from all three throats, charging up his own bioluminescence. Mark remembered Vivienne's comment about the Titans being like gorillas, beating their chests. Except these gorillas were millions of years old, hundreds of feet tall and... not gorillas. But there was clearly a grudge there, maybe one that went back two hundred and fifty million years or more. And here they were in their tiny craft, caught between them.

Godzilla charged. So did Monster Zero.

They slammed together, hundreds of thousands of tons colliding at high speed. The shock wave raced over the ice and hammered the Osprey. Mark felt the sting of it in his ears, and even through the metal hull the air itself felt like a slap in the face.

"Everybody hold on!" Colonel Foster shouted.

It wasn't clear which talon or tail struck them, but it sent their crumpled craft tumbling across the ice until they fetched up against an outcropping. Trying to shake the spots from his eyes, Mark saw the others climbing out of the remains of the Osprey. That seemed like a great idea, one to be emulated, but everything was spinning, and he was having trouble keeping focus. He floundered toward the opening.

Someone grabbed his hand, pulling him forward, guiding him out onto the ice.

Vivienne. He nodded his thanks, breathless.

The ice shook again as Monster Zero landed a tremendous blow on Godzilla that sent him thudding into the permafrost, but the giant saurian quickly regained his footing. The spines in his tail began to glow blue, and the light moved up his spine, blazing ever brighter until it reached his head. Then Godzilla's mouth gaped and a blue beam of atomic fire jetted out. Monster Zero dodged, yanking his necks so the deadly beam threaded between them. Golden lightning crackled from the three-headed monster, striking Godzilla squarely in the chest. The reptile staggered back – into the sinkhole. Energy was still streaming from his mouth as he fell; he went sideways and hit one of the few remaining buildings, blasting debris all around them. Then Godzilla vanished into the abyss.

That was bad. As much as he hated Godzilla, Mark was sort of rooting for him to win this particular fight, or at least keep the other monster busy long enough to let them get away. But now Monster Zero turned his attention back to them.

He and Vivienne ran like hell toward the others, but he still wasn't a hundred percent. He saw Coleman running toward them…

A dragon head darted down, fangs gaping. The tiny hairs on his skin pricked up, and a sharp, sulfurous musk stung the back of his throat.

The huge mouth snapped shut.

And Vivienne was gone.

She couldn't be of course. He must have seen it wrong. She must have been knocked aside or something.

But part of him understood the truth. And he was next.

But he wasn't. Gasping, stumbling, he made it back to the others. Vivienne was nowhere to be seen.

Oh, God he thought, as the details reasserted themselves. The huge jaws closing on her, the unbelieving look on her face.

Oh, God, she's gone.

Serizawa was staring at where she had been. He looked like someone who had just been asked a question he should be able to answer, but couldn't. Then his features began to crumple in on themselves. Mark had never seen him look so beaten or broken.

But Serizawa wouldn't feel that for long, or anything else, for that matter. Because Monster Zero was coming back for the rest of them.

A plume of flame erupted on the monster, and then another, accompanied by deafening concussions. Monster Zero shrieked and gave ground.

The flying cavalry had arrived – the *Argo* and its escort of jet fighters. Missiles screamed overhead, peppering Monster Zero with high-yield payloads.

The three-headed dragon screamed again, overwhelmed by the sudden bombardment. It swept the air with its wings, swatting one of the rockets and deflecting it. It spun out of control.

Right toward Mark.

Before he could take more than a step it detonated. The shock wave picked him up like a giant hand and hurled him through space. For an instant he was in free fall, and then he hit something so hard he heard his bones crunch together. Breathless, ears ringing, he lay there, knowing he had to get up, but completely unable to move. Through blurring vision, he saw a huge head rise up from behind the dragon, from the sinkhole, and then Godzilla pulled himself up and launched himself toward Monster Zero, just as another round of missiles struck the gold-scaled Titan.

It was too much for the newly awakened Monster. Attacked from all sides, he broke from the battle, flapped his heaven-spanning wings, and took to the sky.

Then everything blurred away, and Mark didn't see anything at all.

For the fourth time, Serizawa turned to say something to Vivienne, who wasn't there. She would never be there again, but his heart and mind hadn't accepted it yet. They had been working together for so long, he felt incomplete without her. Half a mind.

He began flipping his father's pocket watch.

His father had worked for Monarch, too. He had been recruited not long after the bombing of Hiroshima and Nagasaki, but Serizawa didn't learn that until many years later. He'd grown up believing his father worked for a cargo company. It was only when he was older that his father had taken him aside and told him the truth.

There were monsters in the world. They had been sleeping for a long time. Now they were waking up.

The detonations in Japan woke the first one – Shinomura, a festering hive-colony of creatures that resembled a nematode with wings. It began preying on remote islands in Oceania.

Then Godzilla appeared and began to fight it – or, rather, them. A torn-off piece of the first one had regenerated into a second creature. Godzilla killed one, but the other escaped. Godzilla went after it, and when they came together, the military dropped a nuclear bomb on both of them.

The bomb destroyed Shinomura. For many years, Monarch believed Godzilla had also perished in that atomic inferno.

But he hadn't. Godzilla's role was to keep the balance. With both Shinomuras gone, he simply returned to whatever deeps he inhabited. When new Titans emerged decades later, Godzilla returned as well.

Now he was back, and it was clear – at least to Serizawa – why. He only hoped he could convince the others. Godzilla was not their enemy.

Sound returned first, the steady roar of jet engines. Light followed more slowly, and recognition came last. Foster and the others talking, somewhere near.

Mark was back on the *Argo*, lying down.

He pushed himself up slowly. He felt like one big bruise, both inside and out. Emma. Madison. Vivienne. Had all that been real?

As much as everything ached, nothing felt broken. He struggled to his feet and headed toward the voices.

They were on the bridge. Serizawa sat alone, flipping his pocket watch, not participating in the discussion. He looked kind of out of it. Vivienne's death had hit him hard. They had been colleagues and friends for a long time.

"Anything on the satellites?" Foster asked.

"Subs have Godzilla hauling ass past Argentina," Stanton said. "We lost Monster Zero in a tropical storm over Brazil. Scanning the entire southern hemisphere. So far, nothing."

"Then scan the northern!" Foster said.

The Colonel turned on Coleman.

"I know what I saw, Sam," she said, "and I'm telling you *she* pulled that trigger."

"All due respect, Colonel, you saw wrong. Okay?" Coleman insisted. "She wouldn't have done that. Christ, she recruited pretty much everyone in this room."

"Maybe Jonah forced her, right?" Stanton suggested. "Maybe he used Madison as leverage."

Coleman stood firm. "No," he said. "It had to be someone else."

Coleman had claimed to be a big fan of Emma's, hadn't he? That was obvious now. And he wasn't going to like this.

"Emma," Mark told them. "It was Emma."

It broke his heart to say it. Like Coleman, he wanted a way around it. Some missing bit of information that would acquit his former wife. But he knew her, and he knew what he saw.

Everyone went silent and all turned to stare at him. He was starting to get used to that.

"Foster saw it right," Mark pushed on. "It was her. No one forced her to."

It wasn't just Coleman. None of the scientists wanted to believe it. It was a tribute to Emma, in a sense, the trust they still had in her.

"Are you sure?" Serizawa asked.

Mark nodded.

Foster turned to face the map of the containment sites. All of them were on red alert.

"First she releases Mothra," the Colonel said. "And now Monster Zero. Anyone else sensing a pattern here?"

"Yes," Chen said. "And not a good one. It's as if she's trying to start a mass awakening."

"Well," Mark said. "It's just too bad that no one tried to warn you that was gonna happen."

"Hang on, guys," Coleman said. "Why the hell would

she want to release them? And why would she team up with Jonah, of all people, to do it?"

Serizawa's face set back into familiar lines. His voice grew firmer.

"We will ask her when we find her," he said. "So let's keep looking."

He met Mark's gaze. He didn't say a word, but Mark understood him. It was time to set their pain aside, to be dealt with later. Now was the time to do what needed doing.

Jonah's men secured their new location and began setting up for the next phase, making sure everything was patched together. Meanwhile, Emma found a room she and Madison could share.

But she found Maddie sitting in an old radio room, settling in.

"I thought we would stay together," she said.

Her daughter didn't say anything, but continued to find places for her things.

"Maddie—"

"Leave me alone," she snapped.

"Look, I know you're shaken up—"

"I don't even know if he's alive," Maddie said. "He was there. You just left him. *We* left him. To die."

"I never meant for that to happen."

Tears were starting in Maddie's eyes, but she didn't look sad. She looked *angry*.

"I don't want to talk about this," Maddie said. "I don't want to talk about *anything*."

Emma paused, and then backed out of the room. She needed to give her some space. There was time for that now.

Of course it had been hard on Maddie, seeing Mark like that. For that matter, it had been hard on her, too. She wished he wasn't involved – it only made things more difficult and complicated. Monarch must have dragged him in to help find her and Maddie through the ORCA.

She went to set up her command post. She found Jonah already there. He'd been quieter than usual since Antarctica.

"Dr. Russell," he said, when she came in.

"Jonah," she said. She sat down with the ORCA and began checking its calibration.

She didn't like Jonah. She never had, and the tighter their association became, the less she could stand him. He was a fanatic with no conscience and little if no empathy. For him, there was no means too dirty to see him through to his desired ends.

But she needed him. And now he seemed to be – as hard as it was to believe – hurting.

"I'm sorry," she said, not looking at him.

"About your daughter? She nearly got us all killed."

"No," she said, checking back her anger. "She was only trying to save her father. She can't be blamed for that."

"She can indeed," Jonah returned. "Keep her curbed, Dr. Russell."

She frowned.

"I meant I'm sorry about Asher," she explained.

"Oh, that," he said.

"You two seemed close."

He shrugged. "He knew what he was into, what he was risking. I've known many soldiers who died never knowing what they were fighting for. Ash died for *something*. So."

Maybe if he hadn't tried to shoot Mark he would still be alive, she thought. But it wouldn't serve her cause to say that, or make anything better. They had to move on, finish what they had started.

"You remember how we met?" Jonah asked her.

"Guam. You tried to hijack the plane I was on. And tried to kill me later."

"And yet when you came around to the one true church, you turned to me," he said.

"Don't be too flattered," she said. "I knew I could never do this alone. You were the only person I knew who was capable of... this."

"But that is flattering, in a way," he said. "It makes me so happy that you saw the light."

He didn't sound happy, but then he never did. Satisfied was about as close as he ever got. He also wasn't right, at least not exactly. He and she shared similar goals, but the outcomes they desired were – quite different.

Mark's head was still pounding. He took a seat, leaned against the window, and closed his eyes, desperately trying to get just a little sleep. He couldn't, though. He kept seeing Emma, pressing that button. And Maddie, screaming. And Vivienne, eaten by that – what to even call it?

"Mark."

He opened his eyes and found Coleman sitting across from him.

"What now?" he asked.

"Mark, we've gotta be sure—"

"Are we still on this?" Mark said. "Yes, I'm sure. I was married to her. I—"

He cut himself off.

"I should have known," he said. "The minute you guys

told me she'd started tinkering with the ORCA, I should have known."

"This must be really hard for you," Coleman said.

"Hard. Yeah."

"Why the ORCA?" Coleman asked. "I mean, she wanted to use it to calm Titans. And she did, at least once."

"Yeah," Mark said. "When I was in her office, I found some of her notes on that. She tried to use bio-sonar to calm that thing – Jinshin-Mushi – twice. The first time it didn't work. She just made matters worse and got a bunch of people killed."

"She learned from that mistake," Coleman said. "When she used the ORCA prototype—"

"What else do you know about it? The ORCA?"

Coleman paused.

"Well, uh, I know that you guys went to MIT together. That's where you first started designing the ORCA, and it's where you, uh, fell in love—"

"Emma tell you all of this?"

"Some of it."

"You said you were a fan of my ex-wife. Just how big a fan were you?"

His blue eyes went wide. "Look, *no*. I mean, I should be so lucky—" he stopped, drew a breath, started again.

"She's a rock star," he said. "She's brilliant, wonderful. Monarch's wonder-worker, what we all aspired to be. And I don't understand what's happened. Why she would do this."

"Do you know what happened when we tested the ORCA?" he asked. "Did she ever tell you that?"

Coleman shook his head.

"Beautiful day on the Puget Sound. We were just going to try to – nudge them a little. Herd them. Make them turn a couple of times. Instead, they freaked out and beached themselves. But they didn't stop at that. They kept trying to go inland. Cut themselves up on the rocks. There were five of them. Three of them died. Because we thought it was a good idea to fuck around with nature. That's why we abandoned it. After our son died, she started talking about working on it again. It's what broke us up. Well, that and my high-ethanol diet."

"I'm sorry—"

"I'm getting off-point," Mark said. "I know her. She thinks she knows what she's doing, just like the two of us were so damn sure of ourselves before we killed those whales. But these aren't whales, Sam. A screw-up with these – monsters – I don't want to imagine."

"Yeah," Sam said. "Okay. Thanks for explaining that."

Mark nodded. "Just out of curiosity," he said, "where are we headed?"

"Mexico," Sam replied. "I hope you brought some flip-flops and swim trunks."

TEN

We cannot command nature except by obeying her.

—Francis Bacon, *Novum Organum*

Keeping track of Godzilla wasn't much of a problem. In the past he hadn't been bothered by submarines and drones in his wake or alongside of him, and he didn't seem to mind now. Mark wondered how they fit into the monster predator's world. Did he think of them as part of his pack, since they were following but not displaying aggression? Or did he think of them the way sailors on fishing boats thought of the seabirds that circled their craft hoping for scraps?

Whatever the explanation, it struck him as odd, given his behavior toward the underwater base. If he had any long-term memory, he surely knew submarines had weapons.

Anyway, Godzilla wasn't their chief priority. Finding Emma was.

Foster pulled up a global map and traced a track depicted on it with her hand.

"Godzilla appears to be following the same path as Emma's Osprey, heading north over South America to here." She zoomed in to a small island. "Outpost 56 in Isla de Mara, Mexico. We touch down there in ten minutes."

La Isla de Mara, an island in the Gulf of Mexico, not far from the mainland. The satellite map detailed a dormant volcano with what appeared to be a geothermal plant built into its mouth.

La Isla de Mara wasn't the only outpost Monarch was worried about. At least six others seemed to have been compromised. Outposts in Thailand, Sudan, Brazil, the American Southwest, and Germany. And one more, in the Pacific.

Skull Island.

Was Emma about to release the Titans in those locations, too? What the hell was she up to, and why? Sure, she'd always respected the things. Liked them, even. Hell, she was a paleobiologist whose wildest wish had come true. Rather than study fossils, she got to play with living creatures millions of years old.

But she wasn't a terrorist, and she wouldn't work with a terrorist unless she had a really good reason.

The problem was, try as he might, he couldn't think of a reason that made any sense.

Antarctica was isolated and unpopulated, the Monarch base and a few research stations aside. These other places, though – Cambodia, Mexico, Sudan – they had human populations. Even if the monsters stayed contained, the fight to win back the bases from Jonah's mercenaries would create a lot of collateral damage. And if Emma managed to release these monsters, it would be much worse.

"What about the people?" Mark asked.

"I'm sorry?" Colonel Foster said.

He pointed to the coastal village near the volcano.

"The people. The people down there in that village who don't realize they're gonna be the special of the day."

"We've sent G-Team to begin an evacuation," Serizawa said.

"Dr. Serizawa," the bridge officer said, "we have a call on the emergency channel – from Isla de Mara."

"Answer it," Serizawa said.

Emma appeared on-screen. She stood in front of a panel of instruments, and she was alone.

He couldn't take his eyes away. Even now she was beautiful to him. After everything. Because history didn't restart every second, or even after something awful happened. And his history with Emma was written too deeply in him to be easily erased.

Which made this all the more awful.

"I suppose I should go first," Emma said.

That snapped him out of it, a little, gave his anger purchase.

"Where's Madison?" he demanded.

"She's right here with me."

Madison stepped into the frame.

"Dad?" she said. "Dad, are you okay?"

The rush of relief was dizzying.

"Madison – you all right, hon?"

"Dad – I'm sorry."

"You don't have to be sorry," Mark said.

"She's fine, Mark," Emma said. "Trust me."

Trust you? he thought. But he held his tongue. He had to know what she was going to say, and if he went at her the way he wanted to, that might not happen.

Emma nodded. She nudged Maddie. His daughter paused, still looking at him. Then she moved out of sight.

Colonel Foster had no qualms about calling Emma out.

"Trust is a little hard to come by, Dr. Russell," she said, "especially after what you pulled."

"I know," Emma replied. "And I can only imagine what you're all thinking. But if there were any other way to do this, I would."

Mark listened to his ex-wife with a growing sense of dread.

"Do *what*, Emma?" Mark demanded.

He could tell she was making an effort to stay calm. This wasn't easy for her.

It shouldn't be. She had blood on her hands. But he knew her too well. Underneath whatever remorse she felt, he sensed absolute conviction.

"I'm saving the world," she said.

"By releasing those things?" he shot back. "That doesn't make sense!"

"As impossible as it seems," she said, "it does. Hear me out, Mark. After we lost Andrew, I swore his death would not be in vain. That I would find an answer. A solution to why the Titans were rising. But as I dug deeper, I realized that they were here for a reason and that despite all the years that we spent trying to stop them, we never dared to confront the truth."

"What truth?"

"Humans have been the dominant species for thousands of years and look what's happened…"

Video appeared on the screen. Scenes of warfare, starvation, deforestation, oil spills played out as she spoke.

"...overpopulation, pollution, war. The mass extinction we feared has already begun. And we are the cause. We are the infection. But like all living organisms, the Earth unleashed a fever to fight this infection. Its original and rightful rulers, the Titans."

The video cut to an insectile MUTO destroying Las Vegas, Godzilla on Bikini Atoll, Kong on Skull Island, a MUTO breaking out of confinement at the Janjira nuclear plant in Japan.

"They are part of the Earth's natural defense system. A way to protect the planet. To maintain its balance. But if governments are allowed to contain them, destroy them, or use them for war, the human infection will only continue to spread. And within our lifetime, our planet will perish, and so will we. Unless we restore balance."

"And what's going to be left if you do this?" Stanton said. "A dead, charred world overrun by monsters?"

"No, Dr. Stanton, the exact opposite."

More video. A forest, shown growing by time-lapse photography, a volcano, the ruins of San Francisco and Las Vegas overrun by plant life.

"Just like how a forest fire replenishes the soil, or a volcano creates new land, we have seen signs that these creatures will do the same: San Francisco. Las Vegas. Wherever the Titans go, life follows – triggered by their radiation. They are the only thing that can reverse the destruction that we started. They are the only guarantee that life will carry on. But for that to happen, we must set them free."

"You're murdering the world," Chen said.

"No," Emma said. "Because as difficult as this will be, I

promise humanity will not go extinct. Using the ORCA, we will return to a natural order. A forgotten order where we coexisted in balance with the Titans. The first gods."

Now her presentation showed images of cave paintings. Monsters and people.

"This is a dangerous path," Serizawa said. "You are meddling with forces beyond our comprehension, gambling with the lives of billions!"

"And what are you gambling with, Serizawa? Monarch is broken. It's on the verge of being shut down by a government whose only objective is to eradicate the creatures and if that happens, what will our chances be?"

Mark had heard way more than enough.

"You are out of your goddamn mind!" he said. "First you put our daughter's life in danger, now you get to decide the fate of the world? That's rich, Emma!"

"I couldn't be more sane and Madison couldn't be stronger. After we lost Andrew, I trained her to survive and at least now she will have a fighting chance!"

"A fighting chance? Why don't you listen to yourself? It's not all math, Emma. Some things you can't control."

"And there are some things that you can't run from!"

That stung, all the more because it was true. He had run, to the bottle, to the wilderness. Anything rather than face what had happened to his boy.

But there were different kinds of running. He'd run away. Emma was running *toward*.

"This won't bring him back to us," he said.

That got her. He'd known it would. He watched her struggle with it, but that certainty of hers was so strong. It always was, when she made up her mind about something.

As he feared, she shook it off.

"I can only urge you all to take refuge," she said. "Over the last sixty years Monarch has prepared bunkers around the world to save and restart civilization. I suggest you find them."

The screen went black.

For a moment no one said anything. Emma could be convincing. As crazy as it all sounded, she made some good points, and he saw a little doubt on some of their faces.

Chen broke the spell.

"That bitch!" she said.

The problem, Mark thought, *was that she could do it*. She had already released two of them, and many more were vulnerable. She must have been working at this for a long time, using her clearance to get the necessary codes and information. Odds were good that she had managed to place some of Jonah's people at some of those sites, sleepers awaiting their orders. The level of coordination was astonishing, but it was – from her point of view – necessary. After Antarctica, the government would move quickly to terminate the other monsters. Emma was making certain they wouldn't get that chance.

But maybe they could stop this one, whatever it was. It wasn't free yet. If there was a kill switch, they might be able to fight their way to it.

"How long until this thing lands?" Mark asked.

"Three minutes," Colonel Foster said.

"You might wanna rethink that," Dr. Stanton said.

"Why?" Foster asked.

"Something's not right. Check this out."

Stanton put up security footage from the containment facility. It was littered with bodies wearing Monarch uniforms.

"Emma's not at Isla de Mara," Stanton said. "I mean, the signal's too weak to be local. She's bouncing it off our satellites. They must be holed up in one of our old bunkers. She could be anywhere."

Great, Mark thought. Anywhere. And Maddie with her, sheltering, waiting for the apocalypse she had set in motion.

An alarm began blaring.

"What is that?" Mark asked.

"Oh, Jesus," Coleman said. "She shut down the containment system—"

"How much time do we have?" Serizawa asked.

"Mateo," Mariana said. "We have to go. Now."

"Naana," her grandson asked, "what's the matter?"

Mariana had been worried for some years now, but in the last few days her bad feeling had become stronger.

It had to do with the volcano.

She was not a newcomer to the island; her father's family had fished these waters for many generations; the line of her maternal grandmothers went back before the arrival of the Spanish.

For them, for her, the volcano was known as El Nido del Demonio, the Nest of the Demon. There were many superstitions about the place; her Huasteco great-grandmother scared her when she was little with tales of the great fire demon that slept in the mountain. She had become skeptical of her great-grandmother's stories after the age of ten or so, and by the time she was grown, and educated, she rarely thought about those tales.

When she was in her twenties, strangers came to the island. Her daughter Marisol was only two years old. They said something about environmental contamination and quarantined much of the volcano. No one ever went to the Demon's

Nest unless they had to, so no one really cared. But it made her and others think of the legends again. Eventually, they built a geothermal power plant in the mouth of the volcano. All was quiet for decades.

But then, five years ago, when she watched on the television as Godzilla and other monsters crushed San Francisco, she began to wonder, and worry. Monsters were no longer merely the tales of a great-grandmother. They existed.

Lately, there had been new activity on the Demon's Nest. Her cousin Valeria had seen helicopters landing, and also strange men making their way from an unknown ship at the docks.

Gunshots had been heard on the mountain. Two young men who worked at the plant were missing.

And now more strangers came, these from Monarch, the organization that hunted Godzilla and other monsters.

She could think of only one explanation. Others felt the same; she already heard bedlam in the streets. Word was that soldiers were evacuating people from the town square, in helicopters.

She looked down at her grandson and thought once again how beautiful he was. He had the same black, curly hair as his mother, and his father Juan's soulful eyes. His father had gone beneath the waves fishing and never returned. His mother, her sweet Marisol, had been killed in a car crash in Tampico, where she had been trying to find work.

She was all Mateo had, now. And he was all she had, except for photographs and keepsakes.

"It's nothing to worry about, Mateo," she said. "We're going for a ride in a helicopter, that's all."

"Oh," he said, brightening up. "That sounds fun. Should I get some things?"

"No," she said. "We're in a hurry."

Even as she said it, she spotted the little cross Marisol used to wear, hanging on a peg beneath her larger crucifix.

Quickly, she pulled it down and gave it to the boy.

"Take this," she said. "It was your mother's."

When he'd put it on, she grabbed his hand.

"We need to be quick," she said. "Do you understand?"

"Yes, Naana," he replied.

At least Dad is okay, Maddie thought. *For now.*

But nothing else was. None of this was happening the way Mom had explained it. She had left a lot of things out. Like how many people were going to die. Like what it was *like* to see someone die, to think your own father was dead. It sounded like a good thing, saving the world. Seven billion people. More people were going to make it than wouldn't, she'd been told, and then all the peace and harmony would begin. Wouldn't it?

Necessary losses. But who got to decide who was necessary and who wasn't? Her dad was right. One person shouldn't get to decide for everyone, especially when they didn't even know a decision was being made. It was more than unfair – it was unjust.

It had been weird, hearing her parents arguing again. On the one hand, it had seemed like old times – the worst part of old times, anyway. As always, with her in the middle. She remembered the feeling that she somehow had to please them both, to keep them together. But then Dad left, and she realized she had to focus on Mom.

But now she was right back where she'd been, but worse. Because this time they weren't fighting about Dad's drinking or Mom working all the time or the ORCA or whatever. The problems in their family were now literally the problems of everyone on Earth. Sure, it had always sort of felt that way to her. But now it was actually true.

She was tired of thinking. She activated the screen and found a station covering the Isla de Mara evacuation. At least they were trying. Monarch. Dad.

It wouldn't be enough. She knew who was in the mountain.

"Containment system bypassed. We're patched in, ready to broadcast the ORCA."

That was one of Jonah's guys – she didn't know his name. Some techie. Normally Asher would be hanging around, too. But Asher was dead.

She thought back to the moment after Asher died, back in Antarctica. She wondered if Jonah had written Asher off as a "necessary loss." Probably.

Jonah looked at her mom expectantly.

"Doctor?" he said.

Her mother walked past Maddie, over to the ORCA. She opened the case. To Maddie, she seemed a little hesitant. And she should be. There were still tons of people on the island. People who hadn't done anything to deserve what was about to happen.

"Mom," Maddie said. "Don't."

Her mother wavered. She looked at her, surprised. Maybe she could be talked down. After all, three Titans were already out there.

"I'm sorry," Jonah sneered. "Did a child just tell you what to do?"

"Maybe Dad's right," Maddie pushed on. "Maybe this isn't the way—"

"By all means, Dr. Russell," Jonah said. "Let's reconsider

our entire plan now, especially after telling your friends about it."

"Madison, we talked about this," her mother said.

"No," Maddie said. "You said we were doing this to help people, that we'd give them a chance to find shel—"

Jonah banged the table with his hand, hard.

"We don't have time for this," he snapped. "Did you really think this would be easy? Painless?"

He sent her a malicious look, but he was still talking to Mom.

"Is that what you told her?"

"Leave her out of this," her mother said.

"Why? You're the one who pulled her into it. Madison, tell me – exactly what did Mommy sell you on? Some grand utopia? Man and monster living together in blissful harmony?"

He was exactly right, but the level of condescension was more than she could take.

"Bite me, dickhead," Maddie said.

Jonah's cold gaze bored into hers. He put his hand on the butt of his gun. The hairs on the back of her neck pricked up, and she felt a chill.

"If I were you," he said, softly, "I would be very careful what I wished for."

"And if I were you," her mother said, fury just barely contained, "I'd learn how to use the ORCA myself before I did something as stupid as threaten my daughter."

There was absolutely nothing about her mother when she was like this that suggested she could be screwed around with. Jonah was a scary guy, as heartless as they came. But right now, he and Mom were toe to toe.

"Sir," the other guy said, "they're attempting to lock us out. It's now or never."

"Emma," Jonah said. "*You* came to *me*. This was your plan. We both want to save the planet, but everything is going to die if you don't see it through."

Her mom looked over at her.

"Please, at least let them get to safety," Maddie said.

Her finger still hovered over the activation button. Mom was listening to her. Maybe…

"Ma'am?" the man said. "Our window is closing."

Maddie saw her mother's hand tremble. But she activated the ORCA.

"I'm sorry, Madison, but this is bigger than just you and me."

Once again, the device began pulsing.

Mom, no, she thought. But now it really was too late. Maybe her mother hadn't lied to her, not exactly. But she felt fundamentally betrayed, in a way she never had before. She'd thought she knew her mother.

She knew now that she did not.

"Signal's good," the tech said, studying his instruments. "Specimen's vitals are spiking. Patching us into the next containment site—"

"No," her mother said. "Not yet. We do this gradually. One at a time." She looked at Maddie as if that was supposed to reassure her.

Madison felt tears starting and fled the room. The idea that Jonah would see her cry just now was unbearable.

ELEVEN

From the notes of Dr. Chen:

> *I saw a Storm Bird in the heavens,*
> *high above us, rising like a cloud.*
> *It was a terror,*
> *its aspect was monstrous,*
> *its mouth was flame*
> *its breath obliteration*
>
> —*The Epic of Gilgamesh*
> Tablet IV

Mark watched the evacuation on the monitors, while keeping one eye on the display of the volcano.

G-Team was supervising the airlift in the town square, but there were hundreds left to go, and the crowd was in a full panic. That only grew worse when the ground began to shake, and the volcano rumbled.

When Barnes and the others first arrived, they found a sleepy little fishing town with a nice town square surrounded by colorful old buildings and not much going on at all.

But now it was freaking chaos. At first it was a rush to the docks, whole families piling into fishing boats, headed for the mainland. But now that all of the boats were gone, and the airlift had been set up in the town square, it was all coming down on them. Too many people, too few aircraft, and not enough time.

"What's got them so rattled?" he wondered aloud. "Nothing's happened yet."

"We're Monarch," Martinez replied. "Five years ago, maybe nobody knew what that was. But now they do. You don't think anyone here believes our bullshit story that the volcano's about to go boom, do you? They have TV here, too, you know. They know why Monarch shows up. Monsters."

Barnes nodded. "Yeah, that's fair," he said, silently counting the people climbing into the Osprey.

A group still waiting surged forward, trying to get around.

"One at a time!" Barnes yelled. "Back up!"

But they didn't, or at least not much. What could he do, shoot them? No. But things couldn't keep going like this, either.

A piercing shriek suddenly split the air. Not a claxon or an alarm – like nothing he'd ever heard.

But it shut everybody up.

Well, that and the earth shaking under their feet.

Weirdly silent, everyone turned to stare at the volcano

overlooking the town. Hell, it looked like their fake story was real, after all.

The quaking grew stronger. Dust and small pebbles danced in the town square. Dogs howled off in the distance.

The top of the mountain burst open, belching flame and black ash into the sky. Eerily, there was no sound, just the rapidly expanding cloud and ejecta streaming off like Roman candles.

A few seconds later, the noise arrived, like a thousand bombs going off at once. Barnes felt the shock against his face.

Things were getting more fun by the second.

A volcanic eruption on an inhabited island was bad enough in and of itself. But if Mark was right, this was just the beginning. He didn't know what specifically to expect. With the exception of the MUTOs that Godzilla duked it out with in San Francisco, no two known Titans looked alike. To his knowledge, anyway. He'd been out of the loop for a long time. But if he had to, he would bet that whatever was sleeping in The Nest of the Demon was unlike anything he'd ever seen before. But it would be big, and it would be deadly.

Amidst the smoke and flame, a silhouette drew up from the volcano and spread – yeah, wings. Big, burning wings that looked as if they were made from half-cooled lava. But at least this one only had one head…

More than anything, this Titan resembled a flying reptile, but it wasn't exactly that. It had a crest spearing out from the back of its skull, but its beak was a cruel hooked affair. Its wings looked like the black skin of a cooling lava flow, still molten within. And, of course, it was hundreds of times larger than any flying creature previously known. And it was on fire. Rodan rose from the volcanic furnace like the mythical phoenix, shedding flame and lava, reaching for the sky.

But it did not take to the air. It seemed to be taking the situation in; eying the town, the Ospreys, the jets screaming by.

"Got a catchy name for this one?" Mark asked Chen.

"Local legends call it Rodan, the Fire Demon," she informed him.

"That's comforting," Mark said.

"I'm picking up the ORCA," Dr. Stanton said. "Looks like she's piping into the base remotely."

That could be useful. They hadn't recorded Emma's Monster Zero soundtrack, but if he could compare the signal she was sending Rodan to the one she used on Mothra, he might be able to tease out how she was doing this.

"Record it," Mark said. "I need a sample."

Stanton nodded.

"Guys," Coleman said, "remember that tropical storm where we lost Monster Zero? Well, it's changing direction. Guess where it's headed now?"

Mark looked at the radar image. It had not only changed direction – it was speeding up. Coming right at them.

"That's not possible," Stanton said. "No storm moves that fast."

"Unless that's not a storm," Chen said.

"Oh, man…" Coleman said, as realization dawned. Monster Zero wasn't *hiding* in the storm. He was *making it*.

"We need time to finish the evacuation," Serizawa said.

"Then you better hurry because it's closing in fast," Stanton said.

Mark stared at the prehistoric beast in its nest of lava. If they fought this thing here, now, the people below would not only have to contend with the monster, but with the missiles sent askew, like the one that had nearly punched his ticket back in Antarctica, along with crashing aircraft, stray rounds of ammunition and who knew what else?

But then he realized something. Maybe they didn't have to fight it at all.

"Serizawa," Mark said. "Let it go."

Everyone stared at him in disbelief.

"Seriously," Stanton said. "What is wrong with you?"

He pointed to the radar image of the approaching storm.

"I think that thing is responding to Big Bird's cries," Mark explained. "That means it's coming here for food, a fight or something more – intimate."

"What do you suggest?" Serizawa asked.

"All fighters, weapons free," Colonel Foster said.

She didn't have to tell them twice. The jets streaked by, unloading their missiles at Rodan, the Fire Demon. Mark doubted conventional explosives would matter much to an animal that had napped for a few million years in a lake of molten rock, but it might just piss it off.

The white contrails of the rockets converged on the monster. They popped on him like bottle-rockets, and seemed to do about as much damage.

But the winged behemoth had certainly noticed them. His angry gaze searched the skies, dismissing the smaller craft and centering his glare on the *Argo*.

It didn't matter whether the missiles had actually caused Rodan pain. What Mark was counting on was the monster interpreting their attack as a challenge to his dominance; an invasion of his territory by another flying top-tier predator. And no self-respecting giant burning monster bird thing could let that slide, could he?

"I think we got his attention," Mark said.

"Everyone strap in," Foster said. "All ships follow our lead!"

The *Argo* banked hard and ran like hell, the jet fighters right behind her. Pissed, Rodan leapt free of the volcano, spreading his wings and taking to the air, dragging flame and lava, smoking like a burning fuel dump.

The chase was on.

Mariana gripped Mateo's hand harder as the demon emerged from the volcano and sat enthroned in flame. Her great-grandmother's tales of Rodan had scared her when she was little, but no words she or anyone else could say could ever live up to the terrifying reality. Satan himself could not be as terrible. Was this the apocalypse? Had the end times come?

"Mateo, we must run faster," she said.

The boy turned to look at Rodan, his face transfigured by terror.

"Don't look," she said. "Just run. And say a prayer."

As her grandson began mumbling a prayer, she said her own.

God protect my little one, she whispered. *Keep my Mateo from harm.*

But she knew God heard everything, not just what was spoken aloud. So he knew what was in her heart.

You took my Marisol too young. You owe me.

* * *

GREG KEYES

They reached the square, but the crowd was thick, and everyone was behaving like they were crazy. Men and women she had known her whole life elbowed her back. They were changed, her people, changed by the wakened demon. He had hardened their hearts.

But at least she and Mateo were in a queue. The soldiers were doing their best to get everyone on a helicopter, she could see that. But there might not be time.

She looked back. The demon was still in his nest. Maybe he would stay there a while longer, maybe they would get to the helicopter...

But then the monster lifted his wings, beat them like a gargantuan bird of prey. He tore free of the mountain and flew toward the village.

Then no one was in line anymore. There was no point; they fled in terror, but Mariana didn't. She stared at Rodan as he approached, watched as the most distant houses in the village seemed to bow down beneath the wind from those terrible wings. Black smoke followed him as if the sky itself was on fire.

The thunder, she remembered from her great-grandmother's stories.

And then the thunder came. She recognized it as a sonic boom like those caused by the fighter jets that sometimes did maneuvers over the sea, but this one shook her to her bones. She still held Mateo's hand, but she knew she had failed him. Down the street the debris-laden wind came, but she could not make herself move.

Then someone grabbed her, dragged her from where she stood rooted, pulling her and Mateo into a lane between buildings.

And then the wind struck, stronger than any hurricane

wind she'd ever felt. Roofs tore from the buildings above her; windows became glittering confetti. The blast picked up cars and sent them end over end through houses and streets. Those still in the square were swept from their feet.

The wind caught Matteo and tried to carry him off, but one of the soldiers grabbed him, kept him from being hurled away by the thunder of the demon's wings.

"Hang on, kid!" the man shouted.

The wind died as quickly as it had come. Mariana gaped at the devastation of her town, at the lava pouring from the volcano.

"Come on, you two," the man who had saved them said. "Let's get you out of here."

"What about our house?" Mateo asked, as they followed the soldiers.

"We have our lives," she told him. "For that we must thank God, and these men and women. I almost lost you, Mateo. How could I bear that? All of our things, our house – they don't matter. These people have preserved for us the only thing that matters. Our house can be replaced."

In the distance, the volcano rumbled. They might die yet, she realized. They probably would.

"Now, be strong," she told her grandson. "Pay attention to the soldiers. Do what they say, and we will be fine."

Rodan caught up with the fleet far quicker than seemed reasonable, hell-bent on destroying the threat to his domain. Gold Squadron – their jet escort – flew interference, trying to slow the monster's advance, but they were paying an awful price. As Mark watched, Rodan snatched jets from the sky with its clawed feet and sent them flaming toward the ocean below. When it caught the *Argo*, they wouldn't fare any better.

But they didn't have to stay ahead of him forever. Just long enough to get where they were going.

But even that would be a challenge.

Rodan was still burning, Mark noted, like an aircraft going down, trailing black smoke. At first he'd hoped that was a good sign. But now he saw the locals had it right. Rodan *was* a fire demon, carrying the blaze with him wherever he went, just as Godzilla had his blue radiation and Monster Zero his golden-lightning stuff.

Maybe the Monarch scientists had it wrong. They kept telling him the Titans were part of the natural order, but he didn't see it. How could *that* be natural? Maybe the Titans didn't arise when the rest of life on Earth did. What if they weren't part of life as we know it at all? What if they came from before, when there was no water or free oxygen, when everything was a volcanic hellscape, the atmosphere a perpetual lightning storm, when radiation sleeted from the sky and pulsed from the ground at levels that would strike a human dead in the time it took to draw a breath of the poisonous atmosphere. The Earth was like that for billions of years, before it started to rain, the sky to cool, seas to form. Before bacteria. Before the first photosynthetic organism started pumping oxygen into the air. Plenty of time for another kind of life to evolve based on some other chemistry that didn't need water or oxygen. It was easy to believe, watching the terrible flaming bird gain on them, that life as they knew it was just a pale attempt to imitate what came before, those earlier creatures that mostly perished when the rains arrived. Only a few adapted, survived to live in an oxygen atmosphere, became immortal...

No, not immortal. The MUTOs had been killed. The rest of them could be as well.

Griffin had almost been caught off-guard by Rodan's sonic boom, or whatever the hell that was. In the last seconds she had managed to turn the rotors to plane mode and kick into the wind, but that hadn't saved the craft from being dinged up pretty well by flying debris. She was running diagnostics, swearing under her breath as they loaded up the refugees.

"Is it gonna fly?" Barnes asked Griffin.

"Maybe," she said. "One of the engines is damaged, I can't tell how bad. There may be more. Might be better to put her in the shop, you know?"

"We have to get these people out of here," Martinez said, nodding at the handful of villagers that remained.

"Why?" Griffin asked. "Big Bird already took off, chasing the *Argo*. They're probably safer here than up in the air."

"Yeah, I wouldn't go that far," Barnes said, pointing to the volcano. Another gigantic plume of ash had just belched out of it, bigger than the last, but rather than just rising into the air, this looked like an avalanche or mudslide coming *down* the mountainside.

"Okay," Griffin said, "I say we get the hell out of here."

"Everybody strap in," Barnes yelled. "Now."

Griffin started the engines and turned the rotors up. One of the engines coughed, and smoke started to pour out.

"Yeah," Griffin said. "Hang in there, baby."

The Osprey seemed reluctant to leave the ground, and the smoking engine was making a funny noise.

Barnes looked back at the volcano; the wall of ash was coming, and fast.

"Hurry it up, Griffin," he said. "Some shit's about to go down!"

"You worry too much, Chief," Griffin said. "You need to do some yoga or something. Relax."

Martinez was trying to calm the passengers down. "It's all right," he was saying. "This is normal. Griffin here is the best pilot on the team."

"I'm the only pilot on the team," Griffin said. "But I'll take it."

They were picking up speed now, but it still didn't look like they were going to make it.

"Above it," Barnes said. "We need to be above it."

"What's 'it', anyway?" Griffin asked.

"Pyroclastic flow," Barnes said. Griffin arched her brows at him, skeptically.

"Hey," he said. "I took a geology class. It's not just the heat and ash, there also gas—"

"Just hang on, Chief," Griffin said.

They had just barely cleared the buildings, and then only because most of them were missing their tops. She tilted the rotors forward and gunned it. They dropped about ten feet during the switch as the wings sought to catch wind.

"We're not going fast enough," he yelled.

Then the wind hit them from behind. He smelled sulfur, and his eyes and nose burned.

It felt like a giant's hand had just slapped the Osprey in the back.

Barnes smelled sulfur and ash now, and realized he couldn't breathe.

* * *

Ahead of the *Argo* stirred a storm that blotted the sky, a boiling mass of iron-colored clouds with burning hearts of lightning.

They were fleeing one monster right into the mouths of another, Mark thought. *Wonderful. Whose plan had this been?*

Oh, right. His.

"*Argo* to Gold Squadron," Stanton broadcast. "Let's lure this turkey away from the mainland and straight toward Monster Zero – ETA, two minutes."

"Copy," the reply came back. The pilot was on-screen, along with his handle, *Cobra*. "Start the clock."

Gold Squadron doubled back and fired on Rodan. A few missiles hit him, which didn't faze the beast much at all. He lifted to fly above the squadron; just as they were beneath him, he clapped his wings with such force that three jets were simply slapped from the sky by the shock wave. The same beat of his wings sent him straight up, like a burning spear aimed at heaven, where he vanished into the clouds.

Was Rodan breaking off the attack? Had they managed to get through that rocklike hide?

But then he came screaming back down from a different angle, like an eagle stooping on sparrows, catching the jets off-guard, crushing two of them with his clawed feet and biting one as it exploded. The wreckage spun down to the ocean below.

Cobra was still there, but Rodan was right behind him and gaining fast.

"On my six!" the pilot shouted. "I can't break off! Ejecting!"

Mark watched as the pilot's ejection seat rocketed from the doomed plane.

Rodan swallowed the pilot, seat and all. Cobra's monitor went offline.

"Cobra's raptor is off the team," Stanton announced. "ETA to Monster Zero, sixty seconds."

Rodan's snack hadn't done much to deter him; he was coming up swiftly on the main squadron.

"Duster two-two-three," Foster said. "He's on your tail! Get out of there!"

"I'm losing control. I'm losing—"

Her craft spun away and crashed into the sea.

Then Rodan rolled, its flaming, pinioned wings sweeping though the air as if drilling a hole in the sky. It seemed to happen in slow motion, but Mark watched in horror as the spinning monster's wings swatted jets from the sky like bugs. When Rodan finished his roll, Gold Squadron no longer existed. The pilot feeds winked out in quick succession. The *Argo* was alone.

"We lost the squadron," Stanton said. "ETA to Monster Zero, thirty seconds."

Engines whining, the *Argo* rattled as they raced into the hurricane, Rodan right smack in their rear-view. The sun vanished as they were engulfed in the rolling fringes of the tempest. The *Argo* shuddered as lightning struck her, repeatedly.

"ETA to Monster Zero, ten seconds," Stanton said.

It was too late. Rodan had caught up with them. He reached out to grab the *Argo* with his talons.

Lightning flared again, and a three-headed silhouette appeared through the clouds. Heads and claws darted for them. Rodan screeched and veered away, abandoning his pursuit of the *Argo*.

But there was Monster Zero, right there. Rodan had the right idea.

"Dive!" Foster commanded. "Dive!"

Weight vanished as the craft turned down and dropped. Above them, the two Titans crashed together, locked claws, and began to fall, writhing and twisting, biting and clawing at each other.

Gravity returned as the *Argo* finally leveled out, little more than inches above the water. The pilot kicked the engines into high gear, trying to get as far from the monsters as possible – as quickly as possible.

How are we still alive? Mark wondered.

But it had worked. All of these things wanted to be top dog. Monster Zero had been on his way to put Rodan in his place already; they had just sped up the process.

Stanton was glued to the radar.

"Jesus," he said. "They're killing each other."

"Better them than us," Mark said.

The radio crackled and then the voice of Chief Warrant Officer Barnes.

"Mayday, mayday – come in, *Argo*, this is Raptor One, do you read?"

"Copy Raptor One," Foster replied. "What's your status?"

"We're screwed, that's what. And we have kids on board. We're gonna need immediate midair retrieval."

Colonel Foster swung around. "Lock onto their position," she said, "and prepare the hangar for emergency landing."

"Hangar doors are unresponsive," Stanton said.

"Manual override?"

"They're stuck," Stanton clarified.

Mark was tired of being a fly on the wall. Maybe he could actually do something.

"Which way to the hangar?" he asked.

"I can show you," Coleman replied.

"Anyone else?" Mark asked.

"I know the way," Coleman repeated. "Come on."

"Hope you have a big wrench," Stanton called after them.

When they reached the hangar, deck officers had already torn open the control console and were desperately trying to patch cables to get the doors open. It didn't look like they were having much success. The place was full of fire and smoke.

"What's the problem?" Coleman asked.

"The hydraulic systems are jammed," the officer said. "I'm trying to jump-start power. It's not looking good."

Serizawa leaned in, studying the two Titans as they fought their way across the sky. At times the battle was hidden by storm clouds, but Rodan's flame and Monster Zero's flashing breath were visible in the murk.

Mark had guessed correctly that Rodan's emergence had drawn Monster Zero's attention, that the three-headed dragon could not tolerate competition. But Serizawa sensed something else was going on. Despite Stanton's comment, he wasn't certain Monster Zero was trying to *kill* Rodan so much as dominate him. That was not the case when he fought Godzilla. That suggested Emma was right in guessing that Godzilla and Monster Zero were in a class by themselves, apex predators that stood above the other Titans. Ultimately, the real struggle for dominance would be between the two of them. If the rest of Emma's thesis was correct – that the last confrontation between Godzilla and Monster Zero had ended with Godzilla triumphant and the dragon frozen in ice – and given how things had gone in

Antarctica, Monster Zero was trying to build his strength before facing his ancient foe again.

He had never been more certain that Godzilla's place in the world was to restore balance. What he was not sure of was what Monster Zero's role was. The MUTOs Godzilla killed five years before had been going about the business of their life cycle – eating and reproducing. But while they had been ruthless killers, he hadn't sensed any particular malice in them. They defied that sort of anthropomorphism.

But Monster Zero seemed – evil. It was a concept that did not sit easily with him. The Titans were part of the world, had been long before humanity. They simply *were*. A carnivore was not evil because it sought living prey; it was simply how it was built. And he was suspicious of his own feelings. Monster Zero had killed Vivienne. It would be all too easy to let grief bait him into the same trap Mark was captive to.

Monster Zero struck Rodan a crushing blow, jagging the other monster with lightning and sending him into the ocean, throwing up a huge plume of water and steam.

Then Monster Zero turned his attention to the *Argo*, and once more Serizawa was sure he saw spite in its triple gaze as it began beating across the water toward them.

The control panel beeped. A call was coming in.

"It's Admiral Stenz," Stanton said.

Serizawa immediately felt wary. Stenz was a good man, a capable leader of men. They had worked together on the MUTO attacks. But he lacked imagination, and he did not understand the Titans. Even after Godzilla behaved as Serizawa predicted – defeating the MUTOs and then returning to the sea – Stenz was still skeptical of the Titan's intentions. Moreover, he was an instrument of the government, which had been trying to pry jurisdiction over the

Titans from Monarch for a while now. About that, Emma was correct: if they got control of the great beasts, they would kill them, or at least attempt to. Like Emma, he believed that the consequences of doing so would be catastrophic. He disapproved of her conclusions and methods, but he didn't disagree with her diagnosis.

Stenz appeared on-screen. A little grayer, a few more lines in his long, rugged face.

"Admiral," Serizawa said.

As usual, Stenz went straight to the point.

"Dr. Serizawa, Colonel Foster – I need you and the rest of your forces to immediately disengage and withdraw to a safe distance."

"Admiral," Foster said, "I don't understand."

"We have been developing a prototype for a new weapon," the Admiral said. "An Oxygen Destroyer designed to exterminate all life forms within a two-mile radius. With any luck it will kill these things and this nightmare will finally be over."

"Admiral," Serizawa said, "we must keep our faith in Godzilla—"

"I'm sorry, Doctor," Stenz said. "You had your chance. The missile is already on its way. May God have mercy on us all."

The screen went dark, but on radar, the missile was now visible.

"He's not lying," Colonel Foster said. "It's coming in hot."

In the hangar, things weren't going well. Far from feeling helpful, Mark was starting to wonder what he was even doing down here. At this point, it was clear to everyone that no amount of tinkering with the electrical system was going to resolve the problem. The Osprey was trailing smoke and flying more unsteadily by the moment. Something had to happen, and soon.

He studied the control panel, knowing it was pointless, that the problem wasn't on that end. But then one of the switches caught his eye, and he remembered the Osprey drop over Antarctica – from this very hangar. They'd been clamped above, and there had been a spare. He looked up, and there it was, clamped above them. Another Osprey.

He didn't feel like talking them through this. They might try to stop him, and Barnes and the others were out of time as it was. So he shoved the deck officer aside.

"What the hell do you think you're doing?" the officer yelped.

Mark ignored him and punched the Osprey release button.

Griffin was doing her best, but Barnes could see they weren't going to be in the air that much longer, not in this weather. They were lucky to be here at all, and if Griffin had been a lesser pilot, they wouldn't be. She had used the gaseous edge of the pyroclastic flow to come up to air speed, but that hadn't been easy on the already-damaged Osprey. If he'd known how bad things were, he might have pointed Griffin toward the mainland instead of trying to rejoin the squadron.

Now it was too late for that. It was the *Argo* or nothing.

The hatch blew open, and something fell through it. It took a heartbeat to realize it was the spare Osprey.

Which they were going to hit.

"Look out!" Barnes screamed; but Griffin dodged just enough. The second craft splashed into the ocean.

It wasn't pretty, but they had a hole to shoot for, now.

"Hold on!" Griffin shouted, and punched the Osprey toward the now-open hangar bay.

The engines coughed as she pushed them to their limits. Behind him, the townspeople were praying together. He hoped it helped.

They came in hot and smoking; hit the deck, skipped and skidded across it, and nearly slammed into the far wall before finally grating to a stop.

He let out his breath.

Okay, he thought. He glanced at Griffin, who seemed unruffled.

Yoga, huh? Maybe there was something to that.

Barnes stumbled out of the vehicle. Mark and Sam were there to meet him.

"Thanks for the lift," he told Mark.

Mark didn't have a chance to reply; rising over the whistling of wind through the open hangar, they all heard a familiar roar, and saw that Monster Zero was almost on top of them, skimming low across the waves.

Damn, Barnes thought. It had been a nice try. He glanced at his passengers and felt for them. He had signed up for this, but what had they done to be thrown into such a mess? To have their homes, their town, destroyed, and now their lives taken?

Dr. Russell had a lot to answer for.

He took a deep breath and waited for the impact. He reached for his sidearm. Maybe if he could put a round or two in its eye...

Below, the ocean bulged, lifted, sprayed up, smashing into Monster Zero. But it wasn't a freak wave; it was a helluva big lizard. Godzilla had caught up with them. He snatched the flying monster in mid-flight and slammed him into the water, like a killer whale taking down a seal.

Everyone in the hangar cheered, even Mark. In fact, from the corner of his eye Barnes thought he caught the zoologist doing a little fist-bump.

But they didn't have time for a long celebration.

"What are you all gawking at?" Barnes shouted at the others. "Move!"

TWELVE

From Dr. Chen's notes:

There was the great flood. At that time, Thunderbird fought with Mimlos-whale. The battle lasted a long time. For a long time the battle was undecided. Thunderbird in the air could not whip Mimlos-whale in the water. Thunderbird would seize Mimlos-whale in his talons and try to carry Mimlos-whale to his nest in the mountains. Mimlos-whale would get away. Again Thunderbird would seize him. Again Mimlos-whale would escape. The battle between them was terrible. The noise that Thunderbird made when he flapped his wings shook the mountains. They stripped the timber there. They tore the trees out by their roots. Then Mimlos-whale got away. Again Thunderbird caught Mimlos-whale. Again they fought a terrible battle in another place. All the trees there were torn out by their roots. Again Mimlos-whale escaped.

Many times they fought thus. Each time Thunderbird caught Mimlos-whale there was a terrible battle, and all the trees in that place were uprooted. At last Mimlos-whale escaped to the deep ocean, and Thunderbird gave up the fight. That is why the killer whale still lives in the ocean today. In those places where Thunderbird and Mimlos-whale fought, to this day, no trees grow. Those places are the prairies on the Olympic Peninsula.

> —Legend of the Hoh and Quileute people of the Pacific Northwest. Told by Luke Hobucket circa 1933.

By the time Mark and Coleman got back to the bridge, the *Argo* had begun to move again, flying up and away from the fight. It was clear Godzilla was in his element now, worrying Monster Zero like a crocodile, rolling him, trying to keep all three heads under at once.

"Twenty seconds to impact," Stanton said.

Impact? Mark wondered.

"What did we miss?" Coleman asked.

Suddenly a dragon head hurtled toward the windshield, its maw gaping at them, and Mark realized they weren't out of range yet.

But then Godzilla yanked Monster Zero back down, and the *Argo* began to haul some serious ass.

"Oh," Coleman gasped.

"The military just launched a weapon that's about to kill them both," Stanton said.

Mark glanced at Serizawa, whose brow was deeply

furrowed. Someone way above his pay grade must have made the call. Serizawa would never willingly allow his favorite monster to get blasted. And despite himself, Mark felt the stirrings of sympathy for Serizawa's point of view. Godzilla had saved their lives a couple of times now, whether he meant to or not. But if the big lizard had to die for them to get Monster Zero too…

"It's not the worst idea," Mark said.

On the other hand, Godzilla was winning. Monster Zero was taking way more than he was dishing out, his golden light flickering, while Godzilla had never looked stronger. The two monsters dwindled as the *Argo* tore away, but there were plenty of cameras on the action as Godzilla grabbed one of Monster Zero's heads – and bit it off. A spray of black blood jetted from the stump. It looked almost like petroleum.

That had to hurt, even if you had a couple of spares. Mark found he was looking forward to what Godzilla would do next.

A flicker of silver entered his peripheral vision. A plane?

He blinked involuntarily as both monsters were engulfed in light. The flash was brief, a brilliant green, and it quickly mushroomed into the atmosphere, casting a chartreuse pall over the sea. As the flash faded and the cloud lifted higher, he saw the Titans were no longer locked in battle. They were thrashing about in the water, grasping for something out of reach, fighting something they couldn't claw or bite.

They were sinking.

Still flailing, both Titans vanished beneath the waves.

Mark had been praying for this moment for five years. For Godzilla's death, justice for his son and all the others who had died in the monster's trans-global rampage. But somehow, now that the moment was here, he wasn't as elated as he'd thought he would be. He realized he didn't just have sympathy for Serizawa's views – he was beginning to *believe* him. And if Serizawa was right, what they'd just done could be a big mistake. Rodan was still out there, and Mothra, and plenty more where they came from.

The sea, still not entirely settled from the fight, began to stir and foam. Bubbles broke the surface, as if some undersea gas cavity had opened up. Thousands of silvery slivers appeared, spreading on the surface.

Fish, he realized, as the sea began to darken and grow red and the bubbling increased, became a fountain, a spray.

Monster Zero exploded from the blood-red sea, now a two-headed dragon, but most certainly not dead. His wings cracked the air as he broke free of the ocean and soared aloft. Mark feared that he would turn back to them, but instead he flapped off toward land. Apparently, the loss of a head meant it was time to call it a day.

The sea quietened back down, settled into its accustomed swells. Serizawa kept staring, but if he was hoping the big lizard was going to come back up, it seemed he was going to be disappointed.

"Dr. Stanton," Serizawa finally said, "can you locate Godzilla?"

Stanton began scanning.

"Yeah," he said, "I've got something..."

He turned up the volume, and once again they heard the thudding of the huge reptile's heart. But not like before. This time it was much weaker and less steady.

"His vitals are fading," Stanton said. "Radiation levels plummeting."

The radioactive aura on the tracking screen was dwindling. The heartbeat continued to weaken. What the hell had they hit him with? And why had Monster Zero been able to handle it so much better?

"Come on, big guy," Stanton murmured. "Fight it."

"No," Serizawa said. He looked stricken.

Godzilla's heart beat once more. The aura faded. Mark kept waiting for the next beat. Any second now it would start again.

But it didn't.

The telemetry displayed only flatline signatures.

"He's gone," Stanton said.

Serizawa was trembling. He looked broken. All of them, everyone in the room looked like – what? Like they had lost a loved one? Or was it just that none of them believed the big lizard could die?

"Looks like you got your wish, Mark," Serizawa said, softly.

It was true. But he took no pleasure in it. He'd wanted revenge for a long time. Now he just wanted his daughter back.

Mateo was sleeping, which Mariana found incredible. But she was grateful for it; he had seen too much today, just as she had. The soldiers had found quarters for them on the big airplane, some food and drink. It wasn't good, but she was happy to have it, as she was happy to be alive.

"How is he doing?" the man sitting next to her asked, indicating Mateo. She knew him a little bit. The cousin of one of her high school friends. Once in a while he would appear for Mass. He was a netmaker, and sometimes went out with the fishermen. Antonio.

"As well as any of us," she said.

"What do you imagine will happen next?" Antonio said.

She shrugged. "The soldier named Barnes said we are going to a Monarch base. From there we will be repatriated."

"To where?" he said. "Our poor island?"

She shook her head. "I do not know," she said. "I don't know if I could take Mateo back there anyway."

"I've never been to the mainland," Antonio said. "I wouldn't know how to live there."

"It's not over yet," Mariana said. "By the time it is, there may be no place left for us anywhere."

Jebel Barkal, Sudan

The pilgrims grumbled about being denied access to the site, and so did the local government, but Nez broadened the perimeter to include the tomb and place it off-limits to visitors. And for a while, nothing happened, except that they got a little more information about who carried out the attack on the Yunnan outpost. Nez finally relaxed enough to have a beer in the cantina during one of her rare off-duty hours. It was a good thing she only had one, because an hour later she was called back to duty. Another base had been attacked, and another Titan released, in Antarctica. A little later, they were called to view a video of Dr. Emma Russell – whose mind had clearly slipped crooked – taking credit for the releases and making it clear she meant to set even more monsters free.

The Colonel was off in Washington, so Kearns turned to her.

"Master Sergeant, part of your role here is to advise," Kearns said. "I know you've been increasing security. But—"

"Kill it," she said, without hesitation.

"Excuse me?"

"The monster," she replied. "I've seen the kill switch. Use it."

Kearns, Esmail, and the others stared at her.

"That's not an option," Kearns said. "At least not at this point."

"It's the only way to make sure it doesn't get loose, sir."

"Freer takes me for a fool," Kearns said. "I hope you don't. I'm well aware the government is trying to make the case to execute these creatures. Trying to find any excuse—"

"Mr. Kearns," she broke in, "two monsters are already loosed on the world, and the crazy doctor just told us she's going to break out as many as possible. That is not an excuse to kill Mokele, it is a mandate."

"Three," Esmail said.

"What?" Kearns asked.

"Mexico," he said. "Just came in. La Isla de Mara. The Demon's Nest…"

On one of the monitors a volcano was erupting, but it wasn't just lava, smoke, and ash coming out. A Titan was spreading fiery wings. It looked like it was made of lava itself.

"Rodan," Lang said.

Be damned, she thought. *That's Tsé nináhálééh, the Rock Monster Eagle.*

"Now can we kill it?" she asked.

"This site will not be compromised," Kearns said. "Mokele-Mbembe will remain contained and unharmed. You make sure of that. It's why you're here."

She sighed, but then she began giving orders.

"Move the helicopter and drone patrols out to ten klicks," she said. "If a mouse moves out there, I want to know about it."

GODZILLA: KING OF THE MONSTERS

* * *

When Monster Zero flew off, he had a destination in mind. Drones tracked him to Isla de Mara, where – beneath a steadily darkening sky – he settled into Rodan's flaming nest.

It looked to Mark like a classic case of asserting dominance. He was not only taking Rodan's territory but also his very seat of power, a usurper sitting on the old king's throne. And yet, that was odd behavior for a wounded animal. They usually returned to somewhere they considered safe, or at least familiar.

And there could be little doubt Monster Zero was badly hurt. Once in the nest, he began writhing and screeching in pain. Maybe – hopefully – the loss of a head was fatal blow, but like a decapitated snake, Monster Zero was taking his time realizing he was dead. Sitting in the lava seemed to make things even worse for the big fellah, which was a shame. Had he made a fatal mistake claiming Rodan's throne? Was he now too wounded to fly out again?

But then Mark noticed something. It wasn't just the necks that still had heads that were squirming like earthworms on a hot sidewalk. The headless neck was, too. It was no longer gouting blood, and in fact the severing wound wasn't there anymore, either. In fact, something appeared to be emerging from the stump.

No, he had read it all completely wrong.

Monster Zero wasn't pissing on Rodan's territory, and he wasn't dying. He'd come to the Demon's Nest for the lava, the radiation moving up from beneath the earth. Searching for the nourishment he needed to regrow his freaking *head*. Like a goddamn hydra from Greek mythology. It was covered in some sort of slimy membrane, but one of the other heads reached over and bit it off, so the baby head could keep forming.

In moments the new head was fully grown, blinking newly formed eyes, just as full of malevolence as the others.

At least, Mark thought, *it only grew back the one. Hydras were supposed to grow two for every one you took off.*

But three was still three too many.

Monster Zero opened his trio of razor-filled mouths and screamed at the heavens.

To Mark, it didn't seem like merely a scream of triumph. It was something else. A challenge, maybe. Or a call.

THIRTEEN

From Dr. Chen's notes:

Of coral wood the flesh of man was made, but when woman was fashioned by the Creator and the Maker, her flesh was made of rushes. These were the materials the Creator and the Modeler wanted to use in making them.

But those that they had made, that they had created, did not think, did not speak with their Creator, their Modeler. And for this reason they were killed, they were deluged. A heavy resin fell from the sky. The one called Xecotcovach came and gouged out their eyes; Camazotz came and cut off their heads; Cotzbalam came and devoured their flesh. Tucumbalam came, too, and broke and mangled their bones and their nerves, and ground and crumbled their bones.

This was to punish them because they had not

thought of their mother, nor their father, the Heart of Heaven, called Huracan. And for this reason the face of the earth was darkened, and a black rain began to fall, by day and by night.

—*The Popul Vuh*, Sacred book
of the Quiche Maya
Book One

Sedona, Arizona
Monarch Outpost 55
Titanus Scylla

Rick drove from Flagstaff to Sedona on the winding road through Oak Creek Canyon, admiring as he always did the great beauty of the place. Forty years he had been making this drive, and he still loved it. He thought about how he'd brought his children here, when they were young, to play in the creek. One day he explained that the stone the canyon cut through had been laid down mostly in the Permian period, and they'd spent the rest of the day crawling on all fours through the horsetails, pretending to be dimetrodons, the top predators of the early Permian.

He was a rock hound and a paleontologist at heart, but that didn't always pay so well, so he'd put his degree to work in the oilfields down around Sedona.

He reached the field and pulled his truck around by the office, a prefab metal building. He climbed out and stood for a moment, watched the pumpjacks bobbing up and down, like giant metal versions of the drinking bird toy he'd had as a kid. The pumpjacks, of course, were drinking oil – or as his youngest, Molly, liked to put it, "sucking the earth's blood."

The operation was mostly automated, but there were workers around, minding things. About half a mile away he saw the government guys were unusually busy. They had commandeered some land a few years back, claiming some sort of bio-hazard. It didn't matter; they could pull the oil right out from under them, and they kept to themselves.

Sawyer stuck his head out of the shed.

"Hey, Rick."

He nodded. "I was headed on west to have a look at the new site," he said. "I thought I would check in here first."

"Did you get my text?"

"I was in the canyon," he said. He pulled his phone out. "There it is."

"I just sent it," Sawyer said. "It's your seismograph. It's going loony."

"Huh," Rick said.

The seismograph was something he'd built, mostly for fun, nearly thirty years ago. His son Evan had helped him update it a few years back, so it recorded digitally, instead of on paper.

Sawyer was right; the usually flat line was looking excited, as if recording a distant earthquake, and a pretty big one.

Or else a little one, right under the ground where they were standing. As he watched, the waves continued to spike.

Now he felt it in his feet. The shed was starting to rattle.

"You think it's one of the rigs?" Sawyer asked.

"I don't know," he said. "But I don't like it."

He stepped outside, looking at the field with a more critical gaze.

"I don't—"

The ground exploded, and something long and black

stabbed out of it, arched over, and slammed back into the ground about twenty yards from the shack. Rick stepped back so fast he banged into the shed.

"Holy mother—" Sawyer swore.

They were sticking up everywhere, jamming into the ground. Jointed, covered in bristle-like hairs. The earth jumped and just lifted up. Almost quietly, the pumpjacks slid into the hole it left.

It.

He was barely aware that he and Sawyer were only a few feet from the pit it had come up out of. His whole nervous system felt like it was shutting down, the thinking part of his mind overwhelmed by a fear hundreds of millions of years old, encoded in the primitive brains of his chordate ancestors when they were prey to things like this. Its spider legs held up a bulbous body, a face of squirming tentacles under two merciless eyes, buried in something like a cuttlefish.

David. Anna. Molly, he thought, picturing their faces.

"The goddamndest thing," Sawyer said.

It was the last thing Rick ever heard.

Near Munich, Germany
Monarch Outpost 67
Titanus Methuselah

The cork came out of the bottle with a loud pop, sailing across the meadow.

"That's littering," Lara said, smoothing out the blanket and placing their little picnic of cheese, bread, and strawberries on it.

"It's cork," Jannik said. "Biodegradable."

"Um-humm," she said, as he poured the champagne into two plastic cups. "Paper is also biodegradable, but if you throw it on the ground, it's littering."

He handed her a cup.

"Prost," he said. They both took a sip.

"Listen," Jannik said. "I grew up right around here, you know. You see that mountain there?"

"You're trying to change the subject from littering," she said. But she glanced behind her and saw the mountain he meant, rising over the trees.

"My grandfather told me it wasn't always there. There was a village instead. And then one day a guy who was traveling in some other country came home. The village was gone, and that mountain was there."

"I see," Lara said. "And when did this happen?"

"Very long ago," he said. "The Middle Ages, maybe."

"Your grandfather must have been pretty old."

"My family has been here for centuries," he said. "But let me tell you the other thing about this mountain. They say if you bring a pretty girl here, and ask her to kiss you, she can't say no."

"Oh, I see," Lara said. "Well, it's a good thing you haven't asked me. I would hate to prove your legend wrong."

He grinned and leaned toward her.

"But I will prove it wrong," she said.

He stopped and reddened a bit. Jannik was used to getting his way with girls, she knew. With his long blond hair and blue eyes, he was almost pretty, and he could be interesting if he wanted to, so maybe someday she wouldn't mind that kiss. Maybe even later today.

But not now.

"Are all university girls so hard to get?" he asked.

"You tell me," she said. "You've gotten plenty of them, from what I've heard."

"What's so wrong with that?" he asked. "I like educated women."

"I like men who don't litter."

"Fine," he sighed. He stood up and wandered off in the direction the cork had flown.

She had a strawberry and looked off into the distance.

"A-ha!" Jannik said. He held up the cork.

And then his gaze went past her. His eyes widened.

"The mountain..." he said.

"Oh, now I'm going to hear more about this magic mountain, am I?" she said. "Come on, you've tried that on me already. Be original."

"No," he said. "The mountain, it—"

His scream was surprisingly high-pitched. It was so surprising it set her skin on edge.

He turned and ran

"Really, he's taking this too far," she said.

But then she felt the earth shift below her.

She turned around and saw the mountain was standing up on four immense legs.

It had a face and horns like a bull from some ancient hell. And as she watched, it put one ponderous limb forward, and then another. The forest growing on its rocky back shivered and shook with each step.

She didn't scream; she kept her breath quiet. It was half a kilometer away, at least. It would never notice her unless she drew its attention.

They had walked here after taking the train from Munich to the little town over the hill. She thought that was where it was going.

When its head was out of sight she picked up the champagne bottle and began drinking.

Indian Ocean
Classified Monarch Outpost
Undesignated Titan

In his office beneath the Indian Ocean, Dr. Kingsley Ikande lay on his cot and watched the surface of the water some ten meters above him. He had tried to take a nap – he hadn't slept in over twenty-four hours – but sleep eluded him. He was too troubled. He'd been meant to fly to Lagos, to see his wife and little girl for a week.

And now all of this.

He knew Emma Russell; his dissertation had been based on some of her early work. He'd had the great pleasure to meet her, at a conference. There, she had recruited him for Monarch.

It was so hard to believe she had gone mad. Two Titans unleashed on the world, and the suspicion was that she would try to release more.

Their floating containment was probably one of the safest; very far from land. Anything flying or moving under the water would be noticed from very far away.

But that didn't stop him worrying, of course.

Let the nap go. He was going back up.

But instead he went to see Kraken.

That wasn't its official name. It still hadn't been assigned one in the Monarch classification. That was fitting, since this outpost was similarly unnamed. But someone – he seemed to remember it was Devlin – had called it Kraken, and the name had stuck.

GREG KEYES

They had discovered the sleeping Titan on a seamount in relatively shallow water, curled around the remains of a nuclear sub that had been missing for decades. They had built the containment around him, sub and all. He was in deep hibernation and didn't seem to have noticed a thing.

The habitable part of the base – the living quarters, the control room, the laboratories – was all either on the surface or near it. But to observe the Titan directly – or take some sort of sample – several elevators ran through the ocean down to various points adjacent to the beast.

They had learned quite a bit about Kraken. X-rays, sonic scans, DNA analysis, had built a picture of what he must be like. His central brain cavity was enormous, far larger than it needed to be to control his body, suggesting a certain amount of intelligence, not unlike his distant cousins, the octopuses – although unlike octopuses and squids, his head was protected by a dense, curving cone of shell. He had dozens of smaller brains associated with his limbs. Like octopoids, he could also change the color and pattern of his skin and shell; when they found him, he had been virtually invisible. They pinpointed his location by radiation signature and his bio-sonic emission.

He had multiple hearts, and there was good evidence that he could regenerate limbs and, in fact, virtually any part of his body.

The elevator came to a stop; Ikande stepped out.

One of the techs, Jane Harris, looked up from her instruments as he came in. Otherwise, the lab was empty.

The large window faced one of Kraken's eyes. It was closed and had been closed since they found him. Jin, the paleobiologist, thought he was in the middle of a sleep cycle that might last another decade, unless he was threatened.

They had been quite careful not to make him feel threatened.

"Anything new?" he asked.

Harris shook her head. "No, nothing. Same as always. All functions are there, but at very low levels. How about topside? Any more Titans cut loose?"

He shrugged. "Nothing new there, either. I almost feel slighted. Why wouldn't our big fellow be invited to the ball?"

"Don't even say it," she replied. She frowned.

"What?"

She fiddled with her equipment.

"Nothing, I guess. There was just a little spike, but it went right back down. No, wait..."

The com light suddenly blinked on. He answered it.

"Ikande here."

"Dr. Ikande, it's Jen. We just got a flood of reports. Titans have been released in at least four other locations, simultaneously."

"Released? By terrorists?"

"It's unclear, Doctor. Things are kind of chaotic at those sites."

"Of course they are," he said. He looked back at Jane, who was now frowning in earnest. "What is it?" He demanded. "Is he waking up?

If he was, the containment field should still hold him, but there was no way to be certain of that. If he woke like the other Titans, it would be best to use the kill switch. Emma had clearly thought of something the rest of them hadn't.

"No," Jane said. "The opposite. His hearts are shutting down, one by one." She looked over at him. "He's dying."

"Why?"

"I have no idea. It's like he's having an allergic reaction

or something. Everything's dropping off, including radiation signature."

He stared at Kraken's lidded eye, trying to decide how he felt. This creature had been put in his charge, and he had failed it. He knew how many of the Monarch scientists – like Serizawa – felt about the creatures.

On the other hand, if it died naturally, he wouldn't have to pull the kill switch.

"Did you get all of that, Jen?" he asked.

"I did," she replied. "I... don't understand."

"Call it in," he said. "Tell Castle Bravo we'll be sending them our data. Maybe whatever happened to—"

His words stopped in his throat. Kraken's eye was open, staring at him.

"Oh, God," he said. "Turn on the containment field."

"Done," Jane said. "Doctor, I'm still getting nothing. This says he's dead."

"His eye is open!"

"Maybe some postmortem reaction—" but then she broke off, too. One of the tentacles was suddenly right there, pushing against the containment field – no, pushing through it, effortlessly.

"What is happening?" Ikande yelled.

"The field works on living Titans," Jane said, getting up from her workstation, knocking a coffee cup off. It shattered on the floor. "Kraken still doesn't read as alive."

"I..."

His skin prickled, and suddenly he felt very cold as understanding dawned.

Oh, shit.

Protective coloration was only the surface of what this thing could do. It could mimic other states. It could make sonar think it wasn't hearing anything, disguise its radiation signature.

Play dead.

The tentacle was reaching for them, but it wasn't here yet. He bolted toward the kill switch.

But the tube suddenly collapsed and water rushed in with such force that it almost knocked him out. He saw the other tentacle that had reached around from the back, quietly wrapped around the elevator tube. He got his bearings and tried to swim toward the surface, but Kraken was way ahead of him, grappling the floating base and dragging it down by the middle. Ikande kicked desperately, until something took hold of his leg and yanked him back down.

Tingua Preserve, Brazil
Monarch Outpost 58
Titanus Behemoth

Mariko crawled through the hatch and into the access tunnel. The alarms were blaring, and everyone was running around like crazy.

Behemoth was awake.

He had been sleeping deep in a cave in the Tingua preserve not far from Rio de Janeiro. Mariko had been on the crew that discovered him, her first job with Monarch. First job, period. After the containment was set up, she had volunteered to stay on. It was actually a great gig. Behemoth was, to her, the most interesting of the Titans, and when free time came her way, Rio and its beaches were less than an hour away – quicker, if she could catch a helicopter ride. Her Portuguese had gotten pretty decent, she'd made friends. She was only twenty-five; the future had looked bright.

But now everything had changed.

She reached her destination, a panel on the wall of the tunnel. She did her job quickly, then continued down the tunnel, opened another panel, and dropped down into the room beyond. Mounted high in the cave, the room was shaped like a hockey puck. The wall of the circumference was transparent, giving her a good view of the giant below.

His legs were folded under him; his mighty tusks curving above him. As she watched, he struggled against the containment field, trying to stand up.

"Mariko? Why didn't you just use the door?"

She turned and found Erik staring at her, his bespectacled eyes full of puzzlement.

"I was checking the wiring in the access tunnel," she said. "The meter downstairs showed some resistance. It looks okay up here, though."

"You could have sent a tech," he said.

"Yeah," she said. "But I wanted the view."

"Are you crazy? He's trying to break out. Like the others."

"I know," Mariko said. "What are you up here for?"

"Backup," he said. "Dr. Singh has us on standby to use the kill switch."

Not all kill switches were the same. Each was tailored to its Titan. And no one was sure if any of them would work. But Singh was pretty confident with their setup.

Behemoth roared, and pushed up *hard*, swinging his head through the containment field and shredding the equipment that powered it. The field vanished. Floodlights snapped on, everywhere. Toward the front of the cave, dozens of security personnel took positions.

"Erik?"

The voice came from the intercom built into a control panel that otherwise had a few indicators and a single switch, locked beneath a cover with a keypad entry.

"Dr. Singh," Erik replied.

"We've had negative results here – we're not sure why. Go ahead and enable the backup kill switch."

"Will do, Doctor."

He punched in a code and flipped up the cover.

"Enabled," he said.

"Do it," Singh said.

Erik reached out and flipped the switch.

Nothing happened.

He flipped it back, and then again.

"Nothing's happening," he reported. He checked the instruments.

"There's no power!"

"No," Mariko said. "There's not."

Erik looked at her, eyes wide, then glanced at the hatch to the access tunnel.

"You were in there. You cut the line that triggers the cascade."

She nodded.

"Oh my God," he said. "Are you one of them?"

"I'm Monarch," she said. She nodded toward Behemoth.

"Look at him," she said. "You think we have the right to just *kill* a god? He was here long before we were. There are cave paintings of him in here that are twelve thousand years old. That's just after people *got* here. The indigenous people still have a name for him – Mapinguary. You heard Emma. We have to let him go."

"You're as crazy as she is. How long have you been working with her?"

"I'm not," she said. "At least not the way you mean. You heard her speech. She's right. Our seas are dying, the rainforests are nearly gone, thousands of species exterminated. I'm proud to help her."

Behemoth rose to his full height. Or at least his full height on four legs. There was a running bet about whether he could go bipedal or not. She was in the "yes" camp. His tusks and thick hair made him look superficially like a mammoth, but he was really built more like a giant ground sloth; his forelimbs were longer than the back, and he rested on the knuckles of hands or paws with thick, sharp claws. The only way he could use those claws was to stand up on his stubbier hind limbs.

She saw muzzle flashes from small arms but couldn't hear the gunshots.

"You've killed us all," Erik said.

"Probably," she said.

Behemoth leaned back, and his forelimbs came up from the floor. His tusks dug into the ceiling, and the entire cave shook. He swatted the soldiers shooting at him with his claws. It looked almost funny from this distance, like he was knocking over toy soldiers. She felt sorry for them, for everyone who had to die. But this was how it had to be.

"I was right," she said.

"About what?"

"Bipedal," she said.

"Goddamn it," Erik yelled. He climbed into the crawlway.

It didn't matter. There was no way he could fix it, not in time.

Blue-white flame jetted toward the Titan from somewhere near her. Behemoth screamed and turned around. He was facing her now; she could see his eyes, the eyes of a god. An angry god, whose sanctuary had been violated.

The fire spewed at him again. This time she saw where it came from, a nozzle protruding from the ceiling. She hadn't known about that.

Behemoth saw it, too. He roared and lunged forward.

"Come on," she whispered. "You know what to do."

The ceiling of the cave was higher, here. This time when he rose up, he was nearly at his full standing height. His face was meters from her when his tusks smashed into the ceiling. Huge chunks of stone tore loose, followed by a tremendous explosion as the reservoir of napalm or whatever it was breached.

Behemoth turned back toward the cave entrance, covered in flame. The fire seemed to find no purchase on his fur, and quickly burned out. He didn't look hurt at all.

The cave, however, was filling with fire, and rock was still falling. The observation room shook, wobbled crazily, and tore loose from the ceiling.

Mariko had one last sight of Behemoth, crashing through the barriers at the cave entrance.

Jebel Barkal, Sudan
Monarch Outpost 75
Titanus Mokele-Mbembe

The ground twitched beneath Nez's feet. She almost didn't notice, but then she saw that nearly everyone in the control room was looking around, puzzled.

Then the floor lurched, and people began screaming.

"Satellite?" Nez snapped.

"I've got nothing," Connaught said.

She turned on her headset.

"Squads," she said. "Everyone shout out, in order. What are you seeing out there?"

None of the helicopters had seen anything, nor had anyone on the ground. The desert was quiet. Nothing on radar, either.

"It's M&M," Keller said. "He's moving."

"Hit the kill switch," she told Kearns.

He shook his head. "Turn on the containment field."

"I'm way ahead of you," Keller told him.

The floor kicked up, hard, overturning tables, sending people and equipment flying.

"What the hell is going on?" Kearns yelled.

"Radiation levels are rising," Keller said. "And I'm getting something on the bio-sonar monitor."

"Mokele?"

"Yes. His heartbeat is quickening. But there's something else, something more distant. Sir, he's pushing against the field."

Nez keyed on the radio. "I want all choppers back here, now," she said. "Recon units, you too. Be ready to fight."

She looked up at Kearns.

"He can't get through the field," the scientist said. "He can push all day. Mothra's field was sabotaged. Ours is intact."

"Sir, that's bullshit," Nez said. "He's breaking free. You know what you have to do. If you don't, I will."

"Sergeant," Lang said. "These creatures—"

"Jesus," Keller swore. The lights dimmed.

"What?" Kearns snapped.

"The containment field just overloaded."

"Evacuate the base," Nez said. "Now." Then she pushed him aside and ran toward the kill switch, only yards away. Before she got there the entire building abruptly flipped on its side. She flailed through space and hit the wall so hard it knocked half a ghost out of her.

Nez came to with the taste of blood in her mouth, a god-awful stench in her nostrils, and a sound like a rockslide that just went on and on. Bodies littered what used to be the wall of the building; the whole place was shaking. The power was out, but light poured in through splits in the metal of the prefab.

As she rose to her feet, the whole building dropped and tilted again, more slowly this time, until it was upright again.

She was two meters from the door. It burst open and sand and gravel began pouring in through the bottom third.

They were sinking.

"Everybody out, now!" she yelled.

Kearns was clearly dead, as were several others. Keller and Esmail were alive, but dazed.

"Out, I said!" Esmail nodded rapidly, scrambling up the mound of dirt and through the door. She managed to get Keller on his feet and dragged him through.

Outside, the once-level ground was now a slope. The three of them scrambled up it as the building behind dropped another few meters, burying the door.

She turned and stared.

It was like watching him being born. He emerged from beneath one of the pyramids. Control had been almost on top of his containment and was now falling into the hole Mokele-Mbembe was leaving behind. Most of the compound was still intact. Monarch personnel were pouring from the buildings, screaming to high heaven, flailing their arms, tripping over one another.

His back broke out first, gray, pebbled like some lizards she had seen. Enormous five-clawed forelimbs pulled at the edge of the pit, and then his long, curved horn knifed out of the sand, followed quickly by his head.

It looked something like an earless elephant, except that its tusks turned down, rather than up. His tail had unwound; it made up two-thirds of his body length.

His trunk flickered out like a snake striking, straight at them. She yanked out her sidearm, but she was already too late; it snatched Keller, pulled him back. The long, elephantine head opened like a crocodile's, revealing thousands of teeth.

Then Keller was gone.

"Run," she told Esmail.

An Osprey shrieked by overhead, and then another, jamming with their fifty-caliber guns, launching rockets. She looked back in time to see a missile explode against Mokele-Mbembe. It didn't seem to bother him much. That trunk was *fast*, whipping around and snatching up people three and four at a time. It was completely out of the pit now, lurching forward on four thick legs. The front legs were a little taller than the rear. Its tail sliced through a pyramid and then flicked up to cut an Osprey in half.

It was as if the world was new again, she thought. The monsters had ruled in the beginning. Now they returned to rule again.

Skull Island
Monarch Outpost 33
Titanus Kong

Alone. Quiet. He sat on the mountain ridge and looked over his territory. The gleaming waters that held the sun in their waves, the shore where land and sea met.

The grassland and the jungle, all quiet. The heat of the sun warmed his fur. The last of his wounds was now merely just an itch along his ribs.

In time, he climbed down from the ridge; he walked his old paths, to the places where the world of both night and day crossed the paths of always-night, the hollows in the stone where the enemies lived. That was quiet too; the smell of the enemies was faint and old. His feet felt nothing in the stone. He went from valley to valley, searching. He went by the little things that spoke to him in voices like wind, but they had nothing to say.

He returned to the ridge and watched the colors in the sky, watched the sun burn behind the clouds, dim, vanish.

He watched the smaller sun appear above. A breeze came, from some distant place, a place he did not know, with strange scents on it.

He heard the call.

He had heard calls before. Not the enemies who killed his parents, the deep-dwellers. Others somehow more like him. When he was young, he did not hear them often. But in recent seasons the calls were more frequent. Once he had heard one of the others, near, very near the island. But it wanted nothing of him. So he did not care.

But this other wanted something. Wanted him to come. To hunt together.

And he heard responses. Many of them.

For a long time, each season was much like the next. The rains came and went. The animals of the island were born and died. And he went on as always.

But something had changed now. It made him restless. It made him a little angry. Change was not good.

Let them stay away from him, these others. He did not

care about their places, their islands. Best they did not come for his.

He felt movement in the stone beneath him, and his anger grew brighter.

The deep dwellers heard the call, too. The crawlers with faces like bone that haunted his sleep. They were waking.

The quiet was over.

He scratched the itch on his ribs and began to hunt.

FOURTEEN

From Dr. Graham's collected notes:

Below the thunders of the upper deep;
Far, far beneath in the abysmal sea,
His ancient, dreamless, uninvaded sleep
The Kraken sleepeth: faintest sunlights flee
About his shadowy sides; above him swell
Huge sponges of millennial growth and height;
And far away into the sickly light,
From many a wondrous grot and secret cell
Unnumber'd and enormous polypi
Winnow with giant arms the slumbering green.
There hath he lain for ages, and will lie
Battening upon huge seaworms in his sleep,
Until the latter fire shall heat the deep;
Then once by man and angels to be seen,
In roaring he shall rise and on the surface die.

—*The Kraken*
Alfred, Lord Tennyson

On monitor after monitor the same thing was playing out. The monsters were all coming out to play. And people were dying, most in fear and panic, some fighting bravely, all outmatched by the return of the sleeping gods to the world.

One by one, the monitors went to static.

"I thought we were going to release them gradually," Jonah said. "One at a time."

He sounded as stunned as she felt.

"I'm not the one doing this," she said.

Only one monitor still displayed an image. Monster Zero, on his throne of fire, all three heads shrieking in unison.

The bunker shook; lights flickered.

I'm no longer in control, she realized. It was Monster Zero. He was doing all this. *This has gotten away from me.*

Jonah got it too. He studied the screen.

"Long live the king," he said. She thought she heard triumph, filtered through his accustomed sarcasm.

Then he left.

Something moved in the corner of Emma's vision. She turned, and to her horror, saw Madison had been standing behind them, watching everything.

"Maddie—" she said.

"You're a monster," her daughter told her. Then she sprinted off, and Emma was alone.

Brooks woke up to a fair, coolish morning in the highlands of Yunnan. He took a Humvee, a science team, and a squadron of soldiers down to the old facility. The bodies had been removed, but rusty bloodstains still covered the floor. The techs confirmed what he'd already guessed, that the security and containment systems had been sabotaged, almost certainly with Emma's help. He hoped to find some other clues. One team had already been through the data, but he thought he might notice something they hadn't.

He'd only been there a couple of hours when he got the call from Hess, a Monarch communications officer.

"Brooks here," he said.

"Dr. Brooks, things are developing. You should probably get back up here."

Ling stood before the waterfall, staring through it at Mothra's cocooned form. Feeling her.

She hadn't told Brooks everything she knew. She felt a little bad about that, but she still wasn't sure of all the facts herself. Only what her mother and aunt told her, and her grandmother. The stories collected not from indigenous peoples or ancient sources, but those passed down from mother to daughter.

We are connected to her, she'd been taught. *Connected for numberless generations.*

She had wondered if it was true, of course. How much of her matriline's mythology was real, and how much fantasy created by time and imperfect transmission? Myths were like a game of Telephone, becoming less like the original every time a different teller learned it.

But Mothra was real. She had learned that at a very young age, and not by telling. Firsthand. It was so long ago, so strange, that at times in her adult life she wondered if she had dreamed it, if it was some sort of false memory.

But the connection was tangible. She'd felt it then, and she felt it now, growing stronger.

In the last few hours, something had changed. Mothra had

shivered, as if she felt a jolt of some sort. Her transformation had quickened in response. And she had a sense of apprehension. And *need*.

The clouds had been gathering above, and now a harsh, cold rain began to fall. Ling continued to stand in it, ignoring the chill, listening to Mothra hurry toward her second birth.

When Brooks got back outside, piles of thunderheads were rolling in, and high winds bent the tops of the council trees. Rain came across the mountains like a solid wall. They had to slow to a crawl, because visibility dropped so low. He wasn't driving, so he stayed on the crackly radio as Hess updated him.

There was another Titan unleashed – Rodan. And now all hell was breaking loose. They had lost contact with Monarch, and all communications were getting sketchy.

The road was close to being a river by the time he got back to camp. He pushed into the command tent.

Inside, all was in bedlam. He made his way through the chaos to Hess, who was on the radio.

"Castle Bravo, this is containment team Mosura, do you read, over?"

He didn't look hopeful.

"Anything?" Brooks asked.

"No, sir, we've lost contact with the *Argo*, Castle Bravo, and the other containment sites—"

"Which ones?" Brooks asked.

"All of them," he replied. "Angkor Wat, Skull Island, Stone Mountain – all the Titans... they're escaping."

He played back the last transmissions they had received from the other containment bases: Behemoth shattering buildings in Rio de Janeiro with his tusks, Methuselah cutting a swath through Munich, Scylla stalking through Phoenix on her spidery legs.

"Jesus," he murmured.

One monitor was still showing something live. Monster Zero, the three-headed dragon, atop a volcano, roaring…

And it clicked.

"It's *him*,' Brooks realized. "*He's* the one doing this. They're responding to his call."

The power flickered and then faded.

"Where's Dr. Ling?" he demanded.

But he knew. She was almost always with Mothra.

He ran back outside, and found her there, in the rain, standing with her back to him.

"Dr. Ling," he shouted, trying to cut through the howling wind and driving rain. "We've lost contact with Monarch."

She didn't turn around.

"Dr. Ling?"

The rain slackened; the winds died down.

Above, the thick clouds parted, and fireflies began to flicker in the highland jungle.

And, beyond the waterfall, something new was happening.

The cocoon was rippling, glowing. Tears appeared in the fabric, and sharp, insectile legs pushed out.

Whatever Mothra had been, she was different now. He was about to see how different. It was a little terrifying but mostly exciting.

The other monsters were free. Now it was Mothra's turn. He hoped Ling was right about Mothra; if Monster Zero was controlling her, too, he and his team were as good as dead.

But it didn't feel like that was happening.

She began to sing, like the night music of insects, but

bigger, more meaningful. A gentle blue light began to shine, as her gossamer wings unfolded.

She was beautiful as she took flight.

Ling followed the Titan's path into the sky, too. She looked a little otherworldly in the blue light, and her expression was nothing short of reverential. He remembered the Iwi people of Skull Island, their attitude toward Kong. He thought he saw something of that in Ling's hazel eyes.

Maddie ran through the corridors of the bunker toward her room, trying to process what she had seen, the sheer amount of destruction that was occurring, the death.

Mom had said monsters and humans could live in harmony. Her experience with Mothra had made Emma think she was right. And there were other examples – Godzilla and Kong.

But from what she had seen, the only relationship these Titans wanted with humans was that of predator to prey. And Monster Zero – she would never shake off the sheer malevolence she'd seen in those eyes. There was no peaceful coexistence with that guy.

No wonder Jonah had sneered at the notion.

"Madison, wait!"

Mom. Following her. She would want to talk. To somehow argue it all made sense. But it didn't. And she was in no mood for waiting. Or talking.

"Get away from me," she shot back.

But her mother persisted.

"Look," she said. "I know things haven't gone exactly according to plan, but I can fix it."

"According to plan?" Madison said. "You said that you

were going to be careful, that you'd release them one at a time, that you would restore balance—"

"And we are," she insisted.

"You also failed to mention the man we teamed up with is a homicidal maniac!"

"They were going to take over Monarch and kill the Titans. Jonah was the only one who could pull this off. I didn't have a choice—"

"There's always a choice!" she said. "You know who taught me that? Dad."

Her mother blinked, and her mouth opened a little, but she didn't say anything.

"You said he left us, that he was a drunk who didn't care about us."

"Because he did leave us," her mother said. "Somebody had to be strong for you and it sure as hell wasn't him. He gave up on me, gave up on you."

"No," Maddie shouted. "You're the one who gave up! You gave up on everything. You gave up on humanity."

"Madison—"

"And if Dad's such an asshole, then why'd he come back? Why is he trying to help people while we're trying to kill them?"

"We *are* helping people, baby—"

"Bullshit!" she said, taking a step toward her mother. "You said you were doing this for Andrew. But do you really think he would've wanted this?"

That made an impression on her.

"I... I don't know," she said.

"Exactly. I'm starting to think you *don't* know more than you *do*."

She ran into her room, slammed the door, and locked it.

Then she ignored her mother pounding on it and calling her name until she went away.

She cast about her room, unsure of what to do next. She really wanted to break something, but there wasn't a lot to break. Her pad, maybe, or some of the old stuff in the room.

But no. The whole world was breaking. She didn't want to contribute any more to that. She had gone along with Mom on this whole thing. She could have stopped all of it at any time, just by telling someone. Dr. Mancini, Chen, Vivienne – her dad. But she hadn't. She had *believed*. She was responsible for what was happening. Because she had trusted her mother.

She had to do something.

The bunker had been built for a lot more people than were currently in it, so Maddie had had plenty of rooms to choose from, but Mom wanted her reasonably near the command center, which limited her choices.

Maddie had picked an old radio room.

Mom said this was one of the first Monarch bunkers to be built, way back in the forties, and it showed. Her room was like a time capsule. She liked the old-fashioned equipment, the poster warning her that loose lips would sink ships. It was like something out of a black-and-white movie.

Her gaze swung back to the poster. *Loose Lips Sink Ships*.

She didn't have access to the Internet here – Jonah had made certain of that. She didn't have a phone.

But what if this stuff still worked? The radio, for instance. The control room had the high-tech stuff. Probably no one had used this equipment in decades.

If it did work, maybe she could do something.

Maybe she could sink a ship.

She examined the gray metal console, found a switch clearly labeled on and off. She switched it on.

Static and voices immediately filled the room. She jerked back a little, not sure what she was hearing. Then she recognized some of the voices. Jonah's men. So that was the intercom. Good to know, but not what she was looking for. She flipped it off, and after a little more searching found another switch. This time dials lit up, little red needles swung to their positions. An angry buzz began.

She leaned toward the microphone and put her finger on the black button on its base. The buzz stopped. She found a knob and began turning it; the sounds changed. Bits of what might be voices went in and out of the static.

She put her mouth close to the microphone and pushed the button again

"Hello...?" she said, experimentally.

Nothing. She kept turning the knob, trying to find a clear channel.

"Is anyone there? I'm trying to reach... Monarch."

She turned it a little more, and suddenly voices poured from the speakers. People screaming, pleading for help.

"Mayday! Mayday! We need help... Everything is burning. Please, is anyone there?"

Horrified, she backed away, got on her bed, and covered her ears. It went on and on, and there was nothing she could do. Nothing. She felt like she was dissolving inside.

Mark was exhausted. He'd spent hours pulling apart animal sounds, analyzing them, playing them side by side with the recordings of the ORCA in action. He wasn't sure anymore that there was a point to it, but it gave him something to do other than think about the fact that his ex-wife was now a mass-murderer on a global scale. He hoped, at least, that she was right when she said Madison was safe. It seemed to him that even the Monarch bunkers might not be secure from what was happening now.

Other than his animal sounds, the bridge was mostly quiet – just a few crew and Chen, working at something as fervently as he was.

"Any luck?" Chen asked, after a while.

"No," he said. "Whatever Emma used to create the ORCA signal – I've never heard it."

He looked over at Chen's console, and what appeared to be ancient texts, murals, inscriptions.

"How are you doing?"

"*Shénhuà shì w men de zh nánzh n*," she said.

"How's that?" he said.

"Myth is our compass. It's something my mom used to say. She believed our stories about monsters and dragons could help us find the Titans and restore our connection to nature."

"Your mother?" he said. "Wait, you're second-generation Monarch?"

"Third," she corrected. "It runs in the family."

Smiling, she showed Mark a photo of her family, including her – and what must be her twin sister, and her own identical twin girls, who looked to be about three. It was more than a little weird.

"That's incredible," Mark said. "Don't suppose your family has any tips on slaying dragons?"

"Slaying dragons is a western concept," she answered. "In the East, they are sacred. Divine creatures that brought wisdom, strength – even redemption."

Mark turned that over in his mind. Was that where Serizawa was coming from, ultimately? The idea that these monsters were divine? Gods? From what he remembered of mythology, divine didn't necessarily mean good or even nice. The gods could be angry, jealous, petty, spiteful.

But something about the way Chen explained it touched a chord in him.

Redemption. He could use some of that.

Quiet time was over. The rest of the team was returning to the bridge.

"I don't get it," Colonel Foster said. "This Oxygen Destroyer. Why wasn't Monster Zero affected?"

"I mean, I'm no scientist," Barnes said, "but maybe it's got something to do with his goddamn *head* growing back."

"I've never seen anything like this," Stanton said. "It violates everything we know about the natural order."

"Unless he's not part of the natural order," Chen said.

All eyes turned toward her.

"What do you mean?" Serizawa asked.

Chen went to her station.

"I was able to piece this together," she said.

She brought up a cave painting, depicting a three-headed dragon surrounded by flames and skulls.

"Well, he looks vaguely familiar," Coleman said.

"It tells of the great dragon who fell from the stars – a hydra whose storms swallowed both man *and* gods alike."

Mark got what she was saying. But really?

"You mean an alien?" he said.

"Yes. He's not part of our natural order. And he's not meant to be here."

"A false king," Serizawa said.

Mark's attention was on another glyph. This one showed Godzilla fighting the three-headed dragon. But the big lizard wasn't alone. He had help from above in the form of some sort of winged monster. And below – humans were fighting with him, tiny though they were.

"An invasive species," Stanton said. "If he is an alien it could explain the storms and the effect he's having on the other Titans. Almost as if he's reshaping the planet to his own liking."

"These legends," Serizawa asked. "What did they call him?"

"Ghidorah," she said. "The one who is many."

"What was that?" Mark asked. "Gheedra? Gridora?"

"I think she said gonorrhea," Coleman whispered.

At the controls, Griffin interrupted.

"Dr. Serizawa," she said, "we're approaching Castle Bravo. But there's something you should see."

Outside, it was pouring with rain, but they could still easily see what she was talking about. The island and "oil rig" that hid the underwater base were surrounded by military vessels and helicopters. A lot of them.

FIFTEEN

From Dr. Graham's collected notes:

Moth: I gave you my life.
Flame: I allowed you to kiss me.

—Hazrat Inayat Khan, Sufi teacher

They took the *Argo* down, and were met not by Monarch staff but by military and government suits.

And Admiral Stenz.

"Colonel," he said to Foster. "I'd like a moment with you and your men." The Admiral nodded at the rest of them. "I'll see you momentarily."

"What's the deal with that?" Mark asked. "I thought those guys were Monarch."

"Sort of yes, sort of no," Coleman answered. "They're sort of on loan. We've never had to test the chain of command."

Mark's mind flashed back to Emma, talking about the government's intentions. If the word had come down earlier to kill all of the Titans, but Serizawa said no, who would G-Team have answered to?

Back in the situation room, horrific scenes played out on the monitors. Cities in smoking ruin, military units pounding a half-dozen different Titans to no obvious effect. Mark was aghast, but his up-close-and-personal experiences with these monsters were making him a little numb. Vivienne's loss had been personal to him, Andrew's death devastating. Even though, intellectually, he knew every one of the thousands if not millions who were dying right now were just as real and important to the people who loved them, he couldn't grieve for them all. His mind wouldn't let him. If he felt for each of those abstract casualties what he felt when he lost Andrew, he would go insane. Anyone would.

That didn't mean he didn't feel anything, though, and certainly didn't mean he wanted it to go on.

When he pulled back from the worldwide tragedy, looked not at the individual events but instead at the global tracking data, some interesting patterns began to emerge, tantalizingly familiar. There was something there, something he almost recognized.

Stenz began the meeting.

"Moscow. London. Washington D.C. All under attack. On every continent, the Titans are triggering earthquakes, wildfires, tsunamis, and disasters we don't even have names for yet."

As he spoke, more images appeared. Ghidorah's storm was now many storms, from super-cells to immense squall lines sweeping through inland areas, spawning thunderstorms and tornados by the thousands.

Rodan was still out there, too. Motion captures from planes and ground bases showed volcanoes erupting as he flew past them, and satellite data presented a string of eruptions that coincided with his flight path, sending megatons of volcanic ash and gases into the atmosphere. Stanton's words came to the forefront of his mind. It really did seem like Ghidorah was trying to tear the earth's ecosystem back down to the bones and start over.

Or maybe Monster Zero just hated everything, and the destruction was a process, a goal in and of itself. Maybe he was a god – but there was nothing that said a god had to be sane.

Yet – whatever his reasons – Ghidorah had tried this before and been stopped. And if you believed the stuff Chen had shown them, human beings had been part of doing that.

"Now, as before, we've been trying to lure the creatures with nuclear materials," Stenz went on, "but they are not taking the bait this time. Their behavior has become random. Erratic. And with our forces spread desperately thin – and these things roaming the globe unimpeded – we are running out of options. And time."

It clicked. What he'd seen in the tracking data.

Mark leaned toward Chen.

"Not random," he whispered.

The Admiral noticed. He turned his steely gaze toward Mark.

"Something to add?" he said.

"Yeah," Chen said. "You're wrong."

"Excuse me?" Stenz said.

"Their behavior is not random or erratic," Chen said.

It came as a mild, but pleasant surprise. Chen probably didn't know what he meant. But she trusted him enough to concur with his assessment.

Mark pointed to the map detailing the movements of the various Titans since their release.

"If I may, sir, as amazing as this sounds, they're moving like a pack. They're hunting. And like all packs from wolves to killer whales they're responding to the Alpha. Grid... Gydar... Girdar."

"Ghidorah," Chen said.

"Yeah," Mark said. "Him. With Godzilla gone, he's the one calling the shots. They're acting like an extension of him."

He stepped forward.

"If we stop *him*, we'll stop *them*," he said.

Stenz stared at him. Mark could almost see him crunching the data. Mark had done the easy part – set the goal. Stenz's mind was geared toward working out the tactics to achieve that goal.

"Is there another creature that might stand a chance against him?" Colonel Foster asked.

"No," Serizawa said. "Ghidorah and Godzilla's rivalry was ancient. And unique. Dr. Graham even believed it was their last battle that trapped Ghidorah in the ice, eons ago."

"So you're telling me we just killed our best shot at beating this thing?" Sergeant Martinez said.

"Outside of a miracle," Chen said, "yes."

She was right. He had identified the problem, but it was an equation with no solution. It was clear that military measures alone couldn't stop him, including their Oxygen Destroyer. And since Godzilla's death, none of the other Titans had even attempted to go against the three-headed monstrosity. That included Rodan, who had plenty of reason to be pissed at Ghidorah. He, too, was taking orders from the Alpha.

So what was left?

Mark looked around at all of the hopeless expressions, at the holocaust engulfing the world. What were they all standing around for? What was *he* doing? Nothing.

He got up.

"Where are you going?" Coleman asked.

"To look for a miracle," he replied.

To say things weren't going the way Emma had expected them to would be an understatement. She'd known there would be death and destruction on some scale. Death was natural, a part of how things were supposed to be. Sometimes there had to be a little more of it than usual to restore balance in a system, especially one as compromised as what many scientists had begun calling the Anthropocene, or "Age of Man." The sheer amount of damage humanity had done to the world's ecosystem qualified it as its own era. And the Anthropocene had been well on its way to hosting the greatest mass extinction in history. Greater than the Permian, when ninety percent of *everything* died. That's what the planet was facing – in decades, not centuries or millennia. When change happened slowly over a long period of time, life adapted. But when the time frame was too short, natural selection didn't have an opportunity to do its thing – unless you were bacteria. Humanity had pushed the natural order almost to a point of no return. That was what she'd been determined to prevent.

But now she saw wildfires the size of small continents, oceans turning red, massive die-offs of fish, birds, coral reefs. Gigatons of ash, smoke, and carbon dioxide were pouring into the atmosphere. Entire ecosystems were being trashed – some already wiped away completely.

She'd thought the human race was bad, but in one day, Monster Zero and the Titans he controlled had done as much damage as humanity had in the last century.

She paced in the control room, feeling like a caged tiger.

"Madison's right," she told Jonah. "We didn't hit the reset button, we hit the detonator."

"Madison is a child," he replied. "This is a war. It's why *you* came to *us*, what we've been fighting for, remember?"

"No, it isn't," she said. "Jonah, we were fighting to restore the natural order. That meant humans and Titans coexisting in balance. But with Godzilla gone, Monster Zero isn't using the Titans to restore the planet – he's using them to destroy it. This isn't coexistence. It's extinction."

"But not for us," Jonah said.

She turned to look at him. What was he talking about?

He poured a scotch.

"Fancy a drink?" he said.

"A drink?" She was incredulous.

He shrugged and poured a second one for her anyway.

"Did I ever tell you how my daughter died?" he asked. "Abducted on her way home from school. They found her six days later in a storm drain while I was out fighting some dirty war for my country – trying to make the world a better place. Like you are."

He knocked back the drink.

"I've seen human nature firsthand. It doesn't change. It just gets worse. So I'm sorry if Monster Zero wasn't exactly what we were expecting – but we already opened Pandora's box. There's no closing it now."

She had been thinking about that – a lot. And she knew the

Pandora story, how she let every disease and hardship out of the box the gods had trapped them in.

But after all the demons escaped, one thing that remained in the box was *Elpis*. The personification of hope.

She nodded at the ORCA.

"Maybe there is," she said. She pointed to one of the monitors showing the evacuation of Boston; Fenway Park was a major hub for the airlift.

"Oh, don't be stupid. You broadcast again and you will expose us all," Jonah said.

She pressed on.

"These creatures communicate like whales, okay?" she said. "They can hear sonar for thousands of miles. So let's send a team, let's broadcast the ORCA from Fenway. It's just a few miles from here. I can use the stadium to amplify the signal. That might break Monster Zero's hold over them and stop these attacks. The city's being evacuated, so it'll be safe."

"And then what?" Jonah asked.

"I'll figure out what the hell Monster Zero really is. And how to stop it."

Jonah's lips thinned.

"Before Monarch finds us? I'm sure your real friends will be very happy to see you again."

"We can't just sit here," Emma said. "This isn't the world we wanted."

"You once said that the world *always* belonged to them. So maybe it's time we give it back."

She shook her head.

"No," she said. "Not like this."

She started toward the ORCA. If Jonah didn't want to stick his neck out, she would do it without him. It had to be tried.

Behind her she heard the *click* of a gun cocking. She turned back and saw him holding a pistol.

"Jonah? What are you doing?"

"The things I've done," he said, his voice grim. "The things I've seen... Humanity *is* a disease and the fewer of them there are the better it is for me." He smiled. "Thank you, Doctor. You cleared the way for us. And when the dust settles, we will live like kings."

He turned to one of his men.

"Sergeant Travis," he said.

"Sir?"

"Do me a favor. If Dr. Russell goes anywhere near the ORCA, slit her daughter's throat."

"Yes, sir," the mercenary said.

Jonah got up and slid the drink he'd poured for her across the table.

"Enjoy your drink."

Even over the intercom, without being able to see him, Jonah's voice sent a chill through Maddie. She hadn't known about his daughter. It was terrible what had happened to her. But it didn't excuse him for all of the murdering he'd done and was planning on doing. Just because someone had taken his daughter from him, didn't make it okay to wipe out most of the human race. Andrew's death had hurt her mother and father, and they had both reacted badly, done bad things. Mom worst of all. But at least she still had a soul. She was willing to try and set things as right as they could be.

But Jonah's soul was long gone. She had no doubt he would cut her throat himself if he thought it necessary. Or maybe even just for the hell of it.

Her mother knew that, too. She was willing to risk pretty much anyone's life – except Maddie's.

Her eyes drifted back to the photo she'd pulled up on her pad. It was of all of them, the whole family, sitting on the stoop of their house in Boston. In front of the blue door. Mom on one side, Dad on the other, she and Andrew in between them. Dad had set the camera up on a tripod and put it on a timer. It had taken four attempts to get the final shot, because Andrew kept making goofy faces. Dad had finally changed the timing without telling anyone.

They had taken it a few days before… it happened.

It was maybe the last time she had felt like everything was all right.

Now they were back in Boston, or at least near it, as the map of Monarch bunkers on her wall confirmed. Bunker 09.

She thought over her mom's plan to amplify the ORCA's signal, and between that and the photo, something began stirring around in her mind. Something better than sitting in this room. Would Mom's idea work? She didn't know. But she remembered how Monster Zero had reacted, back in Antarctica. At the very least it would annoy him. At best – well, it could help. Help Monarch take him out. Help Dad.

Mom couldn't do it now, not with Jonah's men watching her. But *she* could.

On the deck of the oil rig, the rain drove down like nails from the fuming clouds above. Ghidorah's storm was *big*, now, bigger than any weather system ever recorded. How long could the monster keep it up? If he blanketed the earth – or even a considerable chunk of it – in these clouds for weeks or months, it would have the practical effect of a nuclear winter.

Green plants would die, followed by things that ate green plants, and then – well, everything else. Never mind all of the flooding, the saturation of reefs with fresh water…

And they had killed the only goddamn thing that might have stopped him. Of course, if Monarch hadn't kept Zero alive in the first place, if they had euthanized him while he slept, none of this would be happening.

Maybe. It wasn't easy to kill a Titan. They had tried to fry a contained MUTO once, in Japan. It hadn't worked. They had probably upgraded their kill-switch technology in the past five years, but when it got right down to it, the only way to know if something would kill a Titan was to try it on one. They tried to kill Godzilla ages ago with a nuclear bomb, and that hadn't worked. The Oxygen Destroyer hadn't killed Ghidorah. If they tried to fry Ghidorah in his sleep, it might have merely awakened him. Maybe whatever Monarch had done, Monster Zero would be here, now, bringing the rain.

And none of that even mattered, now. It was too late.

"Mark, wait! What are you doing?"

Sam Coleman, following him. Why? Why did this guy keep trying to be his friend?

But he was trying, wasn't he? Or maybe just trying to stop him from stealing an Osprey.

"I can't just sit down there, Sam," he said. "I gotta do something."

"Like what?"

"Like go find my daughter."

"How?" Sam asked. "Where are you gonna go?"

"She's the only thing I got left, Sam," he said. "I wasn't there for her. I'm not gonna let that happen again."

It hung like that for a moment, the two of them standing in the rain.

"Okay," Sam said finally, genuine understanding in his expression. "Good luck."

Mark nodded, then strode on through the rain. He spotted an Osprey and climbed into the cockpit. He wasn't quite sure why – he didn't think he could fly the damn thing. And even if he could, Sam was right. Where would he go? Emma would have her someplace safe, in one of the Monarch shelters, probably. But which one? He didn't even know where most of them were.

He closed his eyes and put his head down.

Please, he thought. *Please.*

The pounding of rain on the Osprey's metal roof slackened off. The wind dropped to nothing, and there was a smell – that moment after rain, when the first kiss of the sun touches the damp earth. But there was no sun. Instead, when he opened his eyes and looked up at the dark clouds, Mark saw a brilliant light emerging.

He stepped out of the Osprey to get a better look, to understand what he was seeing.

The light shone from a pair of enormous wings, as if an angel was descending from the heavens. But an angel with the gossamer wings of an insect rather than feathered pinions. And the body those wings bore between them wasn't remotely human in form. More like an insect. But it *felt* like an angel. Like an answer to a prayer.

It could only be Mothra. The Titan his daughter had been reaching to touch when Jonah's mercenaries arrived. A pupa no longer.

And yet this didn't *feel* like a monster. It wasn't attacking them, for one thing, but just revealing itself – almost as if it expected something from him. Whatever was going on, Mothra wasn't taking orders from Ghidorah.

In fact, Monster Zero's storm continued to recede, as if it could not stand Mothra's light.

This was something new. Even with Godzilla gone, Ghidorah wasn't in total control of *all* the Titans. One still stood apart. He remembered the ancient representation Chen had shown them. Godzilla and humans, fighting side by side with – this.

For the first time since Antarctica, Mark felt hope.

SIXTEEN

From the notes of Dr. Houston Brooks:

But to return to our hypothesis, in order to explain the change of the Variations, we have adventured to make the Earth hollow and the place another within it; and I doubt not that this will find opposers enough.

—Edmund Halley. *An Account of the Cause of the Change of the Variation of the Magnetic Needle; with an Hypothesis of the Structure of the Internal Parts of the Earth,* Philosophical Transactions of Royal Society of London, No. 195, 1692, pp 563–578.

Inside the base, Serizawa witnessed Mothra's arrival and the retreat of the storm. The restoration of balance, at least in this corner of the world. He wished Vivienne could have lived to see this, the vindication of their beliefs.

"Beautiful," he murmured.

All the more wonderful because of the hope she brought in this dark moment. And yet Mothra was only one. With Ghidorah commanding the other Titans, how much could she do?

"Mothra," Dr. Chen said. "Queen of the monsters."

Serizawa thought he heard pride in her voice. He knew her twin sister Ling was on the Yunnan replacement crew, but was there more to her excitement? Her family's history with Monarch was as old as his own, and her knowledge of the mythic import of the Titans was greater than anyone's. Had she suspected Mothra was different? Did she know more about Mothra than she let on?

Just then, Mark came in, soaked to the bone.

"Stanton, are you recording this?" he asked.

"I record everything, man," Stanton said. "Everything."

He turned up the sound, and the room was filled with what might be a choir of crickets and cicadas, but more... musical than that.

"It's like a song," Chen said.

"Is this bug communicating?" Admiral Stenz said.

"There's more, Admiral," Mark said. "It's just outside our hearing range."

"I'll bet that there's only one thing that *can* understand this," Stanton said.

That was right. If Mothra was communicating, who was she talking to? Not Ghidorah.

"Godzilla," Serizawa said.

"Yep," Stanton confirmed. "I'm picking up the reply..."

Another sound joined Mothra's song – a faint thud, a deep moan...

"He's still alive…" Chen said.

Serizawa took a breath. Mothra hadn't come to fight a losing battle. She had come to show them the way. To bring Godzilla back. That was the rational core of the hope he'd felt at the sight of her petal-like wings.

Others, of course, were not so reverent.

Barnes, for instance. The Chief Warrant Officer gestured at the goddess.

"So her and Godzilla have some kind a thing going on?" he said. "Kind of messed up, right?"

"Symbiotic relationships between different species aren't all that uncommon," Sam said.

"Still messed up," Barnes said.

"Can you track him?" Serizawa asked. There was no time to waste. The world was spiraling into chaos. If there was something they could do, the quicker they did it, the better.

"No," Stanton replied. "Signal's too weak."

He turned his gaze to Mothra.

"But maybe she can."

Chen glanced over at Mark.

"You asked for a miracle," she told him. "I think we just got one."

"How many nukes do you have?" Mark asked.

Serizawa wrinkled his brow.

"Why?" he said.

"We can help him."

For the first time in a while, Serizawa smiled.

The plan came together quickly, as it had to. The fleet was fueled, provisioned, made ready for war. Ships were called in from nearby ports and bases. Aircraft carriers, destroyers, one Ticonderoga-class cruiser stocked with Tomahawk missiles, alongside smaller but still deadly vessels. They had half a dozen nuclear subs. One would serve as Admiral Stenz's command center. Most of the others would join the fight as well.

But one was being outfitted for something special.

Serizawa thought this was probably the largest fleet of war deployed since World War II.

They had air power, too. Squadrons of jets and helicopters had been assembled as well. This battle group represented all of the might Monarch and the government could bring together.

But Serizawa knew that without Godzilla, it wouldn't be enough. Everything now rested on the sword's edge.

Which might be a fitting name for the submarine the techs were getting ready for him and his people, loading it up with nuclear weapons. That was his part of the mission.

"This plan," Stanton said, nervously. "It's what we call a long shot, right?"

"No," Serizawa said. "It's our only shot."

"Yeah," Stanton said. "Cool." He took a slug from a flask.

After he was certain he had everything he needed on the submarine, Serizawa went to Vivienne's room. All of her things were still there, although there weren't that many of them. Some clothes and a small assortment of hats. A photograph of the two of them when she'd first joined Monarch, along with the team he'd been working with at the time, including Brooks.

She'd been so young, so full of wonder. So intelligent. What, twenty-two, maybe? She had called him 'Sensei' the first time they met, and she had never called him anything else. She had more compassion than anyone he'd ever met. And until the day she died, she had never lost her sense of wonder.

Besides those things, there was her collection: an Indonesian Garuda bird puppet, a thunderbird mask carved by a Haida artist, a wooden statuette of Minokawa, the moon-swallowing bird monster of Bagobo folklore she'd picked up on their trip to the Philippines to see a fossilized Titan skeleton. Various small pieces of art from around the world that she thought might represent folk memories of the Titans. He picked up one of them, a simple pendant carved from stone, a bipedal lizard with a long, thick tail and ragged dorsal spines. He had given her that one himself, on her thirtieth birthday. His father had given it to him, years before. His father had been given it by a Yapese man who had carved it from memory.

But who should it pass on to now? Vivienne had no children. She'd had a few relationships, but never married, and as far as he knew hadn't remained close to any of them. She was too devoted to her work, something he understood and appreciated very deeply. She had some nieces and nephews, he knew, but they would never understand its worth. She had been close to Emma and Madison these past few years, but it hardly seemed practical to give it to either of them at the moment.

Maybe it had come back to him, then, at least for a time. He put it in his pocket.

He closed the door leading into the hall.

He had never told her how much he appreciated her all those years; how much easier it made his work and his life to have someone who truly understood him and what he was working for. He thought she knew. He hoped she had.

"You are irreplaceable," he told her, and felt a tear trace down his face.

Barnes studied the thermal map Foster pulled up depicting the hurricane engulfing most of the East Coast. It was a real monster, bigger than any storm he'd ever seen. But that wasn't what made it so creepy. That would be the eye of the storm, where he could just barely make out the infrared form of their three-headed friend.

Foster was laying out the battle plan.

"This Category Six hurricane over D.C. is where King Ghidorah is nesting," she said. "Working with all four branches of the military, this will be a joint operation to lure it away from the mainland so that we can continue evacuations long enough for our submersible team to complete its mission."

So it was the Isla de Mara thing all over again. Only with a lot more people to get out of harm's way, on the one hand, but a hell of a lot more firepower on the other. They were going after this monster fully loaded.

"Yeah," Griffin said. "But what do those nerds think they're gonna do down there with a bunch of nukes?"

"Didn't you hear, Griffin?" Barnes said. "We're bringing Godzilla back from the dead."

Sam and Foster stayed with the *Argo* to coordinate the action against Ghidorah. Mark, Serizawa, Stanton, Chen and the others boarded the submarine. Mark wasn't sure if Sam looked mournful or scared shitless. Either way, it felt a little odd that they weren't along on the same ride anymore.

Mark had never been in a submarine before. Nor was it on his bucket list. And as the hatches closed, bells clanged, and the engines started up, he realized he felt a little claustrophobic. Something he hadn't known about himself.

And they weren't even underwater yet.

He was a long way from the open places he had become accustomed to over these many months. Since Serizawa and the others had shown up in Colorado, everything about his life was contracting. His choices. The very spaces he inhabited. His path was working its way toward a tightrope, and his balance wasn't all that great.

They were in motion, however, nosing along toward Mothra, who seemed to be beckoning them on, hopefully toward Godzilla. But could you ever really know what a glowing moth with an eight-hundred-foot wingspan was up to?

Of course not. But it was the only lead they had, a bet they were placing for a whole lot of people.

He could only hope it paid off.

He turned his attention to the moment, and the video conference with Colonel Foster.

"We'll be out of range while you're down there," Foster told them. "But a squadron will stay behind to keep an eye out for you."

"Just don't be gone long, okay?" Sam said. "And Mark – don't worry. I'll keep listening for Madison."

"Thanks, Sam," Mark said.

He meant it. The guy had really rubbed him the wrong way at first. But he meant well.

Everyone around him was in motion. The commander of the submarine, Crane, a square-jawed, dark-eyed, serious fellow, was busy plotting a course with the executive officer,

Bowman. Chen and Stanton were mapping Godzilla's vitals, which seemed a little odd. They weren't thinking about surgery, were they? He tried to imagine how that could be done. Probably they were talking about how to maximize the bomb's energy. Everyone was doing something except for him.

Mark felt like the still point, and for once, that was okay. He had put this in motion, but now he was just along for the ride.

"All right, Bowman," Commander Crane said, now finished with the course. "Let's take her down."

"Dive the ship," Bowman said. "And make depth one-five-zero."

"Good luck," Sam said, from the screen.

"Thanks," Mark replied. "We'll need it."

Serizawa was playing with his pocket watch again. A sign he was thoughtful or nervous, or both. Often both.

Mark offered the scientist some coffee. "What time is it?" he asked.

A wistful little smile drew across Serizawa's face.

"Time to get a new watch," he said.

In an instant, Mark's mind raced back, to a quieter time and the laughter of a young boy. He could almost hear it, the funny little arpeggio his son's giggle composed.

"Andrew's favorite joke," Mark said. "You never could take that thing out without him asking…"

He stopped. Why were even the good memories so painful? Shouldn't it be getting easier? He took in a deep, clean breath and went on.

"If you told me five years ago that saving the thing that took my son was my best shot at saving the family I have left…"

He stopped. He had spent a lot of time avoiding memories

of Andrew. It was the only way he'd been able to stop drinking, and to focus on Maddie. But now the cogs of his mind had slipped. The memories were coming back. He wasn't sure he could bear it.

"Sometimes," Serizawa said, "the only way to heal our wounds is to make peace with the demons who created them."

"You really believe that?" Mark said.

"Don't you?" Serizawa said. "Isn't that why you're here?"

Mark didn't know what to say. Maybe it was, although he certainly hadn't thought so. He'd thought it was all about Maddie, about saving what he had, not dealing with what was lost.

"There are some things beyond our understanding, Mark," Serizawa said. "The laws of nature are beautiful, but they can also be cruel and unfair. But we cannot control these things, or run from them. We must accept them and learn from them – because these moments of crisis are also potential moments of faith. A time when we either come together or fall apart. And nature always has a way of balancing itself – the only question is, what part will we play?"

It was one of the longest speeches Mark had ever heard the usually laconic Serizawa give.

"Did you just make all that up?" Mark asked.

"No," Serizawa said. "I read it in a fortune cookie once. A really long fortune cookie."

Mark smiled, but the moment passed too quickly.

The sub lurched violently and began rocking like crazy. Deafening alarms blared in the close quarters. Had Ghidorah found them, or one of the other Titans? One of the aquatic ones? What was that one in Loch Ness called, Leviathan? Could it have gotten here so fast? He hadn't noticed anything near them in the last tracking data...

But they weren't being battered, or eaten, actually. Since the initial bump they were just sort of *leaning* and twisting.

"Status of the ship?" Commander Crane said.

"Some sort of vortex, Captain," Bowman said. "It's dragging us."

The ship groaned, metal straining and pinging as it began to spiral downward into ever-deeper water.

"Ship still descending," Bowman said, counting down toward the sea floor. "Four hundred feet. One hundred. Fifty."

"Brace for impact!" Crane shouted.

The mostly empty shelter left plenty of space for Madison to work in. Jonah's mercenaries weren't even doing a whole lot of guarding or patrolling. No one on the outside knew they were here, and everyone who might think to look was currently distracted by the impending end of the world. Further proof her mom had fallen in on the wrong side. While she was holed up, safe from what she had unleashed, the rest of Monarch was out there fighting rather than taking to the shelters. Because even the shelters wouldn't be of much use if the atmosphere was fried and every living thing outside besides Monster Zero was dead. Jonah thought he and the other survivors were going to live like kings. Maybe, if by that he meant the miserable lice-eaten thugs in the Dark Ages who had started calling themselves "kings."

She found a bolt-cutter and the storage lockers; with a little help from the first, she opened up the second. And jackpot! Everything she needed: rations and medical supplies, all sorts of stuff that would come in handy. She loaded her pack, and grabbed a stun gun.

Despite her advantages, she knew she had to work fast.

Once they realized she wasn't in her room – that they didn't know where she was – things would heat up. Jonah would put guards on all the exits, and she would be screwed. So get going, Madison.

She quick-walked to the control room. Normally, if someone saw her there, they wouldn't think much about it; but now, with the backpack and all, it would raise suspicion. So when she heard someone inside, she ducked behind a corner.

Just in time. Jonah and one of his killers came out and walked off down another corridor.

She didn't hear anybody else, so she crept up and peeked in. She couldn't see anyone, but thankfully what she had come for was there – the ORCA. She had worried Jonah might hide it someplace or even destroy it, but that wasn't really his style. He enjoyed power over others. He probably thought it was funny that her mother could look at the machine, but never touch it.

His mistake.

She stepped toward it, nervously. Once she actually took it...

Three steps in she realized she had screwed up; she heard a faint scuff of shoes and something threw a shadow on her. Whoever it was must have been in the corner.

She spun around, hoping it was Mom, ready to come up with some kind of story, but instead found one of Jonah's men looming over her. She didn't know his real name, but in her mind she had been calling him "The Mountain" due to his size.

She gave him her best sheepish, "I didn't mean to" grin.

Then shot him with the stun gun.

It worked astonishingly well. He jerked like a fish on a hook, his legs went all wobbly, and he pitched to the floor with a pronounced thud.

The bigger they come, she thought.

Once he was down, she quickly packed up the ORCA and moved on to the second part of her plan. She climbed up on a desk, and used a screwdriver to take out the bottom screws of the grille over an air vent. She first pulled and the pushed the grille, bending it up. When it was wide enough, she shoved the ORCA in. Then she gripped the edge of the vent.

Pulling herself up was harder than she'd thought it would be; her brilliant plan might have already fallen apart. But she dug down deep, jumping and jerking with her arms at the same time. She managed to get an elbow up, and then the other, and from there she pulled until her belly was on the edge and she could wriggle in like a worm.

Sometimes it was good to be small; she managed to turn around in the narrow duct, reach up and bend the grille back down. It wasn't perfectly flush – it jutted about an inch – but it was better than leaving it wide open. Every second she wasn't found out was like gold at this point.

She started crawling as softly as she could, trying to remember the turns from the specs she had pulled up.

It's going to be fine, she thought. *By the time they think to look up here, I'll be out and away.*

She came to another vent and paused to get her bearings. As per her calculations, she was passing the cafeteria.

She hadn't expected to see her mother there. She was just sitting, staring into a cup of coffee.

Maddie considered her, momentarily paralyzed with guilt. She knew her mother. It was all finally catching up with her. Her mom could push her feelings pretty far down, but she couldn't erase them, and now they were coming back up. That might be okay if things had gone the way she planned; she could justify the terrible things she had done. But Monster

Zero had changed all of that. She was already at a low point. Maddie running away was going to crush her.

But there was no choice now. She had zapped one of Jonah's men and stolen the ORCA. He wasn't going to just give her a pass on that. At the very least, he would destroy the ORCA or lock it up someplace where no one could get to it. At worst, he might go ahead and kill her, and maybe Mom, too.

No. There was no turning back.

Her gaze lingered on her mother for another heartbeat, and then she moved on, crawling as quietly as possible.

With each breath she thought she would hear alarms or shouts, or whatever. Surely the man she'd stunned had recovered by now, or someone had found him.

Her heart felt like it was crowding up into her throat, and the air duct felt as if it was growing smaller, tighter.

When she finally reached the emergency exit hatch, she hustled toward it, unlatched it, and pushed it open enough to peek through.

She saw trees and underbrush, but no guards or vehicles. Taking the chance, she climbed out, then closed the hatch.

She was alone, in a patch of woods, but in the distance, she saw swarms of aircraft flitting above a familiar city skyline.

Boston.

Without hesitation, she hefted the ORCA and started toward the lights. It was going to be a long walk.

SEVENTEEN

From the notes of Dr. Houston Brooks:

April 10, AD 1818.
To all the world:
I declare the earth is hollow and habitable within; containing a number of solid concentric spheres, one within the other, and that it is open at the poles twelve or sixteen degrees. I pledge my life in support of this truth, and am ready to explore the hollow, if the world will support and aid me in my undertaking.
Jn. Cleves Symmes, of Ohio, late captain of Infantry.

—From Symmes' self-published pamphlet

Some optimism had crept into Sam as they made their way toward Washington D.C. in the *Argo* and a sky full of jets, helicopters, and a fleet of battleships and submarines with enough firepower to level a medium-sized country. It felt like they could take on anything.

Even when the *Argo* began to chop a bit as they approached the storm, he felt okay about their chances. But as the storm loomed nearer, he started to appreciate the scale of the thing as he hadn't been able to observe it on radar. It was no longer a colorful doppler pinwheel assembled from wind directions and speeds, but hell unleashed.

Dozens of tornados and waterspouts churned though the air and sea, sucking everything they touched up into the bruised gray and sickly yellow sky. He could make out buildings in the distance, but it took a few breaths to understand he could see only the *tops* of things. The summit of the Washington monument, for instance, and the dome of the capitol building.

The storm surge from Ghidorah's tempest had drowned Washington D.C.

"Jesus," Sam said. "It looks like the sky's alive."

"That's because it is," Foster said.

A chain of lightning flared in the black clouds, and for an instant they could see Ghidorah's dreadful outline.

"Here we go," Foster said.

The Osprey dropped out of the *Argo* and into a wind shear so violent they nearly spun around. Griffin compensated, nosing them into the winds.

Barnes had a glimpse of the fleet, far below.

Jets hurtled by overhead. The plan was to get over the eye of the storm and drop some hellfire on Ghidorah. The main fleet would follow them in and pound the monster with everything they had.

He settled himself behind the .50 caliber and searched for a target. Griffin jinked hard, avoiding something ahead. Barnes's fingers tightened on the trigger, but then he saw they had narrowly missed being sucked into a tornado.

He eased off. You couldn't shoot weather.

"C'mon," he muttered.

He caught a streak of flame from the corner of his eye. At first, he thought it was a burning aircraft, falling through a cloud. But lightning flared, and he made out a familiar outline.

"Griffin—" he said.

"I see," she said.

"Ghidorah?" Martinez asked.

"No," Barnes said. "The other one."

"He's on intercept with the *Argo*," Griffin said. "What do you want me to do, boss?"

"Call 'em," he said.

He eyeballed the distance while she alerted the *Argo*. They were too far away for the machine gun to be of any use.

"Are we in range for the missiles?" he asked.

"They're unguided," Griffin said. "I'd rather be closer."

As gunships, Ospreys sucked. It had taken forever for anyone to mount missiles on them, and when they did, they were pretty small ones. But they were better than nothing.

The craft bumped as Griffin turned it into an airplane and sped it toward the track of the fiery bird.

Rodan appeared again through the clouds, circling around toward the *Argo*, using the storm as cover.

"Okay," Griffin said. "One away. Two away."

Two small sparks sped into the storm. One kept going; the other flashed on Rodan's head.

The big bird didn't seem to notice; he vanished back into the cloud.

"Get another shot!" Barnes said.

"That's what I'm looking for," Griffin said.

He moved the gun, looking for a shot. If he led high, he might be able to put a few in at this range.

There was a sudden break in the clouds. But Rodan wasn't there.

"Oh, shit!" Martinez yelped. "Above us, nine o'clock!"

Barnes glanced up to see the monster, filling half the sky, wings folded at its sides, diving straight toward them.

"Griffin!"

"Kind of busy here," she said.

She banked hard and down. Barnes felt the blood drain from his head. He gripped the .50 caliber harder, trying to stay behind it. Rodan's head appeared, plowing right toward them. With a shout he began firing straight at the thing's face.

Then they dropped into a steep dive, and the monster's head was out of frame, although it seemed to take forever for the body to finish going over.

"I think he likes us," Barnes said.

"I think you're right," Griffin said, "'cause he's coming back for another pass."

Lights flickered back on and air began to blow through the vents again. Mark's heart was hammering, though. Underwater, in the dark, with the air growing stale, everything shrinking in on him – what they hell was he doing here? He should be out in a field, with wolves, where you could see what was coming at you. Where the only wall was the horizon.

"Damage report," Crane said.

"Fire in torpedo room is out," Bowman said. "Atmosphere is stable. We're banged up, but we'll make it."

"Make it *where*?" Mark asked.

"Can't fix our position," Bowman said, "but inertial says we're six hundred miles from departure."

Mark wondered if he'd heard that right.

Six hundred miles. Even at a hundred miles an hour that would take six hours, and Mark was pretty damn sure no submarine could go that fast, not even some souped-up Monarch tub. And the lights had been out for a lot less than six hours.

"That can't be," Crane said, echoing Mark's thought.

Weirdly, Stanton was beaming.

"I knew it!" he said. "That vortex was a tunnel into the Hollow Earth!"

Crane looked at him as if he was speaking an unknown language.

"Subterranean tunnel system that connects the entire planet?" Stanton said. "Anyway, it doesn't matter. I told you, Chen!"

"Shut up, Rick," Chen said.

The Hollow Earth was an old idea. It had probably started before humans were fully modern, when they used shallow caves as homes and explored the deeper ones, once they had fire. In the 1600s, Edmund Halley – the same guy the comet was named for – went a little farther and proposed the whole planet was hollow. For a couple of hundred years the notion had been entertained by scientists and crackpots alike and resulted in a fair amount of early science fiction.

To most geologists in the twentieth century, the Hollow Earth was just that – science fiction.

In the 1970s, Dr. Houston Brooks proposed a hybrid model, claiming that the Earth and deep oceans did, in fact, contain cavities of immense size. He tried to test his hypothesis on Skull Island – with catastrophic effects. While he had gathered evidence of deep cave systems, the definitive proof for his larger theory was still lacking.

Until now, maybe. If Stanton was right, Mothra had led them right into a vortex to bring them where they needed to be. To Godzilla. Debate as to what exactly had happened could wait. Whether they had really moved six hundred miles or it was an instrument malfunction, they were where they were, and they needed to get on with their mission.

"One-second emergency blow forward," Crane said.

The sub lurched ahead.

"Doctor?" Crane said, looking to Serizawa.

"Launch probes," Serizawa said.

The feeds from two small drones appeared, illuminating the way ahead with long searchlights. The sub followed along, approaching strange, twisting shapes still too vague to make out. But even from here, they seemed somehow unnatural.

"Lights on," Stanton said. "Cameras good. Range one thousand yards."

The sub and its twin guides crept through the darkness. Mark wondered how deep they were, how many tons of water pressure were pushing against their hull. He decided he didn't want to know.

The occasional flicker of movement in the search beams reminded him that there was life, even down here, where sunlight never penetrated, where photosynthesis was impossible. Land and shallow seas only accounted for about a third of the Earth's surface. Most of the world lay beneath perpetual night.

A dark shape loomed and suddenly resolved as a woman's face, pale and ghostly. Mark took an involuntary step back.

"Jesus!" Stanton exclaimed.

But then the frame widened. It wasn't a corpse or a mermaid, but the figurehead of a ship, a galleon, centuries old.

It wasn't alone. Dozens of wrecks were visible in their searchlights, many piled one upon the other. A Viking knar raised its dragon figurehead from the shatters of triremes, galleys, cogs, and frigates. The harrowed cylinder of a vintage submarine, a diesel-powered beast from the last world war, lay near the broken remnants of a clipper ship and a warship that had probably last seen the surface in the 1910s. All drawn here by the vortex, as they had been, hammered onto the anvil of the abyss.

Mark realized how fortunate they had been to survive, not to end up as part of this ships' graveyard.

But not only ships were rested here. Amongst the wrecks lay immense bones – ribs, long bones, skulls, bony plates.

And Mark noticed something else.

"Wait a second," he said. "Pan right."

There was light in the darkness, a pulsing reddish fog, not coming down from the surface, but rising from the sea floor at the bottom of a trench, where lava was boiling up from fissures in the earth, flowing across the sea floor in braided streams, flooding around fantastic structures that simply could not be natural. Some were more disjointed Titan bones, but others – were not.

Through the murk, crumbling statues the size of skyscrapers appeared, along with temples, state buildings – the remains of a cyclopean city. Breathtaking arched colonnades reminded Mark of Roman buildings like the Colosseum; in other places the architecture seemed more Greek or Egyptian, and here and there resembled the ornate architecture of Southeast Asian temples. And through it all streamed an increasingly larger and brighter river of molten rock.

On many of the buildings and monuments, Mark could barely make out what might be hieroglyphics, bas-reliefs of strange beasts and much smaller humans. One of them clearly resembled Godzilla.

"What is all this?" he asked. "Egyptian? Roman?"

"No way," Dr. Stanton said. "This is something else entirely, something way older."

Much larger murals came into view, and now Mark fully recognized what he was seeing. Depictions of Godzilla, Mothra – and yes, Kong. Beneath them, smaller figures were arranged in various form of respect, or service, or – worship.

"All the legends," Chen breathed. "The stories. They're true. They really were the first gods."

She began taking stills of the ancient carvings.

This changes everything, Mark realized. Emma was right. She had certainly screwed up and gotten untold numbers of people killed, but the link between humans and these ancient beasts was now inescapable.

What he found most remarkable was that absolutely nothing in the poses of the human figures suggested fear, or intimidation. Awe, yes, maybe worship. But also cooperation.

This was the coexistence Emma and Serizawa had so often spoken of. That he had dismissed as nonsense. The Titans were part of the natural order, and always had been.

But there was another story here, too. It was clear the city hadn't been peacefully abandoned and allowed to deliquesce. Almost everything had been scarred, scorched, or blasted. The sea bottom bore the cratered scars of some ancient cataclysm.

The murals of man and monster ended – not because the ancient artists had finished, but because their work had been blasted to pieces. Whatever harmony had once existed in the place had been destroyed, drowned like Atlantis. Had this civilization existed above, in the sunlit world, brought into the deeps by some geological event? Or had this once been a vast cave, filled with air, lit by some unknown light source?

Either way, who – or what – had brought about its downfall? A war of Titans fought with the aid of human beings? If so, given all the monster bones, things didn't seem to have gone very well for anyone.

Except, perhaps, Godzilla.

And what did that mean for them? Was this the fate of his own civilization, to be swept away and forgotten?

"If the earth and stones could only speak," Stanton said, "the stories they would tell us..."

"Dr. Stanton," Serizawa said, "any sign of Godzilla?"

Mark realized that of all of them, Serizawa was the least distracted by the strange wonders of this place. He was still focused on the task at hand.

But of course, what they were seeing only confirmed what Serizawa had already been certain of for years. He was way ahead of them in being able to absorb all of this.

"Yeah," Stanton said. "The probes are picking up a pretty big radiation blob just past that range."

"Set a course," Serizawa said.

Madison pushed through the woods as fast as she could. She kept imagining Jonah behind her, gun in hand. Feeling the bullet hit her in the back. Or would she feel it? Maybe everything would just – stop.

She didn't want to find out.

She came across a winding two-lane road and started down it. She no longer had enough elevation to see the city, but she had a good sense of where it was. She was in suburbia now, passing the entrances to cul-de-sac neighborhoods. Most were quiet, already empty, but now and then she saw a family still packing up. Once some people in an SUV stopped and offered her a ride, but when they learned she was going *into* the city, they shook their heads and moved on.

Her road joined a bigger one, all strip malls, shopping centers, office complexes, and finally to an interstate, and that wasn't quiet at all. Cars packed it bumper to bumper, on both sides of the divide, all going the same way – out. They were mostly ground to a halt, and the drivers weren't happy about it. That was okay; honking and screaming she could deal with. More difficult were the people on foot, weaving between the automobiles; it was like swimming upstream, and the ORCA was heavy. She was already more than tired, and still had a long way to go to reach Fenway Park.

Downtown, the evacuation was kicking into high gear. Sirens wailed near and far. Jets slashed through the skies, and she made out helicopters and Ospreys taking off and landing in the distance.

She stopped to rest, eat, and drink, but never for more than a few minutes.

At least she felt safer now. The odds of Jonah finding her in all of this mess had to be pretty low.

By the time she got within sight of the ballpark, the crowd had turned, no longer flowing out of the city but toward Fenway, which she now saw was one of the evacuation hubs. They were using the ballfield to stage airlifts. She watched hopefully as another group of craft lifted off. The evacuation seemed to be going well. Maybe more people would survive, this time.

No. They *would*. She would see to that. But with all of

these folks pouring into Fenway, it was going to be a little trickier then she had anticipated.

She merged into one of the lines, where people were being herded into the stadium by cops and soldiers. Every few minutes the loudspeakers reminded them all to remain calm, that evacuation ships would be departing every fifteen minutes. It was like being in a theme park, except here if you didn't get on the ride in a timely fashion, you died.

A few places in line ahead, a little girl was clinging to her dad. She looked terrified. Madison made a funny face, and the girl smiled and then turned away.

A moment later Maddie saw her chance. No one official was looking, and the line had gotten her as far as it could. Just ahead a door informed her that only authorized personnel were allowed through it.

She authorized herself, found it unlocked, and slipped inside. She discovered stairs and followed them up, working her way toward the broadcast booth. She had never been to it, but she had seen it from the cheap seats. She had a general idea where it was.

This part was easy. Despite the massive crowds outside, in here it was deserted.

She wondered what her dad was doing right now. They had been here together a few times, just the two of them. Neither Mom nor Andrew had been big baseball fans. She had never cared that much about the game herself, but she liked spending time with Dad, and she liked the atmosphere, the cheese fries, the popcorn.

She hoped he was still okay.

She hoped Mom was okay, too. That Jonah didn't take it out on her. She knew he might.

It took a little longer to find the booth than she would

have liked, but find it she did. From here she had a first-rate view of the evacuation through the giant glass windows, and for a moment she just absorbed the view.

Then she turned around and got to work.

Opening up the ORCA, she began patching it in to the stadium's speaker system.

Someone had left a screen on. She listened as the newscaster droned on.

"Massive storms and other disasters triggered by the Titans have forced millions to flee major cities. And with D.C. hit hard by a Category Six hurricane that has left the capitol completely flooded, this is the single greatest disaster in human history. The grim search continues as people around the world sift through the debris of leveled homes in the hope of finding missing loved ones. And though this sight is heartbreaking, it is in no way unique. Cities around the globe have fallen under the wake of what many are calling 'The Rise of the Titans.'"

Madison pulled up a bioacoustic waveform on the ORCA, then cranked up the volume on the stadium speakers. Now all she had to do was hit the button.

EIGHTEEN

From the notes of Dr. Serizawa:

First of all the deathless gods who dwell on Olympus made a golden race of mortal men who lived in the time of Cronos when he was reigning in heaven. And they lived like gods without sorrow of heart, remote and free from toil and grief: miserable age rested not on them; but with legs and arms never failing they made merry with feasting beyond the reach of all evils. When they died, it was as though they were overcome with sleep, and they had all good things; for the fruitful earth unforced bare them fruit abundantly and without stint. They dwelt in ease and peace upon their lands with many good things, rich in flocks and loved by the blessed gods.

—Hesiod, *Works and Days*, circa 700 BCE

GODZILLA: KING OF THE MONSTERS

* * *

The sub drifted through the spectral city toward something large, much larger than the other buildings. At first Mark thought it was a seamount, or another wall of the trench, but as they drew nearer, and it gained definition, he saw that it was a gigantic sculpture carved into a living stone face. It was a doorway of sorts, not on a human scale, but on a Titanic one. Carved on either side of the structure's base were two huge, three-clawed feet.

Through the cyclopean doorway, lava cascaded along a tunnel that rose in a series of large steps, eventually forming a larger fall that created the river over which they had been sailing. At the far end of the tunnel, a familiar blue glow limned the exit into – somewhere.

"I think we should stop," Stanton said, studying his instruments.

"Why?" Serizawa asked.

"Because I still wanna have kids one day," Stanton replied. "Preferably without flippers."

He pointed to his instruments, which showed radiation readings redlining.

"Full stop," Crane said. "Hover the ship."

The three drones continued on without them, dwindling into the tunnel, but their feed continued.

"It's way hot in there," Stanton said. "Probes aren't gonna last long, but I'm picking up his radioactive signature up ahead. It's weak but it's there."

He had barely gotten the words out of his mouth when the feed from one of the probes ceased, quickly followed by another. The third kept going. A moment later, it entered a vast cavern.

"Okay," Stanton said, "we've got O2, CO2, methane – looks like some sort of air pocket."

"Can you surface into that?" Mark asked.

"You got it," Stanton replied.

Mark stared at the stream as the probe rose into the atmospheric cavity.

Within lay a vast temple complex, and although the probe feed was starting to lose resolution, they could see him, Godzilla, splayed out, a fallen deity in the heart of his own temple, lava breaching up from beneath him.

"Oh my God—" Mark breathed.

"—zilla," Stanton finished.

Then the probe failed.

"Say goodnight, Gracie," Stanton said.

"Pull up the last frame," Serizawa said.

Mark was numb. There was the thing that had killed his son, beaten. Helpless. Logically, he knew they needed the monster alive, but emotionally, he wasn't quite there. He might never be. But that wasn't the point. Serizawa was right. He had to confront this.

Serizawa zoomed in to the volcanic vents surrounding Godzilla.

"There," he said. "Those bits. They're the source of the radiation."

"That's why he returned here," Chen said. "He's feeding. Regenerating."

"This is his home," Serizawa said.

The two scientists shared a look of satisfaction.

"That's how he survived so long," Mark said. "Always adapting. Evolving. It's incredible."

"Welp," Stanton said, "he doesn't really need our help, dude's got this covered, right? He just needs a nap."

"No," Chen said. "This process could take years. Even decades."

"We have to proceed as planned," Serizawa said.

"Hold on," Stanton objected. "We're talking about launching a nuclear torpedo to revive a giant monster. That's not exactly like a jump-starting a car."

"We have one more complication," Commander Crane said. "Our weapons systems were damaged during the crash. We can't launch."

That does put a kink in the hose, Mark thought. Maybe someone should have mentioned this a little earlier.

"Can we repair them?" Mark asked.

"I'm afraid not," Crane replied.

They had come all of this way, found the sleeping Titan – for nothing?

But Chen wasn't discouraged.

"Okay," she said, "so what if we go inside, set a timer, and detonate one of the warheads manually?"

"No way," Stanton said. "If the heat doesn't fry you the radiation will. It might be good for Titans, but it's not so good for us."

"I'll go," Serizawa said.

Mark thought he'd heard wrong. *Wasn't Serizawa paying attention?*

"What the hell does that mean?" he said.

Serizawa didn't speak, but his face said it all. He had skipped to the obvious conclusion: that to bring Godzilla back to health – to have a shot at saving what was left of their world – someone had to die. And he would be that person.

"There must be another way," Chen said.

"There's no time for a debate," Serizawa said. "I'll go."

GREG KEYES

* * *

Sudan

Mokele-Mbembe went through their line like it wasn't even there, crushing tanks beneath his feet, his tail slashing through the hastily erected high-tension lines they'd strung across the mouth of the gorge. Missiles from a jet painted the monster with flame, but he came on, picking up a Humvee with his trunk and lobbing it at the plane as it banked for another shot. The jet turned into a comet, hurtling out into the desert.

After the Titan escaped containment, Nez had managed to rally what remained of her soldiers, crowd them into the few remaining aircraft, and get out ahead of the monster as he followed the Nile north. She only had about twenty troops, but that night, the Egyptian army responded to her radio calls and air-dropped a small army on her position, along with some big guns and a powerful electric generator to charge the "fence." They'd set the trap in the canyon and lured Mokele-Mbembe into it by pestering it with aircraft. The hope was they could damage his legs, but neither the power lines nor explosive charges that went off under him gave him pause. He shrugged off the collapsing canyon walls as if they were Styrofoam rocks in a movie.

None of their preparations had made a difference. Of the two hundred plus troops who had been here at dawn, she now counted perhaps a dozen, and they were all doing what she was – running like hell as the beast thundered after them.

Problem was, it was a box canyon. The far end of it was a steep slope. There were still guns above it, blazing down at the beast, but they were only annoying him, encouraging him to rush up the gorge and silence them.

She hit the incline and started up on all fours, but by the time she was ten meters up, she knew she wasn't going to make it, nor could she escape to the side. The monster was too big and the canyon too narrow.

She drew her sidearm, turned, and began firing, aiming for the monster's eyes. He crashed on, was right on her...

And then he slowed. He took another step and stopped altogether.

For a moment she didn't do anything. She stared at Mokele-Mbembe, wondering what the hell he was up to. Then she decided it didn't matter. Moving slowly, she continued to retreat. She expected him to start up again at any second, but every instant he stood still like that allowed her to gain a little more distance.

Washington D.C. Area

"Come on!" Barnes yelled, firing steadily from the .50 caliber machine gun. "Yeah! You want some of this?! I'll eat your children! I'll eat your mother! I'll—"

Across the cabin, Martinez was at the other mounted gun, also letting loose. Griffin was driving. She had already launched all their missiles.

It had looked good on paper, Barnes guessed. A whole fleet and squadrons of aircraft against one li'l monster. Or, to be fair, two.

Unless you had been up close and personal with the monster, watched Tomahawk missiles pop on its scales without leaving a scratch. But then, nobody had asked him if the attack was a good idea.

But he wasn't mad. Not at the brass, anyway. He got

it; this whole show was about keeping the I-can-grow-my-damn-head-back-dude distracted for a while, so the scientists on the sub could revive the big guy and a few more civilians could be herded to safety. So no, he wasn't mad at the superiors who had sent him in here. They were out there too, fighting as hard as he was, and not doing any better.

But he was pretty goddamn mad at Ghidorah, who as far as he could see was just an asshole, full stop, and he didn't have a lot of love for Rodan, either. Especially now that Rodan and Ghidorah were pals.

Black streaks of disintegrating aircraft fell like rain from the storming sky. The sea below was littered with burning ships chopping on ninety-foot swells, but those fires were going out fast as the raging ocean dragged them under.

And here he was, shooting at monsters he couldn't even see for all the smoke and clouds and shit.

And their brand-new Osprey already all dinged-up.

Not a perfect day, this one.

"Come in, *Argo*," Griffin said. "We can't take much more of this."

"Copy that," Foster said. "We hear you – just hold them off as long as you can."

What was it that Roman mothers had told their sons? Come back with your shield or on it?

Damn straight.

"Come on!" Barnes shouted, firing at a shape in the clouds.

The horrors were coming too fast for Sam to absorb. The sky was on fire, the ocean a wrecking yard full of shattered destroyers and the bodies of the men and women who had manned them.

Up ahead of them, the cruiser *Philadelphia*'s guns were blazing non-stop, and a flight of cruise missiles leapt up into the clouds. They detonated, flaring through the mist, lighting up Ghidorah as he plunged down like an eagle, his hind legs slamming down close to the bow. The ship tilted up, her stern leaving the water entirely.

Jets streaked by, peppering the Titan; the tiny sparks of small arms fire flared from *Philadelphia*'s upper deck. The *Argo* dove at Ghidorah, trying to bring some relief to the *Philadelphia*, but suddenly Rodan was there, diving to intercept them. The *Argo* rolled hard and dropped. Rodan clapped his wings and speared back into the sky like a meteor in reverse.

With a heave of his wings, Ghidorah jumped back into the air, swiping two jets as if they were mosquitos.

The *Philadelphia* snapped in the middle; her two halves settled back on the water like she was okay, but she was doomed.

That wasn't good enough for Ghidorah. Before retreating back into the crowd, he vomited lightning onto the sinking ship. The electricity danced from point to point on the cruiser, and then the ship exploded, spreading flame in every direction.

Rodan was clearly now under Ghidorah's control, and between the two of them they had shredded the once-mighty fleet in much shorter order than even the most pessimistic among them had believed possible.

Admiral Stenz was trying to push a signal through. It flared to life, showing the interior of his submarine full of smoke and water, rocking crazily. Then it was gone. Whether because the sub had exploded or because there was too much interference, there was no way to tell.

The center isn't holding, Sam thought. *Mere chaos...*

But then he noticed something – probably below the level of conscious thought, at first, because so much was going on. But then he realized it was the map of the other Titans. Their positions. Before, they had all been on the move – he remembered Mark likening them to a hunting pack. But now something had changed.

"Hey," he said. "Hey, wait a minute. Colonel, they're stopping... They're stopping! You see this?"

He looked at the live feed of the attacks. Sure enough, the Titans in Barcelona, Egypt, Moscow, Brazil – they were all just standing there, like statues.

"The hell's gotten into them now?" Foster wondered.

Boston

In the broadcast booth, Madison watched the news stream in from around the world; footage of the Titans going quiet.

Maddie smiled. She'd done it. Or at least it was a start. Monarch had a chance to do their thing, now.

On the field below, the crowd was thinned out to almost nothing. A few more airlifts and the evacuation would be complete. If anyone noticed the odd pulses coming from the stadium speakers, no one had come to check it out. But she was staying in case they did. She couldn't let anyone turn off the ORCA.

Anyway, she didn't know where else to go.

Emma tried Madison's room again, but the door was still locked, and she didn't respond to knocking. She left feeling empty. After Andrew's death, after the divorce, she and Maddie had forged a new life together. She'd thought the bond between them was unbreakable.

It hadn't occurred to her that Maddie's connection to Mark would stay so strong, even though he hadn't been there for her, even though she hadn't seen him much at all in the past couple of years.

She supposed it was easier to idealize someone you didn't see every day. You didn't have all of those little arguments about putting away clothes or washing dishes.

And destroying the world.

But it was more than that. Despite his spectacular failure as a husband and father, at his core Mark was still a good man. How difficult had it been for him to leave his comfort zone in the wilderness? Probably very. But he had done it. He was putting his life on the line. Maddie couldn't help but admire that.

Neither could she.

Andrew's death had wounded them both, but in ways that weren't reconcilable. Godzilla hadn't meant to kill Andrew. His universe, his goals, existed at a much higher level than that of the individual human being. Godzilla was trying to keep the planet in balance. He had no malice toward human beings, she was sure of it. If a firefighter putting out a burning building stepped on a beetle in the process, would he even notice?

Her grief had pushed her toward Godzilla's goal. If the natural world had been in balance, the MUTOs wouldn't have emerged – and if they had, they wouldn't have had piles of nuclear materials to feed on. Without them, Godzilla would never have come out of his deep retreat to fight them. Andrew would still be alive. She thought that if she brought the world to harmony, that would be a legacy. For Andrew. So he wouldn't have died for nothing.

Mark saw it another way. He just wanted all of the Titans dead. And barring that, he wanted to forget. She'd been called to action; he'd chosen to run.

No amount of argument would have brought them back together. At least, that was what she had believed.

She went to the commissary and tried to eat, but she didn't have any appetite. Eventually Maddie would forgive her, and they could move on. After all, they were likely to be stuck here for years. There was no hurry now.

She thought about trying to use the ORCA again, but Jonah's warning had been far too vivid. She'd lost her son, her husband, her way in the world. Her certainty and purpose were gone. Only Maddie remained. She had already put her in so much jeopardy, she couldn't bear to put her in more.

She was tossing her uneaten food when the alarms began blaring.

What now? she wondered, straightening. Had Monarch found them? Or one of the Titans?

She hurried to the control center.

She found Jonah there, looking more grim than usual.

"What's going on?" she asked.

Jonah pointed to a screen displaying a signal emanating from Fenway Park. She instantly recognized the cycling biosignatures and piggy-backed master signal.

"The ORCA," Jonah said.

She turned to look for the machine. It wasn't where she'd left it. And yet it was doing exactly what she had planned, before Jonah stopped her.

"I wonder who could've done this?" Jonah asked.

Their eyes met, and she saw he wasn't wondering at all. He

knew as well as she did who had done it. But maybe they were both wrong. Maybe she would find her daughter still sulking in her room. Safe.

She ran to Maddie's room and used her master key to unlock the door. Maddie's things were still there, her laptop, clothes, and books scattered around, her pad…

She picked the pad up and took a sharp breath. It displayed the family picture, the one from their stoop in Boston. The screen was broken, the image covered in cracks.

Maddie, what have you done?

But she knew that, too.

Mark helped Serizawa into the dive suit. The bomb was prepped and ready to go. It was all happening too fast, slipping down a slope that was now almost vertical. There had to be some other way, he was sure of that. It was just that he couldn't think of anything.

"We've removed the warhead's lead shielding and inserted a mechanical timer, so it can function in the radiation," Crane said.

"On first contact you'll start losing your long-range vision," Stanton said, quietly. "After you surface your motor skills will fade. But I added a heliox mixture to your tank. It should help keep you stable longer."

Serizawa nodded without expression as he took in the specifics of his impending death. Stanton was trying to be precise, clinical. To make sure Serizawa's attempt didn't fail.

He wasn't quite succeeding.

"Once you get inside, you'll have about six minutes," Chen said, "before the radiation—"

She was too choked up to continue.

Mark felt his own eyes misting up. Losing Serizawa – it was too much. Everyone felt it. He was part of the very foundations of Monarch, and of most of their lives.

"It was an honor, man," Stanton said, reaching out and shaking Serizawa's hand.

Chen grabbed Serizawa in a hug, gripping him like she didn't want to let go. But she did, her arms pulling back slowly.

"Thank you," Serizawa said. "All of you."

He walked over to Mark and offered him his notebook.

"My notes," he said.

Mark took them, reluctantly.

"Are you sure?" he asked.

"He fought for us. Died for us. He's not only proof that coexistence is possible, he is the key to it. Take care of them, Mark," Serizawa said.

He turned the airlock and then entered the small submersible beyond. The doors were sealed; the water began to rise. Serizawa was on his way.

"He's clear," Crane said.

They watched as the little submersible, like the probes before it, entered the fiery tunnel. Like the drones, Mark knew it would not return.

NINETEEN

When Edmund Halley first laid out his evidence for the Hollow Earth, he said – and I'm paraphrasing here, because old Edmund could be pretty dense in his writing – that if God made Earth to support life, why would so much of the world be uninhabitable? Why so much wasted space? I think in a sense he was right. I've laid out the geological foundations of my theory, but there is other evidence. The Choctaw believe they emerged from an underworld at a place called Nanih Waiyah. The Hopi of Arizona, the Inca of Peru – cultures all over the world speak of vast underground spaces, places where monsters dwell. In some of those tales, the people explicitly leave those underworlds to escape the monsters, but in others they claim some of their ancestors are still down there. Since at least Paleolithic times, human beings have worshipped caves, communed in them, made sacred art in them. We are drawn to caves, and we fear them. Before the first deep ocean dives, it was the received notion that life could not exist in those lightless depths without photosynthesis as the basis of the food chain. But when we got down there we found an ecosystem based on chemosynthesis, driven by chemicals boiling up through deep sea vents. We are surface dwellers on this planet. We know nothing of its greatest deeps, and what might stir there.

—From a presentation by Dr. Houston Brooks

Serizawa tried to control his breathing as he entered the tunnel, to stay calm. To keep his purpose. Like every living thing, from the tiniest single-cell creature to the Titans themselves, his impulse was to stay alive. If he turned back right now, he probably would. He and Mark and the rest could do what Emma said – find a shelter, survive until they could come up with another solution.

But he didn't think there was another solution. Once Ghidorah had destroyed every threat to him in the world above, he would surely turn his attentions down here. He would find Godzilla, still crippled, and finish him. And then it wouldn't matter how well hidden the remainder of humanity was. Ghidorah would root them out, using the other Titans. Wherever he was from, whatever his origin, Ghidorah did not like the world as it was. He was changing it. When he was finished, even those people who escaped his hunts wouldn't be able to survive. And perhaps the other Titans would die as well...

No. Godzilla was their only chance. Earth's only chance.

It was getting hot. The deep sea was cold, but the river of lava flowing down from above was warming it here in the tunnel, where it was enclosed. If it got much hotter, he might not even survive long enough for the radiation to kill him.

The tunnel itself was remarkable. It was hard to imagine how it might have been built. Given the size of it, and the size of the steps, in had clearly been built for Godzilla, the entrance into the temple of the god himself. At the threshold, and thereafter whenever the floor stepped up, the architects had carved enclosures, within which statues had also been carved. Each represented a creature with the body of a bull and the head of a man with a full, thick beard. Bird wings folded at their sides. Although the style was a little different, he recognized them. The Sumerians had called them Lammar, the Assyrians Lammasu. Statues similar to these had been built in palaces and temples all over the Middle East. They were spirits of protection and guidance. Some said they represented certain constellations, or the wheels-within-wheels that made up the natural order. The people who built this place hoped they would protect their god.

Serizawa found them comforting and even encouraging. Protect him, they could not, but he could do with all of the guidance he could get.

Sweat poured from him now; the interior of the submersible was stifling – but it wasn't enough heat to kill him. Not yet.

As he passed the last of the Lamassu guardians, he knew it was now done. He was surely past the point of no return. If he turned around, his only reward would be to spend the rest of his short life in misery. He had seen people die of radiation poisoning. It was no way to die.

The light ahead grew brighter, like a sunrise. Sunrise was usually associated with hope, not death. But even though he knew this sunrise was killing him, it still signified hope. Not for his own small life, but for all life. He was doing the right thing.

But he was still mortal, and part of him was deeply terrified of what was about to happen.

The sub was beginning to sputter and spark, dying as he was. But they didn't have far to go.

He surfaced into... majesty. The feed from the probe had not done this place – this palace of a god – justice. He climbed out of the sub and allowed himself a moment, rooted in awe, to let his eyes drink it all in, before the fierce, invisible rays destroyed his sight.

The cavern was grand beyond his imaginings. Part of it seemed to be natural cavern, but the handprint of humanity was everywhere. Sacred carvings, glyph-covered monoliths, temples, statues that evoked dozens of ancient human civilizations, the prototype of them all. It was fitting, this mixture of man-shaped and natural, as fitting as the relationship between humanity and...

Godzilla.

The Titan lay upon a stone platform in the center of the place, at the top of a long, very broad staircase. Fountains of molten rocks sprayed up around him, draining down the sides of the temples into the waters below.

He felt the presence of holy ground, that sense of simultaneously being very small but part of something immense.

So many years of his life he had spent searching for this creature. First, as a legacy to his father's work, but over the years, he had more and more come to understand Godzilla's place in the world. And thus his own purpose.

A purpose he fulfilled now.

And he found he was no longer afraid.

Carrying the bomb in its case, he started up the stairs. Stanton was right; already the more distant reaches of the cave had become blurry. His limbs trembled. The radiation was sleeting through him, destroying the very cells that composed him. But he put one foot in front of another, each footfall a moment in his journey, each more difficult that the last. The darkness began to close around him.

When he reached the summit, he did not know it at first. But then his failing eyesight focused, and he saw Godzilla was there. His lungs were burning; the heart in his chest – like his pocket watch – no longer kept proper time.

He kneeled, set down the case, and opened it up. With quivering fingers, he started the timer. Twenty seconds. All the time he needed.

He took out his pocket watch and looked at it one last time. Remembering the man who had given it to him.

Things like this should pass from father to son, he thought. But it was too late for that now.

A vast moan of pain shook the chamber.

His body did not want to stand again, but he made it, using all that remained of his dogged tenacity.

He removed his helmet.

The air was harsh with burnt stone and steaming water, the largest sauna in the world. It was nearly too much for him, but that was okay.

Up close, Godzilla's wounds were terrible, and immense. His dorsal spines were barely flickering. But he would heal. He would rise again. And he would fight for their world. He would bring balance.

Serizawa could barely breathe now, and his body felt like the ash of a burned leaf – still holding the form, but none of the color or life.

Godzilla's eyes were open, watching him come. And although it was impossible, he believed that he saw recognition there. Compassion.

He was there now. He stripped off one of his gloves and laid a hand on the Titan's scales.

"Goodbye, old friend," he said. He closed his eyes. There was light.

They couldn't stick around to make sure Serizawa succeeded. If he did, and they were still in the neighborhood, the shock wave from the explosion would rip the sub apart.

It might yet.

"Thirty thousand yards until we're outside the convergence zone," Bowman said, as the sub raced – or at least limped quickly – away from the sunken city and its fallen god.

What if Serizawa hadn't done the job? It was a big *if*. He might have died before arming the bomb. The submersible might have malfunctioned, like the drones. What if there was something in there other than Godzilla, ready to destroy anyone who entered?

They couldn't go back and try again. They had more nukes, but no more submersibles. If Serizawa didn't make it, they were out of options.

But then, behind them, a star was born, pure light shining in the abyss.

Mark breathed a sigh of relief. It was done. Whatever happened to them now...

...became a serious question as the submarine began to shake. "Shock wave incoming! Five seconds," Bowman counted down. "Three seconds—"

When the shock wave hit them, Chen grabbed Mark's

hand. He was so surprised he nearly forgot they were about to die. He gripped back. It felt good. Warm, familiar.

Then it felt like Godzilla had stepped on his chest as the submarine was suddenly accelerated to speeds it was never meant to withstand. Steel groaned, shrieked – snapped, as the ship began tearing apart. He smelled sea water and ozone and – burning. The lights flickered wildly. And still they were deep, surrounded by blackness.

But then a faint light appeared above them, growing brighter, as they were hurled toward the surface by the expanding edge of the explosion.

They broke into the air, tossed up by a tower of water. Mark lost all sense of what was happening; the acceleration faded, was gone, he was weightless—

They slammed back down on the surface of the ocean like a breaching whale.

But when it all sorted out, they were floating. Maybe not for long, but for now. The power was still on, if a bit jittery.

He was still holding Chen's hand.

He didn't let go.

"Are you okay?" he asked her.

Breathless and wide-eyed, she nodded. She didn't let go either. He thought how long it had been since he'd held anyone's hand, had the simple comfort of being physically in touch with another human being. It was especially nice in the face of pure terror…

"Bowman," Crane said. "Send a distress message to the *Argo*."

They donned rainslickers and popped the hatches of the submarine, climbing out on to the upper deck beneath the thundering dark sky. Rain spattered in fits and starts. Waves crashed against the sub, rocking it beneath Mark's unsteady feet.

All he could see in any direction were the gunmetal crests of the sea.

Bowman launched a rescue flare. It shot up, burning brightly, but its glow was dimmed when it reached the low-hanging clouds. It would be a wonder if anyone saw such a feeble light in the gloom of Ghidorah's storm.

Mark looked around them with binoculars, searching for anything peculiar in the sea. Blue light, a strange wave, some sign things had gone the right way...

"Anything?" Chen asked.

He shook his head, doubts creeping in. What if they'd been wrong? What if the bomb hadn't cured Godzilla, but had – well, blown him up? He was in a weakened state. He had survived nuclear blasts before, but that had been decades ago, an earlier technology. What if Serizawa had died for no good reason? Hell, the very idea that anything about these monsters was much better than a wild guess was crazy.

Which made him crazy. It had been his idea. And if he'd been wrong, if he had Serizawa's blood on his hands...

The ocean began to boil and churn – not normal waves or odd crosscurrents, but building up, bulging, like the explosion they had just caused, only slower. The sea was being pushed up from beneath.

And light, blue light, shone through the waves.

The jagged spines of Godzilla's dorsal crest emerged like a mountain range, crackling and dancing with energy. His head breached the surface, rising high above as waterfalls sheeted down around him. Up and up he rose, the tons of displaced water rocking their comparatively tiny craft. Chen took a step forward, tilting her head to watch him tower above them.

The Titan turned his head toward the wild heavens and a blue shaft of energy erupted from between his jaws, stabbed up into the dark clouds, through them, igniting them from within. It seemed like an affirmation, a celebration of his sudden recovery – but also a challenge, casting light into Ghidorah's storm.

Maybe nobody had seen the rescue flare. But someone might notice this...

His victory dance over, the huge saurian bent down toward them, as if noticing them for the first time, his gaze picking over what to him must seem like insects. But Godzilla knew human beings. He had worked with them before. They had just seen the proof of that.

"Mark?" Chen said.

He noticed Crane reach for his sidearm.

"Nobody move!" he said.

He stared straight into Godzilla's eyes, and damned if the son-of-a-bitch didn't stare back. Like it was trying to say something. And he did – or at least something passed between them, something that went into the core of him, and for the first time since Andrew's death Mark didn't... hate.

Godzilla wasn't the enemy.

Everything seemed to slow down, drop away, until he could hear only his own breath and heartbeat – and Godzilla. Like when he listened to the wolves, but deeper, clearer. The rhythms of his own body were melding with the Titan's, harmonizing...

And he understood what Emma had done. What made the ORCA work.

Godzilla broke their mutual gaze, leaving him shaken, amazed, but with a sense of almost religious clarity.

Godzilla turned, dove into the sea, and pushed through the waves.

Mark snapped out of it and turned to Chen.

"I know how to find them," he said.

Before he could clarify, a sonic boom shattered the air above. He looked up, fearing to see Rodan, or Ghidorah, or some other air-bound death-dealer – but it was the *Argo*. She didn't look great – she was battered, and smoke poured from her in several places – but to Mark, she was beautiful. She was here, and she could take him to Maddie.

Sam was there to meet Mark and Chen when they boarded the *Argo*. He must have seen something in their faces, or maybe he had been counting and realized Serizawa wasn't with them. Then he looked at Serizawa's notebook, still clutched in Mark's hand, and his face fell as he realized the truth.

"Let's make him proud and not screw this up," Mark said.

"Oh, God," Sam said. "How did he—"

"By saving us," Chen told him.

"What's the latest, Sam?" Mark asked, as they reached the bridge. Here, too, there were signs of the *Argo*'s travails. Scorch marks, dead control panels. But they were still in the air, so nothing crucial had gone dark.

"Right," Sam said. "Okay. Where to start – uh, we think Emma activated the ORCA somewhere near Boston – that's why Ghidorah and Godzilla are both headed that way. But we still can't pinpoint its exact location without that missing piece of the ORCA signal—"

"I've got the missing piece," Mark said.

Sam's expression became excited and... knowing. As if he had already guessed.

"It's Godzilla, right?" he said. "I mean, I know we already tried—"

"It's not Godzilla," Mark said.

He brought up his earlier work, the ORCA's waveforms all separated out. The others grouped around, watching.

"It's us," he said.

"What do you mean, us?" Foster asked.

"Emma combined the bioacoustics of Godzilla with a *human*'s to create the ORCA's signal. The creatures just think it's another apex predator."

"Well, we are a bunch of horny, murderous carnivores," Stanton said.

"Yeah," Foster said. "It's real poetic. Now what?"

"We track it, we find it, and we get my daughter back," Mark said.

Stanton took a big pull from his flask and gestured at a video feed of Ghidorah.

"Great," he said. "What about Moe, Larry, and Curly over here?"

"Godzilla will bring balance," Chen said.

Stanton, obviously a little tipsy, favored her with a skeptical stare.

"Oh, I get it," he said. "A little of Serizawa's old 'let them fight' action. Always loved it when he said that."

"No," Mark said. "This time, we join the fight."

TWENTY

From Dr. Chen's notes:

> *But when Zeus had driven the Titans from heaven, Earth gave birth to her youngest child Typhon. He was born from the love of Tartarus, by the aid of golden Aphrodite. Strength was with his hands in all that he did, and the feet of the strong god were untiring. From his shoulders grew an hundred heads of a snake, a fearful dragon, with dark, flickering tongues, and from under the brows of his eyes in his marvelous heads flashed fire, and fire burned from his heads as he glared. And there were voices in all his dreadful heads which uttered every kind of sound unspeakable; for at one time they made sounds such that the gods understood, but at another, the noise of a bull bellowing aloud in proud ungovernable fury; and at another, the sound of a lion, relentless of heart; and at another, sounds like whelps, wonderful*

to hear; and again, at another, he would hiss, so that the high mountains re-echoed. And truly a thing past help would have happened on that day, and he would have come to reign over mortals and immortals alike.

—Hesiod, *Theogony*, circa 700 BCE

Sam had told Mark that Emma had turned on the ORCA; he hadn't told him that it had effectively paralyzed most of the Titans. Only three were known to still be active: Ghidorah, Rodan – and Mothra. Emma knew what she was doing. It appeared she had changed her mind. After all, she wasn't trying to kill everyone.

Ghidorah was, though, and the ORCA signal wasn't slowing him up at all. Or Rodan, for that matter, probably because he was so close to Ghidorah.

So right now, if Mothra was still on their side, it was two-vs-two Titanwise. But as for the human part of the army, they didn't have all that much to join the fight *with*. Only a few ships from the fleet had escaped Ghidorah's wrath. More aircraft had made it and were desperately trying to find places to refuel and rearm before rejoining the fray.

Now that he knew what the secret sauce was, Mark was able to fiddle with the signal and get a better fix on it.

Sam was right – the ORCA was thumping out its tones in the Northeast.

In Boston.

It was hard to believe it was coincidence that Emma would return to the city they once lived in to send out her signal. There were better places to do it, if she wanted worldwide coverage. He didn't see Emma's meticulous planning in this. It was improvised. When Ghidorah seized control of the monsters she thought she was in charge of, it must have been a bit of a shock. Now she was doing what she could. But why Boston?

There was a bunker there, he remembered. One of Monarch's hideouts. Had she been there all along – since Antarctica? She must have been.

Maybe she thought it would put Maddie more at ease, to be near her old home. Possibly there was some more practical reason that hadn't occurred to him. At this point it was hard for even him to predict Emma's actions.

By dribs and drabs, the remainder of their fighting force came together, and once more they drove toward a battle with a creature wielding power beyond all understanding.

But this time they had a monster of their own leading the way.

For Emma, it was easy enough to guess what Maddie was up to; she had used the ORCA before to distract Monster Zero. But the signal was coming from Fenway Park, so this wasn't a random shot in the dark by her daughter; she had to have overheard her and Jonah speaking. Maddie was implementing Emma's own plan.

Which meant her daughter had known she was risking her life.

She had always been proud of her girl, but this – this was impressive. She'd managed to steal the ORCA from under the noses of Jonah and his men, make it out of the bunker undetected, cover the many miles between here and the stadium, hook the ORCA to the loudspeakers, and find the right frequencies to transmit.

And only just now was Jonah aware of *any* of it.

GODZILLA: KING OF THE MONSTERS

A little luck and male pride had been on Maddie's side. One of Jonah's men had eventually admitted to being shot with a stun gun by her. When he came to, the ORCA was gone. He'd tried to find her himself rather than tell Jonah. He'd known what kind of hell he would catch from the other guys for being beaten by a twelve-year-old girl. Not to mention whatever punishment Jonah came up with. But when his own search failed, he reported his failure. That's when Jonah went to the control room and found the ORCA gone and the signal thubbing away on the monitors.

It was done. But Maddie was in terrible danger, whether she knew it or not. Boston was evacuated; there was no one to alert. She had to get there herself.

Emma rounded up a few of Jonah's men to help her pack up a Humvee. They were nearly done when Jonah himself showed up.

"What do you think you're doing?" he demanded.

"I don't have time to argue about this, Jonah," she said. "I'm getting Maddie back."

"Not with my men you're not," he said. "Emma, you said this was about the greater good, that the planet deserved a clean slate. But now you're prepared to put all our lives in danger because your little girl is missing?"

Of course. She knew he didn't care about Maddie. He'd threatened to have her killed, after all. But if she framed this in practical terms, maybe he would get out of her way.

"The ORCA—" she began. Jonah cut her off.

"The ORCA no longer matters," he said. "Man does not control the laws of nature. And neither do you."

Emma regarded him, feeling everything slipping away from her. She'd hoped to be gone before Jonah found out. But he wasn't going to stop her.

"Come on," she said to the mercenaries.

But they didn't move. They were Jonah's men, not hers, and he was fully in control of them.

Jonah smiled, but there was no feeling behind it. Just a reflex, a signal of his dominance. He didn't care about Madison, or her, or maybe anyone. Asher had probably been his last real connection, the thing that kept him linked to humanity. Jonah wasn't a person anymore; just a survivor.

So Emma did what she had to do. She pulled out the gun she'd taken from the armory and aimed it at Jonah.

Jonah's men reacted immediately, of course, leveling their weapons at her. She watched them with her peripheral vision. If one of them pulled a trigger, she would damn sure pull hers. She would die, but so would he. She needed him to know that. To see it in her eyes.

"I already lost one child," she told Jonah. "I'm not losing another."

Jonah kept her gaze for a few more seconds. He didn't seem too worried she would shoot him. If she did she would be dead in more or less the same heartbeat. But she no longer cared, and maybe he understood that. Or maybe he did have a little sympathy left in him.

He shrugged.

"Let her go," he told the men. "We have everything we need."

It might be a trick. There was no way of knowing.

She lowered the gun, and when no one shot her she climbed into the Humvee and started the engine. She gunned it down the access tunnel. There was a gate at the end of it that she didn't have the code for. She didn't slow down. The Humvee crashed through nicely, and she sped on toward Boston.

* * *

Once the last helicopter left the stadium, Maddie got a pair of field glasses and took the stairs up to the roof.

The sky was a low, gray ceiling, sickly yellow at the horizons. Gusts of wind mussed her hair and spun stray leaves about. The air felt wet, but it wasn't raining. Something about the atmosphere felt – prickly. It was cool, but now and then a warmer gust came through, and a smell like burning hair and rotten eggs.

The ORCA's song throbbed away in Fenway Park, spreading in waves out and away – beyond Boston, beyond North America, to the furthest reaches of the Earth. All of the Titans were listening.

Played through the powerful speakers of the stadium, the signal sounded almost symphonic, as the machine matched wavelengths with each of the Titans, one at a time, then repeated them. It was still simple, like a heartbeat, but she could hear the difference – like themes. There was Typhon, Behemoth, Scylla, and now – Mothra. The Mothra one sent happy little shivers through her. Had the pupa already transformed? What did she look like now?

Had she, like the others, fallen under Monster Zero's control? Maddie didn't like the thought of that at all.

Boston was now a ghost town, at least as far as she could see. No one was left wandering the streets, no headlights moved between buildings. No honking horns. The sirens were quiet.

She was completely alone.

She had carried out her mother's plan, and it was working. But this was as far as she'd thought ahead. What should she do now?

Hopefully Monarch would figure out what was going on and come to take control of the ORCA. Maybe her father would be with them. That argued for staying at Fenway Park.

Of course, Jonah might come for her, instead. They could detect the signal as well, and he was probably pretty angry and would most likely kill her if he caught her. That was good reason to get lost.

So which was it to be?

The answer came more quickly and decisively than she expected.

It began when the strange feeling, the prickling, intensified. She felt pressure in her ears, like when you were reaching cruising altitude in an airplane.

Then the wind picked up; the flags on the rooftop began flapping harder and harder.

In the distance, something was moving. It was hard to focus on at first, but then she realized it was the sky. The coppery lens of the horizon was gone, replaced by gray clouds so dark they were almost black. They were rolling in like fog, pouring between the buildings with increasing speed, engulfing them, brightened by fitful coils of lightning. Thunder surrounded her, and a strange, deep thuttering, like the sound big propeller planes made in movies when the engine was starting to die. Or like an animal sound made in the back of some really big throat.

Dad wasn't coming for her. Neither was Jonah.

But Monster Zero was, coming for her like an angel of death, dragging the heavens with him. The clouds were closing in on the stadium from every direction.

Heart banging in her chest, she ran back into the broadcast booth and slammed the door behind her. The pressure in her ears increased; the floor beneath her feet pulsed; a plastic cup on the announcer's desk rattled and fell over. The gigantic window vibrated as through it she saw the stadium engulfed in the charcoal fog. The lights flickered, and the song of the ORCA bent into a weird warble.

She heard the beating of wings. Very large wings.

Monster Zero had come for the ORCA.

Maddie backed away from the window, staring, trying to see through the fog beyond the glass, holding her breath. He was there, she knew. The din of his flight grew louder, was right over her...

And then it went on, the drum of its wings growing softer. Then there was silence, and everything was very still.

He didn't know where she was. She felt the pressure in her chest relax, took a breath—

Monster Zero slammed down into the arena. The earth cracked beneath the force of his landing, and the entire building shuddered, knocking her off her feet. She lay there stunned, still able to see out the window because it came all the way down to the floor. He looked agitated, heads whipping around, searching for something. The ORCA, of course – but then why had he flown past it?

Because the sound was coming from the speakers right now, not the little amps on the device itself. Of course. Fear was making her dumb.

Monster Zero was clearly puzzled. This wasn't like before, when she had just randomly turned up the frequency. This time he thought he was hearing another top predator, an unknown beast, challenging his authority over the other Titans. He had come here to kill his competition and take back his throne. But there was no Titan to see, just the stadium...

He didn't let that stop him, though. He located one of the stadium speakers and ripped it from its mounting. When the sound didn't stop, he found the next, and the next, all three heads working at once, destroying the signal, the threat to his power.

Terror froze her in place. She couldn't think. All she could do was *look* at him.

So she decided she wouldn't look. She closed her eyes, trying to focus, tune it out. Get herself moving.

She turned from the window and opened her eyes, realizing she still heard the *thub, thub, thub* of the ORCA coming from just across the room. Now that the outside speakers were dead, this was the only source of the signal. She reached for it, got it in her hands, and very slowly stood up. *Time to go.*

She turned to check his position, and saw all three heads, crowded up to the window. Glaring at her. A yard away.

"Oh, shit," she said.

She sprinted for the door, as behind her the window shattered, and golden lightning flared, following her as she ran, disintegrating the broadcast booth. She felt the heat to her bones, the prickle of electricity on her flesh. She screamed, but she couldn't hear herself over the cacophony.

She took the stairs two and three at a time as Monster Zero savaged the stadium, blasting it with his lightning, slashing it with his tails, ripping out support beams with steel-toothed jaws. He was desperate to find her, his new top predator foe, a Titan clocking in at about five-foot-two. It would be funny if she wasn't about to die.

The stairs ahead of her disintegrated in another blaze of lightning; she dodged between a row of seats, a tail swiping just behind her. Everything sagged as the stadium began to collapse. She fell more than ran the last several yards, spilling out onto the field itself.

The three-headed dragon was waiting, all three heads swiveled to face her. And the ORCA. The malevolence she had seen in his eyes before was still there, multiplied by a hundred – and this time it was directed at her and her alone.

Her only chance now was to get rid of the machine. That sucked, because then the other Titans would fall under his spell again. She could only hope Dad and Monarch had made good use of the time she'd bought them. If she held on to the ORCA, Monster Zero would crush her and it together. Maybe if she gave it to him, she had a chance. Either way, this was over.

She tossed it, so it landed in a pile of rubble near his massive, clawed feet. He looked down at it, then brought his foot down. The ORCA stopped its song.

She hoped that would be good enough. That he would lose interest in her.

But it wasn't good enough. Signal or no signal, he knew her now. He probably remembered her from Antarctica. She had pestered him one time too many. The three heads focused on her and moved forward on their sinuous necks, not in a big hurry. Studying her, maybe trying to figure out how she had done it, how such a tiny creature could have fooled him and the Titans in his thrall.

There was nowhere for her to go. This was it. Lightning rippled across his body, and he began opening his mouths, revealing the crackling energy within.

Maddie screamed. Not in fright, but in defiant, primal fury.

Then a beam of blue energy knocked Monster Zero through the stadium wall, across the street and into the cathedral beyond, setting its bells to clanging.

She stood, staring at the fallen monster, confused and awestruck of the power that had leveled him. She felt the earth shake rhythmically beneath her, and the sound of huge footsteps.

And then Godzilla roared, and she turned around to face him.

She grinned, feeling a sudden, savage glee.

That's right, she thought, grinning. *Come kick his ass.*

Better yet, the big lizard wasn't alone. He was wading in through the harbor, accompanied by jets, helicopters, ships – and they weren't shooting at him. It looked like he was leading them, like they were together, all coming to fight Monster Zero.

And that was great. That was exciting! It was kind of like the best part of Mom's vision, humans and Titans working together.

Only she was right between them. Right smack in the middle of a battleground straight out of some ancient apocalypse. Best change that situation the only way she could – by hauling ass.

She ran through a gap and out into the streets, putting as much distance as she could between her and what was about to happen. Someone could tell her about it later.

Griffin guided the Osprey, following Godzilla as he crushed his way through the city, flattening cars and crashing through buildings as if they were just high grass he was pushing his way through. Mark peered out at the town he'd once called home – or what he could see of it. Most of it was covered in a dense fog.

He pulled out Serizawa's notebook and opened it. Felt the weight of it in his hand. And in a way, he felt Serizawa there, too. He wished the scientist had lived to see this, the vindication of his vision: Godzilla and humanity fighting together against a common foe, trying to put things right. To know his sacrifice had been a worthy one.

They had tracked the ORCA signal to Fenway Park. Emma

must have been using the loudspeakers to boost the signal. That was smart, and it obviously had worked. Maybe too well – it had brought Ghidorah straight to her. The signal had cut out moments before. Right after Ghidorah reached the stadium. Was Emma still there? Was Maddie with her? Or had she had the good sense to cut the thing off and get the hell out of there?

Through the seething clouds and lightning, Godzilla and Ghidorah were black silhouettes against a background of flame. Ghidorah standing his ground as Godzilla charged toward him. This was about to get brutal, and not much of Boston was likely to survive it.

"You know," Barnes said, "I'm starting to think this is Godzilla's world. We just live in it."

Barnes was being flip, but he was also echoing Emma and Serizawa. Watching the Titans come together, Mark finally conceded the point. If it weren't for the fact that these things took millennia-long siestas, would human life have even evolved? Probably not. Trilobites, synapsids, the dinosaurs, brontotherium, the woolly mammoth – all had come and gone, but Godzilla was still here.

He remembered a quote attributed to one of Monarch's early leaders, Bill Randa.

This planet does not belong to us.

The radio crackled. It was Sam, on the *Argo*.

"Guys, you're closing in on the last ping from the ORCA. Fenway Park, dead ahead. We'll keep laying cover fire to keep them off your backs."

"Copy that," Barnes said. "Here we go..."

Mark closed the notebook. Martinez crossed himself and murmured a prayer.

* * *

This is it, Sam thought. The last stand. If Ghidorah won, this time they were cooked for sure. There weren't enough ships and aircraft left to challenge him – not in this hemisphere, anyway. This was all or bust.

To make matters worse, seconds after the ORCA signal cut out, the Titans they still had tracking information on began moving again. Moving toward Boston, if he was reading things right. They had to put Ghidorah down before reinforcements arrived. In the past, Godzilla had managed to take down two MUTOs, but had nearly died doing so. But twelve, thirteen, maybe more?

Not very likely.

Godzilla had almost reached his ancient enemy. What remained of their aircraft were about to engage, and the ships were readying their long-range guns and remaining missiles.

Let's get this sucker, he thought.

Godzilla seemed – brighter. The pulses from his spines grew more radiant every second, and his skin was shining, too. He looked more powerful than the last time Sam had seen him. Not just a little. A lot.

"Is it just me," Sam asked, "or has he been working out?"

"You kidding me?" Stanton said, studying his instruments. "Serizawa's got that lizard juiced."

"Damn right," Foster said.

"Colonel," the bridge officer said. "All squadrons are locked on target."

Foster and Chen and Mark exchanged glances, and then glared out at Ghidorah. Sam knew exactly how they felt. He remembered the sea full of wreckage, the hundreds – thousands – who had already died trying to stop this unholy thing.

"For Serizawa," Chen said.

A hundred trails of fire scorched across the sky.

TWENTY-ONE

From Dr. Serizawa's notebook:

Osiris asks:
My face shall look upon the face of Atum. But how long will I live there?

Atum replies:
It is decreed that you will live for millions and millions of years. Then I shall destroy everything I created when I brought the world up from Nu. I shall return everything there is to the watery abyss.

—Egyptian Book of the Dead
Spell 175, 1550 BCE
(Atum was said to have created the
world at Jebel Barkal. His symbol
was that of a lizard. – S.)

Madison ran.

That quiet moment on the roof, looking out over the abandoned city, seemed an eternity ago. Boston was now a fully active warzone in a battle between the gods.

Everything around her was burning; bricks and steel rained from the sky. Even running as fast as she could, Maddie still hadn't managed to get out of the combat zone. The Titans were just too big. She felt like an ant trying to get out from underfoot of a couple of men wrestling. If she ran a hundred feet, they could cover that distance in a single step. They didn't even notice her anymore, but that didn't matter. The missiles and jet fighters didn't know she was there either; all of those fireworks they were shooting at Monster Zero were made of metal and fire, and they were coming down all around her.

One of Monster Zero's tails sliced through a skyscraper, ripping through its steel-beam skeleton as if it was paper, spraying tons of debris toward her. She desperately dodged her way through it – falling, rolling, springing back to her feet.

Every direction seemed closed off, and the fight was about to roll right over her. Again.

A roar from something that was not a monster drew her gaze to the sky. The big Monarch flying wing – the *Argo* – shot by, spattering Monster Zero with missiles and heavy weapons fire. Driving him away from her.

That seemed like a good thing, but panic was really taking hold of her now. Too many near misses – her luck was not going to hold out. Any second now she would be in the same place as a ton of falling steel. She kept remembering Andrew, how he'd looked when they found him.

She needed to be safe. To find somewhere safe.

Fighting for breath, trembling, she ran on.

Ghidorah crackled with energy, charging up for another volley of gilt lightning.

Missiles speared past the Osprey, their warheads opening on Ghidorah like flowers. The three-headed giant flinched back, and Godzilla slammed full-on into him. Lightning flashed as Ghidorah staggered, but instead of hitting Godzilla the bolts went wild, branching into the sky, three bolts become a thousand fractal streams of energy. One line of lightning crackled by the Osprey, so close Mark felt the heat and smelled the burnt air, but they were spared being struck.

Half a dozen aircraft weren't so lucky; energy arced through and between them, electrocuting the pilots and frying their engines so they hurtled, burning, into the city below.

"Hang on!" Griffin yelled, banking hard to avoid the flaming remains of an Apache attack helicopter.

Blood rushed to Mark's head, and his belly did somersaults. The Osprey was almost on its side, so the window he was next to was facing the flaming city below.

Griffin got them clear and righted the vessel, bringing them back around to a view of the fight as Godzilla impaled Ghidorah's tails with his dorsal spikes; all three heads shrieked in pain.

Griffin circled the Osprey around the fight, dropping toward what was left of the stadium.

"Prepare for landing!" Barnes said.

"Check it out," Martinez said, still watching Godzilla. "Dude's lit up like a Christmas tree."

Through the smoke, Mark saw what Martinez meant. Godzilla was pulsating with a fiery orange light, the air around him distorted by heat waves. This was new – nothing like this had been observed during the big lizard's last trek across the globe.

"Stanton, you guys seeing this?" Mark said, over the radio.

"Oh, we're seeing it," Stanton said. "But definitely not liking it."

Stanton paused. Mark could almost see him going over the readings, calibrating data flow.

The Osprey dropped lower. They were almost on the ground.

Stanton studied his instruments, while Sam glanced nervously from him to the strange light radiating from their friendly Titan.

"Godzilla's radiation levels are going through the roof," Stanton informed him. "We've got about twelve minutes before he goes thermonuclear."

"What do you mean?" Foster asked.

"I mean in about twelve minutes it's gonna be a bad day to be a Red Sox fan."

"Guys," said Sam's voice on the radio. "You need to find the ORCA, grab Madison, and get the hell out of there. Whatever Serizawa did to Godzilla worked a little too well, because he's about to explode like an atom bomb."

Barnes looked around. The Boston skyline burning; jets and choppers flaming out, and two monsters straight out of the apocalypse were going at it hard and bloody.

"Roger that," Barnes answered. "Prepare for landing."

* * *

As the Osprey dropped down, Martinez crossed himself: Barnes closed his eyes. Others – men and women Mark didn't even know the names of – were steeling themselves in one way or another. Preparing to die, if that's what was coming. Looking at the chaos around them, it seemed a fair bet that some or all of them would. Mark felt a lump gather in his throat, and a profound gratitude. Like Serizawa, these people were ready to make the ultimate sacrifice.

The Osprey bumped down onto the field at Fenway Park, and the soldiers surged out.

Golden lightning struck, and the first two out the door were incinerated, their lives cut short in less than a heartbeat.

It was horrifying, but the others piled out anyway, and he was right behind them.

Fenway Park was almost unrecognizable. The once huge left field wall – the Green Monster – had been obliterated, and much of the stadium itself torn to shreds. Mark stared up through the broadcast booth, or at least where it should have been.

That's where Emma and Maddie would have been, right? Patched into the sound system. Ghidorah had figured that out, too.

He leapt out of the Osprey, nearly twisting his ankle on the rubble that covered the diamond. Smoke stung his lungs.

"Maddie?" he shouted. "Madison?"

No one answered. Nothing moved in his line of sight except for G-Team; he didn't see anyone else, living or dead.

They fanned out to search. Godzilla and Ghidorah were just getting started; lightning jagged all around them, along with a flaming meteor storm of dead aircraft. The air stank of burning jet fuel.

He began fearing finding his daughter almost as much as

he feared not finding her. Because to find her like Andrew would be unbearable.

She's not here, Mark thought. *She was never here. Emma came by herself. She left Maddie someplace safe.*

But he had to know, so he couldn't stop looking. Because if she wasn't here, he didn't know where to look for her. The Monarch bunker, maybe. But another chopper had been dispatched to check that out.

"Over here!" Martinez shouted.

Mark rushed to the sergeant's side, fearing the worst, trying to prepare himself. But what Martinez had discovered wasn't Maddie, or Emma.

It was the ORCA, and it wasn't in very good shape. It lay inches beyond the edge of a debris field crushed into the contours of an enormous foot.

He picked it up, studying it, this link to his family. Maybe Emma had just hooked it up to the stadium and taken off. But then why was it down here, and not in the smoking hole that had been the broadcast booth?

On closer inspection, he saw the machine was banged up and singed but maybe not beyond repair.

The ground rumbled, and gas and steam suddenly surged up from beneath them. Godzilla and Ghidorah, still rumbling. "We gotta go!" Barnes yelled. The monsters were coming back their way.

Two of the commandos grabbed Mark and hustled him toward the Osprey, but before they had gone no more than a few steps one of Ghidorah's feet stomped down on the aircraft. The Osprey exploded, sending them all reeling back and adding to the mass of flames already surrounding them.

Godzilla reared up and blasted Ghidorah with his atomic breath, knocking the dragon back toward them.

But then a new light burst down from above, a familiar blue radiance. He saw broad, oval wings sweep back, the orange-ish eye marking toward the ends. Mothra's sonic boom rumbled across the ruined field as she dove into Ghidorah like a hawk diving down on a snake.

This was as close as Mark had been to the giant insect. As her name suggested, she was a bit moth-like, but a lot better armed than most moths he had seen. Her back legs were bent like a grasshopper's and her two front sets of limbs were long, deadly, and clawed like the forelimbs of a praying mantis. But those weren't her only weapons. A long, wicked sting projected from the tip of her thorax. Webbing jetted from her jaws, arresting Ghidorah's fall and sticking all three heads to a skyscraper. One of the heads ripped free and began tearing at the webbing, but then Godzilla was there, plowing into Ghidorah, knocking him clean through the building. Mothra swooped in for the kill.

Rodan burst from clouds, like the flaming avatar of some ancient vengeful god. He speared straight for Mothra, his half-molten wings folded back, striking her like a meteor and tearing her from her flight path. He wrapped her in the furnace of his wings. Mothra shrilled in agony as the soft down on her body caught fire. She struggled to escape his grasp, tearing at him with her claws as the two of them went soaring past.

And Mark and G-Team were alone on the field.

What was left of them. Still reeling, Mark took a head count. Barnes and Martinez were okay; Griffin looked hurt.

The rest of the team was just – gone.

He didn't have a lot of hope that they would fare any better. Gas mains beneath the stadium had ignited; flame and steam jetted from the ground, as if the rain of debris wasn't enough.

Barnes and Martinez helped Griffin to her feet.

Well, they weren't flying out; they would have to walk. But where? The stadium was now an inferno, columns of flame licking at the sky. Any direction they went would end with them as torches. But they had to do something. Find a weak place in the wall of fire, run through it, *fast*...

And then something did burst through the flames – from the other side.

A Humvee.

With Emma at the wheel.

"Get in!" she said.

No one moved. Barnes and the others exchanged suspicious glances.

Mark didn't blame them. She'd caused all this, and now she wanted to help?

Just then, a fighter jet crashed, right behind them. That ended their hesitation in an instant; all of them jumbled into the vehicle, Mark included. It no longer seemed like a time to be picky.

Mark took shotgun, still not sure this was all happening. It seemed completely unreal, like maybe something had smacked him in the head and this was all a coma dream. But dream or reality, he had some questions.

"Where's Madison?" was the first and most important.

Emma's brows came down.

"I don't know," she said. "I thought she was there!" She swerved sharply to avoid the chunk of aircraft that had just crashed in front of them.

"Well, she's not there," Mark said. "Hopefully you're as good at finding her as you are losing her."

"I didn't lose her," Emma said. "She ran away."

"Gee, I wonder why—"

"Oh, don't start," Emma said.

"Don't start?" he said. "You tried to kill me."

"Can't blame that kid," Mark heard Barnes say. "If I had these two for parents, I'd run away from home, too."

Emma slammed on the brakes.

"What did you just say?" she demanded.

"I said, if I had the two of you for parents I'd run away from home too!"

Emma looked at Mark.

"Home!" they both said at once.

Emma stepped on the gas.

Maddie couldn't stop crying, and every minute her panic threatened to strangle off her reason.

Something had given way inside of her.

Nothing lasts, she thought, as her feet slapped the pavement and her heart pounded in her ears.

Nothing. Not Mom and Dad, not Andrew. Not me. Not Boston. Everything's going away.

Boston had always been her happy place, the quiet point in her memory where everything had been good, where they had played bocce on the Common, making up their own rules as they went along. Where her favorite climbing tree had been, her backyard jungle, the sushi place around the corner Andrew always wanted to go to, where he tricked her into eating wasabi by telling her it was green frosting. The zoo, the museums, the boats on the harbor, the *library* where she had checked out her first book.

That place only existed in her imagination now. Looking back on it, the damage had begun when they returned there from San Francisco. The fights between Mom and Dad. Dad leaving. But it was still their home, a place that he might come back to. Those bad feelings could have been mended with better ones. But now, as she fled along Beacon Street, monsters were literally tearing it all down.

She'd felt brave when she started all of this. Determined. But now it was all too much. Too much death, anger, fear, betrayal.

Too many monsters.

She had to make it home. In her core, she knew if she could only reach their old house on Beacon Street, she would be safe, despite everything.

The house was still there, miraculously, in the midst of chaos and hell. The townhouse where they had lived, just on the edge of the Common.

She paused outside, panting, no longer quite sure of her logic. It was just a house, right?

Something huge crashed on the Common just yards away, an inferno with something writhing within it – wings, thrashing claws, long, insectile legs. Not Godzilla or Monster Zero... her mind couldn't sort it out. She didn't want to look anymore.

She ran inside the house, slammed the door, and put her back against it. She slid down to the floor as the house began to shake. She covered her ears, drew her knees up to her elbows, and screamed, as she realized that this place was no safer than anywhere else. It was just a straw house surrounded by very big bad wolves...

Across the room, old family photos rattled on some shelves.

That family in those pictures. She understood now. Like her Boston, those people existed only in her memory.

* * *

It looked to Sam like they were winning. Between their missiles and a supercharged Godzilla, and Ghidorah not being able to heal as fast as he was being wounded. He looked to be trying to fight free and escape again, but Godzilla stayed one step ahead of him.

Their losses were unthinkable. The fleet, all those pilots and sailors, Dr. Graham, Serizawa – all sacrificed themselves to bring them to this moment. There were other Titans out there, but with Godzilla in charge instead of Ghidorah – well, if things didn't get better, maybe they would at least not get worse.

Mothra and Rodan were still battling it out. Locked together, the winged Titans crashed into a bridge. It crumpled on impact, and fire splashed everywhere, like napalm, setting ablaze everything it touched, including Boston Common.

Oh, no, he thought.

Mothra sprang up, found purchase on Rodan's back and slashed her claws deep into him. Rodan screeched and leapt into the air, slamming his wings down, so both of them careened through a skyscraper and vanished from sight. Flame exploded inside the building and began rapidly climbing, floor by floor toward the sky.

Not that far away, Godzilla was still slaughtering Ghidorah, even without Mothra's help. He slammed his opponent with his tail, sent him reeling into a building. Ghidorah flapped frantically and managed to get a few yards off the ground before Godzilla snapped his jaws shut on one vast wing, twisting his head so as to throw the dragon to the ground, sending a ringed shock wave carrying debris and smoke for hundreds of yards through the burning city.

That's gotta hurt, Sam thought. *Come on, finish the bastard off.*

Godzilla seemed to have the same thought. He roared, and from his open mouth the blue beam of his atomic breath pressed Ghidorah back, shrieking in pain.

All the while, Godzilla pulsed brighter and brighter. Ghidorah's golden glow had dimmed to a sickly, intermittent yellow.

The big lizard fell upon Ghidorah, hammering him. Ghidorah, on the ropes, was just trying to escape. One of his heads snaked out, struggling away from its tormenter, as if it somehow thought it could separate from the common body, strike out on its own. Maybe it could. If Ghidorah could regrow a *head*...

But that's not what the dragon had in mind. Sam saw the real target just before Ghidorah's wayward head got there – damaged high-tension lines, showering sparks down into the street.

Ghidorah gaped wide and bit down on the wires.

Despite the damage downtown, most of Boston and its suburbs still had power. Now every light for as far as Sam could see strobed, going dark, lighting back up, dimming again as the power grid struggled to deal with a sudden, massive drain on the system.

Ghidorah blazed back to full charge in an instant; the golden lightning gathered in him and blasted from all three heads, knocking Godzilla off the ground, hurling him hundreds of feet to the harbor, where he crashed into a shipyard.

TWENTY-TWO

The arrogance of man is thinking nature is in our control, and not the other way around. Let them fight.

—Ishiro Serizawa, 2014

Godzilla clambered back to his feet and went at Ghidorah again, but Monster Zero had learned something. One of his heads snaked out and bit into what looked like a power plant. He rose to his full height, wings and heads outspread, the baleful, eldritch light gathering again. Hundreds of branching bolts spread into the sky, jagging through jets and helicopters, a chain reaction that continued even after Ghidorah himself subsided, leaping to every metal object in the sky. Dozens of aircraft, all gone in seconds. A bolt hit the *Argo*, and everything flashed gold. The ship shuddered and pitched, and Sam thought they were done.

But their systems held. He took slow, deliberate breaths, trying get his pulse to ease up.

"Godzilla's radiation's reaching critical mass," Stanton warned. "Six minutes till he blows!"

"Order all the remaining craft to retreat," Foster said.

There couldn't be that many left to retreat, Sam thought. He had lost count of the fallen, long ago.

In the distance, Ghidorah celebrated his victory with another universe-rattling roar. Then his stretched out his great wings and took to the air, headed toward where Godzilla lay stunned. The worst and largest of the gashes on his necks were already closing up.

Mothra was losing her fight, too. Locked in midair, the two Titans tore at each other viciously as they bowled through the city, smashing through buildings, leaving fire in their wake. But Rodan had kept the advantage. Mothra was badly burned, but worse, the flying reptile had pinned her against the top of a skyscraper and had a grip on her wings, which he began shearing into with his vicious beak. Without her wings, she was certainly doomed. Mothra swiped at him with her claws, but Rodan suddenly detached from her and flew off.

But not far. He was only building his speed. He smashed into the giant insect and snapped at her head. Mothra, braced against the building, squirmed out of the way. He made another try.

He missed, and then screeched in agony. He reared back, trying to fight free of Mothra.

But he couldn't. Mothra's sting was buried in his chest, all the way up to her thorax.

Rodan's thrashing weakened. His flames subsided.

She retracted the sting; fire licked within the wound as the flying reptile dropped away, vanishing into the conflagration he'd ignited.

Mothra clung to a toppled building, convulsing, her bioluminescence fading. She had killed Rodan, but it didn't look like she had much longer herself.

The Humvee roared up Beacon Street, swerving around burning aircraft, girders, piles of brick. Through the chaos, Mark caught occasional glimpses of familiar things. The corner store was untouched, the coffee shop was recognizable, although soon the fire raging nearby would destroy them too. Boston Common was ablaze, its familiar trees now torches. Their house was just across the street from it. It should be just up ahead.

Through the smoke, he searched for the familiar roofline. He should be able to see the third stories of the row from here. Instead he saw – distance.

Emma slammed on the brakes, her expression already beginning to crack.

The house had collapsed into a smoking pile of rubble.

Off in the distance, the monsters were still fighting, planes were crashing, ships sinking. The world as he knew it was ending. And as he stared at the wreck of the last place his family had called home, he didn't care.

If Maddie had really been in there – his mind wouldn't let him go any farther. She couldn't be dead. It wasn't possible. Not again.

"Maddie!" he shouted, lunging from the car and diving into the ruins of their townhouse, tossing aside bricks and smoldering planks. Emma worked beside him, a ragged desperation evident in every movement of her body. Barnes and Martinez pitched in, too, pushing aside the wreckage. Mark's hands smarted from a hot spot on one of the boards; sweat and smoke stung his eyes. A weird, acrid scent drifted on the breeze, like burning insects and cotton candy. Something exploded in the distance.

They found Maddie in the bathtub, covered by rubble. She'd done the smart thing, and sought what shelter she could.

It hadn't been enough.

He remembered Andrew, his broken body, all of the life and light gone from his sweet face. How he had wanted to somehow go back to before it happened, make a different choice, be in a different city.

And now Maddie. It was the same. She didn't react when they touched her; her limbs swung limp as they dragged her out of the ruin. Her skin was pale and cold to the touch.

He looked at Emma and saw his despair mirrored in her face.

"Don't go," he said to Maddie, clutching her poor body. "Please don't go."

Together he and Emma held her, held each other. Crying.

Remembering. The fishing trip. Her first day at preschool, her frown, angry because she had to wear a uniform instead of her shark pajamas. Sitting on a rock during a rest on the Appalachian Trail, staring off into the distance, lost in thought. Sleeping next to Emma, a month old, the same little grin, distinctive even then.

Maddie remembered her fear, the tumult outside, the pictures rattling on the shelf. She remembered everything coming apart, her lungs sucking for air and finding none.

Then everything sort of shut off and faded to black. She

was still aware, there just wasn't anything to see, feel, or hear. It was like she was under still water, in the dark, all of her senses turned inward.

She wondered if she was dead. She tried to move, but her limbs weren't there. Her panic had faded, but now it began to return. What had happened to her?

Help me! she tried to shout, but she didn't have a voice, either.

Had she failed? In her terror to escape the fight, she hadn't been able to see the big picture, sort out who was winning. She realized in retrospect that the two Titans on the Common must have been Mothra and Rodan. She had a sort of snapshot of them in her mind, Mothra's beautiful delicate-looking wings, the ugly hook of Rodan's beak, all engulfed in flame.

She tried again to wiggle her hands and feet, but still nothing happened. She wondered if she was even in her body anymore.

But then the darkness grew just a little lighter. A faint blue illumination appeared, just a spot at first, but then it began to expand, as if she was nearing the end of a tunnel.

The glow took on form as it grew nearer, and she became aware of other shapes around her. Familiar shapes. A place she knew. The perfumes of the rainforest, the metallic smell of machinery, the birdsong.

She was back in the Yunnan containment facility. Everything was there – the control room, the carvings on the temple walls – all illuminated by Mothra's bioluminescence. She was as Maddie had last seen her, in her larval form – but this time there was no one else around. Not her mother, not Dr. Mancini, no security personnel – just her and the grub. And as before, she felt a connection with the Titan, and reached to touch her.

This time, she wasn't interrupted.

As her fingers brushed chiton, Mothra transformed. Her face became covered in soft down, and wings unfolded.

Maddie didn't think she had ever seen anything so magnificent.

All of her fear was gone now, and she was at peace. The great insect chittered a strange, lovely song – and although there were no words Maddie could understand, it felt as if the Titan was telling her everything would be all right. She felt Mothra's heartbeat through her hand, harmonizing with her own.

After a few more heartbeats the light began to fade; the Titan's shape unraveled and drifted, a million strands of silk, carried off by the wind. Mothra was gone, and so was her light.

But now Maddie saw a new, harsher light. She heard familiar voices murmuring her name. And crying.

She closed her hand and felt her fingers move. Air filled her lungs.

And Mom and Dad were there, both of them, hugging her.

Maybe I am dead, she thought.

But her body argued otherwise. Every inch of it ached.

Maybe everything wasn't okay. But it was better.

Madison's body twitched; her lips parted, and she gasped for air. Her eyes fluttered open and she looked up at them in confusion.

"Mom?" she said. "Dad?"

Mark couldn't find words. All he could do was hold her, and hold Emma, cherish their familiar warmth, the scent of them. His family.

Andrew was gone, and nothing could bring him back. What a fool he'd been to let go of what he still had left.

He wouldn't do it again.

They finally released one another, although Mark kept hold of Maddie's hand. The others were staring off into the distance, where Ghidorah was killing Godzilla.

Mark didn't understand. They had been winning. What had happened?

Ghidorah's necks wrapped around Godzilla, crushing what life remained from him. His fading dorsal spines began to crack under the stress. Then Ghidorah's wings started to beat, stronger, harder, until – incredibly – he lifted the ninety-thousand-ton lizard from the ground. First slowly, but then more quickly, he ascended hundreds of feet into the air.

As he stood amongst smoke and flame, viewing the Titans high against the storm-wracked sky, Mark felt a sense of dislocation, as if he wasn't in Boston in the twenty-first century, but in a volcanic wasteland millions of years ago, just a little rat-like primate ancestor watching the gods fighting it out, desperate to find a safe place to hide.

Ghidorah opened his claws, and Godzilla fell, a Titan cast from the heavens. He began to burn, and as the flame surrounded him his form blurred, and he looked like a fiery sphere, like a meteor plunging toward the Earth.

The giant reptile struck the ground like a bomb, and when the dust settled, Mark saw him lying motionless in the crater his body had carved into Boston.

He looked dead, but Ghidorah didn't think so – or maybe he just wasn't taking chances. He rose above the fallen giant, his electrical charge building, preparing to end their ancient duel once and for all.

Serizawa had died for nothing, as had Vivienne, and countless pilots and soldiers. With Godzilla dead and the ORCA destroyed, nothing could hold Ghidorah in check, stop him from remaking the world as he saw fit.

And there was nothing they could do about it but watch as the dragon's charge increased, the bottled lightning of a hundred storms. Ghidorah built his fury, and when his body could no longer keep it in, he let it go. The death blow.

Like Ghidorah, Mark had been so intent on Godzilla, he hadn't noticed Mothra. Torn and battered, she pulled herself onto Godzilla, spreading her wings to shield him from Ghidorah. Then, with a defiant screech, she launched herself at the dragon.

She didn't get far. Lightning blasted from Ghidorah's mouth and struck through her, and she vanished in a burst of light. All that remained was a glowing rainbow cloud of particles that began to fall gently upon Godzilla, like a light snow in the moonlight.

Ghidorah's eyes sparkled with dark, malicious glee as he regarded the ethereal cloud that was all that remained of Mothra. It wasn't the expression of one animal that had bested another, or of a predator regarding its prey. Ghidorah *enjoyed* killing. He lived for it.

In no hurry, the dragon returned his attention to Godzilla. At this distance, it was hard to tell, but it looked like the fallen Titan was starting to take on a dull, reddish orange sheen, as if lava was welling up from beneath his skin.

And suddenly Mark realized that they still had a chance. A small chance, but better than no chance at all.

"We need to work fast," Mark told Emma.

"To do what?" she said.

Mark ran back to the Humvee and came out with the

shattered ORCA, the thing they had started building so long ago. Together.

"You can't be serious," she said.

But he was, and she saw it. So they got to work.

Madison's parents began to repair the ORCA. It had been a long time since they had been together, longer still since they had worked at a common purpose.

But now Maddie saw how it must have been, before. Before Andrew died, and Dad started drinking so much, and Mom – lost her mind. They were like dancers, or synchronized swimmers, both working like crazy but somehow not getting in each other's way.

"You sure about this?" Mom asked.

"It's the only way to save him," Dad replied. "We fix it, get on the Osprey, and draw that thing away from Godzilla. Buy him time to get back on his feet."

"Mark, you've seen what that thing can do."

"I know," her father replied. "It'll be tight, but we have to take that chance."

"Patch that cable," her mom said.

"Got it," Dad said.

"No, the red, not the white!"

"Okay, okay!"

"You sure this thing is gonna work?" one of the Monarch soldiers asked. His nametag said Martinez.

Neither of them bothered to answer. In fact, they were so involved in their work they probably hadn't even heard him.

Dad held out a piece of wire for her mom to solder, and Mom suddenly stopped moving, breaking the clean rhythm they had established. She was staring at his hand.

"If you replace this five-pin," her father said, "I can reset the transmitter and we should be good to go."

That's when Maddie realized what her mother was looking at. The wedding band on his left hand.

Then Dad finally got it.

He looked her mom in the eyes.

"I never gave up," he told her, softly.

Maddie felt her throat close up, and tears nearly start once more, but then things began shaking again. Ghidorah was savaging Godzilla with all three heads. Two wrapped around him like boa constrictors, while the other bit into his neck. With each bite, Godzilla's glow grew weaker, while Ghidorah's wounds closed up and vanished. Godzilla cried out, a terrible, mournful sound. The great Titan was dying.

"Whatever you're gonna do, do it fast," Barnes said.

"Are you good to go?" Dad asked.

Her mother nodded. "Yes."

"All right, three, two, one..."

Mom set the solder, Dad sparked it, and Maddie flipped the switch.

The ORCA flickered and powered on. It worked!

"That's it!" Mark said. "That's it."

But maybe they were too late. Godzilla's glow had all but faded. In moments it would be gone.

Overhead, an Osprey descended toward them.

Her mom turned to her. There was something a little off about her expression. But that was hardly surprising, after everything they'd been through. There was a lot that needed saying, but there wasn't time for all of it.

"I love you, Maddie," her mom said. "More than anything."

All of the hurt, her feeling of betrayal, felt like a hard knot in Maddie's stomach. But it felt a little better now. It was a start.

"I love you too, Mom," she said. She knew it would never be the same again. She would never be that kid who thought her mother had it all together, knew everything, understood what was best for everyone. No more than she thought of her father as perfect. But that was for the best, right? To live in reality.

The Osprey touched down, rotors beating at the air.

Her mom started programming the ORCA. Two of the soldiers helped a third who was wounded toward the rescue craft.

"Emma," Dad said. "Let's go!"

"Take her!" her mom said, still fiddling with the controls. "I still have to activate it."

Her dad gave her a skeptical look.

"I'm right behind you," Mom insisted.

Her father lifted Maddie in his arms and ran toward the Osprey. Over his shoulder she saw her mom activate the ORCA, heard its heartbeat song begin.

In the distance, she heard a familiar shriek. Monster Zero's heads came up. He dropped Godzilla's listless body and swung around, searching for the source of the hated sound, the threat to his supremacy that he somehow could not see.

All three heads focused on them.

The monster started toward them with terrible speed, knocking down everything in his path. Skyscrapers crumbled into dust in his wake. They needed to go. She knew what it was like to be face to face with this guy, and every nerve in her body screamed at the thought of being there again.

Her mom picked up the ORCA and ran like hell toward the Osprey.

Dr. Chen and a man she didn't know helped her father get her on board.

"Maddie, thank God," Chen said.

Her dad climbed in, and now they were waiting on Mom. But Monster Zero was coming, *fast*. More full of rage than ever.

"We gotta lift off," a woman in a military uniform said. She wore the marks of a colonel, if Maddie was remembering straight.

The pilot obeyed the order; the Osprey began to rise. Mom still wasn't on board. Dad moved over to the door, so he could pull Mom up when she got there.

We're going to make it, she thought, *all of us. Mom will get on board, we'll take off...*

She tried not to think past that. Which was faster in the air, Monster Zero or the Osprey?

She was afraid she knew.

TWENTY-THREE

From the notebook of Ishiro Serizawa:

In many myths and ancient tales, the world begins with a battle between the gods. In Sumerian myth, the dragon goddess Tiamat fought Anu. In Greece the Titans battled their children, the gods. Cipactli, a sea monster, fought the four gods Huizilopochtli, Quetzalcoatl, Tezcatlipoca, and Xipe Totec in an Aztec myth. In such stories, very often the world is said to be created from the remains of the defeated. Other cultures place the war of the gods at the end of time. Raganorak. Armageddon. I believe both are true. Creation and destruction are two sides of the same coin. The gods go to war, a new world emerges. The new world becomes old, out of balance, and the gods fight again.

* * *

Emma glanced back at Monster Zero, and made a quick, brutally honest calculation.

Mark and Maddie weren't going to make it if the Osprey waited until she was aboard. Even if they managed to get a few yards off the ground, it was hopeless. Monster Zero would follow the ORCA wherever it went, if it was turned on. If she turned it off, he would probably kill them anyway. Either way, he would return to finish off Godzilla.

Unless she stopped him.

So she quit running, and instead watched the Osprey continue to rise.

"Mom!" Maddie shouted.

Emma focused on Mark's surprised face, saw him take it in and understand what she was doing.

"I love you," she said, knowing they couldn't hear it. She said it more for herself than for him. She had kept those feelings walled off for so long…

But it all came back so effortlessly now, the good times. Falling in love. Falling in love in a whole new way when they first saw Andrew, held him, that tiny little primate. And again, when Madison came along. Nothing was ever perfect. There were always tough times and arguments. But they'd had balance, then, so when something went wrong, they always recovered.

But losing Andrew had broken that equilibrium, and they never found another. Mark had blamed her for their son's death; he never said so, but she knew. It was her job that took them to San Francisco. Mark wanted to stay in Boston. They could have, but the San Francisco offer had been too hard for her to resist. It was unfair that he felt that way, and part of her had hated him for that.

Only now did she realize that she had blamed herself – for

all of it. That was why she worked so hard to make it right. Out of guilt. She couldn't forgive herself, and in her heart, she didn't believe Mark could either.

Still carrying the ORCA, she rushed to the Humvee, laid the machine on the passenger seat, started the engine, and gunned it, driving away from her family as fast as she could manage through the wreckage of Boston.

A glance back showed it was working. Ghidorah took a sharp turn, dismissing the Osprey, coming directly after her.

You won't touch them, you son-of-a-bitch, she thought. *You won't touch my family.*

Mark saw Emma's lips form the words. He saw her expression and believed her. That she still loved him. And he knew what she was about to do.

Maddie understood, too.

"No! Mom! Stop, stop!" she shouted. Mark was still at the door. He leaned forward, toward his retreating wife. He couldn't lose her again. He could jump, wrestle her into the Osprey, or – something. They weren't too high yet. Foster might not come back for Emma, but she would come back for him.

But the others grabbed him, pulled him back. He could only watch helplessly as Emma boarded the Humvee and drove away into the ruins of Boston, as the Osprey rose higher.

And Ghidorah turned to follow her, as she had surely planned.

Emma was right, of course. Leading the monster away was the only way to save Maddie. He just wished he'd thought of it first.

Give him hell, girl, he thought, as hot tears of pride, love, and loss burned at the corners of his eyes.

"Daddy," Maddie said, through her tears, hugging him hard.

He hugged her back, his girl, his Maddie. Death might break them apart, but nothing else would.

Emma didn't know how far she would get. Far enough, she hoped, for the Osprey to vanish into the smoke and ash. For Mark and Maddie to fly to safety.

Was Godzilla dead? When she'd last seen him, he was limp, unmoving. If he was, there was nothing to stop Ghidorah. The other Titans would fall in line with his will, and they would continue transforming the Earth into whatever it was Ghidorah wanted. But if Mark and Maddie survived, Chen, a few others – then it still wasn't over. Mark could build a new ORCA, a better one. Or maybe what was left of Monarch would come up with something new – a bioweapon, a drug, a way to short-circuit Ghidorah's energy attack. At least there was hope. Hope that someone could undo some part of the terrible damage she had unleashed. She wouldn't be part of it, or see it done.

Hope would have to be enough for her. And love.

She dodged the Humvee around piles of rubble and the few buildings still standing, working for every second she could get. The ORCA continued throbbing away, and Ghidorah was *right* there. She spun the wheel, careened around a pile of burning debris, straightened up, pushed the pedal all the way down.

Everything went gold, then white, as pain like she had never known jagged through her body, striking every nerve like a match. The agony didn't last long; as it faded, she was away and rolling, bouncing, until the Humvee fetched up against something and stopped.

She'd been thrown clear, she realized. Not that that meant much. She couldn't feel anything. But her vision was still clear. Ghidorah stooped toward her, sniffing...

She wasn't scared. There wasn't anything else he could do to her.

Come on, you bastard, she thought.

Behind Ghidorah, an orange glow appeared, a colossal shape eclipsing the burning city. Emma smiled. She'd done it. Given Godzilla enough time to recover.

Time to restore the balance.

"Long... live... the king," she gasped out.

Godzilla, his body steaming, his dorsal fin pulsing red, burning like a dying sun, charging toward Ghidorah.

She couldn't breathe anymore. That was okay. That was fine. She closed her eyes, saw Mark, Madison, and Andrew. It was enough.

As the Osprey rose above the battlefield, Mark's gaze tracked the Humvee, vanishing behind debris or drifting smoke, but reappearing.

"Jesus, God," Stanton said. "Look."

"Fucking A," Barnes said.

He followed their gazes, to the crater where Godzilla's body lay.

Only he wasn't in it anymore. Massively wounded, he had pulled himself up and was staggering after Ghidorah. First uncertainly, then with stronger and greater strides. He was glowing red, now, pulsing with an inner radiance that shone through seams in his scales, leaked from his eyes, as if his heart was the core of a red giant star about to go supernova.

Mark tore his gaze away, looking for Emma. She could still make it!

He didn't see the Humvee, but he saw Ghidorah. And then, just ahead of him, racing out from behind a crushed building, the tiny vehicle.

Ghidorah came down on her like a hammer, blasting the Humvee with his lightning breath. Energy arced all around it, and the car went flying.

Then Ghidorah blotted out his view, heads swinging down toward where he'd seen the Humvee stop.

The Osprey's rotors flipped over, and they were an airplane now, plowing as hard and fast as the craft was able. Mark felt his ears pop as they gained elevation.

Below, Ghidorah whipped around toward Godzilla, blasting him with lightning, but the big lizard just took it – absorbed it – and kept coming, pulsing brighter and faster. Again and again, the three-headed dragon struck, but Godzilla, despite his wounds, didn't even slow down. He collided with Ghidorah like a walking mountain, wrapping him up in his forelimbs, grappling him close, as his dorsal fin pulsed faster and faster, ignoring the dragon's attacks as he thrashed in his grasp.

The pulses were now so fast they were almost continuous. They sheeted through Ghidorah like a hard wind, ripping his wings and burning them away is if they were made of tissue paper. Ghidorah screamed and blasted Godzilla with all three heads, but then another wave of radiation pulsed out and disintegrated two of the dragon's heads. Ghidorah slumped to the ground, writhing, as Godzilla stepped on his chest, and as another pulse built within the great lizard, Ghidorah's remaining head shrieked.

Mark shielded Madison with his body and tried not to

look, desperately hoping they were out of range.

He saw through his closed eyelids the flash that engulfed what remained of Boston. He held Maddie tighter, as the Osprey suddenly jumped through the air. The blood drained from his head, and then they were in free fall.

But only for a moment; the Osprey slapped onto a thermal; her wings caught, and they were flying again. A little shakily, maybe, but well enough.

When Mark opened his eyes, he saw a mushroom cloud lifting from Boston. The Osprey started a wide turn around the city as the cloud continued to lift, and it gradually began clearing below.

Through the smoke, downtown Boston was a wasteland of blackened ruins, burning streets, twisted steel beams. He was reminded of the ruins of the city beneath the sea. In a few thousand years, would there be anyone left to wonder what had happened to the civilization he had been born into?

The Osprey buzzed a little closer, and he began to discern the crater where he'd last seen the two Titans. But there was no sign of Godzilla and Ghidorah. Had they been completely atomized? If so, what would that mean? Without a king – or a queen – what would the other Titans do?

Something began to shift beneath the wreckage, something big. As it emerged, Mark waited for Godzilla's familiar dorsal spines. Instead, golden horns appeared, then the scaly head and snout.

Ghidorah.

Oh, for God's sake, Mark thought. *Is it really impossible to kill this thing?*

But then the head rose up farther, although its neck looked weird, not the slender snake neck of Ghidorah, but a really thick, green neck.

Then he understood, as Godzilla rose up from the ruins – with Ghidorah's head in his *mouth*.

Ghidorah's eyes snapped open; he was wriggling in Godzilla's jaws, lightning flashing, trying desperately to escape. Godzilla shook it like an alligator would, as if trying to eat it.

But then a blast of blue energy erupted from the saurian's maw, and Ghidorah's final head disintegrated in the withering atomic radiance.

The blast ceased; a little bolt of lightning crackled around Godzilla's mouth.

Godzilla had won. They had won.

But the world was changed forever. So many cities destroyed, so many people dead. Things weren't just going to bounce back to the way they were.

And maybe that was as it should be. If Emma was right, with Ghidorah gone, the global ecosystem would rebound; the ravaged places would become green; forest would cover where Boston had been. The dying ocean reefs would thrive as they hadn't in a hundred years.

He hadn't wanted it to happen this way. But the eggs were broken. They needed to decide what kind of omelet to make.

It was the dawn of a new world. Or the return of a very old one.

Soon he would go and find his wife's body. He had no doubt that she was dead. And he would grieve with his daughter, and together they would find out how they fit into this new era.

He remembered what Chen said about dragons being creatures who might bring redemption. And they had. For him.

For Emma.

"Jesus," Stanton said. "Good thing he's on our side."

"For now," Chen said.

"Dad," Madison said. "Look."

As more of the smoke cleared, they saw Godzilla was not alone after all.

Rodan was back, along with a horror on eight long, spidery legs, a monster that looked like a bull with a mountain on his back, a knuckle-walking mammoth with tusks hundreds of feet long, and a six-legged, hunchbacked MUTO like the one that had broken containment in Japan five years ago. Behind them flitted a flock of smaller forms that resembled pterodactyls – leafwings, from Skull Island.

Ghidorah's cavalry was a little late to save him, but they were here. It looked like this wasn't over after all.

Godzilla glared at the newcomers and drew himself up for battle, head up, arms ready to grapple. Battered and bruised he might be, but he was still ready to fight.

The other monsters stopped their advance; they seemed to shrink from him, then – bowed, each in their own way.

They were standing down. Acknowledging their Alpha.

Serizawa's natural order was restored.

Godzilla threw back his head and roared until the heavens shook.

EPILOGUE

I will not speak of Leviathan's limbs.
its strength and its graceful form.
Who can strip off its outer coat?
Who can penetrate its double coat of armor?
Who dares open the doors of its mouth,
ringed about with fearsome teeth?

Its back has rows of shields
tightly sealed together;
each is so close to the next
that no air can pass between
They are joined fast to one another;
they cling together and cannot be parted.

Its snorting throws out flashes of light;
its eyes are like the rays of the dawn.
Flames stream from its mouth;

GODZILLA: KING OF THE MONSTERS

sparks of fire shoot out.
Smoke pours from its nostrils
as from a boiling pot over burning reeds.
Its breath sets coals ablaze
and flames dart from its mouth.

Strength resides in its neck;
dismay goes before it.
The folds of its flesh are tightly joined:
they are firm and immovable.
Its chest is hard as rock,
hard as a lower millstone.
When it rises up, the mighty are terrified;
they retreat before its thrashing.

The sword that reaches it has no effect,
nor does the spear or the dart or the javelin.
Iron it treats like straw
and bronze like rotten wood.
Arrows do not make it flee;
slingshots are like chaff to it.
A club seems to it but a piece of straw;
it laughs at the rattling of the lance.

Its undersides are broken potsherds,
leaving a trail in the mud like a threshing sledge.
It makes the depths churn like a boiling caldron
and stirs up the sea like a pot of ointment.
It leaves a glistening wake behind it;
one would think the deep had white hair.
Nothing on earth is its equal –
a creature without fear.

It looks down on all that are haughty;
it is king over all that are proud.

Santiago led the men through the corridor. They made him nervous, with their heavy boots and iron gazes. In particular, he did not like their leader. He had known men like this before. But these were not times for caution. The world was changed forever, as had been foretold. Many of his relations and old friends were dead, others were scattered to the four corners of the earth. He had been at sea when Rodan burst from his nest; he had weathered Ghidorah's storm and made safe harbor. Thus he still had his boat, and his fishing gear. But to what purpose? The waters were poisoned. And where would he take his catch?

But again luck had been with him. He'd made a good catch. Now these men had come to pay him for it. Or maybe they would kill him and his men and take it. They were dressed like soldiers, which in his experience often did not bode well. But what choice did he have?

"It is a brave new world, my friend," he told the leader. "Such things as this have become much more valuable since the rise of the king."

The leader said nothing.

"It took nine fishing boats to raise it," Santiago went on. "My men don't ask for much, just enough to relocate their families. They cannot fish here anymore. Everything is dead."

They had reached the warehouse space, where his men waited. Nervous, like him. The stench of death was worse than before.

He flipped on the lights so they could see it, and prayed for the best.

His men did the same, stepping away from it, crossing themselves.

Even in death, covered in seaweed and barnacles, his once golden scales dulled by putrefaction, Ghidorah's head was terrifying. He had seen it happen, seen Godzilla tear it off and drop it in the sea. And he knew those seas better than the faces of his children.

The leader, Jonah, stepped into the light. He stared at the severed head with a most unsettling expression, and then he smiled. But there was no mirth there. It was the sort of smile his grandfather used to call *la sonrisa del diablo*, "The Devil's Grin."

"We'll take it," Jonah said.